WHEN GRACE SINGS

THE ZIMMERMAN RESTORATION
TRILOGY, BOOK 2

WHEN GRACE SINGS

KIM VOGEL SAWYER

CHRISTIAN LARGE PRINT
A part of Gale, Cengage Learning

GALE
CENGAGE Learning·

Farmington Hills, Mich • San Francisco • New York • Waterville, Maine
Meriden, Conn • Mason, Ohio • Chicago

GALE
CENGAGE Learning®

THE LIBRARY OF CONGRESS HAS CATALOGED
THE THORNDIKE PRESS EDITION AS FOLLOWS:

Sawyer, Kim Vogel.
    When grace sings / by Kim Vogel Sawyer. — Large print edition.
      pages ; cm. — (Thorndike Press large print Christian romance) (The Zimmerman Restoration trilogy ; book 2)
      ISBN 978-1-4104-7768-2 (hardcover) — ISBN 1-4104-7768-1 (hardcover)
      ISBN 978-1-59415-541-3 (softcover) — ISBN 1-59415-541-0 (softcover)
      1. Mennonites—Fiction. 2. Large type books. I. Title.
    PS3619.A97W427 2015
    813'.6—dc23   2014043150

[CIP data for the hardcover edition without any alterations]
Published in 2015 by arrangement with WaterBrook Press, an imprint of Crown Publishing Group, a division of Random House, LLC, a Penguin Random House Company

Printed in the United States of America
2 3 4 5 6   22 21 20 19 18

For Kendall Grace,
with love and prayers for you to rest in
His strength
and seek His will always

But he said to me, "My grace is sufficient for you, for my power is made perfect in weakness."

— 2 CORINTHIANS 12:9

CHAPTER 1

Chicago, Illinois
Early September

Briley Forrester

A folded newspaper slammed onto the corner of Briley's desk. His fingers left the keyboard with a jolt, and he sent a scowl in the direction of the person who'd interrupted his focus. He cleared the frown quickly when he recognized his boss. He leaned back in his squeaky chair and forced a light chuckle.

"Did you skip your morning coffee, Len? You look a little tense." Or maybe he needed a hair from the dog that bit him. Len's red, watery eyes and drooping jowls spoke of too much imbibing last night. A habit many of his coworkers practiced, but one Briley had been wise enough to avoid establishing. Aunt Myrt had never approved of drunkenness.

"What I need is a story that'll break us out of our rut and put us on top again." Len perched on the edge of Briley's desk. His bald head shone under the harsh fluorescent lights. He folded his arms over the chest of his rumpled plaid shirt and blew out a noisy breath. The man must be bothered. Rarely did he show up to the *Real Scoop* office in anything other than a crisply ironed shirt and bold tie. He glowered at the newspaper lying half on, half off the desk. "Look at the headline. Look what sells papers these days."

Briley picked up the copy of the *Illinois Times* and unfolded it. A photograph of an Amish barn raising filled a quarter of the front page, and the lead article read "Plain Living Brings Joy and Peace." While Briley scanned the article about the increased yearly tourism in Amish-Mennonite communities, Len continued to bluster.

"You gotta be kidding me. Driving a buggy, wearing pants with suspenders, living in a house without a television or microwave — that's supposed to make a person happy? It's nothing but a bunch of hooey."

Briley set the paper aside. "So let 'em have their moment in the sun. What's it to you?"

Len's frown deepened. "They irk me,

that's what. Ever gotten stuck behind one of their tractors on the highway? What're they doing anyway, driving their farm implements where only cars are supposed to be? And don't get me started on what their horses leave behind in parking lots. Disgusting." Len snatched up the newspaper and glared at the black-and-white image. "Look at 'em in their *Little House on the Prairie* clothes and Tom Sawyer straw hats, climbing all over that barn frame. This is news? But it's the hottest story on Internet search sites this morning. I don't understand it . . ."

A prickle inched itself up Briley's spine. Could this be it — the idea that would take him from bit pieces in the middle of the tabloid to a front-page feature and byline? He tamped down his excitement. He couldn't just blurt it out. Somehow he had to make it Len's idea.

He rocked his chair on its creaky springs and assumed an unconcerned grin. "Aw, you know how people are about the Amish. Probably half the out-of-staters who come to Illinois take a drive through Amish country, gawk at the buggies and clothes flapping on the line and horses pulling plows, and buy a jar of apple butter. It makes 'em feel good to believe those folks in their homemade clothes and houses lit by lanterns have it all figured out." He pretended to examine a small chip in his thumbnail. " 'Course, we know it's hooey, like you said, but it'd be pretty hard to convince the general populace otherwise."

Briley gnawed his thumbnail and watched Len out of the corner of his eye. His boss was thinking — crunched brow, tapping foot, lips twitching around like a fly had gotten trapped in his mouth. But it might take a while for a coherent thought to form, considering the man's dip into a bottle last night. Although impatience nibbled at Briley, he refused to give vent to it. In his two years of working under Len's direction, he'd learned he couldn't push the man any more than he could push a rope. *Just let him reason it out.*

Bending over his keyboard again, Briley applied his fingertips to the keys and tried to tap out a few sentences about the scandal surrounding the selection of the new *American Idol* winner. He'd only managed to form a half-dozen words when Len blasted out a guffaw. Whaddaya know. He'd formed a thought. Briley hid a smile and looked up. "What?"

Len smacked Briley's desk with his open palm. "Hooey. All hooey. We know it, right?

So let's make sure the world at large knows it."

Briley raised his eyebrows in what he hoped was an expression of surprise. "You mean, disprove the Plain-living-means-peaceful-living theory?"

"That's exactly what I mean." Len's red-rimmed eyes sparkled with fervor. He leaned in, resting his elbow on his knee and settling his intense gaze on Briley's face. "No one's ever tried to show the truth — the *real* truth — of living Plain. And I'm willing to bet you my Mercedes-Benz the truth is half those folks wearing bonnets and shoveling manure would rather be living in air-conditioned houses and popping frozen dinners in microwaves."

Briley laughed. "I'm happy with my Camaro, thanks, but it'd be interesting to pursue the story." He'd intended to let Len come up with the whole idea himself, but he couldn't hold back his thoughts. "Consider the trickle-down effect. We could put the visit-the-Amish tourism out of business, bringing those visitors back to the cities to frequent the museums and theaters and bars instead. Every big city near an Amish community would thank us."

Len's lips pursed, the furrows in his broad forehead deepening. "The problem is how to really prove the people living in those communities are dissatisfied with their simple existence. Nobody'd believe it without quotes from the Plain folks themselves. And you can't just ask them. They'd tell you they're perfectly content." He grimaced, shaking his head. "No, a person would have to live among them. Win their trust. Then he could authentically uncover the reality of living Plain."

"*Live* among them?" Briley made a face. An intentionally distasteful face. "No reporter with a wife or kids is going to want to pack up and move to an Amish town for who-knows-how-long to make friends and dig up the truth."

Len squinted an eye at Briley, as if taking aim. "You don't have a wife or kids. You don't even have a dog. Are you volunteering?"

Boy, it was hard to stay in his chair. Briley linked his hands behind his head and faked a yawn. "Well, you're right about me not having anything holding me back. I suppose I could do it."

Len smirked. "Your subtle act is a little too well done. I know you want this story. It's one of those rare ones that can make a reporter in this business."

Briley offered a sheepish grin. Maybe Len

wasn't as oblivious as Briley sometimes believed. But he kept a rein on his eagerness. Len could still hand the story to somebody else, leaving Briley looking the fool. "Okay. I confess, I'd like to do it."

"You sure?" Len lost the teasing look. "This could be the dirtiest dirt the *Real Scoop* has dug up to date. It'll take real focus. Cunning. Pulling the wool over people's eyes. In other words, finding a way to *fit in* so you have access to the real dirt. You aren't exactly known for fitting in."

Len would never know how much anger his last comment stirred, because Briley was well practiced in hiding his true feelings. But the emotion roared through his gut and sent heat from his midsection to his extremities. He clenched his fists on the back of his head and ground his teeth together. After slowly counting to five, he brought himself under control enough to answer.

Forcing his lips into a wry curl, he brought his arms down and propped his elbows on the chair's hard plastic armrests. "Maybe I just haven't had the right motivation to fit in anywhere yet. Doesn't mean I can't do it."

Len examined him for several seconds, and Briley remained still and unflinching beneath his boss's scrutiny. Finally a grin

15

tugged at one corner of the man's lips. "All right. It might take me a little while to get everything organized for a lengthy stay in Amish country, but I'll get it arranged. In the meantime, do lots of reading up on the Plain groups. I mean, research 'em deep, Briley. Get their traditions and religious practices in your head so you won't go offending them the minute you hit town."

Briley raised his hand like a Boy Scout making a pledge.

With a snort of amusement or derision — Briley couldn't quite determine which — Len pushed off from the desk and snatched up the newspaper that had started their discussion. Tapping his thigh with the rolled-up wad of newsprint, he aimed a warning look in Briley's direction. "Don't get too cocky. Those people are supposedly family oriented. That'll be unique for you, who's never had a family to speak of. Don't let some Amish girl sucker you in."

Len's comment about family cut, but Briley covered it with a laugh. "Briley Forrester taken in by a plain-clothed, plain-faced, plain-living female?" He shook his head, hunching back over his keyboard. "Not likely."

CHAPTER 2

Sommerfeld, Kansas
Late September

Anna-Grace Braun

"Sissy! Sissy, you need to come out!" Small fists banged on Anna-Grace's closed bedroom door, adding insistence to the demanding call.

Anna-Grace chuckled indulgently, familiar with the long-practiced morning routine. Who needed an alarm clock when she had an early rising little sister? "I'll come when I'm ready, Sunny." She pinched up one last bobby pin and raised it to her cap.

"But, Sissy, Steven is here and wants to see you now!"

Steven was here? Before breakfast? Even though Anna-Grace had spent the better part of yesterday afternoon with Steven — on the front porch with her folks' watchful gazes aimed out the living room window —

her heart fluttered as eagerly as if they'd been apart for weeks. Anna-Grace dropped the pin on her dresser top where it bounced twice and leaped over the edge. She dashed to the door and swung it open, nearly tripping over Sunny.

Laughing, she caught her little sister by the shoulders and did a side step that put her in the lead. She scurried up the hallway with Sunny trotting along on her heels, her small hand batting Anna-Grace's arm. As she passed the wide doorway to the kitchen, she peeked in and caught Mom's eye.

Mom gave an understanding smile. "Sunny, come here, please."

"But —"

"Help me set the table for breakfast."

With a sigh Sunny changed course and headed into the kitchen, allowing Anna-Grace to enter the living room free of her little shadow. She loved Sunny dearly. She'd prayed for a younger sibling every night from the time she was four until she'd turned thirteen, and she wouldn't trade the little girl who'd come all the way from China for anything in the world. But sometimes she needed privacy.

Steven waited on the patch of tile just inside the front door. As always, the sight of her intended raised a rush of warmth from her chest to her face. Did every girl feel so giddy and light when in the presence of the one she loved? Would this wondrous feeling someday be commonplace, the way Sunny's morning door knocks and calls were now an expected part of a daily routine? How Anna-Grace hoped she'd never lose the heart-lifting pleasure of gazing upon her golden-haired, broad-shouldered beau.

"Good morning, Steven." She wheezed the greeting, a bit breathless from her mad dash through the house. "What a surprise. I didn't expect to see you today."

He swished his thigh with his dark blue ball cap, creating a rhythmic *whisk-whisk.* "Yeah, well, it's a surprise to me, too."

A shy grin lifted the corners of his lips, capturing Anna-Grace's attention. His pale-pink lips, the lower one plump and soft looking, had never kissed her except on her cheek or temple, but she anticipated the day when they would meet her lips for the first time. Only five more months now! In the Old Order faith, being a wife and mother was a woman's highest calling, and February couldn't come soon enough to suit her. She pushed the thoughts aside as Steven cleared his throat and continued in his easy, low-pitched drawl.

"When I went home from here yesterday

evening, my folks gave me some news. They thought you should know it, too, and Mom said I'd better come right away. Otherwise you might hear it from someone else first. You know how word spreads in town."

There were no secrets in Sommerfeld. Sometimes the intimacy of her close-knit community gave her comfort, and other times it rankled. She offered a quick shrug. "What's the news?"

"You know how my brother took off five years ago and we haven't seen him since?"

Kevin Brungardt's departure was a painful chapter in his family's history. It had left a bruise on the hearts of many Sommerfeld residents who'd watched him grow more and more belligerent before finally sneaking off one night under the cover of darkness. Anna-Grace's parents still prayed he'd return someday, but she didn't hold out much hope, given the young man's rebellious nature. Fortunately Steven was nothing like his brother. "Yes, I know." She spoke softly, injecting sympathy in her tone.

Steven pulled in a breath and blew it out. "My grandfather — Mom's father — deeded several hundred acres of land in Arborville to Kevin. But since my brother hasn't claimed it, Dad petitioned to get it into his and Mom's names instead. The court approved the request. And Dad says . . ." An odd expression crossed his face. "He says they're going to sign the land over to me. As a wedding gift."

Anna-Grace gasped. She reached for his hand and he took hold, but his grip felt clammy. He must be nervous about the responsibility. But he wouldn't have to farm it alone. He'd have her to help him. Their own farm! She couldn't curb her excitement. "What wonderful news! Is there a house on the land?"

Steven nodded slowly. "Just a small one, built in the 1930s or early '40s. But Dad hasn't been to the property in years, so he doesn't know what shape it's in. The land's been rented out ever since Granddad Meiers died, with the money from the renters going into an account in Kevin's name. Dad's still trying to get that changed over, but he says once it's done, I can have it, too, in case I need to build a new house or do repairs on the one that's there. I'll also need to buy some equipment."

"Steven, what a blessing." Anna-Grace fought tears of gratitude. She and Steven couldn't help but have a wonderful start as husband and wife with a house, cleared fields, and a sum of money to see to their needs. "I feel badly that Kevin sacrificed his inheritance, but I'm so happy for you."

"I felt funny about taking it, but Dad says it's only right since I'm Granddad Meiers's grandson, too. Granddad died the year before I was born, and Mom says if he'd known about me, he likely would have split it between Kevin and me anyway. So I'm not taking anything that isn't rightfully mine."

He sounded uncertain. Even undeserving. Her heart ached for him. Steven was such an honorable man — so good and kind and giving. Of course he wouldn't want to take something that should belong to someone else. Anna-Grace squeezed his hand. "Your mom's right. Even if Kevin came back tomorrow, he wouldn't want to be a farmer."

Although she was several years younger than Kevin and he'd been gone a good while, she remembered the scowling youth who stood to the side at community workings, only joining in when commanded by his father and then halfheartedly participating. Kevin wouldn't eagerly claim a farmstead. But Steven had a hardworking attitude, and he'd learned farming from his dad. This gift was beyond anything she could have imagined.

She smiled so widely she felt as though her face might split. "Oh, Steven, our own place . . ."

"Uh-huh."

She laughed at his somber expression and gently swung his hand. "Will you go see your land soon?" Maybe she could go with him, if Mom and Dad gave her permission.

"Probably. Dad said we'd drive over some Saturday morning. Or maybe a Friday evening and spend the night. He'll let me know." Steven withdrew his hand and turned toward the door. "I need to get to work. Dad's waiting for me. But I wanted you to know about the land and . . ." His voice trailed off as if he'd forgotten what he was talking about.

Anna-Grace shook her head, a smile of amusement playing on the corner of her lips. The ribbons trailing from her cap tickled her neck, reminding her that soon she'd trade the white ribbons for black when she became Mrs. Steven Brungardt. And then she'd move away from Mom and Dad and the town that had always been her home. Suddenly she understood Steven's reticence. Changes, while exciting, also meant giving up something. It would be hard to be hours away from her parents and sister and everything else familiar.

"We'll be all right, Steven," she said, as much for herself as for him.

A weak smile formed on his face. "Sure. Sure we will." But the lack of confidence in his tone stung Anna-Grace's heart.

Steven Brungardt
Steven climbed into his old Ford pickup, jammed his boot on the clutch pedal, and gave the key an almost vicious twist. The engine rumbled to life, the *chug-chug-chug* vibrating the truck's cab. He put the truck in gear, then eased onto the house-lined street. Soon children with lunch boxes and books in hand would amble out the doors for their walk to school. But for now the dirt streets were empty, tempting him to gun his engine and drive a little recklessly. What would it hurt? Nothing. And it might dispel some of the restlessness that had kept him awake last night and still rattled through him. But he didn't do it. Because reckless was something Kevin would be. And Steven had spent his entire lifetime trying his best not to be his brother.

As Steven drove through the center of town, his gaze drifted across the familiar businesses. Every building freshly painted, the front walkways swept clean, and the smudge-free windows reflecting the morning sun. No cars were parked outside Lisbeth's this morning. The tiny café where

Anna-Grace worked part-time as a waitress — now owned by her aunt Deborah but still bearing the name of its original owner — was never open on Sundays or Mondays. But every other day of the week, cars filled the entire two blocks on either side of the café. Mostly fancy cars driven by outsiders.

When outsiders — non-Mennonites — visited Sommerfeld to eat at the café or purchase hand-crafted goods, rather than bemoaning the unpaved streets or questioning the lack of air conditioning in the businesses, they commented on the tidy appearance of the town, citing how different it was from their own bigger, bustling cities. Steven wished he had the courage to ask them about their cities. What was it like to live in a place that wasn't so small a person knew every neighbor by name, where young people were free to pursue higher education, and where people didn't need to seek the approval of the elders to buy a car or get a telephone or purchase a new piece of farm equipment? Sometimes he wanted to tell the outsiders, "Don't envy us. You're the lucky ones." But of course he didn't. Mostly, he didn't even let himself think it. But despite his best efforts, he couldn't stop thinking about it today.

Because last night when Dad had told him

about the land in Arborville and how Steven and Anna-Grace would raise a family there, he realized with greater clarity than ever that what he wanted didn't matter. All that mattered was what Dad and Mom wanted for him. What the fellowship elders would approve.

He stifled a growl as he turned his truck onto the road leading to his family farmstead. Why hadn't he told Anna-Grace he didn't want to farm the land in Arborville? Why hadn't he shared what he'd thought about last night — selling the land and taking the money from the account built up by the renters and moving to a city where he could finish high school and then go to college?

From the first day he'd entered the little community school and sat in rapt attention under the exuberant instruction of Miss Kroeker, he'd wanted to build a love of learning in other children. No other men in his community had ever become teachers, but in his childish mind he'd decided he would be the first. Until he'd told his brother his dream. Kevin scoffed at the idea. *"If you're gonna be a Mennonite man, you'll have to do what Dad and the elders want you to do, and teachers are always women. So forget it, little brother."* He'd never mentioned it again. But he hadn't forgotten.

He'd started to tell Anna-Grace what he wanted to do with the land, but he lost his nerve. Anna-Grace's delight too closely reflected Dad and Mom's excitement, and he felt trampled and stifled and frustrated. So he'd kept his thoughts to himself. His cowardice troubled him. Shouldn't a man feel comfortable telling the woman who would be his wife the deepest longings of his soul?

The sliding doors on the century-old barn were spread wide, letting Steven know Dad had already taken their fellowship-approved tractor and disc to the field to turn under the dried cornstalks. He'd be watching for Steven to come take over the task so he could move on to burning the wheat stubble. Dad had never given Steven responsibility for burning an empty field, claiming if something went wrong he'd rather face the consequences himself than see his son suffer. Dad might mean well, but his actions communicated a lack of faith in him.

Will Dad follow me to Arborville and do the field burning there, too? The snide thought caught him by surprise. *Forgive me, Lord, for being disrespectful.*

Steven parked the truck in the lean-to behind the barn, then trotted to the house to change clothes. Mom had insisted he wear a button-up cotton shirt rather than a work T-shirt to visit Anna-Grace. He'd considered saying he didn't think it would make much difference to Anna-Grace what he wore, but fearing his comment would be construed as rebellion, he'd simply done as his mother directed. Because he was the good son — the one who didn't pierce his mother's heart.

He clomped directly to his bedroom and hung his shirt in the closet rather than draping it over the end of the bed, then popped a pocketed T-shirt over his head. Still tucking in the tail, he moved into the hallway. Mom was coming from the opposite direction with a load of towels in her arms. Her face broke into a smile when she spotted Steven.

"What did she think?"

Steven needed no further explanation. "She was excited." Remembering Anna-Grace's sparkling blue eyes and the firm grip of her slender hand, he tried to conjure happiness. But it failed to rise.

"I'll bet she was." Mom beamed as brightly as Anna-Grace had. "It will seem strange to her at first, I'm sure, living away from Sommerfeld. But she has family in Arborville."

Steven frowned. "She does?"

"Mm-hm. Remember? Anna-Grace's great-aunt — her dad's mother's sister — and most of her children live there. As a matter of fact, Anna-Grace's cousin Cletus Zimmerman has been renting Granddad's land. With family nearby, it won't take her long at all to feel at home there. And if she's like every other young woman, she'll be eager to set up housekeeping and make the place her own."

Steven released a rueful chuckle. "Yeah. She's eager all right."

Mom laughed and shifted the bundle in her arms. "That's good. Better than fearful, yes?"

"I guess so."

Mom laughed again, shaking her head at him. Her reaction reminded him of the way Anna-Grace had behaved — amused and maybe a little baffled by his lack of enthusiasm. If he told Mom his concerns, would she understand? He formed the words in his head. *"Mom, what I'd really like to do is sell that land and use the money for college. Would you be proud to have a teacher for a son?"*

"Well, now that your errand is done, you'd better head out. Dad left more than half an hour ago already, and he wants to get that field burned before the winds stir to life. So you'd best go on now."

He held back a sigh. "Sure, Mom." He headed outside, setting his feet hard against the drying grass. Maybe it was best she'd interrupted his thoughts. He shouldn't hurt his parents by telling them he didn't want the land. And he shouldn't hurt Anna-Grace by telling her there was something more he wanted than being a Mennonite farmer, husband, and father.

Sometimes being the good son was a difficult burden to bear.

CHAPTER 3

Arborville, Kansas
First Friday in October

Briley

This was a town? Briley propped his forearm on the window frame and slowed his fire engine–red Camaro to a crawl in case he might miss something. By the time he reached the north end of Main Street, which was only a block from the south end, he realized there wasn't anything to miss. A hardware store with oil lamps displayed in the window — oil lamps, of all things! — and a lumberyard on the east side, a grocery store, fabric shop, gifts-and-crafts shop, and postage stamp–sized post office on the west made up the entire business district. What had Len been thinking to send him here? A place this small couldn't hold a story of interest.

But he sure was stirring interest. Or, more

accurately, his car was. The mix of Amish and Mennonite folks — according to his research, the Amish women wore the solid-color dresses and the Mennonite the floral-patterned ones — meandering along the concrete sidewalks all paused to gawk as he rolled by. Little boys pointed, only to have their hands smacked down by their mothers, and little girls hid behind their mothers' skirts to peek at him with round eyes. Hadn't they ever seen a sports car before? He tried to summon a bit of sarcasm. *Take a picture. It lasts longer.* But he had to admit he liked the reaction. Who would've thought ragamuffin Briley Forrester would garner such attention? Now if his article would get the same attention from non-Plain folks . . .

He planted his foot on the brake and stuck his head out the open window. "Hey, there."

The two Amish women and cluster of kids on the corner outside the hardware store aimed curious faces in his direction. The oldest kid, a boy maybe twelve or thirteen with a bowl-shaped haircut and homemade britches held up by suspenders, raised his hand in a wave and called, "What'cha need, mister?"

"I'm looking for the —" He poked the button on his recordable memo-keeper, and his voice stated the inn's name. He turned back to the little group. "The Grace Notes B and B. It's supposed to be in Arborville, but it's not coming up on my GPS."

The kid glanced at one of the women, presumably his mother, and waited until she gave a nod. Then he trotted to the side of the car and leaned down, his gaze examining the car's interior as he talked. "That's out at the Zimmerman farm. Go back to Highway 96, drive north three miles to County Road 42. Then go east two and a half miles. You'll see the sign for Grace Notes at their lane." He made a sour face. "It's all dirt roads out there, mister, so your shiny car'll get plenty dusty."

Briley grinned. "It'll wash. Thanks, kid."

The boy backed up slowly, the heels of his clunky brown boots stirring dust that swirled away on the stout breeze.

His foot still on the brake, Briley revved the motor, earning an open-mouthed look of wonder from the kid. The boy's mother pursed her lips, though. She grabbed the boy's elbow and yanked him onto the sidewalk. Briley winked at the red-faced mother, mock saluted the boy, and took off, leaving a cloud of dust in his wake.

As he pulled onto the highway, he berated himself. Why had he showed off that way? Who cared if he impressed some little

Amish kid in a podunk town? The boy couldn't do anything for him, and if the townsfolk branded him a troublemaker, they wouldn't open up and share the information he needed to complete his article. He'd acted like the cocky seventeen-year-old he'd been instead of the mature, responsible twenty-six-year-old he was supposed to be.

Aunt Myrt's voice chided in his memory. *"You're gonna have to bury that wild side of yours, Briley Ray, or it'll be your ruination."* But it wasn't easy to lose the boy who'd hidden his insecurities behind a shield of arrogance. Aunt Myrt had done her best to convince him all he needed to do was let Jesus work in him and he'd be good as new, but Briley'd never been able to grasp the concept. Aunt Myrt was a nice lady — the nicest he'd met over his years in the foster care system — but she was a little simple-minded sometimes. He'd respected her enough not to tell her so, though. Truth was, he missed her.

He spotted a narrow metal sign announcing County Road 42, and he slowed to make the turn. His tires crunched as they left the smooth asphalt and met the gravel-and-dirt road. He hit the button to raise his window before dust flowed inside. He liked the way the dirt billowed in a cloud behind him, so he picked back up to almost sixty. Fields stretched in both directions, only stubble remaining in some, others covered in small, bushy-looking tufts he presumed were soybeans, and still others looking charred from a recent burning. Off in the distance a plume of smoke alerted him to another field being burned. Good thing he'd closed the window. He'd have quite a time getting rid of the smoke smell if it attached itself to his leather interior.

Just as the kid in town had said, two and a half miles in he spotted a sign. He slowed the Camaro and stopped at the end of the lane, examining the sign. Nothing more than a sheet of plywood mounted on fence posts, painted stark white with free-handed letters in dark blue in some sort of flowing script. Black music notes formed a wavy line along the top and bottom, sandwiching the B and B's name in between. Quaint. Aunt Myrt would probably exclaim over it. But Briley wasn't Aunt Myrt.

Pressing the gas pedal once more, he eased into the lane. A thick row of trees, scraggly ones with big green balls growing on the branches mixed with overgrown cedars, had blocked his view of the house, but once he got a glimpse of it, he released a whistle of amazement. The sign didn't do the house justice. He wouldn't want to live in an old Victorian farmhouse in the middle of cornfields, but he had to admit the place was welcoming, with its porch running the full width and on around the side and a variety of paint colors showcasing the different trims. They didn't build houses like this anymore, and even though he preferred his modern apartment in the steel-and-glass building in Chicago, he could appreciate the craftsmanship of the place.

He inched up the lane, taking in the monstrous barn and the half-dozen dried-up flower beds laid out on the lawn. Wire frames, shaped like notes, filled the center of the beds. During the spring and summer, those frames probably held bright-colored blooms. Now devoid of color, they looked stark and empty. Tuneless. He shook his head. This place was making him whimsical, and he was never whimsical. He parked the car in a graveled spot next to the barn and killed the engine. His radio, which he'd tuned to a classic rock station and cranked up full blast, ended midsong.

The quiet struck like a blow. Even with the windows rolled tight, the wind's whisper and a bird's cheerful song crept through. Briley knew what wind sounded like — where he lived, it sometimes swayed the highest floors of buildings — but he couldn't remember the last time he'd heard a bird sing. Reminded him of summer evenings on Aunt Myrt's sleeping porch. At least it raised pleasant memories even if he didn't have the time to be skipping down memory lane.

After popping open the door, he swung his legs out and unfolded himself from the seat. He stretched, arching backward to work out the kinks in his lower spine. When he'd bought the sports car, Len told him it was a foolish expenditure. *"Why not just walk or take the bus like every other downtown Chicago dweller?"* Then Len had teased him about needing a pry bar to get himself in and out of it. *"A man close to six foot three with shoulders broad enough to give Atlas some stiff competition has no business cramming himself into a sardine can."* But Briley was used to close quarters. All his growing-up years, he'd had little more than a bed and a couple of dresser drawers to claim as his own. And the Camaro's sleek frame made up for the compact space. He'd keep the car no matter what Len said.

He left his luggage and laptop in the backseat and didn't even bother hitting the lock on his key fob — who would disturb anything? Then he ambled along a series of steppingstones that led to the porch. Len had made the lodging arrangements for him. Briley had wanted to stay in Wichita, the closest large city, where he'd be able to enjoy a bit of the nightlife, but Len said if he was going to write an accurate depiction of living the Plain lifestyle, he needed to be in the middle of it. Briley paused at the base of the porch steps and turned a slow circle. He was definitely in the middle of "plain."

A soft squeak caught his attention, and he turned to see the front door open. Briley removed his sunglasses and slipped them into his shirt pocket. A girl with her dark hair pulled back in a simple tail, wearing a straight denim skirt and a pumpkin-colored long-sleeved T-shirt with the sleeves pushed up to her elbows, stood framed behind the old-fashioned screen door. Despite her humble wrappings, he recognized beauty when he saw it. Mennonite or not, the girl was a knockout.

He mounted the four steps in two bounds. Two long-legged strides brought him to the opposite side of the door. He settled his weight on one hip, slipped his fingertips into the slanted pockets of his jeans, and grinned at the girl. "Hi, darlin'. I'm Briley Forrester, and I have a reservation for a long-term stay." Three months would probably seem like forever, but at least the scenery was nice. He peeked beyond her shoulder. The screen distorted his view, but he didn't think anyone else was inside. "Is the owner here so I can check in?" He half hoped she'd say no so he'd have a little more time to flirt. He liked flirting almost as much as he liked writing exposés.

She pushed the screen door open, forcing him to take a sideways step, and moved onto the porch although she remained just over the doorjamb with the screen door braced against her shoulder. Her chin tipped back when she looked into his face, giving him a glimpse of a few light-colored freckles strategically placed on her forehead and cheeks. One larger one — more prominent — decorated the left side of her upper lip. What a perfect location to land a kiss. Maybe he'd find a little nightlife here in Arborville after all.

"I'm Alexa Zimmerman. I manage Grace Notes B and B."

"Really?" He gave her a bold up-and-down look. "You're too young and pretty to be running a hotel."

"It's a bed-and-breakfast inn, Mr. Forrester, and —"

"Call me Briley."

"— my age and appearance have nothing

to do with my ability to run it well." Looking across the yard, she pointed. "Is that your vehicle?"

He nodded, anticipating a complimentary comment.

"Since you're long-term, feel free to pull it into the barn at night. It will need to stay on the side yard there during the day, though, so my uncle can access his equipment. Do you have luggage?"

He automatically formed a smart-alecky reply. "Well, I'm here for a long-term stay, so . . ."

"If you'd like to get it, I'll show you to the cottage."

He placed his hand on his chest, feigning surprise. "What? No bellhop to assist me?"

She let the screen door flop into place. Without a word, she stepped past him and trotted down the steps.

He followed her. "Where are you going?"

She moved along the steppingstones, her gleaming ponytail swaying between her shoulder blades. "You asked for a bellhop. That would be me."

He might be a flirt, even a rogue by some people's definition, but he wouldn't let this slip of a girl carry his luggage. He bounded past her and stopped in her pathway. She came to a halt and looked upward. She didn't even crack a smile. She sure was a serious thing. Too bad. He'd like to have a little fun with her. What would it take to strip away her cloak of indifference?

He quirked his lips into a grin that usually raised a self-conscious giggle from members of the female population. "Where's your sense of humor? I was only teasing, Alexa."

"You may call me Miss Zimmerman."

Wasn't she something else? Maybe living among people who avoided modern technology made her a throwback to an earlier century. He swallowed a chortle and bowed, affecting a highbrow look. "I beg your humble pardon. Miss Zimmerman, it is." The hours spent watching black-and-white classic movies with Aunt Myrt weren't for naught. He could be throwback, too.

Her brows pinched together, reminding him of his third-grade teacher. She'd never appreciated his shenanigans, either. The same deviltry that had led him to torment Mrs. Burton reared its head and aimed its attack at Miss Alexa Zimmerman.

"I shall retrieve my luggage forthwith and carry it with all due haste to your establishment. Furthermore, I —"

"Furthermore" — she folded her arms over her chest in a perfect imitation of Mrs. Burton — "you'll behave yourself. I reserve

41

the right to refuse service to anyone. I might only be a young woman, but I am the manager of Grace Notes B and B, and I would appreciate being treated with respect."

His amusement fled. Irritation replaced it. She didn't need to be so high-and-mighty. Didn't she know how to have fun? But what did he care? Would he let some unsmiling Mennonite girl make him feel small and insignificant? Absolutely not. He shrugged in well-practiced nonchalance. "Whatever you want, Miss Zimmerman. I've had a long drive and I'm tired, so if you'd point me to my room and tell me where I can grab some supper, I'd appreciate it."

She finally smiled. Not a flirtatious smile. Not even a friendly smile. More a smile of success that brought a greater stab of aggravation. "Of course, Mr. Forrester. The cottage is ready for you, and as your boss requested, I stocked the minifridge with sodas, sandwich fixings, and fruit so you can prepare your own simple supper. Please grab your luggage and follow me."

With a little snort he slung his laptop case over his shoulder and then retrieved his leather rolling suitcase. The case's wheels bumped across the steppingstones, hindering his progress, but he followed her past the house and then along a narrow gravel path to a small, square building painted in colors similar to the Victorian farmhouse.

She opened the door and held her hand out in invitation. "Here you are. Your own little home-away-from-home."

He crossed the cracked square of concrete serving as a stoop and entered what Alexa — oops, Miss Zimmerman — had called the cottage. The space reminded him of a project from one of the do-it-yourself home improvement magazines Aunt Myrt liked to read. Quite a change from his masculine, streamlined, glass-and-black decor at home. A designer would probably define the cottage as "charmingly eclectic," and no doubt some would rave about the scattered throw rugs, mismatched furnishings, and high tin ceiling. He felt as though he'd stepped into a time machine and landed somewhere near the turn of the twentieth century. His sense of zipping backward in time increased when his gaze fell on the massive wood-burning stove lurking in the far corner.

He pointed at the big black hunk of iron. "I'm not expected to cook on that thing, am I?"

She laughed lightly. If he hadn't been annoyed with her, he might have enjoyed the trickling sound. "There's a microwave behind the roll-up door in that green-painted cupboard."

He crossed to the cupboard and slid the door upward. A shiny, stainless-steel micro-wave greeted his eyes. He blew out a relieved breath.

"You should find everything you need, but if you discover you're lacking something, please just knock on the back door. I'll do what I can to make your stay comfortable."

He considered voicing a suggestive request but decided against it. Aunt Myrt wouldn't approve, and Len had warned him about trying to fit in with these people. He made a mental note — *no flirting.* Besides, she was being pleasant so he'd respond in kind. "Okay, thanks." He placed his laptop case on the scarred table that held a square red-and-white-checked scarf and a chunky crock overflowing with artificial daisies. How sweet . . . "Any other regulations besides leaving my car outside the barn during daytime hours?"

"Grace Notes B and B is a no-smoking, alcohol-free inn. Even though you're in the cottage rather than in the house, we'd ap-preciate you honoring our preference."

Our? Maybe she was married and that's why she resisted his flirtations. Then he'd definitely curb it. He might be a lot of things, but a wife-stealer wasn't one of them. "No problem. Anything else?"

"On Sunday we attend worship service, so I only serve breakfast at eight o'clock. Every other day, you're free to choose an earlier or later time that suits your schedule."

"Eight is fine every day for me."

"All right. Since you'll be staying for a while, you're welcome to attend service with us on Sundays."

Eventually he'd want to sit in on their worship — Len said he ought to. But tomorrow he intended to kick back and relax, work out the stiffness in his muscles from his long drive from Illinois. "Thanks. I might do that."

"All right then." She'd remained on the stoop. She withdrew a silver-plated keychain shaped like a music note from her pocket and held it across the threshold as if her arm was a bridge. "Here's the key for the cottage. I unlock the back door of the house by seven if you'd like a cup of coffee before breakfast." She backed up slowly, her hands clasped loosely against her skirt front.

He glanced down, but the way she cupped her right hand over her left, he couldn't tell if she wore a ring or not. Not that it would matter. If he remembered his research correctly, the Old Order groups didn't wear wedding rings.

A smile, this one more genuine and definitely more appealing, curved her lips. "Welcome to Grace Notes B and B, Mr. Forrester. I hope you enjoy your stay." She turned and scurried off before he could say anything else.

CHAPTER 4

Alexa Zimmerman

Alexa slammed the back porch door closed behind her. The solid *crack!* failed to chase the image of Briley Forrester from her mind. She pulled in a long, slow breath, willing her clamoring pulse to calm. Gracious, it should be illegal for a man to be that handsome. And doubly illegal — if there was such a thing — for him to be so aware of his own virility.

"Alexa? Are you all right?" Grandmother's worried voice carried from the dining room.

Alexa pressed her palms to her chest and blew out air in a whoosh before rejoining her grandmother at the table, where they had been wrapping silverware in cloth napkins before the sound of the car drew Alexa to the front door. She plopped into her chair, feeling as winded as if she'd run a marathon. "Yes. Sorry about that bang. The door got away from me."

Grandmother raised one eyebrow in silent query. She placed the last bundle of silverware with the others on the table and leaned back in her wheelchair. "That should be enough to carry you through the next two weeks. Unless you get more calls. I presume, since you didn't bring anyone inside, your long-term guest just arrived?"

Funny how Grandmother always used *your* rather than *our* when referring to guests or anything else related to operating the inn. Even though the house belonged to her, she saw the business as Alexa's. Grandmother placing the responsibility firmly on Alexa's shoulders made her all the more determined to make this business work. Thank goodness Mr. Forrester — Briley — had stopped acting like a wolf on the prowl so she didn't have to send him elsewhere. She needed the money from his stay.

"Yes. I hope he's comfortable in the cottage." She'd hated to give up what she'd intended to claim as her own little house, but when the newspaper man in Chicago had indicated he'd be sending a male reporter for an up to three-month stay in Arborville, it had made sense to put him out there rather than have a single man staying in the house with Grandmother. As Uncle Clete said, the people in town might raise their eyebrows. And she wouldn't do anything to cause a stir. Well, at least not more than her arrival in town already had.

"What's he like?" Grandmother asked.

Alexa busied herself stacking the rolls of silverware in a little wicker basket. "Nice, I guess. Definitely big city." She pictured his black-with-white-pinstripes button-up shirt, open at the collar and rolled back at the cuffs yet neatly tucked into what were obviously designer blue jeans. Instead of wearing tennis shoes or boots, like the majority of the men in Arborville, he wore tasseled loafers. With jeans!

She shook her head. "He'll stick out like a sore thumb around here, and at the same time I imagine he'll turn a few heads. He's quite the looker." She waggled her eyebrows and fanned herself, partly for show, partly because her face was heating. She'd never encountered a man as blatantly sensual as Briley Forrester.

Grandmother frowned. "You be careful, Alexa Joy Zimmerman."

Alexa drew back. "I haven't done anything wrong."

"Sometimes you don't have to. With some men, just being a female is enough."

She remembered his flirtatious behavior when she'd opened the door. If Grandmother had been the one to greet him, he probably would have behaved the same way. Flattery rolled too easily from that man's tongue. "I already set him straight. He tried coming on to me, but I let him know it wasn't appropriate."

"Good for you." Grandmother gave a firm nod. Then she sighed. "I'm glad there are other guests staying this weekend. I'll feel a little safer knowing Mr. Brungardt and his son will be here, too, with a stranger from Chicago out in the summer kitchen."

"The cottage," Alexa corrected with a smile.

Grandmother rolled her eyes but she grinned. "I suppose considering all the work you and Paul did out there to turn that sorry little building into a pleasant getaway, I should stop referring to it as 'the summer kitchen.' You really did a wonderful job with it."

Pride swelled at Grandmother's compliment, but Alexa formed a modest rejoinder. "Without Mr. Aldrich's know-how, I would never have been able to transform the old summer kitchen into a guest cottage. I'm glad he had time in his schedule to get it done for me."

"Amazing how much things have changed in such a short amount of time." Grandmother's tone turned reflective. "Six months ago my house wasn't handicap accessible, I was living here alone, you were living in Indiana, and I didn't even know I had a granddaughter named Alexa." A smile trembled on her lips. She reached across the table, took Alexa's hands, and squeezed tight. "You're such a blessing to me."

"You are my gift." Mom's voice echoed in Alexa's memory. Tears stung. She missed Mom so much. All her childhood, it was just her and Mom. How strange to be so far away from her, yet Alexa knew she was where she was supposed to be. Even so, she couldn't wait until Thanksgiving when Mom would visit and see everything Alexa had accomplished in the past few months.

"And I think having a long-term guest is a blessing, too." Grandmother released Alexa's hands to scoop up the last rolls of silverware and plop them into the basket. "I wondered if you'd have any business at all in the fall and winter months."

Alexa had wondered the same thing, especially since the representative from the Kansas Bed-and-Breakfast Inns Association had indicated many inns closed during the winter. But she'd gone ahead and spent the money to advertise anyway, wanting to get her B and B listed on Internet search engines. And that's how the newspaper man from Chicago had found her. So it all worked out well in spite of Uncle Clete and Aunt Shelley's dismal predictions. She wanted to succeed. Not to prove Clete and Shelley wrong, but to prove to them she could do something worthwhile. She needed their approval. Maybe too much.

Rising, she grabbed the basket of silverware and then carried it to the antique sideboard where she stored the plates, mugs, and glassware for guests. She wasn't allowed to keep the guests' dishes in the kitchen with those she and Grandmother used. Being an innkeeper required her to know and follow state guidelines as well as be a good cook, a maid, a greeter, and a bookkeeper. What a challenge! But she could handle it. Her mother had taught her she could do anything through Christ, who gave her strength.

Grandmother rolled her wheelchair around the end of the table toward the living room. "If you need to prepare anything for tomorrow's breakfast, I'll be happy to watch the road for the next arrivals."

"I don't really have anything to do tonight, but thanks." Alexa intended to stir up a sausage-and-hash-brown casserole and bake cranberry-and-walnut-filled apples for breakfast. With all male guests expected, she decided she should avoid making strawberry crepes or miniature spinach-mushroom quiches. She looked forward to preparing the fun dishes for couples next spring and summer.

She helped her grandmother transfer from her wheelchair to the sofa, then retrieved her basket of crocheting hooks and yarn. Once Grandmother was occupied, Alexa crossed to the window and looked out. The bright-red sports car — an unusual sight in little Arborville — caught her eye. Such a pretentious vehicle, one guaranteed to garner attention. The same way Briley Forrester's movie-star appearance captured attention. Alexa folded her arms across her waist as fingers of awareness tiptoed up her spine. As Grandmother had said, she'd need to watch herself. Given his unbelievable good looks and easy means of flattery, the man had probably left a trail of broken hearts in his wake. She didn't want to add hers to the number.

She turned and sent a slight frown toward her grandmother. "The man who's coming with his son . . . the Brungardts? Did you say they have ties to Arborville?"

Grandmother lowered the half-finished doily. "That's right. Mr. Brungardt's wife,

Claudia, was a Meiers. She grew up on the farm next to ours. My Cecil started renting their land when old Mr. Meiers passed away, then Clete took up farming the acreage after Cecil died." Her brows pulled low. "Clete said the Brungardts asked to meet him at the farmstead tomorrow afternoon. I hope there isn't a problem."

"I guess we'll know when —" The sound of a car's approach pulled Alexa's attention to the window again. A solid gray sedan with black spray-painted bumpers, obviously a vehicle driven by a member of an Old Order sect, inched up the lane. She shrugged. "I was going to say 'when they get here.' And I'm pretty sure that's now."

Steven

"Whew." Steven shook his head and stared at the house through the car's windshield. Dusk was falling, but there was enough remaining light to see that the farmhouse was painted like a circus tent. "Anna-Grace told me her great-aunt's house had a new paint job, but I didn't expect anything so . . ." He wasn't sure how to describe it.

Dad pulled his sedan next to a red sports car and turned off the engine. He frowned first at the car and then at the house. "I don't know what to think. A fancy car beside the barn. A fancy house. Your mother would be shocked. It wasn't like this when she lived next door."

Steven wasn't shocked. He was intrigued. But he wouldn't say so.

Dad went on, his expression dour and tone forbidding. "It must be the influence of that granddaughter of Abigail Zimmerman's. She was raised in the world, you know."

Steven vaguely recalled the Brauns talking at a Sunday fellowship dinner about the return of one of the Zimmerman daughters, who brought a grown-up daughter home with her. Mom had been encouraged by the story, saying it meant there was hope Kevin would come back, too, someday, but Steven hadn't paid much attention. What did he care about some family he'd never met? Now he wished he'd listened more closely.

Dad tapped his chin with his finger, his scowl deep. "Maybe we should have waited and come over in the morning instead. Maybe it's not such a good idea for us to give our money to someone who isn't of our sect."

Steven didn't think it would be any different than buying groceries from one of the big chains or a car from the dealer in Salina. Plus, in his opinion, it wasn't right to make

55

a reservation and then not honor it. Obviously the inn-keeper was waiting for them — yellow porch lights glowed a warm welcome. But it was useless to argue with his father. So he waited in silence for Dad to decide what to do.

After several long minutes, Dad huffed a breath, got out, and headed for the house. Even though he hadn't invited Steven to go with him, he followed anyway. The pathway was lined by glass balls that flickered first red, then blue, then green, reminding Steven of tiny fireworks. Color everywhere he looked. So unlike home. A thread of eagerness to see what else was different here sped his steps.

The front door opened and a smiling girl stepped onto the porch. She moved to its edge and waved. Although not attired like an Old Order Mennonite, her clothes were modest, her hairstyle simple, and she hadn't slathered her face with makeup. After getting a look at her car and the way the house was painted, Steven had expected something different. Something more. He couldn't decide whether he was disappointed or relieved by her humble appearance.

"Good evening," the girl called. "Are you the Brungardts?"

Dad stopped at the bottom of the porch

stairs. "That's right."

The girl's smile widened. "It's so nice to meet you. I'm Alexa Zimmerman. Welcome to Grace Notes."

Steven wanted to climb the steps and go right inside, but Dad didn't move.

"Is your grandmother here?"

Alexa Zimmerman didn't seem put off by Dad's brusqueness. Her smile remained in place and she gave a nod, linking her hands and laying them against her skirt front. "Yes, she is. She's been watching for you. I think she's eager to visit with someone from Sommerfeld since her nephews live there."

His face set in an uncertain frown, Dad stared at the girl for a few seconds. Then he gave a nod and turned to Steven. "Go get our case."

Steven swallowed a smile. He guessed they were staying.

CHAPTER 5

Briley

Briley carried one of the ancient chairs — the one that appeared the sturdiest — from the table to the front stoop and settled his frame into it. Had it been up to him, pretty much every piece of furniture in the cottage would have been hauled to the dump a long time ago, but he could make do for three months. He had a lifetime's worth of experience of making do.

He eased into the chair, cringing when its joints complained, and opened the cover on his electronic notebook. As he hit the On button, a movement to his right caught his attention. A dog with shaggy black-and-white fur trotted toward him. For a moment he tensed. Would the thing attack? But then he saw the dog's tongue lolling from its open mouth and its flag-like tail wagging in a friendly swish.

"Well, hi there." Briley stuck out his hand

and let the dog sniff it over. "You live around here?" Of course, the creature didn't reply, but it gave his hand a swipe with its warm, velvety tongue, then flopped down on the stoop next to Briley's chair and rested its head on its paws. Briley laughed, pleased more than he could explain by the dog's presence. He gave its soft ears a quick scratch. "Sorry, fella, but I have work to do. You can stick around, though, if you want to."

The dog rhythmically *thump-thumped* its tail against the stoop as Briley propped the notebook on his knee. The evening air was cool but not overly so, sufficiently blocked by his leather bomber jacket. A single lantern mounted next to the door gave off enough light for him to see. He began typing, his process slow and deliberate as he chose the little squares representing letters.

First impression of A.Z. — a little stuffy; cautiously friendly; dresses like a grandma.

First impression of community — people curious and watchful; town small but neat . . .

He typed a lengthy description of the businesses and of what he'd glimpsed through the windows. Len would laugh about all those oil lamps. Then he turned his attention to the farm that would be his temporary home.

First impression of farmstead — quiet; neat; peaceful.

The third descriptor stilled his fingers. *Peaceful* wasn't something he'd experienced much. Not as a child being shuffled from foster home to foster home, and not as an adult living in the middle of a big, bustling city.

He lifted his head and gave his current surroundings a slow examination. A long clothesline stretched from one end of the yard to the other, the wire shining in the moonlight. No trash blew across the ground or gathered along the house's foundation. Lights burned behind windows in the farmhouse, several on the first floor and two on the second. The glow became a beacon as darkness crept across the landscape. The insistent chirp of a cricket — or maybe a herd of them — combined with the soft whistle of the wind. Scents he couldn't recognize filled his nostrils. Earthy scents. Not unpleasant.

Using the hunt-and-peck method, he tapped out *fresh-smelling,* then glanced at his list and chuckled. So far everything he'd recorded about the locale was exactly what Len said everyone wanted to believe. *"There's gotta be dirt there, Briley,"* Len had told him during his last morning in the office, his expression earnest as he slipped into what Briley called his reporter mode. *"Find the dirt. Disprove all that peaceful, smiley, turn-the-other-cheek nonsense that makes people want to visit their communities and bow down in admiration. Let's show the real truth of being trapped in the Plain lifestyle."*

Sitting there with his new furry pal, drinking in the pleasant quiet, Briley wondered if Len might be wrong. He hoped not, because if he couldn't uncover dirt, he wouldn't have a story. And he desperately wanted the story. His first major byline. The teachers who shook their heads in dismay at his struggle to read, the foster parents who declared he'd never amount to anything, the class bullies who called him "big dummy" — wouldn't all of them be shocked to discover how wrong they'd been about him when Briley Forrester's name appeared under a lead story? And the *Real Scoop* needed a story that would capture the public's eye before it collapsed like so many other periodicals.

He'd keep his ears and eyes wide open. He'd peek beneath the surface of these people. He'd find dirt. One way or another, he'd find it and expose it for all the world to see.

No rooster announced the dawn, but Briley's cell phone alarm blared out the theme from *Star Wars* and brought him fully awake at seven o'clock. He groaned as he rolled off the mattress of the strangest bed he'd ever seen. Before crawling into it last night, he'd given it a careful look-over. Home built of sturdy wood and with a jointed metal frame, it actually folded up against the wall when it wasn't in use. If Alexa — he might have to call her *Miss Zimmerman,* but he wouldn't think of her as anything but Alexa — hadn't already had it down and made up for him, he might not have even found it. The contraption squeaked every time he moved, but he had to admit the mattress was of good quality. Once he'd put in earplugs — something he always used at home but hadn't thought would be necessary in these *peaceful* surroundings — he slept fairly well.

He didn't bother to remake the bed before hefting the mattress into the wooden frame.

A click of the cabinet doors, and not only was the bed hidden from sight, but the space felt much larger. He whacked the dividing curtain aside and padded on bare feet to the bathroom. He dipped his knees to bring himself low enough to see his whisker-dotted reflection in the mirror while he brushed his teeth. The ceiling of the tacked-on room sloped toward the east and was better suited for munchkins than for full-grown men.

But if he decided to take a soak, the claw-foot tub was like the one in Aunt Myrt's old-fashioned bathroom, so it would accommodate his length. For now, though, he wanted a shower. He twisted the knobs until the water temperature satisfied him — the hotter the better — then stepped into the center of a clear plastic circular curtain that protected the walls from spatters. He had to arch backward to fit beneath the rain-shower nozzle, but the water flowed hot the entire fifteen minutes of his shower and felt good.

He shaved, smirking at himself as he did so. Those *Duck Dynasty* guys had nothing on some of the Amish men he'd seen. Maybe he'd let his whiskers grow, too, while he was here so he'd fit in better. Nah. A beard wouldn't be enough to make him fit.

When he'd scraped his face as smooth as he could get it, considering his thick, dark whiskers, he splashed on spicy aftershave and then dug through his suitcase. He chose a deep plum shirt similar in color to the one the helpful boy had worn yesterday and a pair of denim jeans absolutely nothing like the boy's homemade, suspendered britches. The shirt was pretty wrinkled from its journey, but he gave it several sharp snaps and managed to work out the worst of the creases.

As he dressed, he glanced at the bureau lurking in the corner of the sleeping area. He should probably put his clothes in it rather than leaving them in the suitcase. Maybe later today. Or tomorrow. Aunt Myrt's voice tiptoed through his memory. *"Procrastination is just a fancy word for lazy. Laziness isn't a worthwhile trait. Don't put off for tomorrow what you can do today."* With a sigh he yanked open the drawers and transferred his clothing, then plunked the suitcase in the corner.

He shook his head and said with a light chuckle, "There ya go, Aunt Myrt." The sound of his voice startled him. He'd never spoken to an empty room before. Maybe the silence of the place was doing weird things to him. Rather than examining himself, he tugged socks and shoes over his feet and headed across the yard for the door Alexa had indicated would be open when he was ready for coffee. Caffeine ought to chase the weirdness out of him.

He moved with wide, eager strides across the dewy yard. A sloping concrete slab almost creamy in its newness led to the screened porch door, and inside the porch he located the door for the kitchen. It had to be the kitchen door based on the good smells seeping from behind it. His nose detected cinnamon, sausage, coffee . . . a tantalizing combination. His stomach growled and saliva pooled under his tongue in anticipation. Maybe he'd ask if he could be served up right away instead of waiting another fifteen minutes 'til it was eight o'clock.

He gave the square etched-glass window on the door a few taps with his knuckles before pushing it open. The kitchen was empty save for the wonderful aromas, but he heard voices from somewhere in the house. So, feeling a bit like an intruder, he moved past the warm kitchen through a short hallway lined with cupboards from floor to ceiling and stepped into a good-sized dining room, where a table big enough to seat at least a dozen people lurked in the

65

middle of the hardwood floor.

Alexa sat at the head of the table. She glanced at him, her face flooded with pink, and she lurched to her feet. "Mr. Forrester . . . good morning."

Two men — one older, one who looked a little younger than Briley — and a gray-haired woman sat on opposite sides at one end of the table. Based on their clothes, Briley surmised they were Mennonite. Alexa's family, maybe? The men turned backward in their chairs to peek briefly at Briley. Each gave a nod of greeting, then focused again on the contents of their plates. He couldn't blame them. Whatever they were eating smelled great. The older woman held her fork motionless and appraised him with a steady look. A slight smile curved her lips, but he sensed she was taking stock of him. He fought the urge to fidget.

He covered his unease by aiming a smile at Miss Zimmerman. "I know I'm a little early, but you said you'd have coffee ready, so . . ."

She tossed her napkin onto the table and gestured to the chair next to the older woman. Silverware rolled up in a green cloth napkin and a mug were already in place. "Please have a seat and I'll get your plate and some juice. The coffeepot is there on the sideboard, along with cream and sugar. Just help yourself." She scurried out of the room with her ponytail bouncing on her spine.

Briley sauntered around the table — it was a fairly long walk, given the length of the table and the size of the room — and hooked the mug with one finger. Making it spin like a pistol, he moved to the sideboard and then stilled the mug's rotation with a clamp of his hand. He set the mug gently on the wood top. No sense in scratching things up if he could avoid it. Although he'd distinctly heard conversation when he came in, no one spoke now. The scrape of forks on plates seemed extremely loud in the otherwise quiet room. Were the trio at the table watching him? He chose not to look. He filled his mug to the brim and raised it for a sip. Strong and flavorful with a rich, almost nutty aftertaste. Perfect.

Smacking his lips in satisfaction, he turned toward the table. At the same time, Alexa bustled through the doorway with a glass of pulpy orange juice — fresh squeezed? — and a plate so filled with food he couldn't even see the pattern around the edges. She followed him to his chair and set the plate in front of him, careful not to brush his arm as she leaned in.

"There you are. Would you like ketchup or some hot sauce for your casserole? I used spicy sausage, but one man's 'spicy' is another man's 'mild.' "

Briley glanced across the table to the other men's plates and noted they hadn't added anything to theirs. He presumed that meant it would be flavorful enough. "No, thanks. This looks great. Thanks, Miss Zimmerman."

With another quavery smile, she backed away and returned to her chair. She sat and placed her napkin in her lap, but she didn't lift her fork. "Mr. Forrester, let me introduce you to my grandmother, Mrs. Zimmerman, and our other guests. Joe Brungardt and his son Steven are from Sommerfeld, Kansas." She turned to the pair of men. "Mr. Forrester lives in Chicago. He's a newspaper reporter."

He was actually a tabloid reporter, but he wouldn't correct her. He extended his hand across the table. "Hello. Very nice to meet you."

The father rose from his chair to shake Briley's hand, but the son only bobbed his head in greeting.

Briley shifted his attention to Alexa's grandmother. Instead of a dining room chair, she sat in a wheelchair. The new-looking ramps in the front and back suddenly held great meaning, and an unexpected wave of sympathy struck him. He offered her his most charming smile — the one Aunt Myrt had bemoaned could melt butter. "It's nice to meet you as well, Mrs. Zimmerman. You have a beautiful home."

"Thank you." Her words were polite, but her eyes held apprehension. "It would only be a plain-looking farmhouse were it not for Alexa. She gave the house a makeover for my birthday and then set to work fixing things up in here and turning what used to be the summer kitchen into a cottage. Now everything looks like new."

Briley took a bite of the casserole. He chewed slowly, savoring the blend of flavors, then swallowed and wiped his mouth. "Obviously your granddaughter is a woman of many talents. A decorator, a gourmet cook, already operates her own business . . . What else do you excel in, Miss Zimmerman?"

Alexa's cheeks blazed pink. She rose jerkily, blinking rapidly in the Brungardts' direction. "Mr. Brungardt, I see your plate is empty. Would you like another serving? There's plenty left." The man nodded, and Alexa took his plate and disappeared into the kitchen.

Briley forked another bite of casserole to keep from chuckling. Her pretense of caring for the other guests hadn't fooled him. He'd been around females enough to know when one found him attractive. Most young women preened or openly flirted. Alexa, either shy or unaccustomed to social inter-action, did neither. Wouldn't it be fun to break down her barriers? Now that he'd figured out the *us* indicated her and her grandmother — and of course he should have surmised she was single when she referred to herself as *miss* — she was fair game.

He'd have to be cautious, though. The grandmother's legs might not work, but he suspected nothing was wrong with her vi-sion. Or her senses. He could tell she'd already pegged him as untrustworthy, the same way a lot of older people did when they looked at his shadow of dark whiskers, spiked hair, and leather jacket. He might have some trouble winning this one over. *"You've got to fit in if you want them to open up to you."* Len's warning rang through his mind. It wouldn't be nearly as much fun, but he'd behave himself.

Alexa returned with a plate heaping with casserole and a face empty of the pretty blush. Breakfast continued with soft chatter among the two guests — from Summer's Field, was it? — and the Zimmerman women. Briley didn't intrude upon the conversation. Listening with a reporter's ear, he searched for any tidbits that might find their way into his article. To his disappointment, nothing of merit arose.

When the older Brungardt had finished his second serving, he pushed his plate aside. "That was very good, Miss Zimmerman. If you wouldn't mind writing down the recipe, I will take it home to share with my wife. I think it would be a good one to have at our fellowship breakfasts."

Briley perked up. "Fellowship breakfasts?"

Mrs. Zimmerman answered. "Our church membership often gathers together for meals. We share food and our concerns and the things that give us reason to celebrate. We're very much like a big family." She paused and tipped her head, making one of the ribbons from her cap crunch against the flowered shoulder of her homemade dress. "Do you come from a big family, Mr. Forrester?"

Briley broke off a chunk from his baked apple. "No, ma'am." He stuffed the apple into his mouth.

The elder Brungardt turned to his son.

71

"Are you finished with your breakfast?"

"Yes."

"Let's get our things and head to the farmstead, then."

"Yes, sir."

Briley observed the younger man out of the corner of his eye. He was so polite. So serious. Maybe even a little resigned.

Mrs. Zimmerman said, "My son doesn't plan to meet you at the property until after lunch. You can stay here and relax until then, if you like."

Both men stood and pushed in their chairs. The father said, "It's been a long time since we were there, so I'm eager to see how the house and outbuildings look." He flung his arm around his son's shoulders, smiling for the first time since Briley entered the room. "We want to make sure the roof hasn't caved in and the walls still stand."

"Clete has maintained the property, the way his father taught him." Mrs. Zimmerman lifted her chin. "He wouldn't have watched everything fall apart without contacting you. He's a responsible renter."

Briley surveyed Brungardt's face for signs of resentment. According to his research, the Amish and Mennonite were nonconfrontational, but Mrs. Zimmerman had come close to issuing a challenge. Would Brungardt meet it?

The man waved one broad hand in dismissal. "Of course he is, Mrs. Zimmerman. I wouldn't expect anything less from Cecil Zimmerman's son. But as I said, we haven't been there in more than a dozen years. Things change in that amount of time, and if Steven is going to live in the house, then —"

"*Live* in it?" If Mrs. Zimmerman was able, Briley suspected she'd leap out of the chair and grab the man by his shirtfront. Her startled gaze bounced from the pair of Mennonite men to Alexa and back to the elder Brungardt. "But what of the land? Clete grows wheat there every year. We depend on that acreage."

The Brungardt son hung his head. The father's face pinched into a grimace of regret. He patted his son's shoulder. "I'm sorry, Mrs. Zimmerman, but the land belongs to Steven now. That's what we wanted to talk to Cletus about. Steven will be farming it from now on."

Mrs. Zimmerman stared at the man with her mouth open. Alexa crouched down and whispered something into her ear while the two Brungardt men shifted from foot to foot, clearly uncomfortable.

Briley sipped his tepid coffee, his mind whirling. What an interesting turn of events. Might he have arrived in Arborville in time to see a feud erupt between supposedly nonconfrontational people?

CHAPTER 6

Steven

If the floor opened up and swallowed him, Steven wouldn't complain. Standing there with Dad's arm heavy on his shoulders, Mrs. Zimmerman whispering frantic messages to her granddaughter, and the man from Chicago smirking into his coffee cup, he'd never been more uncomfortable. *God, I'm supposed to be able to do all things through Christ who gives me strength. Why can't I find the courage to tell Dad I don't want to be a farmer like him?*

He nudged his father. "Let's get our things and go." He'd spoken softly — hardly more than a whisper — but apparently Mrs. Zimmerman heard because she jerked upright in her wheelchair and aimed a determined look at him.

"Take Alexa with you."

He hadn't expected such a command. But he understood why she'd given it. He'd noticed how the Chicago reporter looked at Alexa, and he'd also seen how Mrs. Zimmerman looked at the reporter. Mrs. Zimmerman didn't want Alexa near the man. Steven wanted to take her along. They'd leave for home after meeting with Cletus Zimmerman, so he wouldn't get another chance to ask her about living outside a closed community. He'd hoped to talk to her after they arrived last night, but Dad ushered him up to their room, and they stayed there until breakfast. The opportunity presenting itself was too good to pass up, but he couldn't be the one to agree. Dad would have to do it.

Dad cleared his throat. "We'll be there a long time — all morning and into the afternoon."

"That's fine." Mrs. Zimmerman patted Alexa's hand. "You go look at the old Meiers place with Mr. Brungardt and his son. As clever as you are, you can probably give them some ideas for fixing up the house again."

Alexa rose from her kneeling position and gestured to the table. "But I need to clear the mess here and load the dishwasher."

"I'll do it. I'm not helpless, you know. You go on with the Brungardts. Clete can bring you home when they've finished looking and talking." Mrs. Zimmerman had it all

76

arranged. Alexa didn't offer another argument.

But Dad did. "Mrs. Zimmerman, I appreciate you wanting to help Steven, but it would be better for him to wait and let his wife suggest the improvements."

Mrs. Zimmerman's head snapped up. "You're married, young man?"

The same uncertainty that struck every time someone mentioned the wedding came again. Steven laughed nervously. "Not yet."

A proud smile formed on Dad's face. "Steven and your great-niece, Anna-Grace Braun, are planning a February wedding. They will live together at his grandfather's farmstead and farm the acreage."

"So you're Anna-Grace's Steven . . ." Alexa gazed at him. "I suppose we should have made the connection already." She turned to her grandmother. "It would be better, Grandmother, for Anna-Grace to —"

"Obviously I don't know your fiancée." The reporter interrupted. He pinned his gaze on Steven and leaned back in his chair, looping one elbow over the ladder back, and gestured toward Alexa with his coffee mug. "But I've seen how Miss Zimmerman here can take something old and make it work. If that farmhouse is old — and I'd wager it is, the way you talked about it earlier — then she ought to be a good one to take a look at it. Give you some ideas to take back to your girl."

Your girl. Steven broke out in a cold sweat. Everyone said Anna-Grace Braun was the sweetest girl in Sommerfeld, and he agreed. The other young men envied him. With his parents' and the fellowship's blessing, he'd proposed. He couldn't change his mind now without disappointing too many people who mattered to him. But in that moment, if he could find the courage — and the selfishness — he'd charge out the door like his brother had done and not come back.

Sommerfeld
  Anna-Grace

Anna-Grace set plates of flaky biscuits swimming in a sea of sausage gravy in front of the two café patrons. Steam rose from the plates, carrying the mouth-watering aroma of Deborah Muller's home-ground sausage. Her stomach twined in hunger — the morning had been so busy she hadn't been able to grab so much as a bite of toast — but she sent a bright smile across the pair. "There you are. Is there anything else I can get for you?"

The woman glanced in her coffee cup. "Maybe a little more coffee."

"I'd like some Tabasco," the man said.

Anna-Grace couldn't imagine putting hot sauce on gravy, but she only nodded. "Of course." She crossed squares of black-and-white tiles to the scarred counter where pots of hot coffee and bottles of condiments waited. She tucked a small bottle of Tabasco sauce in her pocket, grabbed a pot of steaming coffee, and wove her way back between the crowded tables. After taking care of the couple in booth three, she made the rounds and refilled coffee cups for other patrons. Setting the empty pot near the four-burner coffeemaker, she ran a hand across her forehead and released a tired sigh.

Ten o'clock, and the café still bustled with activity. Saturdays were ordinarily busy days at Lisbeth's, bringing in both local and out-of-town patrons, but by midmorning the crowd usually thinned. Not today. Would her boss be able to let her go at her usual eleven o'clock quitting time? She hoped so. She'd been at the café since five that morning, and she was eager to get home and put her feet up for a little while. That is, if Sunny would let her relax. Her little sister probably had her hand-me-down tea set laid out and waiting for Anna-Grace's arrival. And if she did, Anna-Grace would sit, sip pretend tea, and eat pretend cookies, because in a few more months she wouldn't have the opportunity to have tea parties on Saturday mornings with Sunny.

"Would you clear table four?" Cassie Muller, the other waitress, paused beside Anna-Grace and touched her sleeve. "Some people are waiting to use it, and I need to serve the folks in booth one before their food is cold."

Embarrassed that the boss's daughter-in-law caught her daydreaming instead of working, Anna-Grace grabbed the dish bin and rag and hurried off. As she mopped the table clean, the couple waiting to use it walked over. Anna-Grace glanced up and smiled in relief at Mr. and Mrs. Willems from her fellowship. They wouldn't express impatience for the wait, the way some outsiders might. "Hello. It's been a busy morning in here. I'll have this ready in just a moment."

"Don't rush, Anna-Grace." Mrs. Willems fingered the end of one black ribbon trailing from her cap as Anna-Grace swept crumbs into her hand. "Darrin and I aren't in any big hurry. We just wanted a place to sit and sip coffee while we wait for the auctioneer to get past the farm implements to the household items."

"That's why it's been so crazy in here."

Anna-Grace laughed at herself. She should have remembered the auction at the Penner farm. They'd been advertising it for weeks. Apparently she'd gotten too wrapped up in her own little world to be aware of what was happening outside her door.

"You should try to go out there, too," Mr. Willems said, "since you and Steven will be setting up housekeeping soon. In Arborville, I hear. There might be some things you could use in your new place."

"That's true, Anna-Grace." Mrs. Willems nodded in agreement. "Why, that old house belonging to Steven's grandparents will surely need a new stove and refrigerator, and the Penners have appliances listed on the auction bill."

Anna-Grace hid a smile. Just as Steven's mother had suspected, it hadn't taken long for the townsfolk to learn about the gift of land in Arborville. But she wouldn't add to the gossip. Mom and Dad wouldn't approve. She lifted the dish bin and stepped away from the table. "I'll talk to my folks about it and see what they think."

"You do that." Mrs. Willems gave Anna-Grace's cheek a soft pat before she slipped into one of the chairs. "I know the Penners would be happy to think their refrigerator and stove were going to be used by such a nice young couple as you and Steven."

Anna-Grace thanked the woman, then hurried off. Although it was a bit disconcerting to be the topic of conversation by half the town, she appreciated how everyone in Sommerfeld supported her betrothal to Steven. In the past, there had been some couples who met with mild disapproval or outright objection. She could recall twice when the fellowship leaders refused to offer their blessing on a potential union.

She emptied the dirty dishes into the tray beside the dishwasher, then moved to the sink to wash her hands. As the warm water flowed over her skin, warmth flooded her soul. The fellowship's blessing only verified how perfect she and Steven were for each other. Surely she was the most blessed girl in the whole town.

Arborville
  Alexa

Alexa explored the interior and wandered the area around the Meiers house with Steven and his father. Their slow, meticulous examination complete, they stood on the sloping porch where age-grayed gingerbread trim wore ropes of spiderwebbing. She grimaced as she took in the peeling paint and cracked windows. She'd be the first to

82

admit the place needed help. No one had lived in it for over twenty years, and it showed signs of neglect both inside and out. But Steven's father declared the house structurally sound, and Uncle Clete, who had arrived only a few minutes ago, voiced his agreement.

Mr. Brungardt and Uncle Clete ambled toward the barn, discussing land yield and other things Alexa wouldn't even pretend to understand. Oddly, Steven stayed behind, and his father didn't seem to notice. So Alexa felt accountable for entertaining him, the way she would any guest to her bed-and-breakfast.

"You must feel so blessed to receive such an incredible gift." She gingerly placed her fingertips on the railing and peered across the brown yard, more dirt interspersed with clumps of weeds than grass. "It'll take some real work to fix it up, but it's a charming little house." Her mind whirled with ideas for turning the single-story Depression-era bungalow into a warm and welcoming family home, and it took great self-control not to blurt them all at the man who would bring Anna-Grace Braun to Arborville.

Her heart jolted. *Dear Lord, how will I handle having Anna-Grace living on the farm next door?* Alexa pushed aside her worries

83

and focused on the house. "I especially like the built-in cupboards in the dining room and the egg-and-dart trim over the doors and windows. They add lots of character, don't you think?"

"Yeah. I guess."

"Do you plan to start work on it right away so it's ready by the time you get married?"

"If Dad says I should."

Alexa glanced at Steven, puzzled by his lackluster response. She wouldn't expect a soon-to-be-groom to be so . . . reticent. When she'd met Anna-Grace at Grandmother's birthday party last June, she'd been surprised to discover that the girl, who was only nineteen like Alexa, was already pledged to be married. Although Anna-Grace had exercised restraint — she seemed like a quiet, reserved girl — she talked of little else than her upcoming wedding the entire evening. Alexa didn't know of any other young women who married at nineteen. Unless they had to. But apparently that wasn't the case with Steven and Anna-Grace. They simply wanted to get married and start a family.

The idea of marriage frightened Alexa. Maybe because she'd been raised by a single mother, she wasn't ready to even think about being a wife. More frightening than marriage, though, was the idea of Anna-Grace — the biological daughter released for adoption by the woman Alexa knew as Mom — living so close. At least Alexa would have a few months to reconcile herself with the idea before Steven and Anna-Grace moved in next door.

She shifted to face Steven. "Anna-Grace will probably want to help work on it. I know I would, if it were going to be my house. Will you bring her over soon so she can see it?"

"Probably." If she wasn't mistaken, a hint of melancholy colored his tone. Before she could form a question that wouldn't sound too nosy, he said, "Did you finish high school?"

The change in topics took her by surprise. "Yes."

"What was it like?"

How could she answer? "Um . . . good, I guess. I liked it."

"Did you go to college?"

She shook her head.

"Why not?" His gaze bored into hers, his expression serious. "Isn't it allowed by your fellowship?"

Alexa couldn't stifle a short laugh. "Mom and I attended a Mennonite Brethren church, but we never referred to it as 'our fellowship.' It's just . . ." She shrugged. "Our church. Mom really wanted me to go to college, but I couldn't decide what career path to follow. So I put it off. And then I used the money I'd saved for college to turn Grandmother's house into a bed-and-breakfast. I'm not sure whether I'll ever go."

"But you could, if you wanted to."

"Well, sure."

He clamped his hands over the railing and stared outward, seeming to search the empty fields. Watching him, Alexa experienced a rush of sympathy she didn't understand. He had so much — a father and mother willing to give him a start toward his future, a lovely girl who would soon be his wife, a family legacy he could pass to his children and beyond. She and Mom, all on their own without a family support system, had to work for everything, and she didn't even know who her birth parents were. She tried to summon envy, or even disgust at his shortsightedness, but it refused to rise. He seemed so forlorn, she could only feel sorry for him.

Understanding dawned. She released a little gasp that caught his attention. "You want to go to college, don't you?"

He frowned, zinging a look toward the

barn. But his father and her uncle were inside. They couldn't overhear. He almost seemed to deflate, his tense frame collapsing and his head dropping low. "Yes." He swallowed. "Yes, I really do."

"What do you want to do?"

"I want to be a teacher." The longing in his voice proved how much he wanted it.

"Then why don't you?"

He sent a sideways glance that communicated frustration. "Because I can't."

"Why not?"

His face twisted with a snide grimace. "Because in my fellowship, teachers are women. Men are farmers, or furniture makers, or business owners. They aren't teachers."

A chilly blast of wind slapped the house, rattling the windows and releasing a low howl. Alexa pushed her hands into the pockets of her jacket and crossed the flaps. "Just because it's never been done before doesn't mean it *can't* be done, right? My mom grew up right here in Arborville as part of the Old Order fellowship. She went to college and became a nurse. That was new to her fellowship. But her family was proud of her for doing it." Of course, they hadn't realized what else Mom was doing — raising a baby on her own and keeping it secret. But that information wouldn't benefit the confused young man standing on the porch with her.

Steven sighed. His breath formed a little cloud. The temperature had dropped more than Alexa had realized. "My family wouldn't be proud if I asked to go away to school. They'd be —"

"Steven?" Mr. Brungardt waved from the open doorway of the barn. "Clete says a storm is brewing. We need to leave soon, but come look at this barn first. You'll have to do some patching on the roof and on the north side, but the loft is still usable. Come see."

Steven bent his elbows and did a push-up off the railing. The old wood complained as it released his weight. Looking toward the barn, he finished softly, "They'd be disappointed. They want me to marry Anna-Grace and farm my grandfather's land. So that's what I'll do." His expression resigned, he moved slowly toward the rotting steps.

Alexa watched him go, disjointed thoughts tumbling through her mind. He planned to bring Anna-Grace here, but he didn't really want to do it. He wanted to go away somewhere and become a teacher. If he pursued his desire, she wouldn't have to live next door to the girl her mother had given up for adoption. Was it selfish to hope his dream came true so she didn't have to face what would certainly be her worst nightmare?

CHAPTER 7

Arborville
Alexa

Alexa always looked forward to Sunday. Traditionally the Zimmermans gathered for a meal and a time of fellowship after Sunday service. When Grandmother Zimmerman's son and daughters brought their families together, there were fourteen of them in all — a dozen more than had sat at Alexa's kitchen table during her growing-up years. She loved the noise, the happy chaos, even the messes. When she sat at the table with her grandmother, aunts, uncles, and cousins, it didn't matter that they weren't her blood relations. They were her *family,* and she savored every moment with them.

Today they gathered at Shelley's house, and for the first time since giving birth two months ago, the youngest Zimmerman sibling, Sandra, joined them rather than going home to rest. Although Alexa tried hard not to play favorites, she couldn't help feeling drawn to Sandra. Only six years older than Alexa, Sandra seemed more like a sister than an aunt. From their very first encounter, Sandra had openly accepted Alexa into the circle of family, unlike Clete and Shelley who'd struggled with the idea of their older sister having a child without the benefit of a husband. Not until the truth was revealed about Alexa's parentage had Clete and Shelley relaxed around her. But they hadn't completely accepted her yet.

To Alexa's delight, Shelley seated her next to Sandra, and she anticipated the chance to chat with her young aunt. However, the children were especially boisterous. Grandmother blamed their unusual rambunctiousness on the storm that had blown through yesterday afternoon, declaring them "little barometers." Whatever the reason, their loud voices hindered conversation between Alexa and Sandra, but from experience Alexa knew that Shelley would send the children to the kitchen for dessert. She'd be able to visit with Sandra then.

Just as they finished their meal — savory homemade chicken pot pie so good Alexa battled a groan of delight with every mouthful — Shelley rose to cut the pies Alexa had brought along to share. Sandra and Derek's little Isabella wakened from her nap on a blanket on the living room floor and let out a quavering wail. With a sigh, Sandra pushed to her feet. "I suppose it's only fair she's hungry when the rest of us are. Shelley, may I take her to your bedroom and nurse her?"

Shelley began herding the children into the kitchen. "There's not a chair in there, but if you don't mind sitting on the bed, go ahead."

Sandra scooped up the baby and headed for the hallway. "Alexa, I'm trusting you to save me a piece of the peach-pecan."

"Will do," Alexa laughingly promised. She helped Shelley serve half portions to each of the children, from Clete and Tanya's eight-year-old Jay down to Sandra and Derek's three-year-old Ian, then carried plates to the dining room table for the adults. Shelley followed with a pot of coffee. As Alexa started to sit down to enjoy her dessert, an idea struck and she picked up both her and Sandra's pie plates. "Aunt Shelley, would you mind if I took this in to Sandra?"

Shelley hesitated for a moment, pursing her lips, but then she nodded. "Just tell her not to drip pie filling on my quilt."

Alexa flopped a pair of napkins over her arm and then headed to the bedroom hallway. She passed the open doorway where twin-sized beds draped with pink-and-white-checked quilts, nearly buried beneath a pile of stuffed animals, identified the room as Ruby and Pearl's. The door at the end of hall was closed, but Alexa could hear Sandra's soft voice coming from behind it. She tapped on it with her elbow.

"Who is it?"

"Alexa. I have your pie."

"Get in here!"

Giggling, Alexa balanced everything on one arm and opened the door. Sandra had propped a pillow in her lap and draped a blanket over her shoulder. Isabella's little body formed a misshapen lump under the blanket.

Sandra kept one arm wrapped around the baby but held her other hand toward the pie and wiggled her fingers. "Gimme."

Alexa laid a napkin out on the bed next to Sandra's hip and put the plate on top of it. "Shelley said not to make a mess on her quilt."

Sandra grinned. "Of course she did." She took her fork and eagerly stabbed up a bite. "Mmm . . . I love peaches and pecans together." She ate another bite, even closing her eyes in exaggerated enjoyment. Then she pointed her fork at Alexa. "You know, you should experiment with this pie recipe and make a breakfast cake with peaches and pecans. I bet your guests would love it." An impish grin twitched her lips. "I'd be willing to be your official taste tester until you got it right."

Alexa laughed again. Sandra always managed to make her laugh. She sat carefully on the edge of the bed and held her plate under her chin to catch any crumbs. "I might take you up on that. Especially now with a long-term guest in place, I'll probably need a few more recipes so he doesn't get tired of the same things morning after morning."

"Mother said you put him in your apartment."

Alexa already missed the privacy the little summer-kitchen-turned-cottage had given her, but it seemed awkward to have him in the house with Grandmother, even if they did have a nurse come in at night. "Yes. I moved into one of the guest rooms."

"What happens if you get enough reservations to fill all three guest rooms?"

All three rooms filled would be a blessing, but she didn't expect to be that busy until spring. She shrugged. "I'll just camp in with Grandmother for a night or two. We'll make do."

"It's nice you had a place to house a long-term guest," Sandra said. "Of course, eating your good cooking every day for three months, he just might decide to propose by the time he's supposed to leave."

Alexa cringed. "Oh, I hope not."

Sandra burst out laughing. The lump in her lap jerked, and one little arm flung itself from beneath the blanket. Complaining whimpers followed. Alexa averted her eyes as Sandra whisked away the blanket and situated Isabella again. When she draped the blanket back in place, she said, her tone teasing, "What's the matter? Don't you like the hunka-hunka gorgeous type?"

Alexa gawked at her aunt. "Sandra!"

Sandra's entire body vibrated with suppressed laughter for several seconds, making the mattress bounce. She patted what Alexa presumed was Isabella's bottom based on the location of the lump and shook her head. Her twinkling eyes and teasing grin didn't match the mesh cap with its trailing ribbons. "What? I might be a wife and mother, but I still have eyes in my head. A cross-eyed person couldn't help but notice how good-looking the reporter from Chicago is. Even Mother said so."

The heat that often plagued her when Briley Forrester aimed his amazingly handsome, rich molasses gaze in her direction filled Alexa's face again. She whacked at the pie with her fork, her head low. "You're right. He is good looking."

Sandra snickered. "Thought so."

Alexa set her desecrated pie aside and turned a serious look on Sandra. "Can I ask you something?"

"Sure." Sandra went back to eating her pie, her expression devoid of teasing.

"How old were you when you got married?"

"Nineteen. Same as Shelley. Same as Tanya when she married Clete."

An image of Steven Brungardt's sober, uncertain face flashed in Alexa's memory. "Did you marry because you wanted to, or because it was expected?"

"Because I wanted to, of course." Sandra tipped her head, the ribbon from her cap puddling on the bump created by Isabella's little head. A hint of worry glimmered in her eyes. "Are you wondering if you're old enough for courtship?"

Alexa shook her head firmly. "No. I'm wondering why I'm not interested."

Sandra turned her back for a moment, bringing Isabella from beneath the blanket. She adjusted her clothing, then tipped the baby over her shoulder. Facing Alexa again, she gently patted Isabella's back, the last few bites of her pie apparently forgotten. "Maybe you just haven't met anyone yet who makes you want to consider marriage." Sandra spoke, her voice low. "I was only sixteen when I met Derek, but I knew from the first time he and I spent an hour together that I wanted to be his wife. I felt . . . safe with him."

"Sixteen . . ." Alexa propped her hands on her knees and chewed the inside of her cheek. "Wow. That was awfully young."

Sandra smiled. "I suppose so. But you have to remember, Alexa, around here sixteen is different than sixteen in most places. In the Old Order community, by sixteen you've been out of school for two years already, you've learned all you need to know about maintaining a household, and you've spent some time at a job either in your parents' home or workplace or somewhere else. Sixteen is probably elsewhere's twenty."

"I'll be twenty in December." Alexa sighed. "Do you think if I'd been raised in Arborville instead of Indiana, I'd be ready for marriage?"

"I don't suppose there's any way to know that for sure, but I also don't think there's any expiration date, so to speak, for finding the one you want to spend your life with. Don't feel as though you need to rush it just because Shelley and I were settled by the time we were your age."

An uncomfortable feeling wrapped itself around Alexa. For as long as she could remember, she'd wanted to be part of an extended family, to belong with them. She'd finally met her mother's family and had been accepted in their ranks, but her up-bringing outside of the Old Order sect set her apart. Or maybe it was deeper than that. Maybe her birthright set her apart. Mom was born and raised Old Order. Alexa was neither. What was her birthright?

Sandra stood and turned to lay Isabella on the bed. She tucked a soft cloth beneath the baby's cheek and covered her with a little blanket. Her movements were tender, the expression on her face sweetly affection-ate. Alexa could imagine Mom tucking her in the same way when she was tiny. Yet, watching, not even one tiny ember of desire for a child of her own stirred in Alexa's heart. She lacked so many of the motherly traits Mom and Sandra seemed to possess. Was she like her biological mother, who had abandoned her in a box behind a garage?

Sandra picked up her plate and fork and gestured for Alexa to follow her. In the hallway, she offered a repentant grimace. "Alexa, I'm sorry if my comment about the guest from Chicago made you uncomfortable. I was teasing you, and I shouldn't have. Mother says he is a real flirt and she's worried about you. She doesn't want to see you . . . well . . ." — pink stained her cheeks — "be pulled in by a flatterer. She's not sure having him there for weeks on end is a good idea. But she doesn't want to tell you how to run your business."

"I can handle Briley Forrester."

Sandra gave Alexa's elbow a gentle squeeze. "I'm sure you can. You're a sensible, mature girl, and your head is on straight. But if he makes himself too much at home and gives you trouble, then you tell Clete, and he'll step in. Okay?"

Her young aunt's concern warmed Alexa. She smiled. "Okay. Thanks."

Still holding her arm, she ushered Alexa up the hallway. "Don't worry. You just keep praying for God to bring the right man into your life, and when He does, you'll know it. And you'll be ready."

Alexa hoped so.

Chapter 8

Briley

Briley had thought Saturday dragged long, but it passed in a flash compared to Sunday. Next week he'd definitely go to service to use up an hour or two of the day. Even after he'd driven to Wichita and killed an hour at a discount store, where he bought the cheapest flat-screen television and DVD player on the shelves as well as a handful of action flicks, and grabbed lunch at a steak house, the late afternoon and evening still stretched in front of him.

To fill some time he drove slowly up and down the streets of Arborville — all fourteen of them — and shot photographs out his open car window. Of businesses, houses, two cats curled together under a bush, kids playing stick-ball, an elderly couple sitting on a porch swing with a colorful knitted blanket draped over their laps . . . Nothing spectacular, but images that would help him paint a picture of the community as a whole. Arborville didn't look anything like Chicago.

He'd already driven the county roads outside of town yesterday, taking pictures of farmsteads, cows, windmills, more cows, old-fashioned farm implements waiting at the edges of pastures, and — by compliments of his telephoto lens — even a half-dozen pretty good images of Alexa standing on the porch of a sorry-looking house with the younger Brungardt. Chilled by the cold air, he'd rolled up his window between photographs. But today was pleasant, warm enough to leave his window down. Kansas sure had changeable weather.

Even though he felt as if he'd already seen it all, he aimed his vehicle for the highway. Anything to use up the remaining couple of hours before sunset. A half mile out of town he came upon a man and boy walking along the road. Fishing poles bounced on their shoulders. Judging by their empty hands, he assumed the pair's expedition had failed, but they didn't look unhappy. The boy appeared to be jabbering as the man listened with his head slightly tipped, an indulgent grin curving his mouth.

Something about the way they sauntered side by side, their clothes rumpled and mud-stained but their bearing relaxed and content, appealed to him, and he snatched up his camera to catch a photo. He slowed to a snail's crawl as he eased alongside them, unobtrusively lifting his camera. They both turned in his direction, and the boy raised his hand in an exuberant wave. Briley pressed the shutter button and captured the bright smiles and friendly wave perfectly.

He dropped the camera on the passenger seat and waved in return. Before he could drive past them, the man held out his arm in a silent bid for Briley to stop. According to his research, the Amish were squeamish about having their faces photographed, and he'd honored their preference, but this man and boy weren't wearing Amish clothes. Hopefully they wouldn't ask him to delete the photo. He happened to like it even if it didn't prove the dirt Len had sent him to uncover.

Briley braked and put the car in Park. "Yeah? What can I do for you?"

The boy scampered over, his tennis shoes stirring dust, and the man ambled more slowly. In unison they slipped the poles from their shoulders and held them upright with the handles braced on the ground, the way a farmer might hold a pitchfork. With their matching short-cropped brown hair and brown eyes, they looked like a set of bookends. Except for one being much taller.

The man stuck out his hand. "I just wanted to introduce myself. I'm Paul Aldrich. This is my son, Danny."

Briley shook the man's hand, and then the boy pushed forward to shake hands, too. A fishy smell clung to them. Maybe they'd managed to snag a fish or two after all. Or at least had sat on a dead one. "Nice to meet you. I'm Briley Forrester."

"Are you the reporter who's staying out at the Zimmermans'? In Alexa's cottage?" Danny nearly danced in place, energy pulsating from his wiry body.

Briley grinned. Two days in town and already well known. He'd make a note of this exchange. "That's right."

Danny jabbed his thumb at his father. "Me an' Dad are the ones who built it. We built the kitchen and the bathrooms and the ramps for Mrs. Zimmerman's house, too. That's what we do — we build things."

A chuckle threatened, but Briley managed to contain it. He doubted this kid did much to help, but it was cute the way he took credit. Pretty decent of the dad to let him think he'd helped instead of setting him straight. "Well, I'd say you and your dad did a good job."

"Yeah. Alexa let me and my friend Jeremy come over and put the bed in the cottage up and down. Dad says it's called a Murphy bed, whatever that means. It's the best bed *ever.*" The boy's gaze swept from one bumper of Briley's car to the other. "And this is the best car ever. I'd sure like to take a ride in it sometime."

"Danny . . ." Aldrich shook his head, frowning slightly. "Don't be pushy. It's rude."

Danny shrugged sheepishly. "Was I being pushy?"

Briley let his laugh roll. The boy might be pushy, but he wasn't obnoxious about it. Not the way Briley had been as a kid, trying to steal attention wherever and however he could. He kind of liked Danny. Even though he smelled like dead fish. "Don't worry about it. Since I'll be in Arborville for a while, we ought to be able to find time for you to take a ride in the Camaro."

Actually, making friends with the boy could help with his article. He could press Danny for authentic feedback about living the simplistic lifestyle. Kids were less likely to mask their thoughts and feelings. Briley pinched his chin, pretending to think deeply. "In fact, if your dad could hold those poles out the window, since they're too long for my trunk, I could give you fellows a ride to your house right now. Whaddaya think about that?"

Danny turned his eager face to his dad. "Can we, Dad? Huh? Huh?"

Aldrich looked at Briley, his expression doubtful. "You'd have to take us to town, and you seem to be leaving it. Weren't you heading somewhere?"

"Just nosing around. Getting familiar with the area."

The man nodded as if the explanation made sense.

"I did some exploring yesterday, but I didn't see a lake." Briley nodded toward the poles. "Maybe you could show me where it is. In case I'd like to do some fishing."

"It's not a lake. Just a pond," Danny said.

Aldrich added, "And it's on private property, but the Heidebrechts have always let people from town come out and drop a line. They won't mind us taking you out there if you're really interested."

Briley had never experienced a desire to drop a line. Not even from one of the boats that left the piers in Chicago on daylong fishing expeditions. Fishing was an activity shared by fathers and sons. He'd never known a real father, and he had no desire to raise a son. But if the townsfolk frequented the pond, he ought to take a few pictures of it. "I'd like to see it."

"It's not far, but you'll have to drive a pretty rough road."

"I'll go slow."

"And we're a little, er, ripe from our afternoon of catching and releasing."

Ripe was an understatement. "I'll leave the windows down. The wind ought to chase the smell right back out again." It'd also bring in a lot of dust, but he'd deal with it.

Danny apparently lost patience with the delays. He shoved his pole at his father. "C'mon, Dad. Let's go!" He darted to the passenger side and opened the door.

Aldrich stood for a moment with both poles in his hands, looking uncertain. But then he shrugged, offered a grin, and followed his son. Danny clambered into the backseat, which was little more than a narrow bench. But he didn't seem to mind. He plopped in the middle, rested his elbows on his knees, and leaned over the console, his smile broad. It tickled Briley to please the kid so much.

Aldrich had some trouble juggling the poles and the door, but he managed to settle himself in the seat and extend his arm out the window with the poles held away from the car. Briley would be sure to drive slowly so those poles wouldn't bounce against the sides of his Camaro. He doubted there was anyone in Arborville who'd know how to buff out scratches.

Briley flicked a grin at Danny as he shifted into first gear. "All right, navigator, tell me where to go."

Sommerfeld
 Anna-Grace

Anna-Grace loved the time of fellowship after worship on Sunday, but she also liked the time when the dishes were done, the guests had departed, and she could savor a few precious hours with Steven. The rest of the week their time together was either with a group of friends or taken in such short snatches it left her dissatisfied. Her parents still sat across the room, actively participating in the conversation, but she wouldn't complain. Sitting beside Steven, holding his hand, not having to share him with a dozen others was enough to make her happy.

After their company left, Mom had sent Sunny to look at picture books in her bed. In the quiet that followed, it seemed the house relaxed beneath a blanket of calm. Then Dad, as if he'd been waiting for the opportunity, opened a floodgate of questions concerning Steven's plans for the future.

Steven answered all of them, his tone respectful. When Mom requested a description of the property in Arborville, Steven provided an overview of the acreage and all it contained. "The buildings, including the house, are pretty run-down and will take some work. But it's a good piece of land." He offered a slight shrug as he finished his explanation and shifted his gaze from Mom and Dad to Anna-Grace. "I should be able to make a decent living, and we should be . . . happy there."

Anna-Grace had a hard time remaining on the sofa. Listening to Steven tell about what would be *their* land, house, and out-buildings — even though, in his typical understated manner, his descriptions were short on details — built a nearly uncontrollable eagerness to see it for herself. She gave his hand a squeeze in lieu of jumping up and whirling in excitement.

Dad leaned forward slightly, his brow puckered into a mild scowl. "So it's settled then? You're going to take over the farm and make your home in Arborville?"

Steven's fingers twitched. "That's right." He drew in a breath and squared his shoulders. "I'll probably move by the end of the month."

Anna-Grace dropped her jaw. "So soon?"

He grimaced. "As I said, there's a lot of work to be done."

The thought of Steven moving away, of not seeing him every week, was a knife in her heart. She missed him already and he hadn't even left. "Why can't we work on it together?"

"My dad says I need to have it finished before I take you to live there. Dad talked to the carpenter who did the work on your great-aunt's house, and —"

"Paul Aldrich?" Mother's query blasted out on a shrill note of panic.

Anna-Grace looked up in surprise.

Steven nodded. "That's right."

Mom and Dad exchanged a grim look, and Mom's face paled.

Apprehension teased Anna-Grace, raising the fine hairs on her neck. "What's wrong with Paul Aldrich?"

"Nothing." Dad sat back in his chair, as if forcing himself to relax. "He and my cousin Suzy were good friends when they were growing up. We even thought they might choose to marry. But they didn't."

Steven went on, speaking to Anna-Grace but sending occasional sidelong glances across the room to Mom and Dad. "Mr. Aldrich said he could spend early November at the house, updating the kitchen and bathroom, and he would ask the fellowship about arranging a working at the property. The men would help paint the house, re-shingle the roof, and repair the barn. The other things that need doing inside — painting, wallpapering, lots of cleanup — I can handle on my own. Then the house will be ready for us when we get married."

Married . . . What wonderful notions the word inspired. The books her friends checked out from the library in McPherson often featured women with careers. Even a few women in Sommerfeld had businesses. But all Anna-Grace wanted was to manage her own household, the same way Mom had. Anna-Grace released an airy sigh. "I wish I could go with you and help, too."

Mom shook her head firmly. "That wouldn't be appropriate."

"Oh, I wouldn't stay at the house." Mom should know that she wouldn't behave inappropriately. She'd been taught right from wrong. "But I could stay with Great-Aunt Abigail. Or maybe with one of your cousins, Dad. When we were there for Great-Aunt Abigail's birthday, they said we were welcome anytime." The idea grew, gaining merit. "Since Sandra has the new baby, I could be a help to her if I stayed with her and Derek."

Dad frowned. "Well . . ."

Mom turned to Dad. "I don't think that's a good idea."

Anna-Grace observed her parents, apprehension building. Both Dad and Mom had assured her they were pleased about her commitment to Steven. Why did they now seem so forbidding? She supposed they hadn't realized he would take their daughter several hours away from them. She hadn't realized it, either, when she accepted his proposal, and going would be hard because she loved her parents. But she also loved Steven. Why did growing up have to hurt?

Tears stung and she sniffed. "Mom and Dad?" They looked at her, and she forced a wobbly smile. "Steven isn't taking me to the moon. Arborville isn't that far away. We'll still see each other. Please don't worry."

Dad stretched out his hand, and Mom reached across the little table between their chairs and took hold of it two-handed, the way someone would grab a lifeline. Dad spoke in a hoarse whisper. "It isn't the distance, Anna-Grace. It's . . ."

Several seconds passed while Anna-Grace clung to Steven's hand and held her breath, uncertainty making her mouth dry.

Mom finally finished the sentence. "It's the town itself. And who else lives there."

Steven gently pulled his hand from Anna-Grace's grasp and stood. "Maybe I should go home."

Anna-Grace leaped up and curled her hands around his forearm. "No."

Her parents stood, too, and Mom took two steps toward them. Her face held a pleading unlike anything Anna-Grace had ever seen from her normally stalwart, strong mother. Whatever troubled her parents, she believed they dreaded saying it even more than she dreaded hearing it.

"Yes, Steven, please stay." Dad's serious tone and the deep furrows in his forehead increased her level of tension. "You're to be Anna-Grace's husband, so you need to hear this, too."

Dad sank back into his chair, almost as if his legs couldn't support the burden he carried. Mom crossed the floor and slipped her arm around Anna-Grace's waist, pulling her away from Steven and gently easing her onto the sofa. She reached for Steven's hand. He linked fingers with her and then sat down again.

With Mom's arm at her waist and Steven holding tightly to her hand, she sent up a prayer for God to bolster her as well. "Okay. I'm ready. What is it?"

CHAPTER 9

Steven

Raised alongside a brother who possessed not even a fingernail's worth of sentiment, by a kind but undemonstrative father and a mother he'd never seen shed tears for any reason, Steven was helpless against the tears flowing down Mrs. Braun's face and the ones glistening in Anna-Grace's eyes. If Anna-Grace hadn't shackled him with her tight grip, he might slip out the door. Even before hearing whatever news the Brauns intended to share, he was already certain he wouldn't like it.

"We've never kept secret your adoption." Mrs. Braun's lips quavered with a sad smile. She cupped her hand over Anna-Grace's knee. "We wanted you to know how much you were wanted. You were our answer to prayer."

"I know, Mom."

Steven knew, too. The Brauns' adoptions

114

were known by everyone in Sommerfeld. If they'd wanted to, though, they could have kept it secret from Anna-Grace. Unlike Sunny, whose Asian features screamed of her parentage, Anna-Grace's blond hair and blue eyes were a near match to Olivia Braun, even though Anna-Grace was much more slender than her mother.

Mrs. Braun went on, her voice so soft Steven had to strain to hear her. "When we adopted you through the private agency in Indiana, we were told only that you were born to an unwed teenage girl. Although we asked for more information, they said the girl's family preferred anonymity. Each year on your birthday your dad and I have spent time in prayer for your biological parents, asking God to bless them. Well, recently . . ." Her chin quivered. Her hand on Anna-Grace's knee began to tremble. She looked across the room to her husband, her expression pleading.

Mr. Braun sat forward, folding his hands in a prayerful position. Then he placed them on the armrest of his chair. "Recently we were contacted by your mother and father."

Anna-Grace gasped. Without conscious thought Steven tightened his grip on her hand. She aimed a brief, grateful smile at him before turning to Mr. Braun. "First of

115

all, *you're* my father. And you're my mother." She pulled loose from Steven's hand to embrace Mrs. Braun. The two women clung for several seconds before Anna-Grace released her hold and reached for Steven again. She sniffled. "I've always been grateful God gave me to you. I can't imagine better parents than the ones I have."

Steven contributed nothing to the conversation, but he silently agreed with Anna-Grace's assessment. Andrew Braun's reputation in town was stellar — he'd never heard an unpleasant word spoken about the man. Olivia Braun's popularity within their fellowship matched her husband's. When someone had a problem, they came to Mrs. Braun for understanding, sage counsel, and a plateful of homemade cookies. Even though Anna-Grace's origins were unknown, Steven's parents hadn't discouraged him from courting her because they trusted the upbringing she'd been given. He admired Anna-Grace's tenderness, honesty, and strong faith. He couldn't have chosen a better girl to be his wife.

"Thank you, sweetheart." Mr. Braun smiled, but it seemed a little strained. "We've done our best, with God's help, and we've never regretted making you our daughter. In our hearts, you are ours, and you always will be." He pulled in a slow breath, his fingers tightening until his knuckles turned white. "Yet we can't deny someone else gave birth to you. And now that we know who the man and woman are, and that you will soon . . ."

He hung his head and fell silent for several long seconds. Was he addressing God — requesting strength or wisdom or even courage? Steven found himself sending up a prayer for God to give Mr. Braun whatever it was he needed.

Finally the man unlinked his hands, braced them on his knees, and pushed upright so slowly it appeared his joints needed oiling. He crossed the floor and stood in front of Anna-Grace. His face held such tenderness, Steven felt like an interloper looking on. He held both hands to his daughter, and Anna-Grace rose and reached back. "Anna-Grace, when you move to Arborville with Steven, you will be in the same community as your birth father."

Steven jolted, sending his spine against the corner of the sofa. "W-what?"

Mr. Braun took Anna-Grace in his arms. "Shortly after our trip to Arborville for Aunt Abigail's birthday party, your birth mother gave us letters written by her and your

117

father to share with you when you were ready."

Anna-Grace spoke with her cheek pressed to her father's chest. "Does she live in Arborville, too?"

Mrs. Braun rose and wrapped her arms around the pair. "No. But her family does."

Steven shook his head, hardly able to believe what he was hearing. If Anna-Grace's birth parents were from Arborville, they were Old Order — Amish or Mennonite. But either way an illegitimate birth would be cause for scandal in the small community.

Mr. Braun cupped his hand on Anna-Grace's mesh cap, as if afraid she would collapse. "We hadn't planned to give the letters to you until you asked about your birth parents, but if you're going to live in the same town with your mother's family and your father, we think you need to know who they are."

An idea crashed over Steven with as much force as a brick wall. He bowed beneath its pressure and then forced himself to stand. He extended his hand toward Mr. Braun. "Wait. Before you go any further, let me ask Anna-Grace an important question."

Mr. Braun set his daughter aside, and she turned toward Steven. Tears formed two moist tracks down her pale face. She seemed so lost, so confused. Compassion swelled in Steven's chest. Maybe this was God's way of saving Anna-Grace from facing a situation she wasn't ready to face. Maybe this was God's way of saving him from making a mistake with his future. *God, am I being selfish or selfless here?* He didn't know for sure, but he had to at least say what he was thinking.

"Just because Dad gave me the farm doesn't mean we have to live there. If being in the same town as your birth relatives is too hard for you, then I can sell the land. I can use the money to go —" He almost said *go to school.* But that would be selfish. Entirely selfish. He amended, "— to make a start somewhere other than in Arborville." He slipped his hands around Anna-Grace's upper arms and looked directly into her light-blue eyes. "If I do that, then you don't have to be told the names of your birth parents right now. It's up to you, Anna-Grace. You decide."

Arborville
  Briley

"It's up to you, of course, but you're more than welcome to join us next time. I think you'll discover it's peaceful to sit on the

119

bank and cast, catch, and release."

Briley had put his car in Park and left it idling when he pulled onto the Aldrich's gravel drive, expecting the father and son to hop out and go inside right away, but instead they'd sat and chatted for at least fifteen minutes. Oddly enough, despite the fish odor that now filled the interior of the car and his basically stranger-to-stranger relationship with the pair, he enjoyed their company enough not to want to rush them out. His teasing comment about them coming home empty-handed from their fishing trip had brought an invitation from Paul Aldrich for Briley to join them the next time they went to the pond.

With a good-natured chuckle Briley rubbed the side of his nose. "Dunno. It might be peaceful, but fishing seems to make a fellow a little stinky, if you catch my drift."

Both father and son laughed. Paul said, "I'm sure you're catching our 'drift' right now, but it's nothing a bath won't cure. So do you want to go with us next Sunday afternoon?"

"Getting kind of late in the year to fish, isn't it?" A hint of unexpected disappointment wiggled its way through his words. When had he developed an interest in fishing? Maybe he was just interested in watching this father and son interact. The look-alikes were so at ease with each other, the boy open but respectful, the father kind yet firm in his expectations. Could they be putting on a show to impress him? Only time would provide evidence.

Danny poked his head between the seats. "Sometimes Dad and me go to the lake in the wintertime and ice fish."

Ice fishing didn't appeal to Briley at all, but he grinned at the kid. "Oh yeah? You're some hard-core fisherman, aren't you?" Maybe he shouldn't have used the word *hard-core.* He waited for Danny's father to berate him.

Instead, the man winked at his son and then turned to Briley. "Fishing is the mildest of Danny's pastimes. He's an active boy — not one to just sit. So fishing is a good way for him to learn patience. You can't *make* the fish bite. You just have to toss out the bait and let the fish decide if it's interested enough to take it. Some good life lessons can be found on a fishing trip."

Life lessons? From fishing? They'd piqued his interest. Still, he shouldn't show too much enthusiasm. They might have only invited him to be polite. No sense in embarrassing himself if they really didn't want him tagging along. "Well, I might drive by the pond next Sunday. You know, to see if you're there, see if the fish have decided to bite."

Danny's grin stretched from ear to ear. "Great!"

"Sounds fine," his father said.

Although the man's reply was more reserved than his son's, Briley still read pleasure in his tone. His plan went from "maybe" to "will do" in his mind. They said their good-byes, and the pair ambled toward the garage, the boy holding both poles over his shoulder and the father walking with his hand cupped on the crown of the boy's head. Briley put his car in Reverse, but for some reason he remained in the drive, watching them until they closed the door behind them.

When they were out of view, he experienced a sense of loss. Completely unexplainable and more than a little unwelcome. A strange thought flitted through his brain. *Lucky kid.* He shook his head hard. Was he really envious of this little Mennonite kid? He forced a laugh, but it fell short of being convincing. He let his foot off the brake and backed into the street with a slight squeal of his tires. He revved the engine good before shifting into Drive and taking off with a burst of speed that made the back end of his car fishtail a bit.

Out of the corner of his eye, he glimpsed the elderly couple he'd photographed earlier, still sitting together on a porch swing. The woman's round face, previously friendly, now pursed into a disapproving frown, the same disappointed expression he used to put on Aunt Myrt's face. Instantly her voice rang in his memory. *"Briley Ray, think before you act. Try to live without regrets. You'll be happier."*

His foot moved from the gas pedal to the brake and brought his car to a crawl. He bobbed a nod at the couple, noted their stiff shoulders relaxing and the woman's frown melting, and he blew out a breath of relief. Then he followed it with a bigger huff of frustration. At himself. For the recklessness that rose without warning. For the ridiculous feelings that had prefaced the burst of recklessness. Even for caring about what these small-town people thought of him.

He drove with care back to the bed-and-breakfast, parked his car in the barn, then headed across the dry grass beneath a dusky sky. Inside the little cottage he kicked off his shoes and tossed his jacket over the back of a chair. He started to hook up his new television, but then he changed course and pulled his laptop from the case. He unfolded the Murphy bed, and then, giving a limber leap, he plopped on the bed with his legs extended and rested the laptop across his thighs.

While he waited for the laptop to boot, he mentally replayed his day, setting the events in chronological order so he could record them correctly. But when he opened his "The Truth on Plain Living" file and placed his fingers on the keys, the first line that formed concerned his last hour in town.

Paul Aldrich (son: Danny) — carpenter; fisherman; involved father; good dad.

A band wrapped around his chest. He slapped the laptop closed, set it aside with enough force to make it bounce on the mattress, then pounded across the floor to the television. He'd do his notes later. When he'd cleared his mixed-up head.

CHAPTER 10

Alexa

Grandmother's night nurse, Marjorie Wells, arrived promptly at eight thirty to help Grandmother prepare for bed. After spending a few minutes visiting with the friendly woman, Alexa excused herself to go up to her temporary room. She closed herself in the bedroom, kicked off her shoes, then settled on the bed. She pulled the teddy bear Grandmother had given her into her lap, resting her chin on the bear's dapper top hat, and took out her cell phone.

During her first few weeks of living in Arborville, she'd called her mother every evening for a chat. Over time, however, they'd slowly transitioned to talking two or three nights a week. With the arrival of guests, she hadn't taken the time to call Mom, but tonight she needed her.

A few deft clicks with her thumbs, and the sound of ringing met her ears. After only two rings she heard, "Hi, honey!" Mom's cheerful greeting brought an unexpected prick of tears.

She hugged the bear tight and sniffed hard. "Hi, Mom. How was your day?"

"Mine was fine, but what's the matter?"

Alexa stifled a laugh. How well her mother knew her. "What makes you think something's the matter?"

"I hear it in your voice." Worry now laced Mom's tone. "What's wrong?"

"Nothing." Alexa closed her eyes and sighed. "And everything. I don't really know."

"Tell me what's going on."

Her arm coiled around the bear, Alexa wriggled against the pillows and created a little nest for herself. "It's nothing, really. I just feel . . . unsettled." Saying it aloud brought an element of relief. She only wished she could understand the root of the feeling. "It's silly. I have the business up and running — have even welcomed guests already. Grandmother and I get along great, I've attended some of the fellowship's young-people gatherings, and I love time with Sandra when she isn't too busy with Ian and Isabella. Really, everything's good. I should be happy. But I'm not." Her voice broke on the last word. She closed her eyes for a moment, suppressing the desire to cry, then forced a glib tone. "Like I said, it's just silly."

"Honey, feelings are feelings. Don't berate yourself for having them. And just because things are going well doesn't mean you're going to automatically be happy."

"But why not?" Alexa tipped her cheek against the bear's hat. "I've always wanted to be part of a big family. Now I am. When I was fixing up the summer kitchen and the bedrooms to open the B and B, I had so much fun. I was so sure God was paving the way for me. Now that guests are coming, I should still be having fun. It doesn't make sense that I have what I wanted and I'm so discontent. What's wrong with me?"

"Alexa, there isn't anything *wrong* with you." Mom spoke kindly, but Alexa detected a hint of amusement underneath her words. She set her jaw firmly to hold back a defensive protest and made herself listen instead. "Think of all the changes you've had in the past few months. You moved from the town where you were raised to a new community. You placed yourself in the middle of a new family unit. You quit your old job and started a business. Psychologists say the stress from even one such change can have an adverse effect on a person's emotions."

Mom's comments made sense, but one thing remained unclear. She sat upright, tension straightening her spine. "So why now? Why not when we first came to Arborville?"

"Maybe because you're just finally slowing down enough to recognize the changes. You've been going nonstop since you got the idea to renovate the farmhouse, and before that your focus was on finding your niche with your grandmother, uncles, aunts, and cousins."

The amused undertone that had stirred irritation was gone now, and Alexa relaxed. "Maybe you're right."

"Of course I'm right. I'm always right." Mom was teasing, but this time Alexa chuckled lightly in response. "Or maybe I should say Linda is always right. She mentioned a couple of days ago she was worried about the effect all the change would have on you. She's praying for you."

Alexa melted against the pillows as images of dear Linda, the spunky lady who'd been a surrogate grandma to her since she was very small, flooded her mind. Tears stung again. She missed Linda, as well as her husband, Tom, and so many others from the church back in Franklin. "Tell her thanks, will you?"

"I sure will. Now . . . you said you've welcomed guests already. Tell me about them."

Alexa set the little bear aside and shared the details of the Brungardts' overnight stay, including Mr. Brungardt requesting her breakfast-casserole recipe, then told her about Steven Brungardt's plans to move into the old Meiers place and farm the land. But she didn't mention that Steven was going to marry Anna-Grace Braun, the daughter Mom had given up for adoption nearly twenty years ago. Why she wanted to keep the information to herself, she didn't know, but thinking about Anna-Grace deepened her feelings of unrest. "Uncle Clete was disappointed to give up renting the land, but we're praying someone else will rent acreage to him."

"Please tell him I'll be praying, too."

"I will," Alexa said.

"What about your other guest? The long-term one?"

Alexa's spine stiffened again. "How do you know I have a long-term guest?"

"You told me when you scheduled his stay, remember? You were all excited about someone from Illinois knowing about Grace Notes."

She sagged in relief. Grandmother was

129

concerned about Briley Forrester taking advantage of Alexa, and Uncle Clete didn't seem to trust him. For a moment she'd suspected someone from Arborville had contacted Mom about the handsome reporter staying in the cottage. What to say about him? Mom would worry if she knew how the man's flirtatiousness had affected her. She chose her words carefully. "So far he seems to be okay. He hasn't complained about what I've served for breakfast, and he pretty much keeps to himself. I think it'll work all right to have him here. I do miss being in my cottage, though."

"I imagine so, after all the work you put into it. But you'll have it back by Christmas, right?"

"Yes." Something occurred to Alexa, and she let out a short huff of irritation. "But we won't be able to stay out there when you come for Thanksgiving." Disappointment brought a new threat of tears. She'd anticipated one-on-one time with her mother after their months apart. They'd have time together, but it wouldn't be the same, staying in the house with Grandmother.

"Alexa, about Thanksgiving . . ."

Alexa swung her legs off the bed and sat up straight. The bear flopped onto its side and lost its hat. "Don't tell me you aren't coming after all."

"Well, there's a possibility I'll need to stay here."

"Mom!" Alexa rose and paced the room twice.

"I'm sorry." Mom's contrition did little to soothe Alexa. "You know how short-staffed we are here, and the other lead nurse — Bridget, you've met her — has a daughter who's in the midst of a troublesome pregnancy. The baby is due the first of December, but it could come early. Bridget has asked for emergency release when her daughter goes into labor and for two weeks afterward."

Alexa blinked rapidly. She couldn't fault Bridget's daughter for wanting her mother with her. But she wanted her mother, too. *I do want my mother. I want my mom and my mother . . .* The realization struck like a bolt of lightning. She sank onto the edge of the mattress.

"If I can't come for Thanksgiving, I will definitely be there for Christmas. All right?"

A selfish retort formed on Alexa's lips — *No, it's not all right!* — but she held it inside. "I understand. Bridget needs you more than I do, I guess." Her attempt at a glib tone failed. Only resentment came through. Before Mom could offer a reprimand, Alexa went on in a falsely cheerful voice. "Well, I probably should let you go. I know you need to leave for work soon."

"Honey, I —"

"I'll be fine, Mom. Honest. Don't worry about me. I'll call again on Wednesday, okay? Love you! Bye now." She disconnected the call and slipped her phone in her pocket. From downstairs, Grandmother's and Marjorie's soft laughter filtered through the heat vent below the window. She crossed to it and used her toes to close the flap behind the iron grate. The happy sound was instantly muffled.

Loneliness descended. She tugged the wispy curtains aside and gazed across the yard. When she'd first arrived in Arborville, she loved looking out the window at the sturdy, old buildings and the fields unfolding toward the horizon like a giant quilt. The view had given her a sense of peace and homecoming. She tried to stir the former feelings, but they refused to rise. With a sigh, she lowered her gaze and noticed a flickering light behind the windows in the cottage. She frowned. Was a lamp bulb going out? Or — her pulse skipped into nervous double beats — was there a fire?

She headed for the hallway, her thoughts

tumbling nervously. Had Briley returned yet? If he were in there, he'd make use of the fire extinguisher. Unless he was asleep. She quickened her pace, and the thud of her feet on the wooden risers competed with the pound of her heart. Not until she was out the front door and trotting across the steppingstones that led to the cottage did she remember she hadn't put on her shoes or a jacket. The rough stones poked her soles through her socks and the night air nipped at her bare arms and legs, but she couldn't turn back now. All of the work and time and money she'd invested in renovating the old summer kitchen could be going up in smoke.

The windows glowed eerily against the darkened landscape, the flickering more pronounced as she drew near. Then quick as a flash of lightning, understanding struck. She came to a stop outside the cottage. Not a fire. Not even close to a fire. A television screen's changing images created the odd flicker behind the lace curtains. Irritation chased away the worry that had gripped her. She'd signed a contract for Internet via a cable line, but she wasn't paying for TV service. How had he hooked up a television?

Shivering, she hugged herself and shifted from foot to foot. Should she knock on the cottage door and ask Briley to disconnect the television? Or should she ask Uncle Clete to discuss it with her guest? As she debated with herself, a ball of fur charged at her from the direction of the barn. Pepper! She braced herself, then changed her mind and turned to run, but she hesitated a moment too long. The dog plowed into her legs.

Alexa threw her arms in the air and shrieked.

Barking wildly, Pepper jumped again, this time planting her front paws on Alexa's middle. The weight of the dog pushed her backward. She caught her heel on the edge of a steppingstone. Her arms flailing and another involuntary shriek leaving her throat, she fell flat on her bottom.

Briley

Briley scrambled from the bed and darted for the door. At first he'd thought the scream came from the movie he'd popped into the DVD player, but when he heard the second one — shriller, louder, more panicked — he realized it was real. He slapped the push button for the porch lamp and threw open the door. In the yellow shaft of light, he spotted the black-and-white border collie wrestling someone to the ground. Obviously the dog was playing — tongue lolling, tail waving so fast it became a blur — but the person on the ground didn't seem to realize it. She'd rolled into a ball with her hands over her head, and little grunts of terror emerged from behind her crossed arms.

Briley put his hands on his hips and shook his head. Served her right, whoever she was, for sneaking around out here where she didn't belong. "You get'er, Muttski."

The dog barked and then gave a nimble leap to the opposite side of the woman's body where it began poking its muzzle beneath her balled fists, and Briley got a glimpse of a long, mink-brown ponytail spread across the grass. Alexa!

He bounded over with one wide stride and caught the dog by its thick ruff. "Here, now, that's enough! Get off of her!"

With a whine the dog plopped onto its behind and stared up at Briley with bright eyes. Now that he had the dog under control, he reached for Alexa. When he gripped her upper arms to pull her to her feet, she let out another bloodcurdling scream.

"Will you knock it off?" He yanked her upright and shot a glance toward the house. "Somebody's going to think I'm murdering you."

Her eyes flew open and she stared into his face. "B-Briley?"

He hid a grin. She must be scared to forget her manners. "That's right."

She looked frantically right and left. "Where's Pepper?"

"Pepper?" Had she hit her head? She wasn't making much sense.

"That stupid dog!"

The dog, which was named Pepper, rose up and whined as if to protest Alexa's exclamation. Automatically Briley commanded, "Sit." To his relief the furry beast obeyed him. All in all, Pepper was a pretty good dog. He looked at Alexa. "What did you do to aggravate the poor mutt?"

She wriggled free of his grasp and stepped a few inches away from him. She sent a smoldering glare from the dog to him. "I didn't do anything to her. I *never* do anything to her. But she hates me! She must, because she always attacks me. And I don't like her all that much, either." In the space of three seconds, the angry glint in her eyes changed. Her gaze seemed to travel his length, and bold red stained her cheeks. She folded her arms across her middle, hunched her shoulders, and turned sharply away.

Briley scowled, puzzled by her odd behavior, and finally the chill air brought realization. With his adrenaline pumping he'd forgotten he'd pulled on a pair of pajama pants in place of his jeans and had shed his shirt to watch TV. So he stood under the moonlight — under Alexa's embarrassed gaze — only half dressed. In the past he'd taken advantage of opportunities to strike a pose and showcase his muscular form, but to his shock he only experienced a real rush of mortification. For her and for him.

Crossing his arms over his chest, he inched toward the cottage door. "Well, since you're all right, I'm —"

"Alexa!" A middle-aged woman — the nurse who showed up every evening — trotted across the yard toward the cottage. She'd had the sense to wear shoes and even put on a coat. And she carried a frying pan. He swallowed a snicker. The woman was armed for bear. Her gaze landed on Briley, and her eyes narrowed into slits. "We heard you scream. Are you all right? Did he —" She waved the frying pan.

Alexa darted to the nurse. "Pepper jumped on me and scared me. Of course Bri— Mr. Forrester — didn't do anything to me. Except come to my rescue. I'm sorry I frightened you and Grandmother." She looped her hand through the nurse's elbow and steered her toward the house. "But it's cold out here. Let's go in."

Pepper sidled close and leaned against Briley's leg as the pair of women scurried off. Briley absently stroked the dog's head. Had Alexa just defended him? He replayed her words — *"Of course Mr. Forrester didn't do anything to me."* Spoken staunchly. With a touch of you-should-know-better in her tone. She trusted him. The realization should please him, but instead an uneasy knot formed in the pit of his stomach.

CHAPTER 11

Sommerfeld
Anna-Grace

If only this knot in her stomach would go away. Anna-Grace sat on the edge of her bed and stared at the sealed envelope leaning against the scrolled base of the accent lamp on her dresser. The bulb was on, sending down a triangular glow that seemed to spotlight the envelope and its neatly penned, simple line on the front: *For Anna-Grace.* Except she didn't know if she wanted it.

During the night, each time she awoke — and she'd awakened every hour — the envelope seemed to mock her with its presence. With each awakening her thoughts bounced back and forth like a monkey she'd once seen in a zoo cage frenetically leaping from one corner to another in its attempt to find an escape hatch.

Just open it. Get it over with.
Don't open it. Throw it away.

The same back-and-forth exchange roared through her mind again, nearly dizzying in its insistence. But which command to follow? Mom and Dad had told her to open it when she was ready. Would she ever be ready to discover the names of the people who'd cast her aside?

Strange how she'd never really thought about her birth parents when she was growing up. Little Sunny often talked about her Chinese mom and dad, asked questions, seemed to require assurance. But Anna-Grace had always been so secure, so loved. She'd simply accepted that the ones who raised her were her parents. Period. Maybe if she'd experienced curiosity before, the envelope would serve to satisfy her rather than confuse her.

A tap at the door interrupted her thoughts. She called wearily, "Come in." The door opened and Mom peeked her head in. Furrows marched across her forehead and formed a V between her eyebrows. Anna-Grace hated that she'd put the look of worry on her mother's normally relaxed face.

A slight smile trembled on Mom's lips. "Are you okay? You hardly touched your breakfast, and you didn't see Sunny off to school."

"Was Sunny upset?" Her little sister loved

her morning routine. So far she'd managed to concern Mom and disappoint Sunny. The day wasn't off to a good start. Stupid envelope, anyway . . .

"She'll survive." Mom stepped fully into the room and crossed to the bed. She rested her fingertips on the rumpled quilt wadded at the foot of the mattress. She didn't say anything about the unmade bed — something that should have been done before breakfast. "She needs to get used to going off without you standing on the porch and blowing kisses at her. It won't be long now, and —"

Anna-Grace stood and turned to face her mother. "Should I break my arrangement to marry Steven?"

Mom drew back, her eyes widening. "Why, Anna-Grace Braun, what kind of question is that?"

"An important one." Her rolling stomach threatened to return what little breakfast she'd consumed. She pressed her palms to her belly. "I couldn't sleep last night. I kept . . . thinking. Steven's family is from Arborville. My birth parents are from Arborville. Arborville isn't a very large town. What if my birth family and his are related? He could be my cousin and I wouldn't even know it. I can't marry my cousin!" Panic turned her voice shrill.

"Anna-Grace . . ." Mom stepped forward and wrapped her in a loose hug.

The embrace was warm, familiar, raising countless memories of being comforted, cherished, unconditionally accepted. How could she even consider betraying her parents by acknowledging another man and woman had conceived her?

Mom pressed a kiss on her temple and then cupped her face. Her hands smelled like lemon-scented soap and the onions she'd chopped for Dad's morning hash browns — a homey scent. "Honey, don't concoct reasons to worry. Yes, Arborville is a small town, but there are several different families represented there. Your dad and I have already confirmed that you and Steven aren't related."

"You did?"

"Of course we did. We would tell you if you two were related by blood."

Anna-Grace's chest heaved with little puffs of breath. "So . . . you *know* my birth parents?"

Mom nodded slowly, compassion glowing in her eyes.

Anna-Grace stepped away from her mother's gentle touch and glowered at the offending envelope. "Mom . . ." She pushed the words past a throat so tight, her tonsils were surely tied into a double knot. "I think I hate them."

"Oh, honey. You don't mean that."

"Yes, I do."

Mom caught Anna-Grace's hand and drew her onto the edge of the mattress. "Why do you hate them?"

Anna-Grace sat stiffly, her heart pounding. According to the Bible, hating someone was the same as murdering them. Did she really want her birth parents dead? Of course not. She just wanted them to go away. But no matter whether she opened that envelope or not, they would always be in the back of her mind now — forever taunting her with their presence. "They didn't want me twenty years ago, and I don't want them now."

"That isn't a reason to *hate,* Anna-Grace."

Anna-Grace hung her head.

"Hatred is an ugly emotion, and it leads to bitterness and vengeful thoughts. You don't want all that inside of you, eating you up, do you?"

No, she didn't. Her parents had raised her to forgive rather than harbor a grudge. Tears clouded her vision. "I'm sorry, Mom. I just wish . . ." Did she wish Steven's parents hadn't given him the land? Did she wish

143

she hadn't been given up for adoption? She sighed. "I wish Steven's land wasn't in Arborville so I didn't have to deal with this."

Mom slipped her arm around Anna-Grace's waist and tipped her forehead against her temple. "Have you considered, my dear daughter, that perhaps God prompted Steven's parents to gift him with the land in Arborville so you would have the chance to get to know your birth parents?"

She blinked away a rush of angry tears. "God wouldn't want me to know the people who gave me away."

Mom's soft sigh stirred the ribbon trailing from Anna-Grace's head covering. "There are many reasons why people give up a child for adoption, and not all of those reasons are selfish. We shouldn't judge, Anna-Grace. I don't know why they chose to relinquish their parental rights, but I'm grateful, because I have the gift of calling you my daughter."

The tears spilled down Anna-Grace's cheeks. She gave her mother a quavering smile of thanks.

Mom rose. She picked up the envelope and fingered it, her lips pursing into a thoughtful moue. "I'm glad you don't have to go to work today. You can take a nap, catch up on the sleep you missed last night. And you can spend time in prayer."

She put the envelope back where she'd found it and faced Anna-Grace. "Your dad and I both think it would be best for you to discover the names of your birth family before you move to Arborville, but we'll respect your decision if you choose to leave it a secret. But please seek God's will rather than allowing your own stubbornness or fear to guide you. Will you do that?"

Anna-Grace didn't want to pray. She feared what God might instruct her to do. But she nodded.

"All right. I'll leave you to rest . . . and pray." Mom delivered another kiss on Anna-Grace's cheek and then left the room.

For several long seconds the envelope held her captive. She stared at it, unblinking, until her eyes burned. She closed her eyes, but the image seemed imprinted on her retinas, visible even behind her closed lids. *God* . . . The prayer refused to form. She flopped onto the bed, pulled up her knees, and buried her face in the pillow. She'd pray later. For now she only wanted to sleep. Maybe when she woke up, the letter would be gone.

But when Anna-Grace awakened hours

later, the envelope was still in its spot, teasing her with its presence. She ignored it the rest of the day and went to bed without opening it. Tuesday morning she turned it facedown on the edge of the dresser and pretended it wasn't there. Steven visited Tuesday evening and asked if she'd decided whether she wanted him to sell the farmstead. She pressed her face against his chest and battled tears. How could she ask him to part with something that had been in his family for four generations so she could avoid facing her past? The request would be so selfish. But could she live in Arborville? She didn't know what to say, so she mumbled she needed more time — perhaps Friday? He gave her a sweet kiss on the forehead and told her to take all the time she needed, but she saw the tense lines around his mouth and recognized his desire to have the decision made.

Wednesday, after her shift at Lisbeth's Café, she spent the afternoon at the local school, creating harvest-related decorations for the big bulletin board inside the front door. The teacher asked why she was in such a hurry to redo the board. Anna-Grace usually left the welcome-back decorations up until the first of November, but she needed the distraction now. She offered a weak shrug and hedged. "I suppose this cooler weather and the changing leaves have made me eager for Thanksgiving." Miss Kroeker accepted the reply.

She accompanied Mom to the church's quilting circle on Thursday afternoon and then regretted it. The buzz around the quilting frame concentrated on the farmstead in Arborville. If only she could be as excited about the gift of land, which everyone deemed a wonderful blessing, as the fellowship members. She fielded their comments and questions with well-feigned enthusiasm, and by the time she left so she could be home when Sunny returned from school, her head pounded with tension. She had to make a decision concerning the land, and soon.

Steven arrived shortly after supper on Friday. Anna-Grace had spent the entire afternoon closed in her bedroom, praying and seeking God's guidance, but when she looked into his hopeful face, she still had no answer. She sank onto the edge of the sofa and buried her face in her hands.

Steven sat beside her and placed his hand lightly on her shoulder. "Anna-Grace, you're making this too hard on yourself."

An unfamiliar swell of anger tightened her chest. She sat upright and released a huff of frustration. "Well, of course it's *hard,* Steven. No matter what I do, the decision will lead to a host of consequences, none of which feel very positive."

He frowned. "What do you mean?"

Her frustration mounted. Was he really so shortsighted? "Let's say we move to Arborville, and word spreads that I am the illegitimate child of a man and woman from the local fellowship. Word will get out, you know. It's inevitable in a small town. People will have a hard time accepting me — befriending me will feel awkward to them — and they'll start looking at my birth parents differently, too. My birth parents won't want me there. They gave me away. Why would they want me just showing up again?"

Unintentional bitterness colored her tone. She closed her eyes for a moment, struggling to bring her emotions under control. God expected His followers to love even their enemies. She could not continue to harbor these ill feelings toward her birth mother and father.

"Then I'll sell it so you don't have to move there." Steven's reasonable voice intruded upon her inner battle.

She popped her eyes open and fixed him with a disbelieving look. "That isn't any bet-

148

ter! If you sell the land, your parents will be disappointed because you're letting go of a farmstead that's been in your mother's family for a century. The entire town of Sommerfeld will think you've lost your senses, parting with such a generous, valuable gift."

He took her hand and linked fingers with her. "But I don't mind. If you can't live there, you can't live there."

His grip felt too tight — almost cloying. She eased her hand free and rose, then took two steps away from the sofa. "You're willing to do this for me now, but someday you'd regret it, and it would always be a dark cloud hovering over our relationship. I can't ask you to give up something that is so special to your family."

"Anna-Grace . . ." He pushed to his feet and closed the distance between them. The tenderness in his expression melted her irritation in one heartbeat. This time when he reached for her hands, she clung willingly. "You are more important to me than the land." An odd look flitted through his eyes. He lowered his head briefly, and when he raised it again the strange glimmer was gone. "I promise not to hold it against you if you would rather not live in Arborville. There are lots of places in the United States with Old Order communities. We could use the money and move just about anywhere. Even to Alaska."

A bubble of laughter pressed upward. "I don't want to live in Alaska."

He grinned. "Well, okay then, not Alaska." He sobered. "The thing is, we don't have to be tied to the farm in Arborville. Or even to Kansas if we don't want to be."

She sucked in a sharp breath and gawked at Steven. "After what your brother did — you'd move away from Kansas and your mom and dad?"

"I wouldn't be like Kevin, running off without warning and never contacting them afterward. I'd stay in touch." His brows descended and defensiveness put a bite in his tone. "It's not the same."

She shouldn't have mentioned Kevin. His departure was an ever-festering wound. She squeezed Steven's hands in silent apology. "Of course it isn't."

His stern look faded. He released her hands and slid his palms up her arms to her shoulders. His broad hands were warm and firm through the fabric of her dress. "All I'm trying to say is if the thought of living in Arborville is this hard for you, then we have lots of options. I'm willing to go somewhere else, if that's what you want to do."

Anna-Grace leaned into his embrace. He loved her. He loved her enough to give up his grandfather's farm for her. Her heart seemed to swell and fill her chest cavity, and happy tears pricked her eyes. Steven's willingness to sacrifice so much for her raised a desire to please him in return. The answer she'd been seeking finally made itself known.

Still nestled in his arms, she whispered, "Steven?"

"Yes?" His warm breath caressed her cheek.

"I'm going to get Mom and Dad." She stepped from the circle of his arms and moved toward the basement door. Her parents had taken Sunny to the rec room in the basement when Steven arrived, graciously giving her some privacy. "I've decided, but I want them to hear it, too."

Chapter 12

Steven

Steven slowly lowered himself to the sofa, his gaze never wavering from Anna-Grace's face. "Hurry and get them then." She darted off, and he curled his hand over the armrest of the sofa, his fingers flattening the padding beneath the brocade cover with the ferocity of his grip. For the first time since he delivered the news about the farm in Arborville, she appeared relaxed. Self-assured.

Hope and helplessness warred in his chest. Her decision would bind him to the farm or set him free. *Let her say she wants to sell it.* Guilt smacked as the prayer left his heart. But if the desire to sell the farm was hers rather than his, his parents would understand. Then he could use the money to —

Anna-Grace, followed by her parents, entered the living room. She came directly to the sofa and sat beside him, but her parents stood side by side near the wide doorway between the living room and kitchen. Mrs. Braun slipped her hand through her husband's bent arm, and he placed his hand over hers. They looked calm and unworried, the opposite of how Steven felt.

He forced himself to let go of the chair's armrest and moved his hand to his knee. He chafed the rough fabric of his work trousers with his palm and released a raspy chuckle. "Well, we're all here . . ."

Anna-Grace offered him a brief smile and nod, then drew in a long breath. "Mom, you said you and Dad would respect whatever decision I made, right?"

Her father said, "We've been praying for you to make the right decision, and we trust your judgment."

"Of course we do," Mrs. Braun added.

"Thank you."

Would she just tell them? Steven gritted his teeth to hold back his demand for her to hurry up.

"I've been praying, too, but until just now when . . ." She turned from her parents and locked gazes with Steven. "You said, 'If you can't live there, you can't live there.' "

His pulse thudded hard. He gave a jerky nod.

"All week I've been telling myself I can't do it. But how do I know for sure?"

She was still asking questions. Hadn't she made up her mind?

She faced her parents again. "I can't just refuse to move and make Steven give up the land his grandfather left as a legacy to his family. Not without knowing for sure if I can live peacefully in Arborville. And the only way to know whether I can live there is to spend time there. And not just for a day or two. For long enough for me to really, truly *know.*"

Mrs. Braun tipped her head, a slight frown creasing her face. "What are you saying?"

Anna-Grace stood and crossed to her father. "Dad, would Steven be wasting time and money to fix up the farmhouse in Arborville?"

Mr. Braun's forehead crunched into lines of deep thought. "Improving a property is rarely a waste because it increases the value."

"So even if later we decide" — she shot a quick look at Steven before facing her father again — "not to live there, it's a good idea to repair and renovate the house?"

"I would say so."

She scurried back to Steven and stood in front of him, her hands clasped at her waist.

154

"When are you going to Arborville to work on the house?"

Slowly Steven shrugged. His dad had been pestering him to get over there and get started, but he'd put it off in hopes of selling the place to someone else. "Probably next week."

"When you go, I'm going with you."

Her mother pulled in a startled breath.

Anna-Grace continued as if there'd been no interruption. "The only thing I'm not sure about is whether to open the letter from my birth parents before I go. Mom and Dad, I know you think it's better for me to learn their names if I plan to live in Arborville, but I wonder if I should wait until I've decided whether to move there permanently." She shifted to face Steven. "I'll stay with Aunt Abigail or one of Dad's cousins, and if I need to, I'll find a part-time job to pay for my keep. But I have to find out, firsthand, whether or not I can settle into the community."

Steven gawked at her, too stunned to speak. She wanted to *go* there?

"Anna-Grace, you can't just quit your job at the café without giving notice," Mrs. Braun said.

"I agree with your mother." Mr. Braun stepped forward and put his arm across

155

Anna-Grace's shoulders. "It would be ir-responsible to leave your aunt Deborah without warning."

Anna-Grace hung her head.

Mrs. Braun remained in the doorway, hug-ging herself. "Besides, we need to contact your relatives in Arborville and make sure someone has room for you."

Anna-Grace, her head still low, sighed. Then she looked at her dad. "You and Mom are right. I'll tell Aunt Deborah tomorrow that she needs to find another morning waitress. If my last day at the café is the twenty-fourth of this month, I can leave for Arborville the following Monday. Is that a better plan?"

Mr. Braun pulled Anna-Grace against his side in a hug. "Yes."

Steven stood. His joints felt tight and clumsy from holding himself so stiffly on the edge of the sofa. He looked first at Mrs. Braun, who blinked rapidly as if tears were threatening, and then Mr. Braun. "Other than wanting Anna-Grace to give better notice at the café, you don't mind her going to Arborville?" Why wouldn't they tell her no? If they forbade her, she wouldn't go. She respected her parents too much to go against their wishes. *Just tell her no . . .*

Mr. Braun's expression turned tender as

he gazed at his daughter's upturned face. "Part of parenting, Steven, is letting go. Livvy and I have done our best to raise Anna-Grace to be a responsible, capable young woman."

Mrs. Braun approached, a smile trembling on her lips. "We knew she'd be leaving us when she married you, and even though this is a little earlier than we'd anticipated, we trust she'll be all right."

Anna-Grace hugged her dad and then wrapped her mother in a hug. The women clung for several seconds before she stepped aside and faced Steven. "How long will it take to repair the house?"

He repeated what the carpenter in Arborville had estimated. "A month if things go well. Two at the most."

She bit her lip for a moment. "So if I wait two weeks, I'll be in Arborville for two to six weeks while you work on the house." She gave a firm nod. "That should be long enough. By the time you finish the house, I should know whether or not living there is something I can do. If I can, the house will be ready for us. If I can't, it will be ready for someone else."

Steven stifled a groan. Four to eight weeks before he'd know whether he could pursue his own desires? He might explode by then.

■ ■ ■ ■

Arborville
 Briley

Briley closed his laptop and pushed it aside. He cringed as he considered Len's reaction to the lengthy e-mail he'd just sent. One full week in Arborville and he hadn't uncovered so much as a speck of dust. If dirt existed here among the people of the Old Order fellowship, they'd swept it well under the rug. Would Len tell him to give up and come on back to Chicago? Even though he was going a little stir crazy — he missed the bustling Chicago nightlife — he wasn't ready to concede defeat. There had to be dirt here. He just needed to peel back the rug a little farther. And that would take time.

His stomach growled. He glanced at the clock and gave a start. Seven already? He'd sat down at the table at a quarter of four to fine-tune the week's journal entries and e-mail Len. Where had the time gone? He crossed to the little refrigerator tucked in an old-fashioned cupboard and rummaged through it. Lunch meat, cheese, a squirt bottle of mayonnaise, and a half-dozen cans of soda — nothing more than what he'd found every other time he opened the door. He was getting pretty tired of sandwiches. He really wanted a pizza. And not the microwavable kind, either — a soft-dough, double-cheesy, pepperoni-and-mushroom-laden pizza like the ones from his favorite parlor back home. His mouth watered and his stomach rumbled again. He smacked the refrigerator door closed, grabbed his jacket from the back of the chair, and strode out the door.

He tugged on his jacket as he crossed the lawn for the house. He tried not to pester the Zimmermans in the evening, but once the pizza craving hit, he knew he wouldn't be satisfied with bologna. If he had to, he'd drive to Wichita, but he hoped he'd be able to find a pizza place a little closer to Arborville.

Alexa responded to his tap at the door and invited him into the kitchen. The room sparkled from a fresh cleaning, but the aroma from supper still lingered. The savory scent heightened his hunger, and he blurted, "Where's the closest pizza joint?"

A sympathetic grin appeared on her face. "Are you homesick?"

Briley frowned, confused. "Homesick?"

"Yes. I've heard Chicago-style pizza is the best."

He hadn't done enough traveling to confirm if the best pizza came from Chicago. He just knew he liked the pies from Johnny's Pizza Parlor better than any other place he'd eaten in the city. Thinking of chomping through a slice of Johnny's pepperoni nearly made him groan in desire. He gave a quick nod. "It's good stuff all right. And I've got a serious craving. Please don't tell me I'll have to drive all the way to Wichita for pizza."

She untied her apron and hung it on a hook beside the back door. "You're in luck. The convenience store on the highway has a pizza oven. You can buy a slice or an entire pie."

"Convenience store pizza?" Briley made a face. "That can't be much better than the frozen store-bought ones. Those things taste like cardboard."

She shrugged and leaned against the edge of the counter. A few strands of hair had worked loose of her simple ponytail and framed her jaw. She pushed the strands behind her ears, then slipped her hands into the pockets of her denim skirt. "I've never eaten frozen ones from the store — I prefer to bake my own — but the Quick Stop pizza really isn't bad. Why not get a slice and try it out? If you don't like it, then you'll know you have to drive to Wichita or Pratt."

Her idea made sense. As hungry as he was getting, even the cardboard variety sounded good. He inched backward toward the porch. "I'll give it a try. Thanks." He turned to go, but an odd sense of loneliness struck and held him in place. "You busy? Maybe you could go with me." A pretty blush stole over her face. He'd flirted enough to recognize that embarrassment, not pleasure, caused it. He'd better give her an out. He sniffed the air. "Obviously you already ate. Was it meatloaf? Spaghetti?"

"Italian meatloaf."

If it tasted as good as it smelled, it had to have been wonderful. "So if you're not hungry and not interested, it's all right." He coughed a laugh and held up both palms. "No pressure."

The blush deepened. She looked to the side. "Mr. Forrester, I appreciate the invitation, but —"

"Hey, I wasn't asking you out on a date." Defensiveness sharpened his tone. Did she have to act so skittish? He wasn't exactly a monster. And she was too young — and too "plain" — for him anyway. "I just thought you might enjoy getting out of the house. I've been here a week, and the only time you've left is to go to the grocery store or to church. But if you'd rather stay here, it's no skin off my teeth."

She jerked her gaze toward him. "No skin off your teeth? Did you really say that?" Amusement glimmered in her eyes.

Fond remembrance replaced the stab of irritation. He chuckled. "Wow. Aunt Myrt just came out of my mouth."

Alexa tipped her head. Her ponytail swung toward her left shoulder, and the bulb hanging from its twisted cord overhead brought out shimmers of bronzish-gold in the dark tresses. "Who's Aunt Myrt?"

Briley wished he could bite off his tongue. "Nobody important." Such a blatant lie. She was the only person who'd ever been important to him. But he couldn't explain without sharing parts of himself he preferred to keep hidden. Before he said anything else to incriminate himself or shame the dear woman who'd loved him unconditionally, he took a backward step. "Enjoy your evening. I'm going after my pizza." He turned and headed across the creaky porch floor.

Alexa's soft footsteps padded after him. "Mr. Forrester?"

He paused at the screen door.

"I can't go with you because Marjorie hasn't arrived yet and I don't want to leave

Grandmother alone."

Of course. She hung around the house to take care of her wheelchair-bound grandmother. He shouldn't have gotten testy. "Ah, gotcha." He angled his head. "By the way, what happened to her?"

Alexa grimaced. "A hay bale — one of the big round ones — rolled over her and crushed her pelvis."

Briley involuntarily shuddered.

She nodded in understanding. "She's lucky to be alive, but she'll never walk again. And for some reason, evening is the hardest part of her day. Her joints ache worse, which makes it harder for her to see to her own needs. So I need to be here. But thank you for asking me to go along."

Sympathy twined through him — an emotion he rarely allowed himself. He took hold of the doorknob. "No problem. Thanks for letting me know where to find my supper." He turned the etched knob.

"Mr. Forrester?"

The hesitation in her voice bothered him. He'd sat at her dining room table and engaged in light conversation every morning for a week and rescued her from the fuzzy mutt that roamed the farm. She'd claimed to trust him, but her timidity seemed to prove the opposite. What would it take to get these people to relax enough to open up to him? "Yeah?" The single word query growled out.

"I feel bad that you don't have a stove in the cottage, so you can't do any cooking. If . . . if you'd like, you can join us for lunch tomorrow after service. There'll be plenty of food."

He examined her face for signs she regretted issuing the invitation. He saw only sincerity. He nodded. "Sure. That'd be great. Thanks."

A relieved smile broke across her face. "Good. Well, I'll see you in the morning then."

"Eight o'clock," he verified.

She nodded.

He gave the door a push, then stopped before stepping over the threshold onto the concrete ramp. "What time is service?"

"Service . . ." Her eyes widened. "You mean *church* service?"

He nodded.

"You want to come?"

Only an idiot would miss the delight reflected in her expression and tone. Her response reminded him of Aunt Myrt's reaction the Sunday mornings he'd rolled out of bed without prompting and stumbled into the kitchen in his best trousers and shirt. Even though he usually slept through the service, she'd always been so happy when he went without a fuss. He should have stayed awake and paid more attention back then. If Aunt Myrt knew he wanted to attend the fellowship's service just to win the community members' favor so he could spy on them, she'd be disappointed.

He swallowed bitter regret and forced a reply. "Yeah, if you don't mind an outsider showing up."

Alexa laughed, a lighthearted trickle of happiness. "Nobody's an outsider in the house of God, Mr. Forrester. You're more than welcome to attend. Service starts at ten, and you can ride along with Grandmother and me if you'd like."

His sports car would look pretty ridiculous outside the little church building alongside the buggies, dark-colored unpretentious sedans, and pickup trucks. "Thanks. I'll do that."

"Okay!" She laughed again, then waved both hands at him. "Now go get your pizza before you starve to death on my back porch. See you tomorrow morning, Mr. Forrester."

CHAPTER 13

Sommerfeld
Anna-Grace

Anna-Grace settled onto her familiar bench beside Mom and Sunny and glanced across the simple worship room at the folks filing into their seats. Neighbors, friends, uncles and aunts and cousins — all people she'd known her entire life. A knot formed in her throat. In two weeks she would enter a different building in a different town and worship with a different fellowship. Her stomach trembled. Could she do it? Could she really leave Mom and Dad and Sunny and her fellowship family?

Friday night she'd been so certain going to Arborville was the right thing to do. Saturday morning she gave her notice at the café without hesitation. Saturday afternoon she called Arborville and made arrangements to stay with her cousin Sandra, then she and Mom made a list of the things she should plan to take with her. Not even one inkling of doubt had entered her mind.

But now worry descended. Or maybe it was fear. Either way, the thought of leaving didn't seem as wise as it had only thirty-six hours ago. She looked across the aisle to the men's side of the church and quickly located Steven's thick, short-cropped blond hair. She gazed at his profile — the slight lift of his chin, his firm jaw, and his lips set in an unsmiling line. He appeared uncertain, too. Was he also fearful about leaving Sommerfeld? He hadn't come right out and said so, but she'd sensed apprehension each time they discussed his grandfather's farm. Sympathy swirled through her chest.

Sunny shifted close and rested her cheek against Anna-Grace's shoulder, and the nervous tremors changed to the threat of tears. *Dear Lord, this is the natural progression of life — growing up, leaving home, forging a separate pathway. Our worry doesn't please You. Give us peace about the direction we're going and help us stay in Your will.*

The prayer soothed the frayed edges of her nerves. She hoped Steven felt it, too. She kissed the top of Sunny's glossy head of hair and turned her attention to the front as Deacon Muller stepped forward to offer the opening prayer.

■ ■ ■ ■

Arborville
  Briley

Briley chose the bench at the back of the simple, white-painted worship room where he could observe the worshipers without them observing him. His research had already prepared him for the men filling the benches on one side of the room and the women on the other. The lack of hymnals and musical instruments didn't take him by surprise, either, but the singing did. The people's voices blended in the most beautiful harmony he'd ever heard. Even though he'd never been fond of church music — it was too tame for his taste — the delivery of the hymns gave him chills. The good kind of chills.

Between standing to sing, kneeling to pray, and sitting on a backless bench, there was no possibility of sleeping through the service in the Arborville church even though it stretched for two hours — longer than any church service he'd attended before. He didn't sleep but he did fidget. He couldn't help it. How could anyone sit comfortably on a solid wood bench with no backrest to lean against? But everyone else, even the youngest kids, sat still and attentive during the lengthy sermon about a man named Joseph who'd been sold into slavery by his brothers.

He listened in snatches between studying his surroundings, but he honestly couldn't find much reality in the gist of the lesson. Bad things could be used for good in a person's life? The concept was too simplistic and fairy godmotherish to be real. After lunch he'd make careful notes about not only the service but also the naiveté of the people seated on these benches in the stark sanctuary.

The service ended — finally — with one more hymn they sang with gusto. At the closing "Amen," parishioners surrounded Briley. He'd already met many of the people while wandering the local businesses or driving around town taking pictures, but they shook his hand and welcomed him anyway. Danny Aldrich — the little fisherman — reminded Briley to come out to the pond and drop a line that afternoon. He received no fewer than a dozen invitations for lunch, all of which he politely declined since he already had plans, and without exception each promised to ask him again in the future. Briley couldn't wait to share this information with Len. His boss would be thrilled at how readily he'd been accepted by the members of the community.

He shrugged into his jacket and left the church, making sure he exited via the same door the other men used, and jogged across the dry grass to Mrs. Zimmerman's car. She and Alexa were already inside — Mrs. Zimmerman in the back, Alexa behind the wheel — with the engine running. He popped open the passenger door and slid onto the seat. "Sorry I kept you waiting. Lots of people wanted to talk to me."

"It's okay." Even as she assured him, she put the vehicle in Drive and pulled out of the parking area, clearly eager to get going. "The others already left, but if they beat us to the farm, they have a key to get in."

Briley frowned. "Others?"

Mrs. Zimmerman answered. "My family gathers every Sunday for our noon meal and a time of fellowship. We trade hosting duties. This is our week to host."

"I see." Anxiety pinched his gut. He'd envisioned lunch with Alexa and her grandmother, not with a crowd. But he sent a polite smile over his shoulder. "That must be nice, being with family every week."

"Yes, it is." The older woman released a contented sigh. "And now that Alexa is with us, all four of my children are represented around my dining room table. I am very blessed."

Briley's reporter nose itched. He propped his arm along the back of the seat and shifted sideways so he could converse with Mrs. Zimmerman. "Hasn't Alexa always been with you?"

The woman pursed her lips, and Briley wondered if she'd ignore his question. But when she spoke, no reluctance colored her tone. "No, Mr. Forrester, to my great regret I've only known Alexa for a few short months. Her mother and I suffered a lengthy separation, all my own fault, which meant I had no contact with my granddaughter. So you might say the two of us are making up for lost time."

He flicked a glance at Alexa and caught the fond curve of her smile change to an uncertain tremble. He wanted to question the odd expression dancing across her lips, but for some reason the words wouldn't form. He faced forward and remained quiet the remainder of the distance to the bed-and-breakfast.

The truck Mrs. Zimmerman's son drove and an unfamiliar car were parked beside the barn. Alexa pulled past them and parked in a graveled patch near the house. She shut off the ignition and pocketed the keys.

"Looks like Sandra is the only one not here yet."

"She's been slower since little Isabella came along." Mrs. Zimmerman laughed softly, the sound holding affection. "But she's worth waiting for."

Briley and Alexa exited the car at the same time, and he moved to the back door to help Mrs. Zimmerman. But Alexa politely asked him to move aside, claiming it was easier to do the transfer herself than explain the procedure to someone else. He could have told her he knew how to transfer someone into a wheelchair, but it would have created another delay, so he waited until Mrs. Zimmerman was situated in her wheelchair. When Alexa reached for the chair's handles, he bounded forward.

"I'll take Mrs. Zimmerman in. I held you up at church, so you probably need to get inside and see to lunch."

She flashed a quick smile and darted off, leaving him alone with the old woman. Mrs. Zimmerman sat with her hands resting over her purse and Bible in her lap, seemingly at ease in his presence.

He curled his hands around the rubber grips. A memory surfaced of Jeffrey, a foster brother whose father had shaken him when he was a baby and caused cerebral palsy.

Jeffrey always wanted Briley to push his chair because he did wheelies. The boy's laughter rang in the recesses of his mind, and he came close to pressing down and sending Mrs. Zimmerman's feet in the air. Fortunately good sense prevailed, and he gave a forward push instead.

"Here we go."

Alexa had gone around to the back door, so Briley followed her lead. He pushed the wheelchair into a kitchen bursting with wonderful aromas and bustling with activity. The moment the chair cleared the threshold, a blond-haired woman with tense lines marching across her forehead waved her hand at him.

"You'll be in the way in here. The table's already set. Take Mother on to the dining room." She turned to the stove and swirled a wooden spoon through the contents of a kettle.

Mrs. Zimmerman snickered, and Briley hid a smile as he wheeled the chair through the kitchen. When they reached the dining room, where a dark-haired woman also wearing a white cap with black ribbons was setting the table, Mrs. Zimmerman angled a grin at him. "No matter what Shelley told you, I'm not staying in here. Let's go to the front room instead." She took control of the chair, and Briley followed her into the large living room.

Two men — Mrs. Zimmerman's son, Clete, and a man Briley hadn't met yet — and a cluster of children were already in the room, the kids on the floor and the men on the sofa. The men both stood when Briley came in, and Clete strode over with his hand extended.

"Hello again, Mr. Forrester."

"Just call me Briley." He shook the man's hand. Although Clete didn't smile, he nodded and repeated Briley's name. Clete struck Briley as the no-nonsense sort. The second man approached, and Briley shook his hand. "I don't think we've met. I'm Briley Forrester."

"I'm Harper Unruh, Shelley's husband."

Briley's eyebrows shot up. He belonged to the bossy woman in the kitchen? Briley had expected someone who looked henpecked, but Harper stood with squared shoulders, and his handshake was firm.

Harper gestured to a pair of look-alike little girls playing with paper dolls in the corner. "Those are our girls, Ruby and Pearl."

The little girls looked shyly in his direction, so he smiled and winked at them. They put their heads together and giggled. Briley grinned again. "Cute kids."

"Thanks." Harper gazed at the girls with fatherly pride.

The front door opened and a little boy burst into the room. With curly blond hair and big blue eyes, he fit in, appearance-wise, with the other children. He darted directly to their circle and plopped down, his jacket still in place. A petite woman and a tall man carrying a blanket-wrapped bundle entered behind the little boy. The woman paused at the wheelchair and placed a kiss on Mrs. Zimmerman's cheek, then hurried into the kitchen calling, "I'm here! Sorry I'm late!" A flutter of female voices rose.

The man laid the bundle on the sofa and unwound the blanket, revealing a wriggling baby with fuzzy tufts of fine yellow hair. Briley stifled a soft snort — the Zimmerman gene was a strong one. Any fool could pick out the relatives just by looking at their hair color.

The newest arrival settled the baby in the crook of his elbow and joined the men. "Glad to see you aren't all sitting around the table waiting on us. Sandra was worried we were keeping everyone from eating."

"We only got home ourselves a few minutes ago." Mrs. Zimmerman gestured toward Briley. "Derek, have you met Alexa's long-term guest? This is Briley Forrester from —"

Derek stuck out his free hand. "From Chicago. The reporter, right?"

Briley nodded as he shook the man's hand.

"I saw you in service this morning, but Isabella here was tuning up to demand her lunch, so Sandra hurried me out before I could greet you." He grinned, and Briley could have sworn orneriness glinted in the man's eyes. "Of course, I wouldn't have been able to get through the crowd, anyway. You got swarmed." He leaned in, and this time Briley recognized the twinkle for what it was — pure teasing. "You aren't carrying one of those little tape recorders to capture our dinner conversation, are you?"

Briley patted his shirt pocket, where the voice recorder he always carried made a slight bulge. "I've got it, but it isn't on. So you're safe." Derek pretended great relief, making Briley chuckle. Too bad Derek was Mennonite. And married with a couple of rugrats. He suspected the two of them could've ended up being friends if circumstances were different.

Derek moved to his son and tried to help the little boy out of his jacket. One-handed, it proved tricky, and Mrs. Zimmerman rolled closer to help. The other two men faced off, arms folded over their chests in serious poses, and began chatting about farmland available for rent in the county. Briley had nothing to add to the conversation, but he listened intently while pretending not to, hoping for something he could use in his article.

"Okay, everyone." Alexa stepped into the wide doorway separating the dining room from the front room. "Lunch is ready. Come on in."

With a collective whoop the children pounded past her and climbed into chairs. Mrs. Zimmerman shook her head. "Goodness sakes, you act as though you're starving." She rolled her wheelchair through the doorway and parked at the end of the table in the same spot she ate breakfast each morning. Briley waited until Derek, Harper, and Clete chose chairs before moving around to an empty seat.

He glanced at the pans of lasagna, bowls of green beans — whole, not cut up like he found in the cans he bought at the grocery store — and tossed salad, and baskets of crusty rolls crowding the center of the table. He almost licked his lips. Everything looked and smelled great.

The women filled the chairs between their

husbands and children, leaving the lone chair at the head of the table open for Alexa. As she slid into the seat, she held her hands to those beside her. Everyone around the table joined hands, and Briley caught hold, too. Aunt Myrt always prayed before meals — he expected someone to give a blessing — but she'd always linked her hands beneath her chin to pray. Holding hands with one of Harper's twins on his left and Mrs. Zimmerman on his right made his stomach feel funny. And he was pretty sure the feeling wasn't the result of hunger.

Mrs. Zimmerman nodded at her son. "Clete, ask the blessing."

Every head bowed and every pair of eyes closed, except Briley's. While Clete prayed, Briley took a slow look around the table, examining the shining blond heads of the children, the men's short-cropped haircuts, the mesh caps covering the women's hair. Only one female head remained free of a cap — Alexa's. He realized with a start that she was the only one of the Zimmerman females to sport dark rather than blond tresses. Somehow that strong Zimmerman gene must have skipped her. And why wasn't she wearing a Mennonite-style dress and cap?

"Amen." Clete finished, and everyone's

heads lifted in one wave.

They passed the food, and chatter filled the room — happy chatter, something alien to the majority of Briley's mealtime experiences. He wished he could push the button on his recorder so he could listen to the sound again later, process it, isolate each voice, turn it into a story. By the time Alexa carried in the dessert — some sort of gooey, chocolaty, pudding-filled cake shaped like an inner tube and topped with drizzly icing, toasted coconut, and chopped walnuts — he'd relaxed enough to tease some with the kids, answer a few questions about life in Chicago, and ask a few questions about Arborville.

But he didn't ask about Alexa's dark hair or mode of dress even though curiosity burned in his chest. His reporter's instinct told him the answer to those questions could very well lead to another story entirely. And he wasn't quite ready to pursue it. Yet.

CHAPTER 14

Alexa

Watching her family devour the mousse-filled double-chocolate cake made Alexa smile. Even Shelley, who often resisted dessert, ate her entire piece and complimented Alexa on its rich flavor and moist texture. Although her aunt had slowly warmed up to her over the past weeks, compliments were still rare, and she savored this one. She swallowed a giggle when Briley tamped the back of his fork's tines against the crumbs to capture every tiny bit of his serving.

He popped the remaining crumbs in his mouth, sighed, and aimed a grin in Alexa's direction. "Best cake I've ever eaten." He swiped his mouth with his napkin, then patted his taut belly. "Worth the five-mile run it'll take to work off the calories."

Everyone, including Aunt Shelley, laughed. Their response warmed Alexa in ways she didn't understand. She hugged herself, holding in the good feeling, while Briley pushed back his chair and rose.

"Thank you again for the dinner, the dessert, and the company. I enjoyed all three equally."

Alexa remained quiet, but everyone else voiced various responses to Briley's statement, assuring him they'd enjoyed visiting with him, thanking him for his kind words, reminding him he was always welcome at the table. Listening to those she'd claimed as her family draw Briley into their fold, she experienced a jolt of jumbled emotions that confused her even more than the warmth that had enveloped her only moments ago. She tamped the feelings down as firmly as Briley had tamped the cake crumbs as he spoke again.

"I made arrangements to join a certain little fisherman at the Heidebrechts' pond, so I need to change my clothes and get going. Thank you again for a very pleasant dinner." He strode around the table and disappeared through the little hallway that led to the kitchen. Moments later, the slam of the screen door announced his departure.

Alexa stared after him. The "little fisherman" he mentioned was certainly Danny Aldrich, the boy she'd mistakenly assumed was her younger half brother. Although

Danny's father, Paul Aldrich, wasn't her biological father, they became good friends while renovating the summer kitchen, and she experienced a twinge of jealousy thinking about Briley growing close to the man and his son the way she'd grown close to them. Did the Aldriches have to accept Briley as readily as they'd accepted her?

Ruby bounced in her chair. "Momma, can we be excused?"

"*May* we be excused," Shelley corrected.

Ruby repeated, "May we be excused?"

Grandmother tweaked one of Ruby's blond braids. "Yes, you may. Take your sister and your cousins to the barn and play with Pepper. The poor old girl needs some attention."

The crowd of children careened from the dining room, grabbed their jackets, and plowed out the front door en masse. At their departure Shelley began collecting the dirty dishes. She flicked a glance toward the kitchen hallway. "I have to say, he's much more polite than I expected him to be."

Sandra held her coffee cup beneath her chin. "You mean Mr. Forrester?" She took a sip. "Why wouldn't he be?"

Shelley clapped crumb-laden saucers into a stack. "Some of the big-city people who visit Arborville appall me with their lack of manners. Mr. Forrester, however, was nothing like I expected. Frankly, I found him a breath of fresh air."

Had Aunt Shelley ever spoken so kindly of Alexa? She didn't think so. And why was Shelley clearing *Alexa's* table? She stood and took over the task of plate gathering. "Sit, Aunt Shelley. I'll take care of the cleanup."

"Oh, but —"

"Just relax. My kitchen. My mess. I'll clean it up." She softened her words with a smile.

For several seconds Shelley stared at her with her brow puckered, and then she nodded. "All right, Alexa. I suppose it is your kitchen now, and you have your way of doing things." She waved her hand as if granting permission. "Suit yourself." But she grabbed the coffee carafe and refilled her cup and her husband's cup before sitting down again.

Alexa circled the table and filled her hands with dishes. Between trips back and forth from the kitchen, she half listened to the conversations. The men had one, involving winter crops, and the women another, concerning ways to break Clete and Tanya's little Julie of her thumb-sucking habit. Alexa could contribute nothing to either topic, so she finished clearing the table and loading the dishwasher without speaking a word.

When she entered the dining room with a soapy cloth to scrub the table, Sandra reached out and captured her hand. "Alexa, may I ask a favor?"

Her sour reflections of moments ago melted. People only asked favors of those they considered close enough to trust. Whatever Sandra needed, she'd do it. "Of course."

"Mother said you put some really nice mattress pads — the memory kind? — on the beds upstairs."

Alexa nodded. "That's right." She hadn't been able to afford new mattresses for the guest beds, but the four-inch-thick foam pads made the old mattresses feel like new.

"Would you be willing to lend one to me for the next several weeks? That is, if you don't have guests scheduled for the rooms."

Such an odd request. Alexa released a little chuckle. "Do you want to find out if they're comfortable or not?"

"No, I want to make my sleeper sofa more comfortable." She let go of Alexa's hand and turned toward the group at the table. "The sofa works well for a night or two, but to sleep on it for several weeks?" She cringed.

Clete bounced his fist against Derek's shoulder. "Did my baby sister banish you to the basement?"

Derek laughed. "No, I'm not going to be sleeping down there. We have a guest coming."

"Instead of taking one of Alexa's nice mattress pads, why not have whoever is coming stay here at the B and B?" Grandmother frowned. "That's why Alexa fixed up those rooms — for guests."

Sandra made a face. "I don't think this guest can afford to pay for a room, Mother. And . . ." She bit her lip, sending a quick apologetic look to Alexa. "It might be awkward if she stayed here."

Clete's wife, Tanya, leaned forward, her eyes sparking. "Who is it, Sandra?"

"Anna-Grace Braun."

Silence descended like a wet wool blanket. Alexa was nearly smothered beneath its weight. "Why?" She didn't realize she'd blurted the query until every face around the table jerked in her direction. Embarrassment seared her face, and she wished she could snatch the word back.

Sandra took Alexa's hand again and squeezed, the touch filled with compassion. "She wants to help remodel the Meiers farmhouse."

Alexa stepped away from her aunt's light grasp. "Well, of course she wants to help. It'll be her home, after all." She moved to her spot and began swiping the cloth over the patch of table. She didn't look, but she sensed everyone watching her.

Grandmother cleared her throat. "Sandra, did she — Anna-Grace, I mean — mention . . . Does she know?"

Alexa understood the meaning behind the question. Her hand slowed as she waited for Sandra to answer.

"I don't think so."

Her breath — a breath she hadn't even realized she was holding — eased out. She didn't want Anna-Grace to know she was the *real* Zimmerman daughter, granddaughter, and niece. If Anna-Grace didn't know, somehow Alexa could continue to pretend she wasn't a replacement for the baby given up for adoption nearly twenty years ago.

"It will be awfully hard to be natural around her." Tanya sighed, shaking her head. "I almost wish Suzy hadn't told us who Anna-Grace is."

"Don't be melodramatic." Grandmother's tone became tart. "Being aware of Anna-Grace's biological parentage doesn't change the fact she is Andrew and Olivia's daughter in the eyes of the law. You've always known she was adopted, and you've never treated her differently than anyone else in the family. That doesn't have to change."

"But it has changed, Mother." Shelley's tone matched Grandmother's. "Sandra's choice of words fits. It's awkward. How can we *not* be uncomfortable around her, knowing she's our niece rather than our cousin?"

Grandmother frowned and didn't answer.

Harper slipped his arm around his wife's shoulders. "I'll tell you how. We remind ourselves that none of this is Anna-Grace's fault. She didn't ask to be given up for adoption, and she didn't ask to be adopted by her mother's cousin. If we treat her differently now, after previously being at ease around her, she'll feel like she's being punished for some unknown wrong."

Alexa's knees felt weak. She eased into her chair and held the wadded, damp rag in her lap. She didn't even care about the wet patch forming on her skirt. Why hadn't Harper expressed such words of support when Shelley was holding herself aloof from Alexa? She hadn't asked to be raised by a single, unwed mother, yet in many ways she'd been ostracized because of it. Why were Anna-Grace's feelings so much more important than hers had been?

"Harper is right." Derek leaned forward and rested his linked hands on the tabletop. "We have to look at this from a legal standpoint. Anna-Grace became your cousin when the Brauns adopted her. She's still your cousin."

Shelley snorted. "From a legal standpoint, he says. As if we only have brains and no hearts!" She folded her arms over her chest and scowled. "Well, let me remind you, Derek, it wasn't your sister who gave birth to an illegitimate child and kept it secret for nineteen years. I'm still struggling with —"

Harper's frown and quick shake of his head silenced whatever else Shelley planned to say, but Alexa suspected she knew anyway. Shelley might have relaxed around her, but underneath she still viewed Alexa as an outsider. She always would.

Sandra turned toward Alexa. Empathy glowed in her blue eyes. Eyes as sky blue as all the Zimmermans, including Anna-Grace. "If you'd rather not lend me the mattress pad, it's all right. I'll just put some big pieces of cardboard between the frame's bars and the mattress to give it some support."

Alexa wouldn't say no. Family looked out for each other, and she wouldn't want to sleep on a lumpy mattress with bars poking into her back. She couldn't subject Anna-Grace to such discomfort no matter how jealous she was of the girl who really belonged in this family. She opened her mouth, fully intending to assure Sandra it was fine for her to borrow one of the pads, but something else spilled out.

"Why not just have Anna-Grace stay out here?"

Sandra's jaw dropped open. Shelley and Tanya both stared at Alexa as if she'd suddenly morphed into an alien creature.

Clete's eyebrows descended. "Are you sure, Alexa? If she stays until the house is finished, she could be here well past Thanksgiving. That's a lot of potential income to give up." His eyes said, *"Here's your out. You can take it if you want to."*

Alexa clenched her fist around the dishrag. "No. Really. I don't have anyone scheduled for the next several weeks so it isn't as if I'll be giving up income to let her have a room. No offense, Sandra and Derek, but she'd be more comfortable here than she would be in your basement. Plus if she's here, she'll be close enough to the Meiers farmstead to walk over on nice days if she wants to."

Clete reached out and offered her a few clumsy pats on the shoulder. "It's very unselfish of you to open one of your rooms to Anna-Grace."

Grandmother blew out a short huff and muttered, "Unselfish, and more than a little nuts."

Cautious laughter rumbled around the table, and Alexa battled a wry grin. Grandmother was right. She must be out of her mind. Could she really sacrifice her peace of mind and let Anna-Grace — Grandmother's biological grandchild — stay under this roof? She pulled in a slow breath to calm her jangling nerves and said in a raspy whisper, "She's family. You don't close the door on family."

Shelley hung her head. Sandra and Derek exchanged a telling look. Tanya blinked rapidly, as if battling tears.

Alexa tapped Sandra's wrist. "When is Anna-Grace coming to Arborville?"

"She'll arrive the twenty-fourth."

Two weeks . . . "All right then. I'll have a room ready for her."

Grandmother aimed an approving smile at Alexa. Alexa managed a wobbly smile in reply, but inwardly she cringed. She hoped no one searched beneath the surface of her words. If they did, they'd realize the motivation for her unselfish act was anything but selfless. She wanted their approval, their acceptance, their affection. And if it took inviting Anna-Grace Braun to the B and B to gain it, then she'd welcome her mother's biological daughter with open arms.

CHAPTER 15

Briley

Briley stretched his legs out and crossed his ankles. The worn straps of the aluminum folding chair creaked as he adjusted his weight to the edge of the seat. He hoped he wouldn't fall through the sagging old chair. He'd thought it chivalrous when Paul Aldrich offered the seat and moved to the opposite side of the pond, but now he suspected the man had the better part of the deal. As stiff as his muscles had grown during his two hours of sitting beside the pond not catching fish, if the chair collapsed he probably wouldn't have the ability to free himself from the rusty contraption.

He angled his gaze toward Danny, who sat as still as a statue in a similar chair about ten feet away. "Do you and your dad really do this every week?"

"Just about." Danny's mouth barely moved to release the answer. No other muscle in his body even twitched. He seemed completely absorbed in watching the plastic ball — what Aldrich called a bobber — floating on the water's surface.

Briley sighed and looked at his own red-and-white bobber. Stupid name. The thing never bobbed. It just sat there. He looked at Danny again, marveling at his focus. How could the kid be so still and attentive for hours on end? Briley had battled tossing his pole aside for the past hour and a half. Of course Danny'd caught and released six fish in that amount of time — the same number as his father. Briley glanced at his floating bobber and stifled a snort. Fish in a Mennonite pond must only bite worms touched by Mennonite fingers. He should drop the pole and go back to the B and B. What a waste of time . . .

He braced himself to rise, and the red half of the bobber suddenly plunged beneath the surface of the water and bounced up again. Briley stiffened. Had he imagined that?

Danny sat up straight, excitement lighting his face. "You got a bite!"

Briley nodded. He curled both hands tight around his pole's handle and stared at the bobber. It went under again, this time the entire ball disappearing and the tip of his pole bending downward with the force of whatever had hold of the bait.

Danny crowed, "Yank it, Mr. Forrester! Yank it!"

So Briley yanked. His pulse galloped into wild double beats as he felt resistance. He'd caught a big fish, for sure! But then the line snapped free and the hook — empty of either a fish or a worm — flew over his head and sprinkled him with cold pond water. He glared for a moment at the fishless hook swaying at the end of the line and then flung the pole to the ground.

Danny drew back, his eyes round. "What's the matter?"

Didn't the kid have any sense? Briley snorted. "What do you think? I lost the fish, that's what's the matter."

The boy shrugged. "That happens sometimes." He squinted against the sun, his gaze never wavering from Briley's face. "Or it might've been a turtle and not a fish at all. They like the worms, too."

Briley balled his hands into fists and held back a growl of frustration. Danny's logical explanation irritated him worse than losing the fish had. "Don't placate me."

"What's 'placate'?"

Words from his trusty thesaurus fell from his tongue. *"Pacify, soothe, mollify . . ."*

The boy's expression didn't clear.

Briley sighed. Why was he picking on Danny? It wasn't the kid's fault the fish had bailed. He'd probably knocked it off with his overzealous yank on the line. "I mean don't try to make me feel better." He forced a grin. "It won't help. I'm mad."

Danny shrugged again. "Getting mad won't make the fish bite. Want another worm?"

Briley was tempted. He'd seen how Danny lit up when he pulled a fish from the water. It'd looked like fun to clamp the pole between his knees, catch hold of the fish dancing at the end of the line, and then work it free of the hook before giving it a toss back in the water. Part of him wanted to experience it himself. But the bigger part of him — the impatient part — was done. He let the bigger part win. "No, thanks."

"Okay." Danny pulled his line from the water, wiped the soggy worm free of the hook against a rock, then set his pole aside. "I'll quit, too, then." He leaned back and propped his ankle on his opposite knee, as relaxed as a person could get.

Briley shook his head, chuckling. He eased into his chair and imitated Danny's pose. Head back, eyes at half-mast against the sun, he mused, "You're sure one laid-back kid. Don't you ever get riled about any-thing?"

He'd meant to tease, but apparently Danny took him seriously. The boy pinched his forehead into a thoughtful pucker. "Sure I do. Everybody gets mad sometimes. My dad tells me, 'Be angry but sin not.' He said that means I shouldn't let my temper make me do things I'll regret later on. He says if I pray when I start feeling really mad, God will help me not sin."

Briley squirmed in his chair. The word *sin* made him feel as though bugs crawled under his flesh. He wanted to change the topic, yet he realized he was being given the chance to pry into the inner workings of the Mennonite faith. He could push past his discomfort for the sake of his article. He feigned a yawn. "Can you gimme an ex-ample of what you consider 'sin'?"

"That's easy." Danny bounced his sneaker-covered foot. "Don't worship any-thing except God. Don't use God's name as a curse. Don't be disrespectful to your mom and dad. Don't kill anybody. Don't take stuff that isn't yours, and don't *wish* you could take stuff that isn't yours. Don't tell lies."

"Phew." Briley blew out a short breath. All those "don'ts" had jarred him. With the exception of killing somebody, he'd pretty much done them all. "That's quite a list."

"But that's not everything. That's just some of the Ten Commandments — the ones I need to know for now. There are other ones that are more for grownups."

From across the pond a whoop sounded. Briley and Danny both looked up. Aldrich held his line high, showing off his catch. His grin spread from ear to ear.

Danny punched his fist in the air. "Way to go, Dad!"

The man waved, then he released the fish from the hook and gave it a gentle heave back into the pond. He swished his palms together, reached into his bait can, and began threading another worm onto his hook.

Danny settled into the chair again and turned to Briley. "You can ask my dad about the other ones. He knows all of them."

When Danny talked about his dad, his voice changed — became proud and subdued and respectful all at once. Briley couldn't imagine speaking proudly of his old man. He didn't even like thinking about the man who'd fathered him. He formed a snide question. "So what happens when you slip up?"

"Well, when I sin, I get in trouble."

The boy's sheepish expression tickled Briley. He chuckled. "Oh yeah? Get a walloping, do you?"

"Sometimes." Danny dropped his foot to the ground and scuffed his toe against the sand. "But that's not the worst thing. The worst thing is when I sin, I make my dad sad and disappointed. That hurts a whole lot more because I love my dad and I don't want him to be disappointed in me." He peeked at Briley out of the corner of his eye. "You're all grown up now, but didn't it make you feel bad when your dad was upset with you?"

Briley linked his hands behind his head and used his thumbs to massage the knot forming at the base of his skull. "To be honest, I couldn't care less what my *dad* thinks of me."

Danny gawked at Briley. "You don't care?"

"Nope."

"But . . . but . . ."

The kid might self-combust if Briley didn't explain. "My dad's not like yours, Danny. Mine didn't stick around. I haven't seen him since I was three years old."

Danny's eyes grew round. "He *left* you?"

Amazing how much it still hurt even after all these years. "He sure did." The sun slowly slunk toward the horizon, taking its warmth with it. Briley pulled his jacket closed and slipped his hands into his pockets.

"Did your mom help you feel better?"

Briley had very few memories of his mother, but he couldn't say she'd ever made him feel better. Not about anything. "Afraid not."

"Wow . . ." Danny chewed his lower lip, gazing at him with round, sad eyes.

Briley didn't care much for the turn the conversation had taken. And the start of a headache throbbed in his temples. Even though he was collecting some good information for his article — wouldn't Len get a kick out of Danny's recitation of the "kid" sins? — he was ready to go. He pushed to his feet, cringing at the complaining creak of the old chair.

Danny bounced up, too. "You leavin'?"

"Yeah." Briley zipped his jacket and picked up the fishing pole. "Where do you want this?"

"The back of Dad's pickup." Danny snatched up his pole and trotted alongside Briley as they moved toward the vehicles parked near the pond. He hollered over his shoulder, "Dad! Mr. Forrester's leaving!"

"Be right there!"

Briley paused. "You don't have to leave

199

just because I am. Stay and fish if you want to."

Danny shrugged. "Getting close to suppertime. We'd be leaving soon anyway." A hopeful grin broke across his face. "Wanna eat supper at our house? We had lunch at the Earlichs', and Mrs. Earlich sent home a big pot of ham and beans. Dad says it's enough to feed an army." The boy looked Briley up and down, his gaze admiring. "Betcha you can eat enough for an army."

Briley was tempted. He hadn't had ham and beans since he lived under Aunt Myrt's roof. She often stretched their food dollars with beans. He'd never minded. He put his hand on Danny's shoulder. "It's nice of you to invite me, but you probably should check with your folks before inviting people over."

"Dad won't mind." Danny darted toward his father, who ambled in their direction. "Dad, can Mr. Forrester have ham and beans with us tonight? Huh? Can he?"

Mr. Aldrich laughed. Briley did, too. The boy reminded him of an overexcited puppy. The man curled his hand around the back of Danny's neck. "I'd say that's up to Mr. Forrester whether he wants to eat ham and beans or not."

"And I'd say," Briley said, "it's up to your wife whether she wants a stranger brought

200

home without any warning."

Danny ducked his head. A sad smile formed on Mr. Aldrich's lips. "Well, you see, my wife passed on. So it's just Danny and me." He tugged the boy tight against his hip. "And you are more than welcome to join us."

Danny peered up at Briley. His puppy-dog eyes begged. "Please, Mr. Forrester? Dad hasn't told you all about sin yet."

Aldrich sent a startled look toward Danny. "What?"

Briley chuckled. The boy would be shocked if he knew just how familiar Briley was with sin. He said, "Never mind." Curiosity about how the man and boy managed without a woman in the home compelled him to accept their invitation. "Ham and beans sounds pretty good right about now. So I'd like to accept that invitation, if you don't mind."

Danny whooped.

Mr. Aldrich laughed and shook his head, amusement mingling with affection in his smile. "Well, then, let's load up and head home before the sun goes to bed and we're left standing out here in the dark. Can't believe how short the days are getting already."

Briley followed the Aldriches to their

house. While he drove, he used his voice recorder to capture the essence of his conversation with Danny and his thoughts about their afternoon by the pond. He found himself adding, "I feel a little like a fish out of water in my sports car when their vehicle blends so well with all the others in town. It doesn't seem to bother them, though. Amazing how many invitations I was given today."

He clicked off the recorder as he pulled behind Paul Aldrich's truck in his gravel driveway, then killed the engine. Danny burst out of the side door and galloped to Briley's car. He danced in place, waiting for Briley to get out. Laughing, Briley slung his arm across the boy's shoulders and entered the house through the front door.

"I'll get the beans heating. Make yourself at home." Aldrich headed around the corner.

Briley stood in the middle of the living room floor and sent a slow glance around the room. He'd left his camera in the car, but there wasn't much to photograph anyway. The room was plain — brown carpet, white walls, brown-and-tan plaid sofa, green chair. Danny's beaming smile provided the only cheerful thing in the entire space. Briley shook his head, stifling a snort. He was a bachelor, but he'd at least thrown around a few pillows on his matching black leather sofa and love seat and hung pictures on the walls to decorate his living room. He should suggest inviting Alexa over to offer a few ideas to spruce this place up.

Danny hooked his jacket on a stand near the door. "Gimme your coat. I'll hang it for you." Briley shrugged out of the jacket and handed it over. Danny carried it as proudly as a server might carry a prince's robe and placed it carefully over a hook. Then he spun around and held both arms toward the sofa. "Wanna sit?"

All he'd done that day was sit, but he moved to the sofa and perched at one end. Danny started to sit at the other end, then he jolted upright. "I'd better go change my clothes first. I smell fishy." He darted through a hallway before Briley had a chance to say anything.

With both Danny and his father occupied elsewhere, Briley had the chance to explore. He pulled the recorder from his shirt pocket, intending to peek through doorways and describe his surroundings. He needed to snoop. He needed to discover if the sad-looking room indicated sad lives. But he didn't move. Something indefinable held him in his seat. Snooping would betray their trust.

Danny bounded into the room from one direction and his father entered from another doorway. They spoke at the same time. "Mr. Forrester —" Then they both stopped and looked at each other.

Briley stood. "I'd really rather be called Briley, if you don't mind."

"I want Danny to show respect to his elders, so I prefer he calls you Mr. Forester. But I'd be pleased to use your first name. Please call me Paul." The man sank into the green chair. It seemed he fit perfectly in the cushion's indentation. "It'll be a little while before the soup is ready. Sit down, and let's talk a bit."

Danny scurried to the sofa and settled in the way he had before. Briley remained standing, however.

"Actually, if you could point me to your bathroom, I'd like to wash my hands." He looked ruefully at his grimy palms. "For not touching any fish, they sure are dirty."

Paul laughed. "Second door on your left in the hallway. Feel free to grab a clean towel from under the sink because I'm pretty sure Danny's already scented the one on the towel bar with his fishy hands."

Danny grinned and hunched his shoulders.

Briley gave the expected laugh and headed for the hallway.

The man's voice followed him. "When you get back, I'd like to know why you chose to write an article about Arborville."

Briley managed a grin. "Sure thing. Be back in a minute." He closed himself in the bathroom and cranked the spigots on high. While he lathered his hands, he planned an explanation that would satisfy Aldrich's curiosity. *"Don't tell lies."* He cringed as Danny's childish voice rang in his memory. But what choice did he have? He didn't dare tell the truth.

CHAPTER 16

Sommerfeld
Steven

Steven crossed the yard, squinting against the bright morning sun, and settled the last box into the backseat of the new-to-him crew cab pickup truck. He snapped the driver's seat backrest into place and then stood for a moment, admiring the gray and black interior. He'd been satisfied with his old pickup, which he'd bought shortly after his sixteenth birthday, and had balked a bit at trading it in. Letting it go was almost like losing a friend.

But now he was glad Dad talked him into it. His old truck had over two hundred thousand miles on it. He'd feel a lot more secure heading off in this model, which had less than seventy-five thousand miles logged on the engine. Still years of life left in it . . . and with its shorter bed it didn't look so much like a farmer's truck.

Dad approached, his hands deep in the pockets of his work jacket and his boots scuffing up dust. "Got everything?"

Steven glanced at the boxes filling the truck's bed and rear half of the cab. Even if he didn't have everything, there wasn't room for one more item. He'd just have to do without. He nodded.

"Well, then . . ." Dad rocked on his heels, looking everywhere except at Steven.

Before he'd carried out this last load, Mom caught him in a nearly strangling hug and stained his shoulder with a few rare tears. Now it seemed as though Dad was fighting against sorrow. Fury and compassion warred in Steven's chest. It pained him to see his parents in such agony about him leaving, but this move was all their idea. Why did they have to turn morose and make him feel even worse about the situation?

He cleared his throat. "I want to stop by the Brauns', say goodbye to Anna-Grace before I leave, so . . ."

"Sure. Sure." Dad nodded, the movement jerky. "You need to get going."

Steven hesitated another moment, waiting to see if Dad would say anything else. Maybe something like, "Your mother and I changed our minds about the farm in Arborville. You take the money and do what you want to with it." But of course he didn't. With a sigh Steven climbed behind the steering wheel.

Dad lurched forward, stepping into the triangle formed by the open door. He gave Steven's shoulder several firm pats, then left his hand resting there, as if he was too weary to pull it away. "You drive careful now. This truck won't rattle you so much as the other one did, and it'll be easy to speed. Watch the speedometer."

"I will, Dad."

"And soon as you get a chance, pull that radio. I should've had them do it at the dealership before we brought it home. The fellowship in Arborville doesn't allow car radios, either. You don't want to get in bad with the leaders there."

"Don't worry. I'll take it out. And I won't listen to it in the meantime."

"I know you won't. You're a good boy, Steven. You always have been. But then . . ." Dad's voice became gruff. His hand on Steven's shoulder tightened. "You aren't a boy anymore. You're a man. A good man. I'm proud of you."

Dad's words should warm him. Instead, tentacles of panic wrapped around him and squeezed until he could hardly draw a breath.

Dad stepped back. "You go now. There's no telephone at the farm, but you can use the one at the gas station and call when you get to Arborville so we know you made it safe and sound."

"Will do."

Dad closed the door with a solid slam. Steven started the engine, nodding at the steady rev at the first twist of the key. Yes, this was a good truck. Dad had chosen well. He reversed in a U that put the nose of the vehicle toward the road, popped the gear to Drive, and prepared to pull forward. But he glanced out of the corner of his eye and caught sight of Dad standing at the base of the porch, hands once again in his pockets, gazing after him. Mom stood framed behind the screen door. She held a wad of cloth — a handkerchief — to her mouth. Even though he couldn't see her clearly enough to prove it, he knew she was crying. For several seconds he froze, battling the urge to put the truck in Park, leap out, go tell them he didn't want to go to Arborville and farm his grandfather's land.

"You're a good boy, Steven. You always have been."

Telling them what he really wanted

wouldn't help anything. They expected him to be a farmer, like his father and grandfathers and great-grandfathers before him. A good boy wouldn't go against his parents' wishes. He had to go to Arborville. Anything less would break their hearts.

Arborville

By limiting himself to half an hour with Anna-Grace — much shorter than either of them would have preferred — and driving straight through, Steven reached Arborville by noon. He pulled into the convenience store on the highway just outside of town, refueled his truck, and called home. Mom sounded much more cheerful than she'd been earlier, apparently having spent the morning adjusting to her son's absence. He hung up the phone feeling frustrated rather than relieved, and he gave himself a mental kick. Did he want his mother to be miserable? Of course not. Or he wouldn't be here.

To his surprise, when he pulled into the driveway of his grandfather's farm, he spotted two trucks parked near the barn. The door panel on one showed Southwest Kansas Electrical, and the second one had a magnetic sign that advertised Aldrich Construction and Remodeling. Who'd brought them out already? Not that he would complain about having electricity.

He shut off his truck and hopped out just as a pair of men — one in gray coveralls and the other in work dungarees and a flannel shirt — rounded the corner of the house. Obviously the one in coveralls worked for the electric company, so the man in the flannel must be the carpenter. Steven waved a greeting.

Both men lifted their hands in reply, and the electric company worker moved directly to his truck and rummaged around in a compartment in the back. The carpenter crossed the dry grass to Steven and stuck out his hand. "Steven Brungardt?"

"That's right." Steven gave the man a firm handshake.

"I'm Paul Aldrich."

"I figured as much. It's good to meet you." Steven glanced toward the electric company truck. "I didn't expect anyone to be here."

Mr. Aldrich smiled. "We'd hoped to be done before you got here. Your father wanted to surprise you."

Steven watched the worker in coveralls head behind the house again with a coil of wire and a pair of pliers in his hands. Dad had been tossing lots of surprises at Steven lately. He offered a tight smile. "Electricity is welcome."

"Well, he hasn't got you connected yet." Mr. Aldrich made a face. "The old knob-and-tube wiring is giving him some trouble."

If he had to, he'd have the house rewired. If not for Anna-Grace, for the new owners. The house would be more desirable to potential buyers if it had electricity. How much time would that take? Steven pushed back his worry and formed a glib reply. "I came prepared with oil lamps just in case, so if it doesn't work, I'll survive."

"Good attitude." Mr. Aldrich aimed a firm clap on Steven's back. "You'll be warm, at least, if that cold front they're predicting comes through. There's a cord of seasoned wood on the back porch, and I made sure the wood-burning stove is in working condition."

"Thanks." Steven strode to the back of his truck and lowered the tailgate.

The carpenter followed him. "Are you unloading now?"

Steven grabbed the closest box. "Yep."

"How about waiting a bit?"

He paused with a box in his arms. "Why?"

"We can stay out of the electrician's way —"

We?

"And besides, it's lunchtime. Are you hungry?"

Steven's stomach growled.

Mr. Aldrich laughed. He took the box from Steven and placed it on the tailgate. "I'll give you a hand with this when the electrician has finished. Come with me. Your folks arranged another surprise."

Curious, Steven followed the man toward his vehicle.

"I think this is probably more your mother's doing than your father's." Mr. Aldrich spoke amiably as they walked, their feet crunching on the hard ground. There must not have been rain here in quite a while. Would the cold front the man mentioned bring moisture? They reached the back of the truck, and Mr. Aldrich pulled a large cooler from the bed onto the tailgate, then opened the lid. "Here you go. There's enough food in here to last several days, but you'll need to keep replacing the ice packs to keep it all cold if we can't get a refrigerator up and running for you."

Steven peeked inside and then drew back in surprise. Dozens of square packages, each wrapped in aluminum foil, formed neat stacks on each side of the cooler. Baggies of raw vegetables and muffins, assorted fruit, and candy bars filled the center section. He shook his head in wonder. "Who made all this?" He looked at Mr. Aldrich, who grinned from ear to ear. "You?"

The man laughed. "You wouldn't want my cooking. Just ask my son! No, Alexa Zimmerman — from Grace Notes Bed-and-Breakfast Inn — put this together for you. Those sandwiches are on her homemade bread, and she also baked the muffins. You can eat without fear of being poisoned. Alexa is a very good cook."

Steven already knew this. His mother had made Alexa's breakfast-casserole recipe two times already at Dad's request. His mouth watered as he stared into the cooler. Each of the aluminum squares had writing on them, and he chose one marked *Chicken Salad with Swiss*. He held his hand toward the cooler. "Help yourself. As you said, there's plenty."

The man reached in eagerly. "You don't have to ask me twice." He selected a roast beef and cheddar. They perched on the tailgate, each prayed silently, and then peeled back the foil and took big bites.

"Mmm," Mr. Aldrich murmured.

Steven nodded in agreement. He finished the sandwich in half a dozen bites, then helped himself to an apple-cinnamon muffin. The muffin was moist and flavorful, but even so he was thirsty when he finished. "The electricity isn't working. What about water?"

"Everything out here is connected to a well, but I wouldn't drink from it until you replace the old copper plumbing with PVC pipe and get the water tested for parasites."

Steven grimaced.

"I put a case of bottled water in the kitchen so you'll have drinking water. And you can, er, use the outhouse until the plumbing is all functional again."

He had his work cut out for him. But he'd do it. He wouldn't give his parents any reason to think he wasn't completely on board with making this farm the best it could be. He'd be the good, responsible, obedient son. And the whole time he was fixing this place up, he'd be hoping Anna-Grace would decide she wanted to live somewhere other than Arborville. Then he could still be the good son, and also be the good husband. And maybe, someday, even a very good teacher. *Open the doors, God, please?*

"Aldrich?" The electrical worker called from the corner of the house.

Mr. Aldrich hopped down from the tailgate. "Let's go see if you're connected."

Steven followed the carpenter to the

splash of shade where the worker waited.

"This is Steven Brungardt," Mr. Aldrich said. "He's the owner."

The worker swiped his dirty hand along his coverall leg, then extended it to Steven. "I have to tell you, this wasn't the easiest job I've ever had. But you're hooked up to the transformer. It'll probably be tomorrow afternoon or so before the company gets the power turned on out here, though."

Steven shrugged. "Tomorrow is soon enough to satisfy me."

"They'll probably want me to change out the meter. Since there hasn't been power out here for a good twenty years, that thing is way out of date." The man scratched his head, making his sweaty hair stick up. "And speaking of out-of-date . . . Some of the wiring in the house needs replacing — I wouldn't put that off. The last thing you want is a fire."

Steven started to reply, but Mr. Aldrich jumped in. "I'll be doing the carpentry work out here. I'll make sure a certified electrician comes in and looks everything over."

"Good idea." The worker hitched his tool belt a little higher on his waist and took a backward step. "I tacked a business card to the back doorjamb in case you have questions — the phone number's on there, and my name is Ronnie. You can ask to have me come back out."

"All right. Thanks, Ronnie." Mr. Aldrich spoke over Steven again.

Steven aimed a short, disgruntled look at the man. This was *his* house. He blared, "Yes, thank you, Ronnie. I appreciate your work."

Ronnie grinned, saluted, then turned and trotted off, his tools clanking.

Mr. Aldrich turned to Steven. "Now that he's done, let's get you unloaded, huh?"

Steven stepped into the other man's pathway. "I can do it."

A puzzled frown formed on Mr. Aldrich's face. "I don't mind helping. In fact, if you could wait a few minutes, I can round up another pair of hands. It'll go a lot faster with three of us."

His parents would say he should be grateful, and they'd be right, but instead only resentment welled in his chest. The offers of help felt too much like intrusion. "Really, I can —"

"The man I'm talking about is Briley Forrester. He's a reporter staying at the B and B, so he's close by. And he asked about taking some 'before' pictures of your barn."

Steven frowned. " 'Before' what?"

"Before the barn raising." Mr. Aldrich

chuckled. "Well, it's more of a barn repairing, I suppose. It's arranged for this Saturday."

He gawked at the man. "Already? But . . . but I haven't even attended a service with the local fellowship yet. Why would they do that?"

Mr. Aldrich drew back slightly, his expression turning from cheerful to puzzled. "Why wouldn't we? Your grandfather was an active member of the local fellowship. He even served as a deacon for many years. The people here are all happy to know that one of Ben Meiers's grandsons will be living on the place." He put his hand on Steven's shoulder. "We want you and your new wife to feel at home here."

The man smiled and stepped aside. "Hold up for a few minutes and let me drive to the B and B and get Briley Forrester. Then I intend to spend the afternoon making a big mess in your kitchen." A wobbly grin lifted his lips. "Surprise number three — I cleared my calendar so I can focus on getting your house ready to welcome your bride." He backpedaled in the direction of his truck. "I'll be right back."

Steven rested his arms on the edge of his truck's bed and watched Mr. Aldrich pull off the property. He coughed and blinked against the cloud of dust raised by the man's tires, but he didn't turn aside. The community was welcoming him and Anna-Grace with open arms, just the way Mom and Dad said they would. If Anna-Grace accepted their welcome — if she felt at home, the way Paul Aldrich had said — then he'd be stuck here. If she resisted them, decided it was too uncomfortable to be here, he could sell the place and move on. Moving on now meant not only disappointing his parents but also a host of townsfolk he hadn't even met.

A breeze stirred bits of old, dry cornstalks and dirt across the toes of his boots. He kicked the brown curls free but the dust remained. He stared at the smudges left by Arborville soil. *God* . . . Words wouldn't form. Steven lowered his head and groaned.

CHAPTER 17

Sommerfeld
Anna-Grace

As Anna-Grace placed the last of the clean plates in the cabinet, the telephone rang. Her mother was busy swishing suds from the sink, so Anna-Grace crossed to the phone and picked up the receiver. "Braun residence. This is Anna-Grace speaking."

"Anna-Grace!" A cheerful female voice came through the line. "Just the person I wanted to talk to. This is your cousin Sandra in Arborville."

"Hello, Sandra." She smiled without effort. Sandra was one of the sunniest people she'd ever met. Even though they'd had little time together — for reasons beyond Anna-Grace's understanding, the family had ceased getting together for holidays after Dad's mother passed away — she automatically felt drawn to Sandra. She had what Mom would call a magnetic personality. Sandra attracted people to her.

"Are you still planning to come to Arborville at the end of the month?"

Mom mouthed, *Is it for me?*

Anna-Grace shook her head, pointed at her own chest, and answered Sandra at the same time. "Yes, I am. It's all arranged from this end." Mom left the kitchen, giving Anna-Grace privacy for the call. As Mom rounded the corner to the living room, worry attacked. Anna-Grace gripped the telephone. "Does it still work for you to host me?"

"Oh, of course! But I wanted to bounce an idea off of you. If you don't want to do it, it's no problem at all — we can just toss you in the basement like we'd originally planned."

Anna-Grace couldn't stifle a laugh. Sandra's way of hosting sounded more like condemning someone to a dungeon than welcoming a guest. "What's the idea?"

"Well, you know our family farmhouse has been turned into a bed-and-breakfast inn, compliments of my sister's daughter, Alexa. This time of year is slow in the B and B business, so she has rooms available. My mother wondered if you'd rather stay out at the farm where you'd be next door to the Meiers farmstead. She said it would be easier for you to go back and forth and help work there if you weren't in town."

"Oh . . ." She sought a diplomatic way of addressing the topic. "I, um, I'm not sure I can afford to —"

"They don't intend to charge you!" Sandra's sweet laughter spilled. "Silly girl, you're family. It would be just like you were staying with me . . . except you'd be staying with Mother and Alexa."

Anna-Grace chewed the inside of her lip and considered Sandra's suggestion. Part of her liked the idea of being closer to the house that could very well be her home in the next few months. But if she were at the farm, away from town all the time, how would she know if she could settle into the community?

"Anna-Grace? Are you still there?"

Apparently she'd left Sandra waiting too long. "Yes. I'm here. I'm sorry. I was thinking."

"Did I offend you?" Real concern came through the line. "I don't want you to think I'm trying to get rid of you."

"I'm not offended at all." And she wasn't. She hoped Sandra believed her. She didn't want to ostracize anyone before she even arrived in town. "I appreciate knowing there's another option, and you're right that it might simplify things if I was closer to the farmhouse. I do want to help in the renovating as much as possible."

"That's exactly what Alexa said." Anna-Grace was certain she heard Sandra smile. "You'd want to be as involved as possible since it will be your home."

Well, maybe it will be . . . "Do I have to tell you right now if I want the room at the B and B?"

"No. As I said, Alexa doesn't have any guests scheduled for the next several weeks, so she doesn't mind holding a room for you."

"I'd like to talk to my parents." Anna-Grace fingered the curly cord on the telephone, her thoughts tripping ahead of her words. "See if they think it would be okay for me to stay closer to Steven. I wouldn't want to start tongues wagging."

"With my mother keeping an eye on you, you won't have a chance to get into mischief." A giggle met Anna-Grace's ear. "You can tell your folks I said so."

Anna-Grace laughed. One of the best parts of being in Arborville would be getting better acquainted with her cousins. "I will. Thank you, Sandra. I'll call you soon and let you know for sure where I intend to stay."

They disconnected the call, and Anna-Grace remained in the kitchen for several minutes, the pros and cons of the lodging options forming in her mind. Oddly, she found an equal number of reasons both for and against each location. Mom and Dad would have to make the decision.

She entered the living room and sat next to Mom, who'd lifted out her basket of mending and put a needle and thread to work. For a moment Anna-Grace sat and watched the needle go in and out, closing the tear on the skirt of one of Sunny's little dresses. Mom stitched with such care, the tear slowly disappearing into a nearly invisible seam. Such a gift her mother had, to make worn things seem like new. She wished she'd inherited it. She could sew but not with the natural ability her mother possessed. But that was probably because Mom wasn't her real mother. Tears stung and she sniffed.

Mom stopped midstitch and looked at Anna-Grace. Concern lined her brow. "Was the phone call bad news?"

Anna-Grace shook her head. She explained the purpose of Sandra's call while Mom listened carefully. When she finished, Mom took her hand. "You're not feeling cast aside, are you?"

"No!" Her answer was half-true. Every time she thought of her biological mother she felt cast aside. But Sandra hadn't done anything wrong. She tamped down the brief stab of guilt and said, "Sandra made it very clear I'm welcome with her. She just wanted me to know there was another place if I preferred it."

"I see." An unreadable expression on her face, Mom seemed to examine Anna-Grace for several seconds. Then she spoke quietly. "You don't have to go at all, you know. Steven would understand."

He'd said as much before he'd driven off that morning. Her heart warmed, recalling his tender embrace and whispered assurance that whatever was best for her would be best for him, too. A smile tugged at her lips. "I know he would. But I want to give it a chance. I can't make Steven give up his inheritance without knowing for sure living there would be too difficult for me."

"That's unselfish of you, sweetheart."

"I want to be unselfish, Mom. And fair. I really do."

"Of course you do."

Mom spoke so matter-of-factly, with such sureness, more tears stung. These of gratitude. "If you didn't have a needle in your hand, I'd hug you."

Mom laughed, set aside the little dress pierced with a silver needle, and held open her arms. Anna-Grace melted against her, savoring a few minutes of being little again, being comforted, feeling secure. Somehow the letter from her birth parents had sucked much of the security out of her world — the opposite of what parents were supposed to instill in their children.

She pulled back and stood. "I'm going to go write Steven a letter and then walk it to the post office. Do you need anything from town?"

"No. Tell Steven hello from your dad and me."

"I will." Anna-Grace went to her bedroom and sat at the little student desk where she'd finished homework, written dramatic poems in her diary, and penned letters to friends over the years. She laid out her stationery and picked up a pen.

Dear Steven, she wrote in her neatest handwriting. Steven had beautiful penmanship for a man, and she always felt as though she should write just as neatly. *I know you only left this morning, but I miss you already. I'll be counting down the days until the 24th, when you come home for the weekend. And after that, I'll get to see you every day.*

A lump formed in her throat. She swallowed hard. Gripping the pen, she continued writing. *I love you so much, Steven. When you told me to do what was best for me because it would be best for you, too, I almost cried from happiness. I want to make sure what I do really is best for both of us. I'll be praying every day for God to help me see His will in this situation, and I know you will be praying for the same thing.*

She wrote until she filled the page, then she signed with her customary *My love always, Anna-Grace* and sealed the letter in an envelope. Gazing at the plain envelope with Steven's letter inside reminded her of the envelope she still hadn't opened. Even though she'd closed it in a drawer, putting it out of sight, it continued to tug at her to peel back the flap and remove the missives.

Leaning over the envelope on the desk, she hurriedly added Steven's new address, stamped it, and then headed for town with his letter gripped between her fingers. As she dropped it into the outgoing mail slot, she recalled her mother's affirmation that of course she wanted to be unselfish and fair. The remembrance solidified her decision to leave the truth of her parentage sealed inside that envelope. Because if she didn't know their names, she could go to Arborville and face the people there without any preconceived notions about the ones who gave birth to her and then gave her away. She could treat everyone fairly and kindly.

Until she figured out who they were. Then being fair and kind would be a test beyond anything she'd ever experienced before.

Arborville
Alexa

Alexa watched as Grandmother tore the check from her checkbook and laid it on the corner of the bed. She stared at the slip of paper, unwilling to pick it up. "I'm sorry you're having to pay the utility bill this month." She'd refigured the amounts in her checkbook every day that week, hoping for some miracle that would multiply the amount, but Friday morning's finding was no better than Monday's had been.

"Don't worry about it." Grandmother dropped the checkbook in her lap and wheeled her chair to the dressing table. She transferred the checkbook to the drawer in the dressing table, then turned and rolled back to the bed. She picked up the check and pressed it into Alexa's hand. "I think you forget I've been taking care of the bills for this house for more years than you've been alive. I certainly don't expect you to cover everything just because the house is

228

going to be shared with guests now from time to time."

When she opened the bed-and-breakfast at Grandmother's farm, Alexa had vowed to cover the bills so Grandmother could keep her money for herself. Having to dip into Grandmother's account to cover basic expenses left her feeling as if she'd failed. Alexa released a heavy sigh. "But I expect it of myself. I really want the B and B to pay for itself and even experience some profit."

"Give it time, Alexa." Grandmother shook her head, the ribbons from her cap gently swaying beneath her chin. "You only opened for business two months ago. It can take two years to get a business up and running. Be realistic."

"Well, you aren't going to cover expenses for that long! I'll find some other way to bring in money." She rose and paced the room, fanning herself with the check. "Steven Brungardt's mother paid me well for putting together that cooler of sandwiches. Maybe I could start catering parties or picnics for people."

"Picnics in October?" Grandmother sounded skeptical.

Alexa's defenses prickled, but she kept her tone in check. "Okay, maybe not picnics, but with the holidays coming, people will be hosting get-togethers with family and friends. Wouldn't there be an interest in hiring someone to set out a variety of hors d'oeuvres or to bake cupcakes or pretty cookies? Maybe I could even do wedding cakes." Hope built in her chest. She looked at her grandmother. In one glance, her hope disintegrated.

Amusement tinged Grandmother's face. "In Arborville? Every person I know does her own cooking and baking. And when they have get-togethers, everyone contributes to fill the banquet table. I can't imagine anyone in town hiring someone to prepare food for them. We don't even hire caterers for weddings. We do it all ourselves."

Alexa plopped onto the edge of Grandmother's bed and bounced her fist on the mattress. "Well, then, I'll advertise in some of the towns around us."

"Would that really be cost effective? You'd have to add transportation expenses to your services. I imagine the larger towns already have caterers available, making the competition tough."

Even though her grandmother spoke reasonably rather than condescendingly, Alexa felt foolish for making the suggestion. She threw her arms wide. "Then what? I can't just sit here month after month with no income. I need to pay my way."

Grandmother rolled her chair close and took Alexa's hand. "You'll have the check from the newspaper in Chicago when Mr. Forrester has completed his article. Given the length of his stay, it should be sizable."

Alexa nodded slowly. Even though she'd offered a discounted weekly rate rather than charging the full daily rate, she still anticipated a profit. "Yes, and I'm grateful for that income. I just wish . . ." She hung her head.

"You wish what?"

She murmured, "I wish I didn't feel like a freeloader."

"Alexa!" Grandmother caught Alexa's chin and raised her face. She looked sternly into Alexa's eyes. "Why on earth would you say such a thing?"

"Because it's true."

"It's not true!"

"Yes, it is."

The V between Grandmother's snapping eyes sunk deeper.

Alexa sighed. "It's at least partly true. I took over your house, promised to pay for the privilege, then couldn't do it. What else is that besides being a freeloader?"

Grandmother's frown remained intact. "A freeloader does nothing to earn his keep. A freeloader is lazy. Something you certainly are not." She pinched Alexa's chin, driving home her point. Then she patted Alexa's cheek before lowering her hand to her wheelchair's armrest. "Think of all the ways you've contributed to this household other than with money. You cook and clean, and your decorating makes it feel like new. And — more importantly — you are my grand-daughter. Family members are never consid-ered freeloaders, even when they behave like ones."

Alexa managed a weak smile. "Thank you, Grandmother."

"A freeloader . . . honestly . . ." She tsk-tsked and rolled her eyes. "The things you say . . ."

The telephone jangled, stealing Alexa's opportunity to defend herself. She scurried to the kitchen and grabbed the receiver from its cradle. "Hello. Grace Notes Bed-and-Breakfast Inn. How may I help you?"

"Hi, Alexa, it's Sandra."

Alexa erupted with a sigh.

"What's wrong?"

Did she really want to tell her favorite aunt she'd hoped a prospective guest was calling? Sandra would think she wasn't welcome to call. "Sorry. Nothing. Just caught me off guard."

"Okay. Two things . . . First, the fellowship men plan to meet at the Meiers farm tomorrow to repair the barn. I had volunteered to be in charge of the drinks table, but Ian started running a fever last night."

"Is it serious?"

"I don't think so — just a cold. But I shouldn't take him out until he's been fever-free for a full day. I wondered if you'd fill in for me."

She'd wanted to go and watch the men work, anyway. "Sure I will."

"Thank you, Alexa. I knew you'd come to my rescue."

Alexa smiled, envisioning herself in a cape, flying in to save the day. "What's the second thing?"

"I finally heard from Anna-Grace."

The amusing images disappeared. "And . . ."

"She agreed it would be better to stay closer to the Meiers farm. She'll take the room."

Alexa eased against the wall, in need of support. "Oh." She swallowed. "Good."

"Good?" Sandra's voice held hesitance. "Are you sure?"

She straightened her spine. "Of course I'm sure. I offered, didn't I? It'll be better for her to be here, close to Steven and close

233

to . . ." She couldn't bring herself to add *Grandmother.* She didn't want to share the grandmother she'd only recently met with the girl who truly belonged in the family.

"So you know, I did tell her if you got calls to rent the rooms, she'd need to come stay with me instead."

Alexa appreciated Sandra more by the minute. "Thanks." She blew out a soft breath. "But given how many times the phone hasn't rung with requests to stay here, I don't think we need to worry about it."

"Just the same, if something changes, the hideaway bed is available."

"All right. Thank you, Sandra."

"Thank *you* for being such a sweetheart. Your mama raised you right." They laughed together before Sandra disconnected the call.

Grandmother rolled her chair into the kitchen. Anticipation glowed in her eyes. "Was the call about a guest?"

Alexa forced a smile. "Yep. Anna-Grace will be staying with us instead of with Sandra."

"Good for her." Grandmother gave a brisk nod that crunched her cap's ribbons against the shoulders of her gray-checked dress and then sent them springing. "And good for us, too. Even though she won't be a paying guest, her being here will give you a chance to practice your hotel-keeping skills and also provide you with some company besides a crotchety old lady and her outspoken nurse." Her expression softened. "And I confess, Alexa, I'll enjoy having two girls in the house for a while. This old house needs the voices and laughter of young people." She turned the chair and wheeled out of the room, leaving Alexa alone.

Alexa chewed her thumbnail and tried to imagine what it would be like to be with Anna-Grace every day. Instead of images forming in her head of the two of them getting along together, she pictured herself donning a cape and flying far, far away.

CHAPTER 18

Briley

He'd heard of Amish barn raisings, but he'd always been a little cynical. Putting up a shed maybe, but an entire barn in a day? Yeah, right. But by noon that Saturday, Briley's cynicism had packed a bag and moved to another state.

Despite the promised cold front dropping the temperature a good twenty degrees and sending a nose-numbing breeze across the plains, twelve men with tool belts clanking on their hips and seven boys eagerly waving paintbrushes arrived by eight o'clock in the morning. Armed with a load of lumber, pouches of nails, and buckets of red paint, they swarmed the barn, as industrious as a hive of bees. Briley snapped close to a hundred pictures, but even though he recorded the event frame by frame, he could never determine who was in charge. Shouldn't there be an unofficial foreman directing everyone? If one existed, he remained well hidden. The workers simply seemed to know what needed to be done, and they did it, all sharing equally in the barn's reconstruction.

While he watched, something Aunt Myrt had told him eased through his memory. *"Every man has two equal abilities — to build up or tear down. The challenge lies in knowing which is the right choice."* The Mennonite men had decided to build up the barn instead of tearing it down and starting over. Briley wasn't sure he'd have made the same choice given the appearance of the structure, but watching the barn's transformation made him think they'd chosen wisely.

When the walls and roof were repaired and the building bore a proud new coat of rusty-red paint, the boys cleaned their brushes in the gushing flow of water from the pump behind the barn, and the men gathered around the food table set up by a half-dozen women. Alexa was off to the side at a second, smaller table. Pitchers of lemonade and tall, silver, spigoted urns and stacks of mugs covered the table. The sandwiches, two inches thick and filled with slivered ham and slices of white cheese, looked wonderful. He hadn't done any work on the barn, so he didn't feel as though he should take a plate, but he'd gotten a whiff of what filled those urns, and he couldn't resist asking Alexa to fill a mug for him.

He drew a deep breath as she lifted the spigot handle and a stream of steaming apple cider flowed into the mug. The spicy scent carried him backward in time. Aunt Myrt stirred up a kettle of cider mixed with Red Hots candies for Christmas every year he'd been with her. The memory warmed him as much as the mug he gripped between his palms. He sipped, enjoying the tang on his tongue, and waggled his eyebrows at Alexa. "Mmm. Good stuff."

She offered a shy grin. She looked very girlish and cute with furry pink earmuffs forming puffballs on both sides of her head and a thick blue-and-green plaid jacket buttoned all the way to her chin. "One of the fellowship members has a small grove of Granny Smith apple trees, and he recently purchased an apple press to make cider. This is from one of the first batches. It's much better than store-bought."

Briley mentally recorded this piece of information. "You people are pretty self-sufficient, aren't you?"

Alexa blinked at him twice, as if he'd startled her. Or maybe offended her. He decided to explain himself.

"Look at this." He waved his arm, indicating the immediate surroundings. "I bet the lumber used on the barn came from the lumberyard in town. And no grocer sold the bread or sandwich fixings, right? The bread probably started with wheat grown in the fields nearby, the ham from pigs raised behind the barn. You'd definitely want pigs far from the house." He chuckled at his own joke. "I'd wager the cheese was made by one of the ladies in her kitchen, using milk from a neighbor's cow." He raised the mug as if making a toast, careful not to waste even a drop of the flavorful cider. "If you had a kiln in town, you'd probably even make your own cups and plates."

Her eyebrows pinched together. "Is there something wrong with purchasing from local merchants?"

Briley repeated something Len had told him. "You people are more than eager to sell your wares to visitors in your town, but when it comes to spending your dollars and making purchases, you keep it close at hand. Kind of a double standard, isn't it?"

Her gaze narrowed and she set her rosy lips in a firm line. He'd irked her. Maybe deliberately. But how else would he get underneath the cheery, helpful, all-is-well veneer to the truth of the person? He took another sip of his cider, waiting to hear what she'd say.

Two men ambled over. The older of the two nodded toward the waiting mugs. "I would take some of that hot cider, please."

Without a word Alexa filled a mug and handed it to him. The second man lifted a pitcher and poured lemonade into his mug. Lemonade Man wandered toward the porch, where others were sitting along the edge with plates in their laps, but Cider Man turned his gaze on Briley.

"I saw you taking lots of pictures." His thick eyebrows, above eyes so brown the pupils were nearly swallowed by the color, formed a worried line. "What will you do with them?"

Briley curled his hand protectively around the digital camera hanging from his neck. "Most of them are for my own use — satisfying my curiosity about the Old Order practice of barn raising. A few might end up being used as illustrations in my article. Why?"

Cider Man crunched his lips into a crooked scowl, as if contemplating whether or not to answer. "Some of our members . . . having photographs taken makes them uncomfortable. They feel it goes against the biblical warning about making graven images. Before you use them in a publication, would you please show them to the men who worked here today and be sure they approve having their pictures printed?"

The stubborn, rebellious side of Briley Forrester raised its head. "I tell you what . . ." He was prepared to inform the man that this was *his* article, and *he* would decide which photographs were used, but the spicy scent of cider rising from the mug — its essence a reminder of the woman who'd tried so hard to straighten his defiant bent — brought forth a different reply. "I'll get the pictures I took this morning printed and bring them to your church service tomorrow. Anyone who's interested can take a peek at them, and if someone opposes me using any specific photos, I'll mark them so they won't turn up in the newspaper. Fair enough?"

A relieved smile appeared on the man's face, softening his chiseled features. He nodded. "Yes. Yes, that is very fair. Thank you, Mr. Forrester." With plate and mug in hand, he headed to the porch and joined the others.

Briley shifted to find Alexa staring at him, wide-eyed. "What?"

She shook her head slowly. "I can't figure you out. One minute you're annoyingly obnoxious, and the next you're understanding and agreeable."

He placed his hand on his chest and feigned innocence. "Obnoxious? Me?"

She didn't say anything, but she didn't have to. Her expression spoke volumes.

He burst out laughing. "Oh, Miss Zimmerman, you are priceless." With effort he brought his amusement under control. "You're right, I admit it. I lean toward obnoxious. I always have, and it's a hard habit to break. You can thank the apple cider for helping me rein it in today, but I make no promises for tomorrow." He drained the mug, placed it on the table, then took two backward steps and lifted his camera. "I got photographs of the barn workers and the women at the food table, but I neglected to record the lovely lady providing us with beverages. Say 'cheese.' "

She squawked, cupped her hands over her fuzzy earmuffs, and ducked.

He took the picture anyway. And he laughed all the way to his car.

Alexa

Alexa peeked over the edge of the table to make sure Briley really was leaving. When she spotted him climbing behind the wheel of his car, she straightened and glanced

242

around. Had anyone noticed her impulsive dive for cover? She wasn't opposed to photographs. Mom had a digital camera, and Alexa often made use of the camera on her phone. But being captured wearing her earmuffs and with her nose probably redder than Rudolph's, given the crisp breeze, would be far from appealing. To her relief everyone seemed engrossed in their own conversations. She blew out a grateful breath, then looked toward the road, where a cloud of dust hid Briley's departing vehicle.

Good riddance! Mercy, what a tease he was. She bristled, then battled a grin. *"I lean toward obnoxious,"* he'd said, and he was so right. Or maybe not obnoxious. Maybe just so sure of himself he didn't care how he appeared to other people — he just *was.* She couldn't decide if being overly self-assured was better or worse than being obnoxious.

She poured herself a cup of cider and sipped. Something else Briley had said replayed through her mind. *"You people . . ."* He'd said it twice, that exact phrase, lumping her in with the members of the Old Order fellowship. With the mug held beneath her chin and aromatic steam curling around her face, she sent a slow look across those who'd come to share in the work.

The men all wore solid navy or dark-green jackets and work trousers in a variety of browns and tans — a type of uniform of their own. The women's white caps topping their coiled hair and black hosiery showing beneath the hems of their flowered skirts marked them as a group. *"You people . . ."* Her sweater and ankle-length denim skirt, although very conservative from a worldly standpoint, set her apart from the others, as did her ponytail falling along her spine. Even so, Briley put her with them.

A spiral of longing wove its way through her chest. She wished she did belong. With the community members. With her family. Somewhere. Anywhere. Would the truth of her unknown birthright always make her feel isolated? If only she could go back to the days before Mom had told her about her foundling status. If only she could forget she wasn't Mom's biological daughter. If only . . . Her vision blurred, her eyes flooding with tears. She ducked her head and blinked rapidly. A quick swipe across her eyes restored her vision. And her resolve.

Briley apparently saw her as belonging, so she needed to view herself the same way. She needed to make everyone see her as a part of their fellowship. And she couldn't do that by keeping her distance. In a burst of determination, she filled four mugs with cider, then hooked her fingers through the handles — two in each hand — and turned toward those perched along the edge of the porch. "Who's ready for more cider?"

Hands flew in the air. She delivered the mugs, then scurried to the table to fill more. As she carried them to others waiting for a hot drink, an errant thought whispered in the back of her mind. A smile grew on her lips. She hoped there'd be some cider left by the end of the lunch. She had plans for it. Briley Forrester wasn't the only person in the world who could be obnoxious . . .

Briley

Briley tapped on the back door before stepping into the kitchen Sunday morning. Alexa was at the oven, thick potholders shaped like mittens hiding her hands. She turned as he entered.

"Good morning," he said. A bibbed apron protected the front of her skirt and blouse, but a spatter of something decorated the apron's square bib. A rich scent escaped the oven, and he licked his lips in anticipation. "Baking this morning, are you?"

An odd sparkle lit her eyes, as if she held back a secret. "Quiche Lorraine."

He'd never eaten quiche — egg pie, really?

And he was sure he detected a hint of cinnamon. Would cinnamon be in egg pie? But what difference did it make? The aromas flooding the kitchen sent his hunger to a fever pitch. Yesterday evening's canned ravioli couldn't possibly compare to what waited in that oven. He slapped his belly. "Bring it on."

Her lips curved into a delightful smile, and she tipped her head toward the dining room doorway. "Go on in. I'll serve in just a few more minutes."

Briley gave a mock salute and strode through the kitchen with an eager step. He rounded the corner to the dining room and moved directly to the long, old-fashioned sideboard where the coffee and mugs were always ready. Except for this morning. He frowned first at the empty top and then at the table, where Mrs. Zimmerman sat across from, of all people, Steven Brungardt.

His mild irritation changed to surprise. "Well, hello, Steven. Are you staying here instead of at your house?"

The younger man shook his head. "The Zimmermans were kind enough to ask me to take breakfast with them until the carpenter gets my kitchen put together."

Of course they had. These people looked

after their own. Briley shifted his attention to the mugs in front of the pair at the table. They had coffee. He pointed. "Is there any of that left?"

Mrs. Zimmerman raised her cup and peered at him over its rim. "You'll have to ask my granddaughter about that."

With a soft snort Briley pulled out a chair and sat. Smelling the coffee but not being able to drink any was torture, and he didn't try to hide his aggravation that none was available. Neither of the other two at the table seemed to notice his surliness, however, which increased his ire.

Mrs. Zimmerman aimed a bland look in his direction. "Will you ride with Alexa and me to service again this morning, Mr. Forrester?" She took a slurping draw from her cup.

"Not today." He explained his need to stay after the church service and show the photographs from Steven's barn raising to the concerned men. "I have no idea how long I'll be, and I don't want to keep everyone waiting. So I'll drive myself to church." Even if his car did stick out like a sore thumb.

"What about lunch, then?" The woman taunted him with noisy sips from her cup.

He flicked a glance toward the kitchen.

Where was Alexa with that coffeepot? "I can fend for myself today." He gritted his teeth. He might have to fend for himself by visiting the convenience store and grabbing a cup of joe on the way to the church.

Alexa breezed around the corner. She balanced two plates on her extended arm and held a third in her other hand. "Here we are!" She placed the first plate in front of her grandmother, then served Steven and Briley. "I'll be right out with your drink, Mr. Forrester. My hands were full." She zipped back through the hallway.

Briley looked at the contents of his plate and changed his mind about quiche in one heartbeat. With chunks of ham and onions dotting the egg mixture and covered with melted cheese, it looked hearty and filling, nothing like he'd expected. Two slices of thick toast, browned to perfection, formed a frame for the wedge of egg pie, and juicy orange crescents and a spattering of cherries added a splash of color. He'd give her one thing — she knew how to make food look inviting. Now if she'd just bring him his coffee before he crawled out of his skin.

As if reading his thoughts, she bustled back into the room with a mug in her hand. She plopped it in front of him, then stepped back. "Anything else?"

Briley frowned. What had she put in his cup? The liquid wasn't black and pungent. Instead, it smelled suspiciously like cinnamon. And apples. Understanding dawned, and he whirled on her with his mouth gaping. "Is that cider?"

She blinked, the picture of innocence. "Yes, it is. You said cider keeps your obnoxiousness at bay."

How could she maintain that expression? Briley threw back his head and laughed, delighted beyond words by her unexpected act of impishness. He wagged his finger at her, swallowing his chortles. "Oh, Miss Zimmerman, be careful. If I didn't know better, I'd think you were flirting with me."

Her gaze whisked downward and then up again. She looked directly into his eyes and said, completely deadpan, "I never flirt."

"More's the pity . . ."

Had he said it out loud? Apparently he had because Alexa's face flooded pink, Mrs. Zimmerman clapped her empty coffee cup onto the tabletop, and Steven released a funny little sound like a dry gargle.

Mrs. Zimmerman spoke, her voice loud and shrill. "Steven, would you please say grace? Yes? Good. Pray so we can eat." Her eyes narrowed into slits of disapproval. "We have a service to get to."

Briley bowed his head along with the others. Steven's prayer was pretty standard — asking a blessing for the food and for the hands that had prepared it — but he suspected Mrs. Zimmerman was sending up a different silent prayer, that he would seek forgiveness for his brazen behavior. A useless request, in Briley's way of thinking. A man couldn't change who he was. His entire life he'd been called a lost cause. He'd come to accept it. So she could, too.

Chapter 19

Briley

At the completion of the worship service, Briley found himself surrounded just as he'd been the week before. But instead of invitations to dinner, he received requests to see the pictures. He laid them out in two neat rows on the last bench on the men's side, and the workers from yesterday's barn repair as well as half a dozen men who hadn't come, including the one who'd delivered the morning's sermon, crowded close.

Briley moved out of the way and let them look to their heart's content. He'd examined the photographs and found nothing unacceptable in any of them. Well, except maybe the one of Alexa peeking over the edge of the upside-down mugs, her brown eyes like a deer staring at oncoming headlights. He'd left that one behind. No sense in embarrassing her. Not publicly anyway. After her breakfast stunt, he might find a choice time and place to share that photograph.

The men circled the bench, murmured, pointed, shook their heads, or nodded approval. Steven Brungardt approached, his flat-brimmed hat held against the front of his black suit coat. He glanced at the cluster of men, then turned to Briley. "What are they looking at?"

"My photographs of your barn repair."

"Oh." He didn't move toward the bench.

Briley examined Steven out of the corner of his eye. The young man, although sturdily built like a farmer and attired in the Mennonite style of dress, didn't seem to fit with the others. He just couldn't quite decide what made him stick out. Then he looked into Steven's somber face and discovered the difference. His expression never changed. He always looked . . . resigned. But why? Briley aimed a pat on Steven's stiff shoulder, trying to knock some life into him. "You ought to be happy. One day's work, and that barn is like new."

Steven remained as still as a statue, no flicker of a smile twitching on his lips. "Yes."

"Are you going to have a house raising, too? Get the place painted and spruced up so it looks as nice as the barn?"

The young man's shoulders rose and fell

in a shrug. "I doubt it. My dad hired a carpenter. Between the two of us, we'll get the interior done. I probably won't try to have it painted until spring unless it warms up again in the next weeks. It was pretty cold for painting yesterday, but Mr. Ohr said they used extra thinner to help the wood soak up the paint."

"Which one is Mr. Ohr?"

Steven pointed out the one Briley had dubbed Cider Man.

Briley nodded. "Neat trick."

"Yes."

They stood in silence for a few seconds while the man who'd approached Briley yesterday began putting the photographs into two stacks with input from those gathered.

Steven cleared his throat. "Were there any pictures there . . . of me?"

Briley nodded. "A few." He tipped his head, intrigued by the various emotions flashing in Steven's eyes. "Did you want to see them?"

Steven shook his head. "No. That's all right. My dad . . . he doesn't approve of photographs. So I probably shouldn't look."

"Yield not to temptation?" Briley asked, half teasing.

Steven stared straight ahead. " 'There

hath no temptation taken you but such as is common to man: but God is faithful, who will not suffer you to be tempted above that ye are able; but will with the temptation also make a way to escape, that ye may be able to bear it.' " He flicked a glance at Briley. "That's from 1 Corinthians, chapter 10, verse 13. I memorized it a long time ago."

Briley swallowed a chortle. Obviously Steven wasn't trying to be funny, but he found humor in the response. So much concern over a few photographs! How much damage could looking at pictures of a bunch of men repairing a barn do? It seemed a little silly, and he fought the temptation to say so. "Betcha that's kept you out of trouble over the years."

The young man gave him an odd look. Then he turned toward a pair of men — Mr. Ohr and today's preacher — approaching with the photographs. The other men exited the church, and Briley expected Steven to follow them. Instead, he stayed put, his head low but obviously listening.

Ohr placed a short stack of photographs in Briley's hand. "These are fine." The preacher kept hold of the larger stack. Ohr gestured toward them. "These, though, we'd rather you didn't use. So if you'll tell me how much it cost you to print them, we'll pay you that amount and then burn them."

He reached for the stack of photos, but the preacher pulled them back slightly. Briley raised one eyebrow. "If you're going to reimburse me, I need to know how many are there."

"Seventy-two."

He gawked at the man. Out of the ninety images he'd printed, they'd only approved eighteen? "What's wrong with them?"

The two men exchanged a glance. The preacher spoke. "Some showed full front view faces. Others seemed designed to draw attention to a man's strength or muscles. Some just included men who didn't wish to be photographed. How much do we owe you?"

Briley stifled a frustrated huff. He'd printed them at a one-hour kiosk in a Wichita drugstore, which added the equivalent of four gallons of fuel to the bill, but he stuck to the photo cost. "Fifteen cents per photograph." He pulled out his phone and brought up the calculator. "Seventy-two times fifteen is —"

"Ten dollars and eighty cents," Steven said.

Briley poked in the numbers and punched the equal symbol. He looked at Steven in surprise. "You're right. How'd you figure that so fast?"

The man shrugged. "I taught myself shortcuts. Instead of multiplying by fifteen, I multiplied by ten — that got me seven hundred twenty, or seven dollars and twenty cents. Five is half of ten, so I halved that amount to get the three dollars and sixty cents. I added the two sums together for the final figure." He shrugged again. "It goes quick in my head." His tone held not an ounce of boastfulness.

"Huh . . ." Briley blew out a breath, carried on a chuckle. "I wish I'd learned those shortcuts. Then I wouldn't have to use this." He waved his phone, the calculator still showing on the screen.

"I could teach you." For the first time interest sparked in Steven's eyes. "If you want. For those days you don't have . . . that." He glanced at the phone.

The preacher cleared his throat. "Do you want the tax, too?"

Briley grinned and pocketed his phone. "If Steven wants to figure it." To his surprise Steven ducked his head and released a short laugh. Briley said, "No, that's fine. In fact, you don't need to pay me at all. It's a business deduction for me, so I'll get it back eventually anyway."

The pair of men frowned, and Ohr said,

"Are you sure? We don't want to cheat you."

No, they just wanted to rob him of the privilege of using his own photographs. "It's fine." Briley slipped the few approved photos in his shirt pocket.

The two gave identical nods. They turned to the rack on the back wall, plucked their hats from pegs, then strode for the door. Just before leaving, Ohr turned back. "Would the two of you like to come with me for lunch? I'm going to the Pletts, and Mrs. Plett always cooks extra. You would be welcome there."

Briley answered first. "No, thank you." He wanted to hurry back to his computer and figure out which photographs had been deemed inappropriate. Len would surely get a kick out of their reasoning.

"Mr. Brungardt? What of you?"

"Thank you, but I have food at my house that needs to be eaten or it might spoil."

"All right then. Good-bye." The man departed.

Briley lifted his bomber jacket from the bench, where he'd draped it instead of using one of the pegs, and jammed his arms into the sleeves. "Guess we better get out of here, huh? Odd there's no janitor still here to lock the door behind us."

An amused smile played on Steven's

mouth. "A janitor? Locking the door?" He shook his head. "You don't know much about the Old Order fellowships, do you?"

Apparently his extensive research hadn't covered everything. Briley fought a grin. "Wanna teach me that while you teach me those math shortcuts?"

Once again Steven took Briley's teasing seriously. "If you'd like. You can come to my house and eat sandwiches with me, and we can . . . talk."

"About math?"

"And the fellowship."

Given the man's taciturn behavior, he'd probably tell a different tale than others in the community. Briley patted the pocket where his trusty recorder waited. "That sounds great. Lead the way, Teach."

Steven

They ate two sandwiches each, drowned by bottles of pop they purchased at the convenience store on their way to the farm, and then dug into the muffins. Steven only had one, but Briley ate three. Since Steven didn't have a table and chairs, they sat on upside-down buckets from the barn and brushed the crumbs onto the floor. With evidence of his past week's activity scattered across the scuffed pine floorboards, a few crumbs wouldn't even be noticeable.

After he popped the last bite of chocolate-chocolate-chip muffin in his mouth, Briley stood, grimaced, and rubbed his hindquarters. "You need to get some furniture in here, my man."

Steven shrugged. Why bring in furniture until he knew for sure this would be his home?

Briley arched backward, pressing his hands to his lower spine, then straightened and stretched his arms over his head. Even as tall as he was, his fingers didn't come close to touching the spider-cracked, ten-foot-high ceiling. "How have you managed a week without anything to sit on besides buckets?"

"I sat on this." Steven patted the cooler and then peeked inside of it. One sandwich, two muffins, and a wrinkled apple lay in its bottom. It would be empty by nightfall. He snapped the lid closed and gestured toward the sturdy plastic box, inviting Briley to make use of it. "But mostly, I don't sit. I work all day, and then I go to sleep." The twin mattress on the floor of the bigger of the two bedrooms suited him fine. Being too tired to care helped. He'd worked like a dog all last week peeling layers of brittle wallpaper from every wall in the house, patching cracks in the plaster, and stripping paint from the woodwork because Anna-Grace didn't like painted woodwork. He had to admit, the egg-and-dart trim above the windows and doors would be pretty with a coat of stain and varnish.

Briley plunked down on the cooler and scuffed his toe against the floor, creating a half-moon shape in the mixture of sawdust, plaster dust, and dust-dust. "And a broom. You definitely need a broom."

He had one. He just hadn't seen the point in using it. Mr. Aldrich swept the kitchen every day before he left, but Steven chose to wait until he'd finished all the messing in the other parts of the house before he started a cleanup. He'd sweep before Anna-Grace arrived next week, though, whether he'd finished messing or not.

Weary of the topic of his housekeeping skills, Steven said, "Want me to show you those math shortcuts now? I have easy-to-learn shortcuts for addition, subtraction, and multiplication. The division ones take a little more thinking, but —"

"Actually, I'd rather talk about the fellowship."

Steven's spirits sank. He'd been looking forward to sharing his mathematical tricks with someone, even if the someone was a grown man rather than a roomful of students. But he only shrugged. He sat back down on the bucket. "Well, let me start by explaining why we don't have a janitor."

Briley pulled a small rectangle of black plastic with buttons marching across one short side from his shirt pocket. "Do you mind?"

"What is it?"

"A recording device. It'll record our voices. Later I'll plug it into my computer, and my voice-recognition software will type out what we've said."

"Oh." He'd never heard of such a thing. Did college students use these devices? He should watch Briley closely and learn how the recorder worked, just in case.

"Is it okay with you if I use it? My handwriting . . ." Briley chuckled, the sound self-conscious. "Not that I'd ever have earned a penmanship award, but now that I'm on the computer most of the time, it's gotten really sloppy. Sometimes I have a hard time deciphering my own notes. Especially when I'm writing quickly."

If he had a pad and pencil handy, he'd offer to keep the notes for Briley, but he hadn't bothered to bring any with him. He'd called Anna-Grace from the convenience store pay phone in response to her letter. "Yes. Go ahead and record us." Steven sent up a silent prayer for guidance. He'd better form his answers to Briley's questions carefully since they'd be recorded and then typed later, word-for-word. "Now . . ." He pulled in a slow breath. "What do you want to know?"

Briley clicked one of the buttons and laid the recorder on his knee. "Start by telling me why the church doesn't have a janitor."

Steven explained haltingly, a little intimidated by the black box capturing his voice, the fellowship practice of sharing the upkeep of the house of worship. "Families take turns coming in to clean and dust and make the windows shine. If they find something that needs fixing — like a leak in the roof or a cracked windowpane — they alert the deacons and someone is hired to do the repair."

"Someone from the fellowship?"

Steven shrugged. "Whenever possible, yes. Our fellowship in Sommerfeld doesn't have anyone with electrical or plumbing skills, so when we need those services we go outside the fellowship. But most everything else — painting, roofing, construction — we can do ourselves. So we do it."

Briley asked questions about why they sang without a piano, why different men instead of one minister had stepped behind the pulpit the two weeks he'd attended, and why the Mennonites allowed electricity and cars when their Amish neighbors didn't. And then he asked about courtship practices. Steven's face heated a bit as he talked about courting. The topic was more personal than the others. But he answered honestly, and as he spoke, a feeling of pride swelled in his chest.

Divorce and single parentage was common outside his community, but within the fellowship he'd never seen a marriage fall apart. Surely the solid start — the shared faith, the friendship-forming, and the time of being published before becoming man and wife — contributed to the successful unions in his fellowship. Entering a relationship with a pure heart, and knowing your intended came with the same purity, meant the marriage could begin with a strong base of trust and security.

"And you'll be getting married soon, huh?" Briley grinned. "Did you pick her, or did your parents say 'Here's the one'?"

Once again Steven formed an honest answer. "Of all the girls in the fellowship, my parents liked Anna-Grace best. They told me so. But I'd already decided I wanted to court her. I just had to wait until she was old enough. She's four years younger than me."

"How old are you?"

"Twenty-three."

"Really? That's all?" The reporter narrowed his gaze and examined Steven for several seconds.

Steven did his best not to squirm beneath the scrutiny.

"You seem older. Maybe it's because you've got your own farm. Or maybe —"

Steven waited, but Briley didn't finish the sentence. So he spoke. "*I* chose Anna-Grace." It was important Briley understood this. There were many things over which he had no control, but he wanted to make it clear that the person he took for a wife was his decision. "My parents and the deacons approved me courting her, but I chose her."

Briley nodded. He stretched again, this time with his arms outward rather than up, and yawned. "You know, Steven, I've talked to quite a few people in Arborville over the past couple of weeks, and I've asked all of them what they like most about living in a Plain community. I've gotten the same response, or a variation of it, from all of them. They tell me they like the sense of close community, the assurance that they and their families will be cared for no matter what might happen, and being able to openly live their faith. Do you agree with that?"

Steven thought for a few seconds about what Briley had said. He couldn't argue with any of it. He nodded.

"Okay then." He picked up the recorder and then rested his elbows on his knees. Holding the little recording device on his open palms between them, he angled a serious look at Steven. "Let me ask you a different question. One I haven't asked anyone else."

Steven stiffened. "Why ask me?"

A sly smile appeared on the man's face. "I have my reasons, but I'm going to claim journalistic privilege and keep them to myself."

Well then, Steven just might keep his answer to himself. He wondered about the question, though. "What do you want to know?"

Speaking slowly and with precise enunciation, Briley said, "What do you like least about living in a Plain community?"

Steven took the recorder, turned it button side up, and then punched the Off button. He pressed it back into Briley's open hand and stood. "That, my man, is none of your business."

CHAPTER 20

Alexa

Over the course of the week prior to Anna-Grace's arrival, Alexa developed a new routine. She served breakfast to both Briley and Steven and then packed lunches for three men. For reasons he didn't explain — and she wasn't going to ask! — Briley had begun spending his days at the Meiers farmstead with Steven and Mr. Aldrich. He'd been the one to ask her for box lunches, even offering to pay for all three, but Steven insisted on paying for his own, and after the first day of delivering the lunch to Mr. Aldrich he, too, called and told her to keep a running tab so he could settle up with her at the end of the week.

She had fun making the lunches for the men, always tucking in some of her home-baked cookies or brownies, wedges of pie, or man-sized slices of cake. Mr. Aldrich especially liked tea flavored with peach slices, so she bought some refillable bottles and kept several handy to add to his lunch box. Grandmother thought she was nuts for doing it. "This is a bed-and-breakfast, not a café," she'd scolded, but Alexa assured her she didn't mind. Besides, it meant a little more money coming into her account. She couldn't turn it down no matter how small the profit.

Each evening, Briley put the three empty lunch boxes on the back porch so Alexa could wash the containers and ready the boxes for the next day. And for reasons she couldn't fathom, he began an odd routine of leaving little somethings in his box. On Monday evening she found a piece of very old wallpaper, musty-smelling and brittle and bearing the faded image of a bluebird. Tuesday there were a half-dozen rusty, square-head nails, each bent into odd shapes. Both day's findings earned a chuckle — they reminded her of treasures a small boy might gather — and then went into the trash bin.

A rumpled, food-stained napkin waited in the bottom of the box on Wednesday, which brought an odd sense of disappointment. Had she offended him by throwing the things away? But when she plucked the napkin out, she discovered he'd used it to wrap a walnut-sized chunk of coal that had nearly fossilized. The black lump was as hard and glossy as polished glass. She set it on the kitchen windowsill so she could enjoy the play of sunlight on the smooth surface.

Thursday she opened his box and found a single page from an old book. A line drawing of a bare tree climbed one side of the page and spread its branches along the top edge. A saucy crow perched on an uppermost branch. The bottom of the page bore a spattering of dots, some more time faded than others, and Robert Frost's poem "Dust of Snow" filled the center in an old-fashioned script. Reading it brought a smile. Even though the sheet was yellowed, the bottom-left corner permanently smudged with dirt, and the edges frayed, she couldn't resist keeping it. She showed the page to her grandmother, who also commented on its charm, and then she put it safely in her desk drawer. She'd seek a vintage-looking frame and hang the poem on the wall in the cottage when she was able to move back in.

All Friday afternoon while she baked and decorated a batch of sugar cookies to share with her passel of young cousins, she looked forward to the hour when Briley would deposit the lunch boxes on the back porch. The hands on the clock seemed to move at half their usual rate, but suppertime finally came and went, and shortly after, she heard the clump of Briley's boots on the porch.

She waited until the screen door snapped into its frame, then dashed out and retrieved the boxes. She pushed Mr. Aldrich's and Steven's plain black, arch-topped boxes to the back of the counter and unzipped the lid on Briley's newer, insulated box. Holding her breath in anticipation, she peeled the cover back and peered inside. At the bottom an envelope waited. The other items had all been old, but this envelope was crisp and white, obviously not something he'd found in Steven's house. What might it hold?

Biting her lower lip to hold back an eager giggle, she pulled it out and unstuck the flap. A partial image showed in the V-shaped cutout. She frowned at it for a moment, confused, and then her eyes widened and heat rushed to her face. "Oh! Oh, that — that obnoxious stinker!" She dropped the envelope back in the lunch box and smacked the lid closed. Muffled laughter reached her ears, and she turned toward the sound. Briley, his hands cupped beside his amused face, peered through the square window on the upper half of the kitchen door.

With a little growl she marched to the door and gave the curtains a brisk yank that hid his face from view. His laughter boomed louder. She jerked the door open and glared at him, one hand on her hip. "I suppose you think you're funny, don't you? As if I'd want that awful picture!"

"You don't like it? But I had it printed just for you."

His hurt tone and wide-eyed expression didn't fool her. "You had it printed just to torment me, you mean."

He held his hands out in a pose of surrender. "Why, Miss Zimmerman, the things you say. Me? Torment you? Never . . ."

She folded her arms over her chest and gave him an I'm-not-buying-it look.

He waggled his eyebrows at her — an annoying gesture made even worse because he was so cute when he did it. "Don't forget, you started it with the apple cider. And then you ended it, because you only gave it to me on Sunday. Didn't I tell you it's the only cure for my obnoxiousness? Be happy it didn't wear off sooner or who knows what you might have found before now."

"Don't worry." She pushed her words past gritted teeth. If the laugh building in her chest erupted, she'd never forgive herself. "You won't go one day without apple cider from now on." She yanked the envelope from his lunch box and pulled out the photograph. Holding it where he could easily see, she tore it in two. She stomped to the waste can and, with a dramatic flourish, tossed in both halves, swished her palms together, and smiled at him in triumph. "There!"

His lips twitched into a mischievous grin. "One down and . . ." He aimed his gaze upward, pinching his chin as if in deep contemplation. "How many to go?"

Alexa rushed at him. "Do you mean to tell me there are more of those things?" The image — tufts of pink fuzz from her unflattering earmuffs poking out between her clamped fingers and her shocked face above a stack of mugs — was etched in her memory. She didn't want anyone else seeing that picture.

He stood with his feet widespread and his fists on his hips like Paul Bunyan and laughed at her.

"Briley!"

"Alexa!" He imitated her tone exactly. Leaning forward until his nose was only inches from hers, he whispered, "There's only one way to find out how many of those prints exist."

She wrung her hands, half-afraid of what he would say next.

"Withhold the apple cider." Then he

turned on his heel and strode out the door.

Alexa gawked after him for several stunned seconds, then she growled in aggravation and gave the door a firm whack that slammed it into its frame. She spun from the door, then jumped in surprise. Grandmother's chair filled the opposite doorway. Alexa's face flamed. What had her grandmother seen? She cleared her throat. "Um . . . hello. How long have you been there?"

"Long enough."

Alexa put one hand on her chest and held the other toward the door where Briley had just departed. "None of that was my fault. He played a trick on me!"

An odd smile quivered on the corners of Grandmother's lips. "I know."

"And I wasn't flirting." She spoke firmly, convincing herself as much as her grandmother. Flirting with Briley would be foolhardy, and she made it a point to never be foolhardy. She frowned, suddenly uncertain. "But . . ." She hurried across the floor to Grandmother and knelt in front of her. "Was he flirting with me?"

Grandmother smoothed a few stray wisps of hair from Alexa's face. "Couldn't you tell?"

Alexa sighed. "No. Not really. Sometimes

I think he is because that's just *who* he is. He's good looking and he knows it, so he can't help himself. Other times I think he's doing it just to tease."

"Teasing and flirting . . . aren't they the same?"

"No." She'd been at the receiving end of both in junior high and had learned the difference. "Flirting can seem like teasing, but it's done to capture the other person's attention. Teasing is purely to rattle someone."

"And are you rattled?"

She was. But she didn't know whether it was his behavior or her reaction to his attention that had rattled her more. She rose and crossed to the waiting lunch boxes to begin cleaning them. "It doesn't matter, I guess. Flirting or teasing, whatever he's doing, he'll probably keep it up until he leaves so I just have to learn to ignore it."

Grandmother chuckled.

Alexa angled a look over her shoulder. "What's funny?"

"I was just remembering . . ." Grandmother chuckled again, her face crinkling with merriment.

Alexa turned around and leaned against the counter, smiling even though she had no idea what had tickled her grandmother. "What?"

"The way you two were going at it in here — both acting hopping mad but trying so hard not to laugh."

Alexa's embarrassment returned with full force. She battled hiding her face behind her hands.

"You reminded me of Clete and your mother when they were young, always cooking up schemes to outdo the other one. Except in reverse, of course, because Clete was the littler of the two. But my, how they sparred, and always in good fun." She sighed. "I miss those days. You and Mr. Forrester — or should we start calling him Briley? — just carried me backward in time." She sat for several seconds, staring into nothing, then shifted her gaze and winked at Alexa. "You know, I'm going to stop worrying about that young man's effect on you. You just proved to me you can hold your own." She caught the wheels of her chair and pulled, rolling the chair backward and out of sight.

Alexa chewed her lip, thinking about what Grandmother had said. *"Always in good fun . . ."* Her teeth lost their grip as a smile took control. She grabbed the lump of coal from the windowsill and held it in front of her, envisioning Briley's smirking grin in its place. "Okay, Mr. Obnoxious, you started it, but I intend to finish it. Consider the game 'on.' "

While Briley fixed his supper — cheap, off-brand canned chili heated in the microwave — he replayed Alexa's reaction to finding that photograph, and he chuckled. She'd played right into his hands, as he'd known she would. She reminded him of an eager puppy digging up a fresh bone when she opened that lunch box tonight. He chuckled some more. Maybe it was wrong to tease her. Aunt Myrt would probably call it a childish thing to do. But he couldn't help it. The girl was too serious, and somebody needed to get her to lighten up. Otherwise she'd be as sour and sullen as Brungardt by the time she reached her midtwenties. "And that would be a travesty."

He carried the chili to the table, sat, and dipped his spoon. But instead of raising it to his mouth, he stared into the bowl and lost himself in thought. An entire week . . . He'd spent an entire week side by side with Steven Brungardt, and not once had he witnessed the man smile. Aldrich smiled. A lot. The carpenter was like those dwarfs in the old Disney film, whistling while he worked. But Steven? Oh, he worked. With

275

unwavering efficiency. But not with any joy. And even though his unsmiling face told Briley the man wasn't happy, he wouldn't say anything to confirm it. Until Steven lost his reserve and talked, Briley had nothing to add to his article. So he'd stick around until he finally gained Steven's trust enough to find out why he didn't reflect the peace people expected the Plain folk to exude.

The spicy scent of the chili broke through his reverie, and he took a bite. He made a face. The beans were soggy, the sauce flat, and he'd never encountered beef with such a grainy texture. But he had to eat something. Would Alexa give him some leftovers if he asked? The kitchen had smelled like fresh bread and something Italian. He huffed out a brief laugh. What was he thinking? After he'd made fun of her, she wouldn't share anything good with him. He muttered, "Just eat the chili."

He took a second bite of the bland chili as his thoughts rolled onward. He'd enjoyed watching the transformation of the kitchen at the old house. His first day in there as he stared at the crumbling plaster walls, the rusty plumbing pipes sticking up from holes in the floor, and the single light bulb hanging from some weird, twisted wire in the middle of the ceiling, he couldn't envision the room being anything except a disaster. But that Aldrich knew what he was doing.

Even though it wasn't finished yet — probably wouldn't be for another week — Briley could now see the potential. In a week's time Aldrich repaired the plaster and painted the walls and ceiling an eggshell-like off-white that brightened the space better than a hundred-watt bulb, replaced the old linoleum with gray-and-white tiles in a checkerboard pattern, and refinished the woodwork so it was as smooth as silk and glowed with the color of spun honey. If he proved as adept at building cabinets as he had with plaster, paint, and stain, there should be no complaints about the kitchen when he was done.

Briley finished his chili and washed the bowl in the bathroom sink. The porcelain gleamed from a recent scrubbing, letting him know Alexa had come in during the day to clean. He pinched his forehead. Were B and B's like motels, where you should tip the maid? Not that Alexa was a maid, technically, but she did come in each day while he was away to sweep the floor, give his bathroom a going-over, and put out fresh towels if he left his wadded in the tub.

A grin pulled at his cheek. No, he wouldn't tip her. At least not the way he'd tip a maid

277

in a hotel. But he had some ideas on what to leave for her to find. He plunked the bowl with the others in the painted cupboard and then retrieved one of the prints he'd made of Alexa's frantic duck for cover. There weren't many opportunities for entertainment in Arborville, so he'd have to design his own. Fortunately, he'd always been creative.

CHAPTER 21

Sommerfeld
Steven

Mom and Dad welcomed Steven home after his brief time in Arborville as enthusiastically as if he'd been away at war. Not that any of his community members would serve in the armed forces as anything other than a medic — the Old Order Mennonites were strict pacifists. But maybe in a way he had been fighting a battle. An emotional one.

Lying in the bed he'd slept in from the time he was old enough to leave the crib, his stomach achingly full from Mom's good cooking, he played back over his first days in what his parents presumed would be his new home. He couldn't honestly say he'd had a bad two weeks in Arborville. The fellowship members were helpful and kind. Mr. Aldrich offered advice on fixing up the house when Steven asked for it but left him to his own devices when he didn't, unlike

Dad, who tended to follow him around and give unsolicited advice that left Steven feeling inadequate to the tasks. He liked being in charge of his own projects.

Living out of boxes wasn't a lot of fun — he missed his neatly organized-by-Mom dresser drawers and closet — but he could do it. He'd memorized the contents of each box by the end of the second day, making it a little easier to locate what he wanted. Once Anna-Grace made up her mind, he'd know whether or not to completely unpack those boxes.

His chest went tight, his body hot. He kicked aside the covers and sat on the edge of the mattress, staring into the shadows of the room. He'd been so busy the past days he hadn't stopped long enough to really think. But all the suppressed worries and wishes and wonderings now rose in a mighty torrent. In his busyness there was something else he'd pushed aside. He couldn't remember the last time he'd prayed. Really prayed. Not just a thank-you for the food or a quickly uttered request for strength or patience.

When he was very young, Mom had always come in and sat on the edge of the bed while he and Kevin knelt side by side and prayed. Kevin prayed first, and then

Steven, because Kevin was older. For years Steven had mimicked his brother's prayers. When Kevin reached his twelfth birthday, Mom deemed him old enough to pray without supervision, so she'd only listened to Steven's, and he'd finally learned to form his own praises, confessions, and requests.

After Kevin left home, Steven told Mom how Kevin had stopped the practice of prayer once she left him on his own. The look of pain on her face remained cemented in his memory. Determined not to inflict that kind of anguish on his mother, he'd never skipped a night of talking to God. Until now. The remembrance of her stricken face drove him to his knees beside the bed. Head bowed, eyes closed, he turned his attention to the One he'd claimed as Father when he was eight years old.

"God, my heavenly Father, forgive me for neglecting You. Being busy is no excuse. Forgive me, also, for any displeasing words, thoughts, or behaviors, whether intentional or unintentional. Thank You for sending the fellowship men to the farm" — he couldn't bring himself to call it *my farm* — "and bless them for the work they did on the barn. Thank You for giving me the strength to work hard in the house and accomplish much. Thank You for Briley Forrester's helping hands this week, and thank You for helping me hold my tongue around him. I don't want my confusing thoughts to make me say anything that would lead him to think less of Your faithful followers."

He took a deep breath, gathering his concerns to lay at God's throne. "Father, about living in Arborville . . . It's a nice town with nice people. A good place to live and worship with fellow believers. But am I meant to farm my grandfather's land? Dad and Mom think so, and I know I need to honor them just as Your Word commands. If this is Your will for me — to live and farm in Arborville — then let Anna-Grace find her peace in the community. And if Anna-Grace finds her peace, then I trust You . . ."

For long seconds Steven gritted his teeth together and held back his final words. He wouldn't say them if he didn't mean them. He wouldn't lie to God. He carefully examined his heart before completing his prayer in a breathy rush. "To give me the desire to be a farmer so I can be at peace, too." His shoulders wilted.

He pushed to his feet and flopped back onto the bed. Pulling the covers to his chest, he sighed. A sigh of contentment? No, more one of relief for finding the courage to openly state his trust in God. He couldn't imagine being as enthusiastic about farming as he felt about teaching, but God had performed miracles in the Bible. He could perform one in Steven's heart, too.

Saturday morning Steven awoke at seven thirty — much later than he'd intended. He leaped out of bed and scrambled into his clothes so he could hurry out and help Dad with the chores. Mom handed him a bacon, egg, and cheese-on-toast sandwich as he passed through the kitchen. He thanked her with a kiss on the cheek, which made her smile, then headed through a gray, damp-feeling morning to the barn.

Dad was lifting the milk pail from beneath Old Blossom, their trusty cow, when Steven entered. He gulped down the last bite of his sandwich, then trotted forward to take the pail. "I hoped to catch you before you started milking. I was going to take care of Old Blossom this morning. Milking was always my chore." Well, not always. Once it had been Kevin's. But it became Steven's a long time ago.

Dad gave the cow's rump a light slap, encouraging her to step toward the feed trough. "She got used to my fingers this past week. Your hands would feel like a stranger's to her now."

The comment was meant to tease. Steven recognized the rare glint in Dad's eyes. But for some reason it pricked like a burr under his skin. In such a short time had he become a stranger? What would he be by the end of a month — forgotten? He turned to carry the pail to the house where Mom's hand-operated separator waited on the back porch.

"Steven?" Dad's voice followed him. "You can stay in the house and visit with your mother. I hired Henry Braun's boy, Theo, to come out and help in the mornings. He'll be here by eight."

"Henry Braun's son . . ." Steven sent a puzzled look in Dad's direction. "But I thought his boy helped in his automotive shop."

Dad paused in stabbing a forkful of hay into Old Blossom's box. "Oh, he did. But Theo decided he didn't much care for getting grease under his fingernails. So I told him he could come out and get good old-fashioned dirt under them instead and see if he liked it better." He shook his head, chuckling indulgently. "Sometimes these young men need to experiment with different things until they know for sure what they want to do with their lives."

Joy leaped in Steven's chest. If Dad understood the Braun boy's desire to do something other than his dad's vocation, would he understand his own son's desires? He licked his lips in anticipation of finally spilling his secret. "Dad, I —"

"I was glad to give Theo a chance to explore farming. Maybe it will keep him around while he figures out what he wants to do with himself." Sadness tinged Dad's features. "I'm glad you aren't restless like Theo Braun. He's given his parents a few reasons for worry in the past years. That's one thing your mother and I are grateful for. Our younger son doesn't make us stay up nights, fretting and praying over his future the way Henry and Marie do over Theo." He scraped the fork clean on the edge of the box, hung it on its hook, then scuffed to Steven and squeezed his shoulder. "Our prayers for you are only ones of gratitude. As much as we miss you around here, we're too happy for your secure future to bring you back."

Steven swallowed the words he'd hoped to say and nodded.

"That land in Arborville has put out a good yield every year for the renters. No reason to believe it won't do the same for you." Dad clapped his shoulder, then stepped back, his smile wide. "Thank the good Lord above, you have a bright future ahead of you." The sound of a car's engine intruded. Dad looked out the barn doors. "There's Theo now. Head on in and enjoy a morning of leisure. You don't get any of those when you're the farm owner, you know."

Yes, Steven knew. He left the barn, giving Theo Braun a nod of greeting as the younger man raced past him. On the back porch he poured the milk into the aluminum bowl of the separator. He situated clean basins beneath the spouts and grabbed the wooden handle to begin spinning the liquid in the bowl. As a boy he'd enjoyed watching the milk spin outward while the cream remained in the center, thinking it somewhat magical that the milk knew to depart down one spout while the cream flowed down the other. He watched the liquid now, trying to recapture some of that wonder.

"Steven, what in the world are you doing?" Mom's startled voice came from behind him.

He glanced over his shoulder. "Separating the cream, Mom. I'll bring it in when I'm done."

"Will you stop that?" Mom waved both hands at him, as if shooing off a cloud of flies.

"But —"

"That's my job."

"But I —"

Mom propped her fists on her hips. A mock scowl formed on her face. "Young man, are you going to argue with your mother?"

Steven released the handle and stepped away from the separator.

Mom laughed. She took over the task. "I saw Theo pull in. Did Dad send you up from the barn?"

"He said he didn't need me."

The corners of Mom's eyes crinkled with her smile. "I think that's his way of saying Theo needs to earn his keep."

Dad could have told Theo to stay away this weekend — that his son was home and could help. "I suppose."

"It isn't often a farmer gets a weekend off. Why not take advantage of this one?" Mom kept pumping while she spoke, the squeak of the hand-crank machine sending out an offbeat accompaniment to her words. "Anna-Grace doesn't expect to see you until service tomorrow, right? Why don't you drive into town and surprise her?"

Steven offered a slow shrug. "I suppose I could do that."

Mom's eyebrows rose. "Don't you want

to see her?"

Of course he did. He just hadn't quite set aside his hurt feelings over being so easily replaced out here. Which was pretty ridiculous when he stopped to think about it. He hadn't wanted to be stuck on his dad's farm in the first place. He gave himself a mental shake. "I always want to see Anna-Grace."

Mom's smile returned. "So go. Stop and pick up a box of chocolates from the gift shop before you go to her house."

"What for?"

Mom burst out laughing. She released the handle long enough to swat Steven's arm. "For Anna-Grace! You've been away. Bring her a little present to show her you missed her."

Seeing her beau show up a day early should be present enough, to his way of thinking, but he wouldn't argue with Mom. "All right. I guess I'll see you at lunchtime."

"I guess I'll see you later than that." Mom shook her head, her eyes twinkling with suppressed laughter. "You know as well as I do Olivia Braun will insist you stay for lunch, and then Anna-Grace will probably want to spend the afternoon with you."

Steven frowned. "So you don't have any need of me around here today at all?"

"Not one bit." Mom had no idea how

much her glib reply pierced him. "So go on and have fun. Enjoy your day."

Steven drove to town under a cloud-filled sky that threatened rain. The gray color of the heavy clouds too closely matched his mood, and he sent up a quick prayer for God to brighten his spirits. He didn't want to greet Anna-Grace with a somber face.

CHAPTER 22

Anna-Grace

The doorbell rang, an intrusion against the cheerful melody of raindrops on the roof.

Sunny let out a squeal and dropped her crayon onto the coloring book. "I'll get it!" She jumped up, bumping the table in her rapid movement.

The tea in Anna-Grace's mug sloshed over the edge and spattered the papers she'd been grading. "Sunny, please be careful!" She reached for a napkin from the little basket in the center of the table. Sunny didn't pause in her dash for the door. Shaking her head, Anna-Grace mopped up the mess. Miss Kroeker always said weather changes made the students fidgety. Sunny proved the teacher's words true — she'd bounced from activity to activity this morning, and it wasn't yet nine o'clock.

Anna-Grace carried the stained napkin to the little laundry room behind the kitchen and tossed it in with the load of towels already agitating in the washing machine.

"Sissy, Sissy, come see who is here!"

"Yes, Sunny, I'm coming." She chuckled to herself at her sister's shrill, excited voice — her parents had chosen well when they named this child, who found reasons for delight in nearly everything — and headed for the living room. She rounded the corner, then came to a startled halt when she saw who waited just inside the door. Her frozen pose of surprise lasted only three seconds. Then her excitement rose, her feet took wing, and she dashed across the floor with her arms outstretched. "Steven!"

He captured her in a hug. His clothes and hair were damp, and he smelled of fresh rain and wet wool and spice from his aftershave. She buried her face in the curve of his neck, savoring the sweet essence of the man she loved. She would have stayed there much longer if her little sister's giggles hadn't reminded her they had a small witness to their embrace.

She stepped away, her face flaming, and locked her hands behind her back. "I didn't expect to see you until tomorrow."

"Dad has your cousin Theo doing my chores, so he said I could take the day off."

Having him near again sent her pulse tripping at twice its normal rate, but she kept herself in check to set a good example in front of her impressionable jabberbox of a sister. She hoped his solemn countenance was pasted on for Sunny's sake. She smiled twice as brightly to compensate for his grim expression. "So you're free the whole day?"

He nodded.

Sunny pulled at Anna-Grace's skirt. "Sissy, can Steven color with me?"

Finally Anna-Grace remembered her parents weren't home. She slapped her hand to her cheek and groaned.

Sunny's face fell. "Does that mean no?"

She tugged Sunny to her side and turned an apologetic look on Steven. "Dad's at the stained-glass studio — he needed to finish a project for a customer in Wichita and said he'd probably be out until late this afternoon. Mom isn't here right now, either. She went to do her weekly shopping. I don't know when she'll be back."

Steven nodded. "I understand."

She wanted to cry. "I'm so sorry." An entire day with Steven after two weeks apart would be a wonderful treat. But unless they had a chaperone in the house, he couldn't stay. The fellowship would never approve, and she understood the wisdom of them not being alone. Only Sunny's presence kept her from slipping her arms around his torso and holding tight.

"You don't need to apologize." Finally a hint of a smile showed on his face, but the timing was all wrong. He shouldn't smile about leaving. "I should have called first instead of just coming over."

"No, the surprise was perfect. I loved having you just pop in without notice." She glanced at Sunny and chose her words carefully. "It was a romantic thing to do."

He stuck his hand inside his jacket and pulled out a flat rectangular box. "I brought this, too."

Sunny squealed and lunged. "Candy!" She hugged the box to her chest. Then she turned a sheepish look on Steven. "Oh. This is for Sissy, isn't it?"

Steven's lips curved into an impish grin. He went down on one knee and Sunny immediately crowded close to him. He slipped his arm loosely around her waist and whispered into her ear. "Shh, don't tell Anna-Grace, but the chocolates are really for you. I think you'll have to let me give the box to your sister, though, since she's my sweetheart. Otherwise she might get jealous."

Sunny nodded wisely, then stuck her mouth close to Steven's ear. "Okay, but you'll tell her to share with me, right?"

"Right."

The rasping whispers carried plainly to Anna-Grace, and she bit the insides of her cheeks to stifle her giggles. Sunny plopped the box into Steven's hand and stepped back, her round face wearing an expression of nonchalance. She swung her arms, swishing her hands against her skirt, and began to hum. Anna-Grace looked quickly away from her sister before the laughter building in her throat escaped, and she caught the tender way Steven watched Sunny. Her pulse skipped. He was so good with children — natural, never stiff or overly jovial the way some men tended to be. He'd be a wonderful father someday.

He shifted his face and his gaze connected with hers. He replaced the smile with a mock-serious expression. "Here you are, Anna-Grace. I hope you'll be unselfish and share with Sunny."

She gave a little bow as she accepted the box and matched his formal tone. "Thank you very kindly. Of course I'll share with Sunny." She examined the box, pretending to think deeply. "Hmm, there are twelve candies in this box, so I'll let Sunny have . . ."

Sunny stopped humming. She stared at Anna-Grace, her dark eyes shining.

"One."

Sunny's jaw dropped open.

"Okay, one and a half."

"Sissy-y-y-y-y . . ."

Anna-Grace burst out laughing. She captured Sunny in a hug and planted a kiss on her warm hair. "You can have half of them."

"Yay!"

Steven put his hand on Sunny's head. "If you get half of the candies, and there are twelve all together, how many candies will be yours?"

Sunny screwed her face into a look of concentration. "There's, um . . ." Her face lit. "Six! I get six! As many as I am old!"

"Exactly right. Good job."

Sunny beamed.

Anna-Grace gave her sister the box. "But you can't have them all at once, and you have to wait until after lunch to eat one. All right?"

The little girl sighed, but she agreed. She bounced into the kitchen with the box cradled in her arms, humming again.

Anna-Grace turned her attention to Steven. "You know, we — Sunny and I — could bundle up, and we could all wait on the porch for Mom to come home. No one would have cause to disapprove if we were out in the open without a chaperone."

Steven's brows pulled into a sharp V. "Sit out there in the rain?"

She laughed at his sour face. "The porch roof would keep us dry. And I happen to like rain. Especially the kind we're getting today, falling straight down like a curtain. It's a cleansing rain."

"It's gray and gloomy and *wet.*"

"Why, Steven, I didn't know you disliked rain showers." Unlike many people, she never found rainy days melancholy. She touched his arm. "God brings both the rain and sun, and each has its purpose."

"I guess." He didn't look convinced.

She caught the ends of the ribbons trailing beside her cheeks and gave them a toss over her shoulders. "Let me check on Sunny, make sure she isn't in there devouring the box of chocolates you brought. Then I'll get our heavy jackets. We'll sit on the porch and watch the rain, and I'll see if I can put a smile back on your face."

He lifted his hand and grazed her cheek with his knuckles. "If anyone can do it, you can."

His words warmed her. She backed up to keep herself from leaning into his sturdy frame. "I'll be right back." When she returned with Sunny, their jackets draped over her arm, she found Steven beside the kitchen table examining the test papers Miss Kroeker had given her to grade.

He tapped the stack with his finger. "What are these?"

Anna-Grace helped Sunny into her jacket. "Just something I'm doing for Miss Kroeker. Every now and then she asks me to grade things that don't require me to know the material. Those are all multiple-choice questions. Easily done." She felt guiltier about giving up her volunteer work at the school than she did leaving her paid position at the café. Deborah Muller had already hired someone to fill the waitress position, and she hoped someone would step up to assist Miss Kroeker. The teacher had her hands full, covering all eight grades by herself.

He shifted the stack slightly and began sliding his finger down the line of questions. "I remember studying about the explorers. Magellan, the first captain credited with circumnavigating the world even though his crew finished the journey without him, and Cortés, who cheated the Aztecs out of their gold." He shook his head. "This student must not have been paying attention. Five wrong just on the first page."

Steven flipped the test to the second page and scanned the questions. "Six wrong here.

Wow. Thirteen out of twenty-four correct is only —" He rolled his eyes ceilingward for a few seconds, then looked at the test again. "Fifty-four percent." He blew out a breath. "That's not very good."

Anna-Grace gazed at him in amazement. "How can you remember all that?" If she were to take the grade-six test today, she'd probably fail it. "And how did you figure the percentage in your head?" She coughed out a disbelieving laugh and held up the grading scale Miss Kroeker had loaned her. "I have to use this thing. You're amazing."

Oddly, he didn't smile in response to her praise. Even more confusing, he slid into a chair, picked up the red pen she'd been using, and began grading, his forehead crinkled into a series of serious furrows. Sunny sent a questioning look at Anna-Grace, but she only shrugged, completely baffled by Steven's behavior.

He graded three tests, even adding comments on the back page of each, before he suddenly seemed to realize what he was doing. He dropped the pen and jumped up, taking a huge step away from the table. Then he looked at Anna-Grace. He must have recognized her bewilderment because he said, "Sorry. Kind of lost myself there for a minute."

She laughed lightly. "Obviously. You must have really enjoyed studying about the explorers to get so caught up in the questions."

"History intrigues me. To really understand where we are now as a nation, we have to look back at where we've been. Here in our community, we sometimes forget there's a world outside of Sommerfeld that has an effect on us and how we live. History — the events of years ago and the things happening today that will be the next century's past — is important."

He spoke with such intensity, the fine hairs on Anna-Grace's arms tingled. She stared at him, trying to understand. Steven tended to be quiet and introspective. She liked that about him — he wasn't thoughtless or flippant like some of the other young men in the community. Although still young he possessed a maturity that made her feel secure in his presence. But this sober, almost grim man seemed a stranger.

His stiff shoulders wilted. "And why am I lecturing you?" He huffed an amused-sounding snort and shook his head. When he looked at her again, he seemed more like his old self. "We were going to sit on the porch and watch your rain curtain. We better go before your mom comes home and catches us in here alone."

Sunny piped up, "You're not alone. I'm here, too!"

Steven laughed. Whatever odd mood had struck, it appeared to slip away with the light sound of merriment. He chucked Sunny under the chin. "Yes, you are, and you're all bundled up for the outdoors. So let's go." He held out his hand, and Sunny caught hold. They headed for the door. Halfway there he stopped and looked over his shoulder. "Aren't you coming, Anna-Grace?"

She hadn't realized her feet remained glued in place. She offered a nervous chortle. "Yes. Yes, I'm coming." She hurried after them and tried to toss aside the uncomfortable feeling that had gripped her while Steven studiously graded those papers and then spoke of the importance of history. But even though the rain fell softly in a fresh-scented shower that pleased her senses and Sunny entertained them by playing a noisy game of hopscotch back and forth across the porch, a niggle of unease remained in the back of her mind.

After years of acquaintanceship, months of courting, a pledge to marry, and plans to spend a future together, she should know her intended husband well enough not to be taken aback by his behavior. His actions were troubling, but the deeper concern came from her feeling of uncertainty.

Mom's car pulled in a little before eleven. The rain had slowed to a drizzle by then, but Steven grabbed up his umbrella and trotted across the soggy yard to escort her to the porch. Then he made several trips from the car to the house, carrying in the sacks of groceries she'd purchased. He unbagged everything while Mom and Anna-Grace put things away and Sunny scampered around, getting in the way. Then Mom shooed them to the table while she fixed a simple lunch of tomato soup and grilled-cheese sandwiches, which Steven stayed to share.

When they finished eating, Mom rose. "I'm going to take a lunch to your dad. He gets so caught up in his projects, he forgets to eat if I don't remind him."

If Mom left again, Steven would have to leave, too. Anna-Grace said, "Why not let Steven and me take it? You've already been out most of the morning. Stay home and relax now." She looked at Steven. "Is that all right?"

Steven gazed at her for several seconds. The same serious expression that had captured his face when he graded papers returned, bringing with it another rush of unease. He spoke slowly, as if weighing his words. "What if . . . you stay here with your mom . . . and I take the lunch to your dad? The rain has stopped, but everything is muddy. No sense in both of us getting mucked up."

"Oh, but —"

Sunny grabbed Steven's hand. "Will you come back after you take Daddy his lunch? We haven't colored together yet."

Steven gave Sunny a little smile and nod before turning to Anna-Grace again. "I don't mind getting muddy. Farmers are used to getting muddy." A slight touch of sarcasm seemed to enter his tone, but his face didn't reflect it. "It'll give me a chance to talk a bit with your dad — something I don't do very often."

Mom started for the kitchen, talking over her shoulder. "Well, it sounds as though we have a plan. Anna-Grace and Sunny, clear the table, please. Steven, I'll have that lunch ready to go in just a few minutes."

"I'll get out of your way here." Steven headed for the living room, an eager bounce in his step.

CHAPTER 23

Steven

Steven pulled up to the curb outside the stained-glass studio on the edge of town where Anna-Grace's father had worked for as long as Steven could remember. Even though Andrew Braun's father and brothers farmed for a living, he was an artist. An *artist*. Something no other man in the community had ever been. If anyone would understand Steven's desire to break free of the traditional occupations of his faith, Andrew Braun would. And Steven silently applauded the opportunity to talk to the man one-on-one.

He cleaned the mud from his boots on a metal scraper outside the door before entering. He'd never been in the studio. Based on the dozens of framed, bright-colored stained-glass pieces hanging behind the large plate-glass windows, he expected the entire place to be feminine. The smell took him by surprise. There was nothing feminine about the overpowering scent of hot machinery and turpentine. Underneath the odors he detected a slight essence of vanilla — probably an attempt to mask the metallic scent. But it failed. He rubbed his nose.

The high-pitched whine of a power tool pierced Steven's ears, and he moved farther into the building past worktables and displays of books, sheets of glass, and unfamiliar tools and hardware, seeking the sound. He located it, and the worker causing the noise, in the far corner of the building. Mr. Braun, his face covered by a clear plastic shield, stood behind a tall wood counter and ran the edges of a bright-red glass diamond along a rapidly spinning cylinder. Tiny bits of glass flew in an arc, catching the light as they fell toward the floor.

Steven waited until he pulled the diamond away from the sander before speaking. "Mr. Braun?"

The man straightened, flicked a look at Steven, then snapped the little switch on the sander. The quiet that fell left Steven's ears buzzing. Mr. Braun lifted the shield from his face, dropped it on the counter, and swiped his forehead with his sleeve. He popped off his leather gloves as he rounded the wood barricade. "Well, Steven. Hello.

It's good to see you."

They shook hands, and Steven matched the older man's grip. Then he held up the lunch Mrs. Braun had prepared. "I brought you something to eat. Your wife was worried about you."

Mr. Braun laughed. "She's always worried I'll forget to eat. Skipping a meal now and then won't hurt me. I don't get as much exercise as I should." He patted his stomach through his tucked-in flannel shirt. "But since you brought it, I'll eat it." He took the sack and moved to a bench stretched along the back wall. "Come. Sit."

Steven didn't need a second invitation. He bowed his head while Mr. Braun asked a blessing for his meal, then patiently waited until he'd taken the sandwich and small thermos of soup from the bag. When the man seemed settled, he opened his mouth to finally ask the question only Mr. Braun could answer.

"How's the work coming on the house?" Mr. Braun spoke before Steven had a chance.

He cleared his throat, forcing his question aside. "Pretty well. Still a lot to do, but it's a lot better than it was when I first started."

"As long as it sat empty, I'm sure it was in disrepair." Mr. Braun took a big bite of his sandwich, chewed, and chased it with a draw from the thermos. "But your dad says it has the potential to be a real nice place. Livvy and I are eager to drive over and see it." He took another bite before adding, "Of course, we'll wait until you're ready for company."

"You can come anytime," Steven said, mostly because it was the right thing to say. He rubbed his palms up and down his thighs, gathering his courage. "Mr. Braun, I —"

"You know, Steven, I think it would be all right if you wanted to call me Andrew. It won't be long now, and we'll be related." He grinned, but his eyes seemed sad. "Maybe if we get a little friendlier, I won't have such a hard time letting you take my daughter away."

Steven swallowed. "All right. Andrew." It seemed strange calling one of his elders by his given name, but it also seemed to put the two of them on more equal footing. Maybe it would make talking to him easier. "May I ask you a question?"

"Sure." He lifted the thermos for another drink.

Steven examined a half circle-shaped window with some sort of purple flowers on a vine hanging from the ceiling by thin silver chains. "How did you know you wanted to do this kind of work? It's not exactly . . ." He sought a word. "The *norm* for an Old Order Mennonite man."

Anna-Grace's father laughed. "No, it sure isn't. And to be honest, it isn't something I planned to do."

Steven looked at him in surprise. "It wasn't?"

"Nope. I knew I liked creating things. Even dabbled a bit in a woodworking shop shortly after I finished school, but somehow it wasn't quite right. Then when Beth Quinn — you probably remember her as Beth Mc-Cauley — came to town and decided to open this shop, she needed help. At first I helped because it was wintertime, not a lot to do on the farm, and she was my uncle Henry's stepdaughter so it seemed right to give her a hand. But in a very short time of working here, I realized how much I liked stained-glass art." He turned a serious gaze on Steven. "It satisfied me, down deep. I finally came to recognize this was God's plan for my future. I've been here ever since."

Steven nodded slowly. "And your parents . . . they didn't mind?"

Another laugh burst out — this one full of self-deprecation. "Oh, they minded all right.

307

Especially my dad. But he was mostly worried about whether I could make a living with stained-glass art. It's the man's responsibility, you know, to support his family. Dad just couldn't see it happening." He nudged Steven with his elbow. "But you know, God worked that out, and now Dad's one of my best supporters. Especially since Beth and her husband moved to the Kansas City area to open a second studio and left me in charge of this one."

He placed the empty thermos on the bench between them and wadded up the paper sack and sandwich wrapping. He rose, smiling at Steven as he did so. "When you really set out to find what God wills for your life, things fall into place. Seems to me there's even a Bible verse to that effect." He scratched his head for a moment. "From Psalm 139, verse 3, I believe. 'Thou compassest my path . . .' To me, that means He has a road mapped out for me to follow. If I ask for His guidance, He'll direct me in the way He wants me to go."

A bitter query found its way from Steven's mouth. "But what if someone else puts a roadblock on your path?"

"Well, then, I would say you should step up your prayers, because either you're on the wrong path or the other person needs to hear God's voice more clearly. Pray God would move the roadblock if you're meant to continue, or ask Him to open a new path that is more of His choosing for you." Suddenly he frowned. "Steven, are you having second thoughts about marrying Anna-Grace? Because if you're uncertain —"

Steven leaped up. "No, sir. I love Anna-Grace." Sometimes he worried they were marrying too soon, but he couldn't imagine marrying anyone but her.

The man blew out a little breath. "That's good to know, because she loves you and is very committed to you. Her mother and I are pleased, too." He rose and put his hand on Steven's shoulder, the touch fatherly. "We know you'll be a faithful husband and a good provider for our girl."

"Yes, sir."

Andrew turned and shot his wadded-up lunch bag like a basketball into the trash barrel. Then he picked up the thermos and pressed it into Steven's hands. Putting his arm across Steven's shoulders, he aimed him for the front door. "Farming is an honest trade, and you're starting off much more secure than many young men your age thanks to your parents' generosity. Whatever challenges you're facing right now getting the house in order will all be worth it the day you harvest your first crop, whether that crop be in Arborville — if that's where you and Anna-Grace decide to keep your home — or somewhere else."

Andrew opened the door and ushered Steven through it. He lifted his hand in a wave. "Thanks for bringing me the lunch. It was good to talk to you, but I'd better get back to work. I'm a little behind on this project since my order of glass didn't arrive on time. Please tell Livvy I'll be home by six." He closed the door before Steven could respond.

Steven dragged his heels along the wet sidewalk, one hand in his pocket, the other gripping the thermos tightly enough to dent its sides, and his head low. He'd been certain Anna-Grace's father would recognize his desire to step outside the norm and pursue a vocation different from any of the Old Order men before him. He paused, looking toward the studio. Should he go back inside and tell the man what he really wanted to do?

"Step up your prayers . . ."

Andrew's advice whispered through Steven's mind. With a sigh that formed a little cloud in front of his face, he aimed himself for his truck. He'd go back to Anna-Grace's house for an hour or two. He'd color with Sunny, talk some more with Anna-Grace and her mother. Then he'd close himself in his bedroom at home — his parents' home — and step up his prayers, the way Andrew Braun had told him to do. He only hoped God would answer them by tearing down the roadblock, not forcing him on a different route. Because those few minutes he'd spent going over test papers were the most satisfying minutes he'd spent in years.

Arborville
  Alexa

The weekend before Anna-Grace's arrival at the B and B passed so slowly it seemed as though time stood still. And Alexa didn't mind one bit. Despite her careful preparations, despite the prayers for God to ease her discomfort, despite telling herself again and again it would be fun to have someone her age staying at the farmhouse with her, she still wasn't ready. Not emotionally. Had it not been for the copy of the awful photograph Briley had taken at the Meiers farm that she found taped to the backside of a pantry cabinet door, she wouldn't have smiled once the entire weekend. If Monday wanted to wait another week to arrive, she wouldn't complain.

Sunday after she and Grandmother returned from Shelley's house, where they'd had lunch with the family, Grandmother went to her room to nap and Alexa wandered upstairs to the room she'd blocked off her scheduling calendar for Anna-Grace's use. At first she'd intended to give her the room with the attached bathroom, but Grandmother talked her out of it. *"If someone calls, they'll be more likely to want the private bath than the shared bath. But Anna-Grace will be grateful no matter where you put her, so save the private bath for a paying guest."* She hoped her grandmother was right and Anna-Grace wouldn't feel as though Alexa gave her second best.

She wandered the room — the one she called "Ruth 2:10" — and examined every detail to be certain it was ready for its occupant. Of the three rooms, this one was the most feminine with its pair of white iron twin beds covered by matching Roman Square quilts pieced and tied by Grandmother's quilting circle at church. The quilts' calico patches of palest shell pink, moss green, and eggshell gave the beds a dreamy, step-back-in-time feeling. Cream-colored eyelet curtains at the windows matched the flounced dust ruffles on the beds, their delicate softness a perfect contrast to the dark burled-walnut dressing table and bureau.

She paused and touched the carved acorn drawer pulls, shiny from yesterday's polishing, then slid her finger along the dresser top. Not a speck of dust anywhere. Not even under the edges of the doily providing an anchor for an antique pitcher and bowl filled with artificial flowers. The other items on the dresser were practical rather than pretty — a box of tissues, a small bowl holding a few individually wrapped peppermints, and a pad of notepaper and a pen imprinted with the name of the B and B. She set the pad so its top edge was parallel with the dresser's edge, then angled the pen on it, just so, with *Grace Notes B-&-B* showing.

After one more trek around the room, during which she examined the floral area rug and exposed strips of stained yellow pine for an errant dust bunny, she sat in the reproduction French Provincial chair in the corner and stared at the framed sampler hanging on the mint-and-white-striped opposite wall. Linking her hands together, she rested them in her lap and tried to imagine how it would feel when Anna-Grace stepped through the front door tomorrow.

She'd met the girl several months ago when the family gathered for Grandmother's sixtieth birthday. They'd had little time to talk, but during those brief exchanges she found her pleasant and unpretentious — the kind of person who could be friends with anyone. But at that first meeting she'd thought Anna-Grace was only her grandmother's great-niece. Now that she knew the truth — that Anna-Grace was really Mom's biological daughter adopted by Grandmother's nephew and his barren wife — everything was different.

Whispering in case her voice might carry out the door, down the stairs, and through the house to Grandmother's ears, she read the words stitched in a flowing calligraphy on the sampler. " 'Why have I found grace in thine eyes, that thou shouldest take knowledge of me, seeing I am a stranger?' " A knot formed in her throat, and she blinked against the threat of tears.

When she'd searched for verses including the word *grace* to feature in each of the rooms, she'd chosen this one in the hopes she could emulate Boaz's kindness to Ruth, providing guests with whatever was needed to meet their needs for the time of their stay, and in so doing give them a glimpse of God's care for His children. But now the words from the Bible seemed to mock her. Anna-Grace wasn't the baby abandoned and taken in by one of the Zimmerman offspring. Anna-Grace wasn't the imposter in the family. She truly belonged here, unlike Alexa, whose birthright set her apart.

She groaned, bending forward in the chair and burying her face in her hands. She had to be gracious. She'd promised Grandmother and Sandra that hosting Anna-Grace wouldn't be a problem. Anna-Grace was coming tomorrow — she couldn't change the plans now. She *had* to be gracious to this girl whose blood tied her to the family Alexa wanted to claim for her very own. The only way she could separate herself from Anna-Grace now was if she received calls to fill all three rooms. Then she'd have a reason to ask Sandra to host the girl instead.

Straightening, she looked toward the ceiling — toward heaven, where the only Father she knew resided. "I don't think I can do this, God. Begrudgingly maybe, but not graciously. So make the telephone ring. Send some guests to Arborville. Fill these rooms. Please?"

But the telephone didn't ring. Not that afternoon. Not that evening. And not the next morning, no matter how many times Alexa repeated the prayer. So at eleven thirty, when Steven Brungardt's pickup

315

pulled into the lane, Alexa gritted her teeth, pasted on a smile she hoped would fool both Grandmother and the arriving guests, and stepped out on the porch to welcome the girl who rightfully belonged in this place.

CHAPTER 24

Anna-Grace

The tummy-trembles that started when she and Steven pulled out of her parents' driveway became a full-fledged uproar when Steven drew the truck up to the patch of gravel next to the Zimmerman farmhouse porch. Great-Aunt Abigail's granddaughter stood at the top of the steps with her arms crossed over her chest. She was probably just chilled, but her pose looked forbidding. Without conscious thought Anna-Grace reached across the seat and took a gentle hold on Steven's elbow.

He shifted into Park, then turned a puzzled look on her. "What's wrong?"

She pulled in a ragged breath. "I'm . . . scared."

Steven placed his hand over hers. "If you don't want to go in there, we can always turn around right now and go back to Sommerfeld. You don't have to stay."

His words stirred unexpected anger. Couldn't he encourage her rather than tell her it was all right to give up? "Yes, I do, Steven."

His brows pulled down. "No, Anna-Grace, you don't. I meant it when I said if it's too hard for you to be here, I can sell the farm and —"

"Don't tell me that!" A touch of hysteria made her voice come out more shrilly than she intended. She gripped his elbow hard and prayed for God to calm her. When she'd gained control, she loosened her hold and spoke again. "Please don't tell me to quit before I've begun. I'll always wonder if I made a mistake if I don't at least try to be a part of this community."

He gazed at her, his lips set in a firm line, for several seconds. Then he gave a short nod and reached for the door handle, dislodging her hand with the movement. "Then let's go in."

She threw open the door and slid out, adjusting her skirt as she did so. Cool air touched her legs and she gave an involuntary shiver. She met Steven at the front of the truck, and he offered his hand. She grabbed it, grateful for the anchor, and they walked together up the wide stairs to the porch.

"Hello. I've been watching for you. Did

318

you have a good drive?" Alexa Zimmerman's words chirped out on an unnaturally cheerful note.

Anna-Grace's throat felt dry, so she let Steven do the talking.

"Yes. The roads were wet but not slick."

"That's good."

Steven scuffed the toe of his boot back and forth on the porch boards. "Did you get rain this weekend? We got a lot of rain in Sommerfeld."

"Some, but not a lot."

Such a stilted conversation. Anna-Grace's unease increased by the minute. Even though Alexa had been friendly at their previous meeting, she now acted skittish and uncertain. Anna-Grace had feared she would feel uncomfortable in the town, but she hadn't anticipated others immediately being uncomfortable around her. Did Alexa sense her inner anxiety? If so, she needed to behave normally and put her hostess at ease.

Anna-Grace forced herself to speak. "Thank you for inviting me to stay here. The house is so pretty the way you painted it. I remember how nice the living and dining rooms were decorated when I was here for Aunt Abigail's party. I'm sure you did just as good a job fixing up the guest rooms." Once she started talking, she seemed to lose her ability to stop. "I'm not terribly creative when it comes to decorating, so I admire your ability to make everything look so warm and homey. I imagine I'll get lots of ideas from you for fixing up the house Steven inherited. That is, if you don't mind sharing ideas."

Alexa stared at Anna-Grace, her mouth slightly open. "Um, no. I'm glad to share ideas."

"Oh, good. I'll plan to pick your brain then." Anna-Grace released Steven's hand. "Would you get my suitcases?"

He was looking at her oddly, too, as if he'd forgotten who she was, but he nodded and headed down the steps.

Anna-Grace held her hand toward the front door. "Can we go in? I'm eager to get settled in my room, because once I get everything put away I can go to the Meiers farmstead. I can't wait to see the house Steven's grandparents lived in." Acting cheery and unaffected helped her feel less uncertain, and when she smiled again it felt much less forced.

The smile Alexa offered in return also lost some of its stiffness. "Sure. Come on in."

Anna-Grace followed Alexa over the threshold into the small vestibule. A scrolled iron rack hung on the wall just inside the door, and Alexa gestured toward it. "If you'd like, you can leave your coat here. There's a closet in your room, but it's more convenient to have your coat close to the exit."

"Thank you." Anna-Grace placed her coat on one of the hooks, then trailed Alexa into the living room. Aunt Abigail was waiting in the middle of the floor. The moment the girls entered the room, she held her arms open.

"Anna-Grace . . . welcome!"

Her enthusiastic greeting brought an immediate sting of tears to Anna-Grace's eyes. She hurried across the carpet and leaned down for a hug. Aunt Abigail had hugged her when she came for the birthday party last summer, but this embrace was tighter, longer, somehow more emotional. Anna-Grace stayed in the bent-over position until the older woman loosened her hold even though the angle was far from comfortable. She straightened as the screen door opened and Steven came in with her suitcases, one in each hand and the smallest case tucked beneath his elbow.

He looked at Alexa. "Where do you want these?"

Alexa reached for one of the two larger cases. "I put Anna-Grace in the room you and your dad shared when you were here." Her gaze flicked in Anna-Grace's direction. "I'm using the shared bath, too, but I don't have any guests scheduled" — did regret enter her voice or did Anna-Grace imagine it? — "so it'll just be the two of us up there."

Anna-Grace smiled. "That sounds fine." She bustled forward. "Let me take that bag."

"I can do it." Alexa started up the stairs, raising the suitcase with her knees as she went. "But I won't unpack for you."

Even though Alexa still sounded a little stiff and formal, Anna-Grace decided to respond in a teasing manner. "Well, then, no tip for you."

Neither Steven nor Alexa chuckled in reply, but Aunt Abigail laughed heartily enough for all of them. She rolled her wheelchair to the bottom of the staircase and called after them. "Alexa has a Crock-Pot of stew simmering in the kitchen. When you're done up there, come join us for a bowl."

Anna-Grace was fairly certain her nervous stomach would reject food, but she couldn't deny her great-aunt's request. "Thank you. Stew sounds very good."

She topped the stairs on Alexa's heels with Steven close behind and entered an octagon-shaped upstairs landing. Brief expanses of cheerful wallpaper in a tiny rosebud print alternated with closed, raised-panel doors painted glossy white. No windows looked onto the landing, but the single bulb in a small antique brass fixture hanging from the center of the rosebud-papered ceiling proved adequate when reflected by the many bright-white doors and the softer-white background of the wallpaper.

Alexa opened the first door on the right, then stepped aside and gestured for Anna-Grace to enter the room. This was it — her new, temporary home. With her linked hands pressed to her jumping stomach, she moved across the threshold, and when she got a look at the room Alexa had set aside for her, she couldn't hold back a little gasp of delight.

She forgot about her nervousness as she touched her fingertips to the top rail of the white iron footboard of the closest bed and gazed around in pleasure. "Oh, Alexa, I think this is the prettiest room I've ever seen."

Alexa set the suitcase next to a pale-pink velvet upholstered chair and turned to face Anna-Grace. "I'm glad you like it. It's my favorite of the three guest rooms, to be honest." She spoke softly, subdued, but pleasure glimmered in her eyes. "Each of the rooms are named for Scripture, and I call this one the Ruth 2:10." She pointed to a stitched rendition of the verse hanging on the wall.

Anna-Grace couldn't hold back a second gasp. She rushed toward Steven, who remained in the doorway with the suitcases dangling from his hands. "Did you hear that? Ruth 2:10." He nodded, and she turned to Alexa, eager to share the significance of the verse. "I'm sure Aunt Abigail told you I'm adopted. My parents initially planned to name a baby girl Anna-Ruth. Anna is for my mother's grandmother, and they chose Ruth in remembrance of the biblical woman who honored Naomi despite their lack of blood relationship. But when they held me for the first time, they decided to name me Anna-Grace instead because a woman they'd never met had been gracious to them, gifting them beyond description, just as Boaz was gracious in giving to Ruth."

Alexa seemed to listen with interest, but she didn't say anything.

Anna-Grace went on. "When I was much younger, I wished my parents had named me something more modern — like your name, Alexa. But once I learned the reason behind their choice, I began to love my old-fashioned name."

Alexa blinked twice, her face unreadable.

"I'm Alexa Joy, named for a nurse who took care of my mother and for the emotion Mom felt when she held me for the first time."

"That's beautiful." Anna-Grace crunched her brow, thinking. "Your mother is Aunt Abigail's oldest daughter, right?"

Alexa nodded, the motion slow and deliberate.

"Aunt Abigail is my grandmother's sister, so my dad and your mom are first cousins. That makes us first cousins once removed, if I remember correctly." She sighed. "And we're so close in age . . . It's too bad we didn't have a chance to get to know each other sooner. We probably would have had a lot of fun together, growing up." She smiled. "I'm glad we'll have some time now to get acquainted. And I don't want you to treat me like a guest in your B and B. I'm just a visiting relative, okay?"

Alexa inched toward the door. "I should go stir my stew and get the biscuits in the oven. Take as much time as you need to settle in, then come to the dining room. I'll have lunch hot and ready for you." She eased past Steven and clattered down the stairs.

■ ■ ■ ■

Alexa

Alexa careened around the corner and nearly plowed into Grandmother, who hadn't vacated her spot near the base of the stairs. She reared back, scrambling to catch her balance. "Grandmother! What are you doing there?"

"Eavesdropping." Grandmother's tart reply didn't surprise Alexa in the least. "And praying." Her second statement emerged with compassion. She tipped her head, furrows of concern marching across her forehead. "Are you all right?"

No, she wasn't all right. When Anna-Grace had started talking about familial relationships, she'd felt as though her chest would burst. She scurried behind her grandmother's chair, grabbed the handles, and wheeled Grandmother to the kitchen. She talked while she kneaded the dough and then patted it flat on the worktable's floured top.

"I can't decide if it would be better or worse for her to know what we know. I feel like I have to think so hard before I say anything that might give something away. It's making me not want to talk at all. And

that'll make her feel like I don't like her."
Did she like Anna-Grace? Initially she had.
This new knowledge hadn't changed who
Anna-Grace was, so she should still like her.
Alexa pushed her reflections aside and
continued. "But if she already knew, I'd feel
funny around her, too, because then she'd
know my mother is really *her* mother."

Grandmother wheeled close and took over
the task of pressing the biscuit cutter
through the soft dough. "I understand. It
was all I could do not to start bawling when
I hugged her today. My first hug as grandmother to granddaughter rather than great-
aunt to great-niece." Tears winked in Grandmother's eyes, but she blinked them away.
"I keep telling myself what happened twenty
years ago is done. Anna-Grace, legally, is
my great-niece, not my granddaughter, and
I must think of her the same way I have
since the beginning."

Alexa paused in transferring the circles of
dough to a cookie sheet. "But you've always
known Anna-Grace was your granddaughter. Even though Andrew and Olivia never
knew who gave them a baby, you did. How
did you keep it secret all those years?"

"Guilt kept me silent. Guilt for forcing
my young, frightened daughter to do what
she didn't want to do, all so I could save

face." The tears returned. One spilled down Grandmother's cheek. She smacked the wetness away and set her chin at a determined angle. "But it isn't guilt keeping me silent now. God forgave me and I've released the guilt. As much as I'd love to be able to claim her as my grandchild, I'll continue to call Anna-Grace my great-niece because it's what is best for her. I won't be selfish the way I was selfish with your mother. I learned what selfishness can cost."

Alexa caught her grandmother's hand. "Grandmother . . ." She almost felt like a fraud using the term, but what else could she call the mother of the woman who had raised her? "Is it selfish of me to wish I didn't know that I'm not really part of your family?"

A fierce scowl formed on Grandmother's face. She yanked on Alexa's hand — a hard, attention-demanding yank. "Don't you ever say something like that again. Do Andrew and Olivia call Anna-Grace and Sunny their non-daughters or their daughters? Blood doesn't matter one bit. What matters is the heart, and you are my Suzy's child in every way that matters."

"But . . ." Alexa crouched so she could be at eye level with the woman in the wheelchair. "Mom and I aren't the same as

Andrew and Olivia with their adopted daughters. Anna-Grace and Sunny legally belong. A court changed their names to Braun and made them an official part of the family. But I —" The ache that had tormented her over the past weeks intensified. "I don't belong to Mom. Not by birth, and not by any legal means. I'm not a Zimmerman. I don't know who I am."

Grandmother cupped Alexa's cheeks. Her hands, warm and dry and dusted with flour, offered comfort and strength. "You are our dearly loved Alexa Joy."

Alexa forced her trembling lips into a smile. "All right, Grandmother." She rose, put the biscuits in the oven, and went on with the lunch preparations as though she'd cast off her concerns so Grandmother wouldn't worry. But underneath the torment remained. Who was she? And where did she belong?

CHAPTER 25

Briley

Briley, car keys in one hand and his trusty electronic notebook in the other, headed across the grass and the last of the fallen leaves. For years he'd tromped along concrete sidewalks in Chicago, listening to the pound of his soles and the noise of traffic. The soft whisper of wind and the crunch of dried grass still took him by surprise. But not a bad surprise. As a matter of fact, he'd grown a little attached to the music of the prairie. But he hadn't mentioned it when he spoke to Len that morning. He'd set himself up for merciless teasing — much less good-natured than any of the banter he and Alexa had exchanged of late.

He came up even with the front of the house and spotted Steven's truck parked in front of the porch, almost on the walkway. His steps slowed. So Steven was back. Had he brought his fiancée, as he'd intended?

Briley made a mental note to take his camera to the house from now on so he could capture interactions between the pair, who were — of all the strange ways to put it — published to be married. Would a published couple in a Mennonite community behave like engaged couples on the outside?

He'd already determined they weren't cohabitating, which was different from many of the couples he knew. Steven would stay at his house, and his fiancée — what was her name again? — would stay here with Mrs. Zimmerman. He chuckled. That wily lady wouldn't allow any hanky-panky under her roof. She tolerated his sparring with her granddaughter. She even forgot herself and chuckled sometimes. But her hawk eyes watched him, and he knew if he stepped out of bounds, she'd come down on him worse than Aunt Myrt ever had.

Even so, he'd had great fun teasing with Alexa over the past week. She proved she could give as good as she got. She had a quick wit — never cruel, just snappish and fun. And her sense of humor! One day she left the wrapper on the cheese in his sandwich, and another time she put in a raw egg in place of a hard-boiled one. What a mess that had created when he cracked it on his knee. But all he could do was laugh while he plotted the next place to post a pic of her wide-eyed look of horror. The cost to print an even twenty copies of that photo was the best three dollars he'd ever spent. Maybe he'd ask Mrs. Zimmerman to help him out. She'd probably think of some really good spots.

He reached his car, and the slam of the front screen door pulled his attention to the porch. Steven trotted down the steps. Instead of climbing into his car, Briley turned around and jogged toward the younger man. "Hey, when did you get back?"

"About twenty minutes ago."

"Are you heading to the house now?" Briley had begun calling Steven's farmhouse by the same term Steven used. Strange that he never referred to it as "my" house. Maybe it was an Old Order thing — not wanting to sound possessive. He'd heard dozens of seriously uttered comments about how God received the credit for the blessings in their lives, the people seeming to forget they had to work plenty hard to hold on to those "blessings."

"After I eat some lunch." Steven opened the passenger-side door on the truck and reached inside. "Mrs. Zimmerman asked Anna-Grace and me to join her and Alexa."

Anna-Grace . . . that was her name. Briley jangled his keys. "I took Paul's box lunch to him this morning but didn't have Alexa make one for me." Robbing her of the opportunity to sneak something in on him. "Since you weren't here, I decided to do some other exploring today. So I'll probably join you at the house tomorrow if that's okay."

"Sure. That's fine, if you don't have anything else to do." Steven emerged from the truck cab with a plain brown purse in his hand.

Briley couldn't resist teasing. "Get yourself a new fashion accessory, did you?"

Steven's lips quirked into a half smile, half grimace. "Um, no. This belongs to Anna-Grace."

Briley laughed and slapped Steven's shoulder. "I already surmised that, my man. Just ribbing you."

Steven nodded. He gave the door a slam and turned toward the house. Then he angled his gaze at Briley. "What are you doing today?"

"Gonna hang out at the hardware store, do some people watching." And some listening. Not only to the words, but to the tones, reading between the words for deeper meanings. Hopefully he'd hear something that would smack of discontent. Len wasn't too happy about the lack of fodder he'd discovered thus far. In fact, his boss had muttered about wasted funds and time. If Briley didn't hurry up and uncover something, he might be pulled back early with no chance for that byline he wanted.

"Before you go, want to come in and meet Anna-Grace?"

Only an idiot would miss the pride in Steven's voice. And Briley might be a lot of things, but stupid wasn't one of them. He aimed his feet for the house. "Sure."

When they entered the house, the sound of laughter — light, trickling, relaxed — carried from the dining room followed by Mrs. Zimmerman's low-toned voice. Apparently Anna-Grace held the older woman's affection. Steven deposited Anna-Grace's purse on the first riser of the staircase, then accompanied Briley to the room where he'd taken nearly two dozen breakfasts as well as a couple Sunday dinners. The table was set for four, his regular place empty of a bowl and silverware.

Mrs. Zimmerman sat in her wheelchair beside the table, and Anna-Grace stood near the chair with her back to the doorway. At a glance Briley noted Steven's intended was slender, blond haired, and full-fledged

Mennonite from her little white mesh cap to her brown hose and oxfords. He prepared himself for her to be homely.

"Anna-Grace?" Steven touched her shoulder as he spoke, and she turned to him with a smile that could light up the darkest night.

Briley gave a start. Anna-Grace homely? Not even close. No wonder Steven spoke of her with such pride. With a little makeup and her hair hanging loose around her face, she'd be what Len called drop-dead gorgeous.

"I want you to meet Briley Forrester. He's the one who's been helping at the house."

Anna-Grace shifted her smile from Steven to Briley, but when their gazes collided, her lips quivered, her eyes widened, and she drew back slightly. "M-Mr. Forrester." She rubbed her palms along the skirt of her dark-blue dress and then hesitantly extended her hand to him. "It's good to meet you."

He shook her hand, trying not to stare. Partly because she was so china-doll pretty, but partly because something about her seemed vaguely familiar. "Likewise."

She withdrew her hand from his light grip and reached for Steven who linked fingers with her. Briley took note of the affectionate gesture while keeping his attention pinned on Anna-Grace. A weak smile continued to quiver on her rosy lips. "Steven t-told me you've been a big help at his house. Thank you."

"No problem. I enjoyed it."

Alexa entered the room, carrying a covered crockery bowl.

Briley slipped his notebook into the crook of his arm and added for Alexa's benefit, "It's kept me out of trouble." He watched her face for signs of amusement, but she didn't even glance at him before heading back through the short hallway to the kitchen. He frowned. He'd given her a perfect lead-in. Why hadn't she taken it?

Mrs. Zimmerman said, "We're going to sit down and have a bowl of stew and some home-baked biscuits. Would you like to join us, Briley? Alexa made plenty."

Her invitation tempted him. The kitchen at the Grace Notes B and B had to be one of the best-smelling places on earth. "Thank you, but I made plans for the afternoon, and I need to get going. I'll just grab a slice of pizza at the convenience store since *somebody*" — he raised his voice, determined for her to hear him — "didn't pack me a lunch today."

She whirled around the corner again, this time carrying a basket of beautifully browned biscuits and a fat jar of some sort of preserves — probably strawberry, judging by the color. She stuck her nose in the air. "That's because *somebody* didn't request a lunch for today. You must ask in order to receive." She turned on her heel and returned to the kitchen.

That was more like it! Briley laughed at her retreating back, then looked at Anna-Grace again. She was watching him, the corner of her lower lip caught between her teeth. He smiled, and a blush stole across her face. "It was nice to meet you, Miss —"

"Braun," all three of the other people in the room chorused.

"Miss Braun," Briley said, "enjoy your lunch. I'd better get going." With their farewells ringing in his ears, he headed for the door.

Anna-Grace

Anna-Grace held her breath until the front door closed behind Briley Forrester. Then she let out the air in one whoosh. She looked at Mrs. Zimmerman. "He's the reporter from Chicago Sandra told me about?"

"That's right."

She shook her head, the image of the man's dark, good looks strong in her mind.

"He's so" — she glanced at Steven and chose her words carefully — "young. For some reason I expected someone . . . older."

Alexa carried in a tray with a pitcher of tea and four ice-filled glasses. "Okay. Everything's here now. We can eat."

Steven held a chair for Anna-Grace, and she slid onto the seat. She looked up to thank him, and he surprised her by leaning down and placing a kiss on her temple. The thank-you got caught by a lump in her throat. She wished she could respond in kind, offering her lips, but not with an audience. And not until they'd exchanged vows.

While they ate, Aunt Abigail asked Steven several questions about the progress of the house. Even though Anna-Grace had pried similar information from him on the drive over, she still listened closely. As Steven spoke, she formed a picture in her head of the house and tried to imagine herself living there. The images were too fuzzy to take shape, her arrival in Arborville still too new. Maybe when she saw it in person it would be easier to envision herself making the old farmhouse and this little town her home.

Steven pushed his bowl aside and rose. "That was very good, Alexa. Thank you."

Alexa hadn't said two words the entire lunchtime, and she didn't answer Steven now, but she did offer a weak smile.

He gave one of Anna-Grace's white ribbons a light tug. "I'm heading to the house to work for the afternoon. Do you want to come with me, or would you rather stay here?"

Eagerness to see the house rolled through her, and she started to state her preference.

Aunt Abigail said, "Let her stay today. She can go over with you tomorrow morning after breakfast."

Anna-Grace swallowed her desire and sank back onto the seat.

Aunt Abigail went on, seemingly oblivious to Anna-Grace's disappointment. "I assume you'll join us for breakfast in the morning, Steven?"

He nodded. "Yes, ma'am. For as long as you're willing to put up with my presence, I'll keep coming back. And, Alexa, if you'd plan on putting together a sack lunch every day, I'll pay you at the end of the week for both meals."

"Sure. I can do that."

Aunt Abigail frowned. "We won't charge you for *breakfast.* We invited you to join us."

Anna-Grace thought Alexa made a sour face at Aunt Abigail's proclamation, but it disappeared so quickly she couldn't be sure. Alexa said, "Grandmother's right. Don't worry about breakfast. You're welcome to eat here with us and . . . Anna-Grace . . . until your kitchen is operable."

Steven grinned. "I won't argue. I might even ask Mr. Aldrich to delay finishing the kitchen just so I can keep coming over here. You always fix something good, Alexa."

A pang of jealousy stabbed through Anna-Grace. She caught Steven's hand. "As soon as your kitchen is done, I'll come over and cook for you. No sense in troubling Alexa."

Alexa bounced up and began collecting their empty bowls. "It's really no trouble. I have to cook for Bri— for Mr. Forrester, Grandmother, and me anyway. What's another two people around the table? But I understand if you'd like to cook for Steven, Anna-Grace, so the house will begin to feel like your home."

Steven stepped away from the table. "You decide what you want to do. For now, I'm leaving you here to visit with your aunt and get better acquainted with your cousin." He waved, his gaze bouncing across Alexa and Aunt Abigail before returning to Anna-Grace. A soft smile that seemed to hold a hint of sadness curved his lips. "I'll come see you this evening?"

Anna-Grace turned to her great-aunt. "Is that all right with you, Aunt Abigail?"

"Fine as spiderwebbing."

Steven laughed. "All right then. After supper, Anna-Grace . . ."

She waited until the front door closed behind him before rising and reaching for the scattered silverware. "Let me help you, Alexa."

"No need. It's my job."

"But I don't mind helping."

"You're a *guest,* Anna-Grace."

Anna-Grace scooped up the spoons and held them tight in her fist. "Please? I'd rather be treated like a member of the family than like a guest." Her heart caught at her statement. She wanted to be a family member both in name and blood. Maybe if she focused on her adoptive family, she'd think less about the unknown blood relations who lived somewhere outside of these farmhouse walls.

Aunt Abigail chuckled. "Well, it appears both of you are in possession of the Zimmerman stubbornness. I'll let you two battle it out." She wheeled her chair into the living room.

Anna-Grace looked at Alexa.

Alexa looked back. Finally she heaved a sigh. "All right. If you want to help, I won't argue."

Anna-Grace smiled. "Good." She placed

the spoons in one of the glasses and followed Alexa into the kitchen. "While we're cleaning up, we can do what Steven said — get better acquainted."

Alexa's long denim skirt and royal-blue sweater told Anna-Grace the girl hadn't joined the Old Order church. Which meant she was free to pursue relationships with men outside of the Mennonite faith. The way she and Briley Forrester had joked with each other made Anna-Grace wonder if a romance might be blooming between the two. As soon as she felt comfortable with this cousin, she would ask.

CHAPTER 26

Steven

Steven entered the house through the back door, and an intense chemical smell nearly sent him running for cover. Ick! Pinching his nose, he made himself move through the small mudroom and into the kitchen. Sawhorses filled the middle of the floor, with cabinet doors laid flat on the wooden frames. Paul Aldrich stood amid the sea of doors, a can balanced on one hand and a small brush in the other.

He looked over when Steven entered and broke into a wide smile. "Hey. You're back."

How could he look so happy when the odor was strong enough to send an elephant to its knees? "Uh-huh." His voice came out nasally. He released his nose, then grimaced. "Is it okay if I open the window?" If he didn't clear some of the smell, he wouldn't be able to work in here today. Already a headache began to form in the center of his forehead.

"I opened one in the front room."

A cross breeze would take more of the smell out. "What about this one?" Steven pointed to the square window above the sink.

"That window looks north." Mr. Aldrich slid the brush along a cabinet door from top to bottom in one smooth sweep. "The way the wind's blowing, it'll bring dust into the house. Don't want anything to mar the surface of these doors."

Steven put his hand over his mouth and nose and moved closer. He didn't like the smell in the room, but he had to admit the doors looked great. Mr. Aldrich had suggested a honey-oak stain, not too dark but not too light. Steven had little experience in choosing stains, so he'd told the carpenter to use his own discretion. The cabinets were only inexpensive pine, unfinished, ready-mades, but thanks to the carpenter's careful sanding and added embellishments, they looked better than Steven would have imagined.

He watched the older man draw another line of varnish, the path as smooth and shiny as ice on a pond. "You were right. That stain is perfect."

"Thank you." Mr. Aldrich went on working as he spoke. "I mix it myself. When you're working with pine, it can be a little tricky not to go too dark. It's a softer wood, so it absorbs faster than oak. But if you get the color right, it can look just as pretty as oak or cherry for a lot less expense." He paused and shot a scowl in Steven's direction. "What are you planning to do today?"

Steven backed away several feet. The stink followed. "Finish sanding the walls in the second bedroom. The Spackle ought to be dry enough since it sat all weekend. Now that Anna-Grace is here, she can pick out paint colors. I hope to start painting tomorrow."

Mr. Aldrich's hand paused for a moment, and his forehead pinched into sharp lines. Not lines of thought, but the way a person grimaced from pain. "She's staying at the B and B, is that right?"

Steven nodded. "Yes."

The man lifted his face toward the east — the direction of the Zimmerman farmhouse — as if searching for something. Then he turned with a jerk of his neck to the cabinet door and dipped his brush. "Could I talk you into holding off?" His hand trembled slightly, and the line of wet varnish formed a squiggle.

"Why?"

"No matter how hard you try to block it, the fine dust from the Spackle finds its way out of the room. These cabinet doors need to be completely dry before you do any sanding."

Steven stifled a huff of displeasure. The sooner he got the place finished, the sooner it could go on the market. If Anna-Grace agreed. *Let her agree* . . . "How long?"

"I'd give it a good twenty-four hours at least."

So tomorrow afternoon . . . "Is there anything I can work on in here today then?"

Mr. Aldrich paused, worrying his lower lip between his teeth. "You really need to finish the sanding and get all the dust cleaned out of the house before you start painting or putting the tile in the bathroom or just about anything else. That dust wreaks havoc on nearly every project."

"I guess I'll work outside today then." With Briley's help, he'd cleared the over-grown brush from around the foundations of the house and barn and cut down several sapling trees that had sprung up in odd places around the yard, but the garden area still needed clearing. Weeds had overgrown the spot. Working outside would take him away from the pungent stink that was making his head throb. He inched toward the mudroom, careful not to bump any of the wet cabinet doors.

When he reached the mudroom doorway, Mr. Aldrich spoke. "Will Anna-Grace only choose the colors, or will she help you paint the rooms?"

They hadn't discussed her involvement beyond selecting shades for the walls, but if he knew Anna-Grace — and he knew her pretty well — she'd want to wield a brush. "She'll be helping."

The man nodded slowly. "Okay. Remember, don't plan on painting until you've got all the dust cleared out. That'll take a couple of days for sure — it tends to settle over time, so you'll need to clean, leave, then clean again." He paused, swallowed, then went on almost as if he'd forgotten Steven was listening. "So Thursday. She'll be here working on Thursday." His hand visibly quivered as he dipped the brush into the can.

Had inhaling the varnish fumes made him wobbly? "Are you all right?"

"What? Oh. Yes, I'm fine." Mr. Aldrich coughed out a short laugh. "Just thinking about what I'll be doing in here on Thursday. Probably putting in the tile backsplash." He frowned. "Are you planning to stay in Arborville on the weekends, or will you go back to Sommerfeld?"

"I only went back this past weekend to get Anna-Grace. We both plan to stay here now until the house is finished."

"So you'll work . . . on Saturday?"

He wanted this project done. "Probably."

"And Anna-Grace, too?"

"I'd say yes."

Another frown. "Do you mind if I bring my son along with me on Saturday? Would he be . . . underfoot?"

The boy had joined his dad on previous Saturdays. Steven liked Danny — a polite boy who asked lots of questions and then listened intently to the answers. He'd enjoyed chatting with the youngster. "It's fine with me."

"And it wouldn't bother Anna-Grace to have him here?" He drew the question out, as if it were difficult to form the words.

Steven shrugged, puzzled by the man's odd behavior. "Why would it?"

"Just making sure." Now Mr. Aldrich spoke briskly. He turned his attention to the cabinet door and scraped the brush on the edge of the can. "I'd better get busy on these things. I want to varnish the cabinets for the bathroom, too, before I leave today, even though it'll be a while before we can put them into place in there."

Steven took that as a hint to get out of the way. He left the house and headed for the barn, where he stored his tools. He lifted the rake from its hook and propped it on his shoulder, but then he stood still and replayed Paul Aldrich's reaction to the news that Anna-Grace would work at the house. He hadn't seemed pleased. And he acted hesitant to have his son around her.

Steven frowned, remembering Alexa Zimmerman's less-than-enthusiastic welcome that morning even though Mrs. Zimmerman appeared happy to have Anna-Grace with them. How would others in the community respond to her presence? Would they accept her as readily as they'd accepted him, or would they hold themselves aloof?

He set off for the garden, his thoughts seesawing with each clomp of his foot against the hard ground. *Accept* her, *reject* her, *accept* her, *reject* her . . . As his left boot reached the edge of the garden plot, his mind reverberated with *reject* her. An unexpected twinge of protectiveness pinched his chest. Rejection would hurt her, and he didn't want her hurt. Yet if people shied away from her, she'd be more likely to want to live elsewhere, more likely to approve his desire to do something other than farm for a living.

He hung his head. *I know I'm cowardly, Lord, not telling my parents I don't want to be a farmer, but how can I tell them without disappointing them? It's got to be Anna-Grace who decides she can't live here. Dad and Mom will understand if it's too hard for her.* He lifted the rake high and then drove the forked tines into the tangle of weeds. He gave a mighty yank, tearing the weeds from the soil. He shook the dried stems loose, then aimed another blow. His jaw clamped tight, his muscles straining, he finished his prayer. *But don't let her be hurt too badly, please? It isn't fair that no matter what I do, somebody I love has to suffer.*

Alexa

How frustrating to have Anna-Grace traipsing around in the kitchen, opening cabinet doors and putting things away as if she owned the place. The prickle of resentment took Alexa by surprise. She'd anticipated feeling awkward around the girl who'd grown in her mother's womb, but she hadn't expected to battle anger. But that's exactly what burned in her chest — anger. She bit down on the end of her tongue to prevent telling Anna-Grace to get out of her kitchen, out of her house, out of her family's affection.

Dear Lord, help me . . .

Anna-Grace clicked the silverware drawer closed and turned a smile on Alexa. "All done." She glanced around. "With all the people in here for Aunt Abigail's party, I didn't get a chance to really see the kitchen. It's so different from the way I remember it as a little girl when my family visited. Did the carpenter working on Steven's house do this kitchen, too?"

Alexa swallowed against the knot in her throat. She feigned great interest in hanging the tea towel just so over its bar. "Mm-hm. It was a big mess for a long time. He pulled everything out, lowered the height of the counters so Grandmother could reach them from her wheelchair, and reconfigured the design. Even though it was all planned with Grandmother's needs in mind, it works well for me, too, in cooking for guests. I'm very happy with it."

"I can see why." Anna-Grace wandered to the baking center and slid her fingers along the butcher-block top. "I really like this area. I wonder if the kitchen in Steven's house will have something like this."

She knew it was spiteful, and guilt descended with the thought, but Alexa hoped the kitchen at the Meiers farm was nothing like the one Paul Aldrich had constructed here. She turned and leaned against the counter. "I usually take Grandmother in to do our grocery shopping on Monday afternoon." Saturdays were hectic in Arborville with out-of-towners, local farmers, and townsfolk descending on the shops. Grandmother's wheelchair and the busy aisles weren't a good combination, so they preferred the quieter weekday. "Would you like to stay here and rest after your drive?" She knew she should offer the option of coming to town, too, but she needed a little distance. Some time alone with Grandmother. A touch of normalcy to face the uncomfortable changes to which she'd opened the door but now found difficult to accept.

Anna-Grace smiled brightly. "Actually, I'd like to see the town. Steven drove straight out here, so I didn't get more than a passing glance."

Alexa's lips twitched with the effort not to laugh. "I think you'll discover you don't need much more than a passing glance when it comes to Arborville. There's not a lot to the town."

"Oh, I know it's very small. Before my great-grandparents died, we came to Arborville every year for Christmas and again each summer for a short visit. I was pretty young when we stopped making the yearly trips, though, so my memories are fuzzy."

"Probably because there isn't much to remember." Alexa hadn't intended to be snide, but her tone emerged on a sarcastic note. Anna-Grace's smile faded. Her hurt reaction stung Alexa. She found herself adding, much more kindly, "We're just going to the grocery store, but you're welcome to come along, if you'd like."

Her smile returned. "I would. I'll go get a sweater." She darted off.

Alexa rolled her eyes and clunked her forehead with the heel of her hand. Why had she agreed? Hadn't she decided she needed a little separation? But she couldn't deny some of her guilt had dissolved when she'd asked Anna-Grace to join her and Grandmother.

Grandmother set her handwork aside when Alexa came into the front room. "Have you finished in the kitchen?"

"It's all spick-and-span." Alexa forced a cheerfulness she didn't feel. "Are you ready for your Monday afternoon excursion?"

"I sure am. Anna-Grace went upstairs to wash her face and recomb her hair. She said she felt mussed." Grandmother chuckled. "I think she wants to present herself well to whoever we encounter today."

Alexa glanced down the length of her

sweater and skirt. She'd worn an apron in the kitchen, but a tiny dot of gravy decorated her skirt, and her sweater showed a slight smudge of flour from the biscuits. She brushed at the flour. "Maybe I should change."

Grandmother waved her hand. "Oh, you're fine, Alexa." She wheeled her chair to the piano, where her purse waited on the keyboard cover. "It'll be a treat for me, having two girls along today. After today Anna-Grace will probably spend her days at the Meiers farm, or I guess I need to start calling it the Braun farm. So I intend to make the most of this outing."

She peeked inside her purse. "I've got enough cash for us to have a treat at the quilt shop's soda counter. I'd also like to take Anna-Grace on a little tour of the town, point out the house where my sister and I lived when we were girls and the school where her pare —" She stopped, shook her head hard, and started again. "Where the local children attend class. Just to help her become familiar with everything."

No one had offered Alexa such a tour when she came to town. Jealousy poked her, and she shrugged its persistent prickle away. "I'm sure she'll appreciate it."

"She has a history here. Even though she

354

isn't aware of her full connection, I want her to *see* the town." Tears winked in Grandmother's pale-blue eyes. "I want to be the one to show it to her."

The patter of footsteps on the staircase alerted them to Anna-Grace's return. Grandmother brushed her fingertips across her eyes and put on a smile.

Anna-Grace breezed around the corner, her hair neatly swept under her cap and a light-blue sweater over her dress. "I'm ready!"

"Give me a push to the car, Anna-Grace."

Alexa held back a disgruntled huff. She always pushed Grandmother's chair to the car.

With a little giggle Anna-Grace darted behind the chair and took hold of the handles. "Here we go." She rolled Grandmother through the little vestibule and, after a little juggling to prop the door open, onto the porch.

Alexa followed the pair. She yanked her jacket from its hook and jammed her arms into the sleeves, punching her fist through the openings. Then she slung her purse strap over her shoulder and tromped down the steps while Anna-Grace and Grandmother made use of the ramp. She hurried across the yard to the car with Grandmother's comment — *"She has a history here"* — tormenting her.

She might be the one to call Abigail Zimmerman "Grandmother," but Anna-Grace was already being claimed as the grandchild. More than ever Alexa recognized that her history was rooted somewhere else.

CHAPTER 27

Briley

From his perch on the hardware store's windowsill, Briley observed Anna-Grace Braun pushing Mrs. Zimmerman up the sidewalk on the opposite side of the street. Alexa trailed behind. The older woman and her great-niece appeared to laugh and talk, but Alexa's lips remained in a sullen line — unusual for the girl. He'd seen her be serious but rarely sullen. His reporter instincts kicked up a notch.

The gray-haired Old Order man and the store's clerk, who'd been leaning against the tall counter and chatting about casual topics for the past half hour, suddenly fell silent. Briley flicked a look in their direction. Their gazes seemed to follow the three women, and not until the trio entered the quilt shop did they start talking again.

"Do you suppose that's the girl who's published to the Brungardt boy?" the customer asked.

"*Ja.* I imagine it is."

The man clicked his tongue on his teeth. "I wonder at her parents, sending her over here already when the two of them aren't married yet. It's a sure way to open the door to temptation."

Briley laid the notebook on his knee and began transcribing their conversation while pretending to pay no attention to them.

The clerk released a throaty chuckle. "Oh, now, she's staying with Abigail Zimmerman at the bed-and-breakfast her granddaughter started. Aldrich says the boy lives at the farm even without a stick of furniture out there. I figure Mrs. Zimmerman will make sure that mile between the two farmsteads is an adequate barrier to them getting into trouble."

"She didn't do so well with her own daughter, now did she?" A hint of recrimination entered the older man's tone. "That granddaughter who showed up last spring is proof of it."

The clerk cleared his throat. "I don't think we should talk about that, Irwin. It was a long time ago, and it's God's place to judge, not ours."

"I'm not judging," Irwin said, "just stating facts. There's no husband, and she's got a daughter, so she fell from grace. And right under her mother's nose."

The clerk muttered something else, but he lowered his voice and Briley couldn't hear. But he didn't need to hear anything else. They'd said enough to stir his interest. He could pursue the topic elsewhere on his own.

Tucking his notebook under his arm, he rose, faced the men, and touched his forehead in a mock tip-of-a-hat. The two nodded in reply, and he left the store, cringing at the loud clatter of the cowbell hanging above the door. There were no cars coming, so he darted directly across the street and entered the quilt shop.

He ignored the curious look from the woman behind the counter and marched through the shop, turning his gaze right and left in search of Mrs. Zimmerman, Alexa, and Anna-Grace. He found them in the far corner where three round metal tables and chairs with bent wire frames created a little sitting area. The women sat around one of the tables, sharing a banana split.

He grinned and ambled over. "Well, look at that. Who would have guessed you could buy ice cream in a fabric store."

"It's one of the best-kept secrets in town." Mrs. Zimmerman spooned up the blob of whipped topping holding a bright-red mara-schino cherry. "I'm surprised, though, that you didn't discover it, given your examina-tion of every store in town over the past weeks."

Her statement let him know the towns-people had been talking about his prowling and picture taking. Briley laughed, not insulted in the least. "I admit, I should've found it by now. But this is the one store I never entered. I just peeked in the window. All I could see were bolts of cloth, and, no offense, that didn't interest me much."

"Sometimes you have to look deeper to see what's really there."

Briley processed the woman's statement. Had she intended to present a double meaning or was she only making small talk? He decided on the latter. "Now that I've seen what's really here, I think I'll order a banana split for myself. It looks great."

"Order over there." Mrs. Zimmerman pointed to a bar straight from the old cowboy movies, complete with tall stools and a low brass rail where a person could rest his feet. He whipped out his notebook, clicked the camera app, and took two snapshots before swaggering over to the bar. He propped one boot on the rail and bounced the peg in an old dome-shaped brass bell. Several hollow jangles rang. The same woman who'd watched him from behind the counter on the fabric side of the store bustled over and asked what he'd like.

He jammed his thumb over his shoulder and drawled, "I'll have what they're having." A snort and a giggle erupted behind him, and he didn't even have to look to know Alexa released the snort and Anna-Grace the giggle. He acted as though he hadn't heard a thing and slid onto one of the stools. The padded seat rotated, so he turned to face the little table and rested his elbow on the scarred wooden counter. "Are you ladies painting the town?"

Mrs. Zimmerman pursed her lips. "That's hardly an appropriate question, Mr. Forrester."

He grinned. "Sorry, Mrs. Z." He'd never abbreviated her name before, but this setting — the century-old counter, the little tables, the informality of the three of them dripping chocolate, strawberry, and butterscotch sauces across the table's top — inspired a casual approach. "I'll rephrase. Are you two giving Miss Braun here the full nickel tour of Arborville?"

Anna-Grace answered. "Aunt Abigail had Alexa drive me by the house where my grandmother lived as a little girl. We also went by the school, the church, and the cemetery. Now we're going into each store so I can become familiar with what's available in case I end up living here."

In case? Briley dove on the statement. "I thought you and Steven intended to live here after you get married."

Alexa and Mrs. Zimmerman looked at Anna-Grace in puzzlement, too. The girl's face turned pink. She gave a one-shoulder shrug. "We haven't completely decided yet. We're still . . . praying about it."

Alexa leaned in. "Why fix up the farmhouse if you're not going to live in it? That doesn't make sense."

If Briley wasn't mistaken, Alexa seemed more pleased than perplexed.

"Steven says the house will fetch a better price if it's fixed up."

Mrs. Zimmerman slapped her spoon onto the table. "Well, of course you're going to live in it. Why go to all that work for someone else?"

"We're just not sure yet." Anna-Grace fidgeted in her chair. "We'll decide after the house is all done."

"Here you are, sir." The store worker slid a boat-shaped glass dish in front of Briley. "Anything else? Something to drink?"

The scoops of ice cream were the size of

362

baseballs, and the toppings oozed over the sides. He'd never seen a bigger banana split. "No, thanks. This is perfect." He picked up the long spoon and chose chocolate smothered in marshmallow sauce for his first bite. The sweetness filled his mouth, and he gave the worker an approving smile. She smiled in reply and headed back to the other side of the store.

The interruption offered the opportunity to shift topics. He knew what he wanted to pursue. "So, Miss Braun, tell me a little bit about yourself. You're from Sommerfeld, yes? Is your father a farmer like Steven?"

"No, Dad builds stained-glass windows." The girl licked her spoon and set it aside. "He's a very good artist. You'll find his windows in churches all over Kansas, Nebraska, and Oklahoma."

The little church where the Zimmermans and Paul Aldrich attended had clear glass windows. "That's a unique occupation for someone of your religious sect."

"I suppose. But he loves it."

"Does your mom have a job? Outside of the home, I mean." After watching Aunt Myrt labor at homemaking and raising a half-dozen kids who weren't her own, he wouldn't presume taking care of a house and children wasn't *work*.

"No, not officially, although she does take in sewing now and then. But that's mostly because she enjoys it so much."

"I see." He paused long enough to take another bite, this one of strawberry, which tasted a bit tart after the chocolate. "Alexa, your mom is a nurse — I remember someone saying that. But I don't think I've ever heard what your dad does."

She clattered her spoon into the empty bowl and rose. Her focus on her grandmother and cousin, she pushed in her chair. "Are you ready to go grocery shopping now? We should probably get to it since I'll need to start supper in a little over an hour. The pork chops I laid out need to slow bake for ninety minutes."

"Then let's go," Mrs. Zimmerman said.

The three gathered their things. Anna-Grace offered a weak smile and wave in parting, but Alexa took hold of the handles on Mrs. Zimmerman's wheelchair and pushed her away without even glancing in Briley's direction. He watched them depart, his ice cream forgotten. Twice before he'd seen the opportunities for a good story escape him. The Zimmermans had accepted without a fuss losing the land they'd rented for years. They also seemed accepting of Alexa, receiving her into the fellowship even though she didn't adhere to the dress code. But this subject — the subject of Alexa's parentage — had the potential to break the facade of perfection.

Apparently an Old Order Mennonite girl had not only given birth out of wedlock, but she'd decided to keep and raise the child. In a religious group that touted traditional values, her choice was far outside the accepted dictates. And according to the man in the hardware store, people hadn't forgotten. He could build an entire story around the Zimmerman woman who "fell from grace," as Irwin had said.

He tossed a few bills onto the counter to pay for his uneaten ice cream, then hurried out of the shop and to his car. Once he was inside and behind the steering wheel, he pulled out his cell phone and jabbed the button to speed dial Len. His boss answered on the second ring.

"Len, I've got it. They're not so squeaky clean after all. Listen to what I found out . . ."

Anna-Grace

Anna-Grace sat in the backseat of Aunt Abigail's car and listened to her aunt and cousin talk, but she didn't contribute. If she tried to talk, she'd probably end up crying instead. She wanted to go home. She wanted to go home *now.*

When Briley Forrester asked about her mom and dad, she'd answered honestly, images of Andrew and Olivia Braun strong in her mind. But then he'd questioned Alexa, forcing her to admit with action rather than words her status as an illegitimate child, and her stomach had begun to churn. Only strength of will prevented her from losing her share of the banana split. Back in Sommerfeld in her top dresser drawer rested letters from her birth mother and father. If they gave her away, it was almost a certainty they weren't married when she came into the world. Which meant she bore the label "illegitimate," too.

The car hit a bump, and she clasped her hands over her stomach. *Don't throw up. Don't throw up!* She brought herself under control, and that unpleasant title returned to taunt her. Why hadn't she ever considered such a thing before? Probably because Mom and Dad were such stellar members of the community, and in the eyes of everyone in Sommerfeld, she was theirs. But here in Arborville her father resided. And her mother's family still lived. She might have passed some of them on the street today without even knowing it.

She closed her eyes and tried to envision the few people they'd encountered during their time in town. Had any seemed uncomfortable to meet her? Had any seemed especially mindful of her? They'd shown various levels of friendliness, some more shy than others, but she couldn't recall any out-of-the-ordinary reactions when Aunt Abigail introduced her as her great-niece. So in all likelihood she'd managed to make it through today without crossing paths with one of her relatives.

But now that she'd been reminded of how small Arborville really was — Aunt Abigail said the town's population was less than seven hundred — she would come face-to-face with them eventually. She didn't know who her parents were, but they knew her or they wouldn't have been able to send those letters.

Her stomach was spinning again. She leaned forward and tapped Alexa on the shoulder. "How much farther to the house?"

Alexa met her gaze in the rearview mirror. "About five minutes." She frowned, her gaze flicking between the mirror and the dirt road. "Are you all right?"

"I feel kind of sick." She released a half cry, half laugh. "The ice cream isn't settling very well."

"Do you want me to stop?"

"No." Anna-Grace swallowed. "I'll be fine. I just need to . . . to . . ." She needed to go back in time before Mom and Dad gave her that envelope of letters so she could be blissfully ignorant again.

"Pull over, Alexa." Aunt Abigail barked the order.

Alexa slowed the car and pulled off to the side, the crunch of the tires on the gravel becoming a hollow sound as two wheels met the grassy ditch. She put the car in Park but left the engine running. Alexa turned sideways and sent a sympathetic look into the backseat. "Maybe if you get out and walk around a little bit — you know, pull in some big breaths of air — it'll help. Want me to get out with you?"

How comical. One illegitimate child reaching out to another. For some reason, a memory surfaced from years ago, even before Sunny came along. Their family had gone to the mall in Wichita and she became separated from her parents. A huge display of televisions — something alien in her small corner of the world — captured her attention, and she stopped to gawk at the images projected on the screens. One of the channels was tuned to a talk show, the guests a woman and three men who intended to find out, on live television, which of the men had fathered the woman's child. Mom found her and yanked her away, scolding, "Anna-Grace, for shame." At the time she'd thought watching the television was the shame, but now she wondered if the shame was really the uncertainty of parentage.

She and Alexa could form a club. The "Who's Your Daddy?" club. A hysterical laugh built in Anna-Grace's throat. "No. Stay put." She threw the door open and staggered across the road to the opposite ditch, away from the car's exhaust, and lifted her face toward the wind. As Alexa had suggested, she drew in great drafts of cool air, filling her nose with the potpourri of rich soil, decaying leaves, and a hint of wood smoke, probably from an Amish farmer's wood-burning stove. The tactic worked. Her stomach calmed, and the sick feeling faded.

But she stayed in place for several more minutes, letting the wind tug at her skirt and sweater and toss the ribbons from her cap over her shoulders. If she spread her arms, would the wind pick her up and carry her back to Sommerfeld where she could pretend she had no other parents than Mom and Dad?

A cloud of dust rose from the road in the east. Another car was coming. She jogged across the road and opened the door to slide into Aunt Abigail's backseat, but when the vehicle's nose topped the rise, Anna-Grace recognized the dark-green truck. She threw both arms in the air and waved them in a wild bid for the driver to stop. The moment it came to a halt she raced to the driver's side and pressed her hands to the glass.

"Steven!"

CHAPTER 28

Anna-Grace

Unshed tears distorted her view of Steven's dear face.

He rolled down the window and reached out to touch her cheek. "What's the matter?" The concern in his voice increased her desire to cry.

She gulped several times, swallowing the sobs that strained for release, and gathered her thoughts. The longing to go home was still strong, but looking into his worried face sent the selfish desire scuttling for cover. How could she have forgotten the work he'd done on the house? How could she have forgotten so quickly the reason she'd come? She couldn't run home right away. She had to at least give herself a chance to settle in.

"Anna-Grace?"

Instead of begging him to take her home, she told a half-truth. "I'm homesick."

A crooked smile appeared on his lips.

"Already? It hasn't even been a full day."

"I know." She forced a short laugh. It sounded strained, but he didn't appear to notice. "Silly, huh?"

He shook his head, amusement glinting in his eyes. "Maybe an excursion will take your mind off of it. Do you want to go to the hardware store with me, see what kind of cabinet handles they have?"

"Let me ask Aunt Abigail." She trotted to the car. Alexa had already rolled down the window, so she stooped over and addressed her great-aunt. "Steven is going to look at cabinet handles and asked if I could go along."

Aunt Abigail waved one hand and blew out a little breath. "You don't need my permission. Go if you want to."

"Thank you!"

Alexa said, "Will you be back in time for supper?"

Anna-Grace straightened and called to Steven. "What about supper?"

"I'll have you back in time."

Aunt Abigail hollered, "Come eat with us, too, Steven."

He raised his hand in reply.

"I'll see you later then, Aunt Abigail. Bye, Alexa." Anna-Grace scampered around to the passenger side of the truck and climbed in. She sank into the buttery soft seat as Steven put the vehicle in gear and pulled forward. He reached across the center console for her hand. She linked fingers with him and released a slow breath, tension easing with the gesture. She hadn't realized how uptight she'd been over the past few hours until she relaxed in Steven's stalwart presence.

Eager to put the worrisome thoughts to rest, she adopted a cheery tone. "I figured you'd stay out at your house until evening since you didn't go over until after lunch. Are you finished for the day already?"

"I couldn't work inside, so I raked out all the weeds from the garden plot. It only took a few hours."

"Why couldn't you work inside?"

"Paul Aldrich, the carpenter, was varnishing cabinet doors and wouldn't let me stir up dust."

She turned slightly in the seat so she could look at him while they talked. "He redid the kitchen at Aunt Abigail's house, and it's so homey yet functional. I can hardly wait to see what the kitchen in your house looks like. When will I get to see it?"

He worked his jaw back and forth. "Well . . . probably Thursday."

Disappointment struck. "Not until then?"

He sent her a brief, apologetic look. "I don't think you'll want to be over there until we finish sanding the Sheetrock and clear out the dust. Mr. Aldrich said as much, too."

What would she do with herself until Thursday? Alexa didn't seem to welcome her assistance in the kitchen, and Aunt Abigail and Alexa had a routine in which Anna-Grace had no part. "I really would like to see the place, Steven." She squeezed his hand and begged with her eyes. "Just a quick tour? Not to do any work or get in the way or anything, but just see what it looks like?"

"You're a pest." He laughed as he said it, letting her know he wasn't perturbed.

She loved the two tiny creases that appeared at the corners of his eyes when he smiled or laughed. Ever since his parents gave him the farmstead, she'd seen less of his smile. She wanted to encourage its return. So she affected a mock pout and fluttered her eyelashes. "Only one peek, ple-e-ease?"

He shook his head, chuckling under his breath. "All right. After we've looked at cabinet door handles, if it isn't too late, we'll go by the house before I take you back to your aunt's. But we'll have to be careful not to touch the cabinet doors. The varnish is still wet."

The hardware store in town only had a half-dozen varieties of handles for cabinet doors, but Anna-Grace found a scrolled design finished in antique brass she liked. Steven counted out the number needed and paid for them. She held the sack in her lap as they drove to the farmstead. The weight against her legs gave her a comforting feeling, as if she were contributing toward something important.

Steven pulled off the paved highway onto the same gravel road that led to Aunt Abigail's. But three miles in, he turned again. She sat on the edge of the seat, searching ahead for the first glimpse of the farm Steven's parents signed over to him. Her heart pounded, and a dozen half-formed images crowded her head. She'd envisioned the place so many times. She could hardly wait to see if the real thing matched the pictures she'd conjured.

Up ahead a huge barn, its roof a patchwork of old and new shingles and its wood siding bearing a coat of dark-red paint, stood tall and proud on a cleared expanse of ground. She pointed. "Is that your barn?"

"That's it." Steven spoke quietly, as if his voice was an intrusion.

"Where's the house?"

"You can't see it from this angle. The barn hides it."

She tipped sideways, her hands tight on the bag of cabinet handles to keep it from sliding off her lap, and strained for a glimpse of the house. But it remained hidden until the truck rolled past the barn and onto a dirt lane. When she finally saw it, she understood why it wanted to hide behind the barn.

Steven parked the truck and turned off the engine. He curled his hands around the steering wheel and gazed out the front window, his lips set in an unsmiling line. "That's the house."

Anna-Grace examined it by increments, letting her gaze drift from the wooden shingles to the peeling siding, age-weathered gingerbread trims, and warped porch rails. After seeing Aunt Abigail's beautifully painted two-story, this one seemed more like a shack. She fought disappointment. She'd expected small. She knew it had sat empty for many years. But she still wasn't prepared for the reality of it. Sympathy swelled in her chest. Such a sad-looking little house, long neglected and sorely in need of tender loving care.

"I know it doesn't look like much on the outside."

She resisted nodding in agreement.

"I haven't done any work on the exterior yet. But the inside's coming along." He finally turned toward her. "Do you still want to go in?"

If the inside proved as sorry as the outside, she might have nightmares. But he'd driven her over for a peek, and she would take it. "Yes. Let's go."

He slid out, then trotted around the front to open her door for her. She handed him the bag of handles before climbing down. Together, they crossed the hard ground and stepped onto the porch. The boards creaked, and Anna-Grace froze in place. Would the floor collapse?

Steven shot her a weak smile. "Don't worry. It sounds worse than it is."

She formed a glib reply. "Mom always says a creaky floor means a place has character."

He chuckled. "Well, then, this place has more than its fair share of character." He twisted the tarnished brass doorknob, and the door groaned on its hinges. He ushered Anna-Grace over the threshold and punched a button on the wall right inside the door. Light from an old, four-arm, pressed-tin chandelier flickered and then flooded the room.

Anna-Grace moved gingerly across the

floor until she stood directly beneath the antique light fixture. She turned in a slow circle, taking in the unpainted plaster walls marked with crooked whitish paths where he'd apparently patched cracks. Tall base-boards, at least ten inches high, stretched along the bottom edge of each wall. Crown molding in the same pattern as the trim above the windows — embossed with a row of alternating ovals and arrows — high-lighted the place where the walls met the ceiling. Her gaze dropped to the floor, where four-inch wide boards created a basket-weave pattern that ended with a square in the middle of the room.

She looked at Steven in complete relief. "This is charming." Her voice echoed, as though she stood in an underground cavern.

His eyebrows rose. "You think so?"

"I do." She meant it, too. Even though it was far from finished, she could see the potential. "Will you show me the rest of it?"

He led her into a short but wide hallway. Single doors both right and left stood ajar, and she peeked into what were obviously bedrooms. He'd taken up residence in the one on the left. Boxes lined one wall, and a mattress with rumpled blankets sat under the window. "There are just these two bedrooms, and they're both pretty small."

He sounded so apologetic, she experienced the need to reassure him even though the rooms were much smaller than the ones at Aunt Abigail's. "I think they're a nice size. Close to the size of my room at home."

The door at the end of the hallway was closed, but he opened it and then stepped aside. "This is the bathroom."

She moved into the stark space. White plastic pipes stuck up from the floor in two different locations, and a wadded towel filled a hole.

Steven leaned against the doorjamb. "The plumber's already changed out the old lead pipes. They were in pretty bad shape. The sink, stool, and bathtub are in boxes out in the barn. Mr. Aldrich — he's the carpenter, remember? — said we've got to do the walls, floor, and ceiling before we bring the fixtures in."

She frowned. "Is there another bathroom?"

"No."

"Well, if there's no working toilet, where . . ."

"I use the outhouse."

She gawked at him, horrified.

"And I use the pump in the barn to bathe."

"Oh, Steven . . ."

He slung his arm across her shoulders and tugged her tight to his side. "It's not so bad. As soon as the kitchen is finished, Mr. Aldrich will get started on the bathroom. I should have a toilet and tub in another week. Maybe two. I can manage that long."

When she returned to the B and B, she would ask Aunt Abigail if Steven could rent one of the empty rooms. He'd catch pneumonia, bathing in cold water from a pump in the barn!

"Do you want to see the kitchen now?"

"It's not as empty as the bathroom, is it?" The bare spaces were a little depressing.

"No, the original kitchen only had one short stretch of cabinets, which were falling apart. So instead of rebuilding them, Paul took everything out and started over with new. It's actually pretty close to done."

"Then I definitely want to see it." She followed Steven with an eager bounce in her step. She hoped the kitchen would be as nice, or maybe even nicer if everything in it was new, than the kitchen at Aunt Abigail's.

They walked through another empty room — the dining room, Steven said, although she could envision it being used as another bedroom if necessary — and finally entered the kitchen. Anna-Grace came to a halt just inside the doorway. Five pairs of sawhorses holding three doors each turned the floor into a maze. Steven had warned her the doors were still wet, so she didn't try to go in, but she looked. And admired. And couldn't hold back a pleased "Ohhhh."

Steven grinned at her. "Does that mean you like it?"

"It's wonderful!" Three full walls of cabinetry, the open cases exposing the crisp, white shelves, formed a horseshoe-shaped work space. Even though there wasn't a baking center like the one in Aunt Abigail's kitchen, she was thrilled with the kitchen's layout. "Anyone would love to claim this kitchen."

"Do you think the appliances your folks got at the auction would fit in here?"

Anna-Grace scanned the openings for a refrigerator and stove. "I don't know why not. And I like how they'll be positioned — the stove at an angle to the sink, and the refrigerator on the wall close to the dining room in case I need to run in and grab extra butter or milk."

Steven sucked in a sharp breath.

She peered up at him, alarmed. "What?"

"You said, 'in case *I*,' as if you've decided this kitchen will be yours."

"I did?"

"Mm-hm."

She drew back, replaying her words. "I guess I did."

"You haven't . . . decided that already, have you?"

Was he hopeful or reluctant to hear her answer? She wouldn't lie to him. "No. I haven't decided. I think I just got caught up in excitement for a minute."

He nodded, and his breath eased out. "Okay."

She caught his arm. "Are you disappointed? You're working so hard on the house and spending money on it, and Alexa said today it doesn't make sense to go to so much trouble to fix it up for someone else. She made me wonder if it's wrong to think about selling it. I know you said you wouldn't mind letting it go to someone else, but are you sure?"

His brows descended. "I'm sure."

He didn't look sure. He looked tense and uncertain. She moved close and rested her temple against his shoulder. "You can tell me the truth, Steven. I want you to be happy."

For several seconds he stood as stiff and still as a statue, his breath coming in short little puffs that kissed her forehead. Then his chest expanded as he drew in a big breath. He shifted slightly, dislodging her head from his shoulder. He cupped her chin, his callous fingers scratchy against her skin, and raised her face. "I can let it go."

"Even after doing all this work?"

"Even after that."

She still thought he appeared less than certain, but she wouldn't accuse him of dishonesty. She smiled. "All right then." She took the bag of handles from him. "Could we hold one of these next to a door and see how they'll look?"

His lips curved into a sad kind of grin. "Just in case they become your cabinets?"

"Just in case."

"All right." He removed one of the handles and very carefully hovered it above the closest door. "What do you think?"

The dark bronzy color of the handle looked wonderful against the warm, honeyed tint of the wood. She nodded. "I like it."

"Me, too." He dropped it back in the sack, then set the sack on the floor.

Anna-Grace returned to the dining room and stared for a moment at the bare walls. Steven moved up behind her and wrapped his arms around her waist. She folded her arms over his, relishing the feel of his rope-like muscles, his sturdy frame seeming to bolster hers. A swell of love rolled through her, and it was all she could do to keep from turning around and melting into his embrace.

He whispered in her ear, "What are you thinking?"

Would he be shocked or flattered if he knew where her thoughts had drifted? She forced herself to focus on the house. "I was looking at the bare walls. So many bare walls in this house . . . and they'll all need paint or paper." She tipped her head to peek at him. "Have you chosen colors yet?"

"No. I thought I'd let you do that."

She chewed her lower lip. She hadn't done badly choosing the cabinet handles, but the thought of decorating an entire house intimidated her. "I hope I don't mess it up."

He chuckled. "Unlikely." He rocked her gently to and fro, his chin pressed to her temple. "I'd better take you to your aunt's now. It's close to suppertime, and people might talk if they find out we were out here by ourselves."

She stepped away from his touch. "You're right. Let's go."

As they drove the short distance between the two farmsteads, Anna-Grace decided she couldn't eliminate her concern about people talking. She had no control over what others chose to do. But she could address her concern about decorating the house. Alexa had decorated all of Aunt Abigail's house plus the old summer kitchen. When it came time to paint the walls, she'd ask for Alexa's advice. It might draw the two of them together.

After all, they had a lot in common. They were both members of the "Who's Your Daddy?" club.

CHAPTER 29

Alexa

As soon as Grandmother's night nurse arrived that evening, Alexa left Grandmother, Marjorie, Steven, and Anna-Grace at the dining room table sipping tea and munching cookies, and she trudged upstairs. Anna-Grace had seemed disappointed when Alexa excused herself, but she needed some time away from the girl. The mumble of their voices followed her, and when she reached the upstairs landing, a burst of laughter made her consider going back down. It sounded like they were having fun. After a moment's hesitation she went on into her room and closed the door.

She kicked off her shoes, crossed to the chair in front of the window, and pulled out her cell phone. She brought up her mother's number and aimed her finger at the Send button. But she didn't hit it. How could she talk to Mom concerning her mixed feelings toward Anna-Grace? Even though Mom hadn't raised the baby girl to adulthood, she still would feel an attachment to her. How could she not? It wouldn't be fair to pull Mom into her worries.

Instead of calling her mother, she set the phone aside and then rested her elbows on her knees, slumping forward and closing her eyes. "God . . ." Before the prayer could take shape, the doorbell rang. Alexa zipped out of her room and clattered down the stairs, calling, "I'll get it, Grandmother." She yanked the door open.

Mr. Plett from church stood on the porch with his hat in his hands. He greeted Alexa with a sheepish smile. "I'm sorry to bother you, but I picked up a couple and their daughter on the highway. Their car broke down, and it'll be an hour or more before a tow truck gets here. They're tired and need a place to stay the night. I remembered you have rooms, so I brought them out. But if you don't take people unless they make a reservation, I'll drive them on into Pratt."

"I have a room, but it isn't set up for more than two people. How old is the daughter?" If she was very young, she might be able to sleep on a pallet on the floor.

The man shrugged. "It's hard for me to tell. Girls today — the way they dress sometimes, they look older than they should be. But she isn't a little girl."

Then the pallet was out.

Grandmother wheeled up behind Alexa. "Who is it?"

"Mr. Plett is here with some people who are stranded. He wondered if we had rooms."

"Did you tell him yes?"

"Not yet." She wished she could have this conversation with Grandmother privately instead of in front of one of the church members. At least the stranded people weren't listening in. They must be waiting in Mr. Plett's car. "Since Anna-Grace is here, I only have the one room, and he said there are three of them."

"A man, his wife, and their not-so-little daughter," Mr. Plett said.

Grandmother gave Alexa her no-nonsense look. "So put the couple in 2 Corinthians 9:8, give your room to the daughter, but ask if they'll share their bathroom with her. Then you go in with Anna-Grace for the night. The Ruth 2:10 has the twin beds, so there's a bed for each of you." She held out her hands as if to say, *Problem solved.*

Alexa swallowed a groan. Stay with Anna-Grace?

Mr. Plett turned toward the porch steps.

"I'll go get them then."

Apparently it was all settled. And this was supposed to be her B and B, not Grandmother's!

Grandmother reached out and bopped Alexa on the arm, making her wonder if she'd read her thoughts. "Weren't you saying you needed to bring in more money? Well, here are some guests. Don't turn them away." Her voice softened as she added, "Besides, it's the right thing to do. If they're stranded in a strange town, they need hospitality. Show them a little of Christ's love by meeting their needs."

Alexa hung her head. Her thoughts had been of herself — all selfish thoughts. She nodded. "I will."

"I know you will."

She stepped out on the porch as Mr. Plett led the trio of travelers up the walkway. The adults each dragged a rolling suitcase, and the not-so-little daughter carried a guitar case.

Mr. Plett gestured to the couple. "This is Curtis and Kathy Kirkley, and their daughter, Nicole."

They seemed so stressed, Alexa's sympathy stirred. She offered a genuine smile. "Hello. Welcome to Grace Notes B and B. I'm Alexa Zimmerman."

The man and woman greeted her wearily, but the daughter just looked Alexa up and down in the snooty way the popular girls at school used to behave. Alexa had never let those girls in school bother her, and she wouldn't let Nicole bother her, either. "Please come in."

They all trooped into the house, deposited their bags near the door, then stood in an awkward group near the piano. Alexa introduced them to Grandmother, then said, "Mr. and Mrs. Kirkley, I have a room ready for you, but I'll need to go up and change the sheets on the bed" — and grab her clothes from the closet — "in the room for Nicole."

Nicole sent a disparaging glance across the front room. "Is this really a hotel? It just looks like an old house."

"Nicole!" Her mother sounded mortified. "Be polite."

The girl slumped her shoulders and folded her arms over her chest.

Alexa decided it was best to ignore the girl's theatrics. "Mr. and Mrs. Kirkley, your room has its own bathroom, but the room for Nicole has to share the bathroom with another room. Would you mind letting her come in and use your bathroom since I already have a guest" — technically, Anna-

Grace wasn't a guest, but the Kirkleys didn't need to know everything — "making use of the shared bath? She'd probably feel more comfortable sharing with you than with a stranger."

Nicole made another sour face, but the adults nodded in agreement.

"Thank you." Alexa inched toward the staircase. "If you'd like to join my grandmother and our other guest in the dining room, we've got cookies and tea." She looked at Nicole. Despite her trendy, mussed-looking haircut and abundance of oversized jewelry, Alexa guessed her to be around twelve or thirteen. "Or milk, if you'd prefer." The girl rolled her eyes. Alexa almost mimicked her. "Make yourselves comfortable, and I'll let you know when the room is ready."

"Come with me." Grandmother led the way, and the Kirkleys followed her.

Mr. Plett approached Alexa and lowered his voice. "I didn't mean to cause you trouble. If you want me to, I'll tell them it won't work for them to stay here."

Alexa smiled, hoping to reassure the man. "It's fine. That's what I'm here for — to provide a retreat for travelers."

He nodded. "All right then. Thank you for making them welcome. I'll come out tomorrow morning and check on them. Good night now."

She closed the door behind him, then darted upstairs. Within twenty minutes she'd finished remaking the bed, performed a quick dusting and sweeping, and transferred the clothes to Anna-Grace's room. She hurried back to the dining room to let the Kirkleys know their rooms were ready. Surely by now Grandmother was ready to wring Nicole's skinny little neck. Old Order children were taught better manners than this one seemed to possess.

Soft chatter — lighthearted, relaxed — greeted her as she rounded the corner from the staircase. As she drew closer, she realized the one doing the talking was the Kirkleys' daughter. She stopped in the doorway rather than interrupting so she wouldn't chase the smile from the girl's face.

". . . long shot, but Mom and Daddy said if it's what I really want, then they'll help me as much as they can."

Steven said, "You're lucky to have a mom and dad who support your dreams. I hope you let them know how much you appreciate it."

Nicole hunched her shoulders and flicked a sheepish glance at her parents. "Probably not as much as I should. But I am thankful."

Grandmother looked up and spotted Alexa. She waved her into the room. "Nicole here was telling what she and her folks are doing on the road. There's a talent contest in Branson, Missouri, and she's going to compete. She sings and plays guitar."

"Is that right?" Alexa moved to an empty chair and sat. Anna-Grace offered her the cookie plate, but she shook her head. "What do you sing, Nicole?"

"Country-western tunes mostly, but sometimes I add a little bit of pop." She tossed her head, sending her floppy bangs away from her dark black eyelashes. She must have used an entire bottle of mascara to get her lashes that thick and gloppy. "Depends on the audience."

Her eyes wide, Anna-Grace leaned toward Alexa. "She's been performing since she was six years old. She even sang 'The Star-Spangled Banner' at a professional football game."

"Not the pros, just college play-offs," Nicole corrected.

"Even so, with all those people in the stadium?" Anna-Grace shook her head. "I would have been scared to death."

Nicole shrugged. "You get used to it." Her

eyebrows rose. "Wanna hear a song? I didn't get a chance to practice this afternoon." She didn't wait for a reply but scampered to the front room and retrieved her guitar. She slung the strap around her neck and stood at the head of the table. "You all are religious people, so I'll sing 'Jesus, Take the Wheel.' It's a country song, but it's kind of religious."

Without further preamble Nicole positioned her fingers on the strings and broke into song. For someone so young she had a strong, sure voice. Alexa didn't know a great deal about music, but she knew a pleasant sound when she heard it. She joined the others in enthusiastic applause when the girl finished.

Nicole beamed a smile across the group. "Thanks." Then she sighed. "I hope our car gets fixed fast so we can get to the competition. I don't want to miss it. Agents and producers come to these things. It could be my big break."

"Well, we will pray you make it on time if you're meant to be there," Grandmother said.

The girl turned a scowl in Grandmother's direction. "What do you mean, 'if'?"

Grandmother chuckled. "What I mean is you have a gift, just as Alexa here has a gift for cooking. When God gives people gifts, He has a special purpose for the gift. If your purpose is to become a performer, the way you said you want, then God will make it happen for you."

Nicole stared at Grandmother as if she'd lost her senses. "But —"

Mr. Kirkley pushed away from the table. "Since our rooms are ready, I think we'll turn in."

His wife also rose. "Yes. It's been a very long day."

Alexa rose. "I'll take you up." She carried Mrs. Kirkley's suitcase and led the family to the upstairs bedrooms.

Nicole bounced on the edge of the bed, then flopped backward across the mattress. Alexa hoped she wouldn't pop any of the careful hand stitches on the patchwork quilt. The girl raised one hand as if conceding defeat. "This'll do. Close the door, Mom."

Mrs. Kirkley pulled her daughter's door shut and then turned a weary smile on Alexa. "Thank you for the refreshments this evening and for opening the rooms to us. We appreciate it."

Alexa smiled. "You're very welcome. Breakfast at seven thirty?"

The adults exchanged a look. Mrs. Kirkley said, "How about eight thirty?"

She'd have to fix two batches — Steven and Briley ate earlier — but she nodded. "That's fine. Do you have any food allergies?"

"Kathy and I are vegetarians, and Nicole is a vegan," Mr. Kirkley said.

Alexa would have to do some quick research before she cooked breakfast. "Okay. Well . . ." She inched toward the stairway opening. "If you need anything, just knock on this door." She pointed to the door of the Ruth 2:10.

"I'm sure we'll be fine. Good night." Mrs. Kirkley ushered her husband into their room and closed their door.

Alexa started down the stairs, and she met Anna-Grace who was coming up. The other girl offered her a sympathetic grimace and spoke in a near whisper. "Aunt Abigail said you moved your things into the room you gave me. I'm sorry you got ousted from your room."

"It's okay. It'll probably just be one night. I'm sorry I had to invade your space."

"It's no invasion." Anna-Grace's smile grew hopeful. "It'll give us a chance to really talk. Get to know each other better. I'd like that."

Why did Anna-Grace always have to be so

nice? Under other circumstances the two of them would probably be great friends. But trying to keep secret Anna-Grace's parentage left Alexa on edge. Being overly friendly would lead to spilling things she wasn't supposed to spill. She didn't know how to respond.

The girl's smile faded. "Or . . . if you'd rather, I can take my things to Sandra's in the morning."

Say something! "You don't need to do that. As I said, they'll probably be here only one night. I'll be back in my own room tomorrow."

"Okay." Anna-Grace lifted her foot to the next riser but didn't climb the stairs. "Steven went home. I feel so bad for him, sleeping on a mattress on the floor and having to use an outhouse. He bathes in the barn!" She cringed. "I wish he could stay here once a room is available. I asked Aunt Abigail, and she didn't say no, but I could tell she had apprehensions."

The door to Nicole's room flew open. The girl pounded across the landing on bare feet and banged her fist on her parents' door. "Mom! I need to brush my teeth!" They let her in.

When it was quiet again, Alexa spoke. "She's probably concerned about what people would think or about what it might tempt you to . . . to . . ." She didn't want to say anything disparaging, but Anna-Grace and Steven were published. She'd seen the looks flying between the two of them. They loved each other, and their impatience appeared to be growing. Mom and Paul Aldrich had given in to temptation, and their choice carried consequences still today. "Grandmother is trying to protect you."

"I know." Anna-Grace ducked her head for a moment, then offered Alexa a shy smile. "And she's right. We shouldn't be alone."

Alexa swallowed a knot of jealousy. What was it like to be so in love?

Anna-Grace grabbed Alexa's arm and tugged. "Let's go to my room. We can talk there instead of on the stairs."

A part of her wanted to resist, but she let Anna-Grace propel her up the stairs and into the room. She clicked the door closed, sat at the foot of the closest bed, and draped her elbow over the top rail of the footboard. An impish grin appeared on her face.

"I've been dying to ask you something, and now that we're finally alone, I can do it."

Alexa sat on the edge of the second bed and braced herself.

"Are you and Briley Forrester, um, you know . . . interested?"

"Interested?"

"Yes." Anna-Grace shrugged one shoulder. "In each other."

"What? No!" Heat exploded in Alexa's face. She fanned her flaming face with both hands. "Gracious sakes, *no.*"

"Oh." Anna-Grace looked surprised. "The way you tease each other, I just thought —"

"I only give back what he gives me." Alexa's tone clipped out more briskly than she intended. "When you've been around him more, you'll discover he flirts with any female who breathes. I could *never* be interested in someone like Briley Forrester."

Anna-Grace fiddled with the brass finial on the footboard. "That's too bad. That he's a flirt, I mean. I've never seen a better-looking man."

"Did you really just say that?"

The girl had the audacity to giggle. "Well, you have to admit, his looks are kind of hard to miss."

Sandra had said something similar. Sitting there with her blond hair tucked under her cap, her innocent expression unable to mask the ornery glint in her eyes, Anna-Grace even resembled Mom's youngest sister.

Alexa jumped up and reached for her

pajamas, which she'd placed on the chair in the corner. With her back to the other girl, she began dressing for bed. "Good looks aside, Mr. Briley Forrester is trouble waiting for a place to happen. Only a fool would take his teasing seriously."

"Oh." Anna-Grace's soft voice carried to Alexa's ears. "That's disappointing."

To her chagrin, Alexa agreed.

CHAPTER 30

Briley

Briley stepped into the kitchen Tuesday morning, took one look at Alexa, and burst out laughing.

She lifted her frown from the computer screen and aimed the glower at him instead. "What's so funny?"

"You. Your face." He laughed again, then drew his hand over his mouth to stifle the sound. If he didn't know better, he'd suspect she spent the night barhopping. But wouldn't she look out of place in a bar in her tunic-style sweater, long twill skirt, and tennis shoes? "Sorry, but I've never seen you so bleary-eyed."

"You'd be bleary-eyed, too, if you only got three hours of sleep."

He rested his hip against the counter and crossed his arms over his chest. "And just what stole your sleep last night?"

She gave him a look that said she had no

intention of answering.

He chuckled again. "Okay, aside from being tired and cranky, what's the matter?"

She pointed at her laptop screen and huffed out an annoying breath. "I have a guest upstairs who is vegan, which means no food from animals — no meat, eggs, any kind of dairy product . . . I've been hunting for a vegan breakfast recipe, but I don't keep tofu or chard or black beans in my cupboard. I have no idea what to fix for her!"

Briley pinched his chin. "Do you have potatoes, onions, and peppers?"

"Well, *of course.*"

She really was in a foul mood. He could have some fun tormenting her, but she might decide not to serve him breakfast. The scent of bacon seasoned the entire kitchen. He wouldn't risk it. "Then make O'Brien hash browns — fried in vegetable oil instead of bacon grease — and toss a piece of dry toast on the plate."

"Dry? Why not with jelly?"

"The strictest vegans won't touch anything with jelling agent in it." He remembered something. "Oh, and unless your bread is free of animal-based oil or eggs, it's a no-go, too. So hash browns and whatever fresh fruit you have around — a banana, an apple, or an orange — and call it good."

She gawked at him. "How'd you know all that?"

"My boss is vegan. I've gone to enough breakfast meetings with him to know what he orders." He fought a smile, remembering Len's excitement about the possibility of turning the public's eye on an illegitimate birth in the midst of a Plain community.

"Well, thanks for the suggestion. I can do hash browns without too much trouble." She closed the computer and set it aside. "For the vegetarians I'll add scrambled eggs and a sprinkle of cheese."

"A vegan and vegetarians in the inn, huh?" Briley waggled his eyebrows. "My, my, you're branching out."

She frowned as she moved toward the refrigerator. "A family from northeastern Colorado got stranded in Arborville, and they ended up here by default. Their daughter is supposed to compete in a talent show in Branson on Thursday, so they're eager to be on their way."

He'd likely be on his way soon, too. Len had encouraged him to pry out the details of his discovery and hightail it back to Chicago as quickly as possible. Yesterday the prospect of returning to the newspaper office made him eager to go. The sooner he got the story written, the sooner he could see his byline in print. Len had promised front-page status — a huge step up from the middle-of-the-paper articles he'd done in the past. But at that moment, leaning against the counter in Alexa Zimmerman's clean, good-smelling kitchen, he experienced a reluctance to leave this place behind. *You gettin' soft, Forrester?*

He straightened and headed for the dining room doorway. "Good luck cooking for those veggie lovers, but remember I'm not one of 'em. I want some of that bacon I smell frying."

"Don't worry, you'll get some."

As he reached the doorway, she called his name. He turned and found her pinning him with a repentant look.

"I shouldn't have been so snappish with you this morning. I laid awake last night worrying about —" A delightful blush stole over her cheeks. "Well, just worrying. And I kind of took it out on you. I'm sorry."

In his circle of acquaintanceship, the girls had forgotten how to blush. Sad, because he found the pink flush adorable. He grinned. "I figure I've given you a reason or two to snap at me in the past, and you held your tongue. We'll just call this one payback for those times, okay?"

A weak smile crept up her cheek, making her seem much less tired and cranky. "Thanks, Briley."

"You're welcome. Now, pay attention to what you're doing and don't burn my bacon!" He waited for her huff, then entered the dining room laughing. He poured a cup of coffee and sat in his regular spot at the table. In the closed bedroom behind him, Mrs. Z and her nurse chatted, creating a soft mumble. From the kitchen, clanks and clunks told of busyness. He inhaled the aromas of coffee, bacon, and bread, and he heaved a sigh. As much as he hated to admit it, even to himself, he'd miss the homeyness of this place.

Alexa zipped around the corner with a plate of muffins and a sectioned dish containing whipped cream cheese, butter, and strawberry jam. She placed the items on the table.

He raised one eyebrow. "That is *not* bacon."

She rolled her eyes. "It's coming, it's coming . . ." She flashed a grin, then trotted back into the kitchen.

He sighed again. Even harder to admit, he'd miss her. He'd grown rather attached to the not-quite-Mennonite innkeeper. He sipped his coffee, frowning. Would Len agree to let him create pseudonyms for the people in his article? He hoped so. He fully intended to share the story he'd uncovered. He had to tell the story. But he'd do what he could to protect Alexa at the same time. He might be a tease, but he wasn't a traitor.

Alexa

The Kirkleys' vehicle, which needed a new water pump, wasn't finished until Wednesday afternoon, so they chose to stay one more night and get an early start on Thursday. Nicole threw a minitantrum over the decision, but her father remained firm. Alexa was glad to see it. Over the short time with them, she'd been given the impression Nicole ruled the roost, and although she had no experience with parenting, she was wise enough to recognize that the girl didn't possess the maturity to be in charge.

Everyone ate breakfast at seven thirty Thursday morning so the Kirkley family could get on the road as quickly as possible. Alexa had a hard time not giggling at Nicole's reaction to Briley sitting beside her. The girl was young, but she knew how to use her feminine wiles. To Briley's credit, he remained friendly and attentive without lapsing into flirtation. She considered commending him, but then decided he didn't need anyone giving him compliments.

More importantly, she needed to hold her distance from him. Over the past three days, he'd gone beyond curious to pushy, questioning her about why she'd been raised in Indiana instead of Kansas, why she didn't dress like the other Zimmermans, why she wouldn't talk about her father.

Sometimes he caught her when she was working on something else — cooking or cleaning or checking e-mail, which meant she answered before she thought. Other times he started out talking about himself, little pieces of growing up in the foster care system without a mom and dad to claim as his own, and it seemed natural to share about her life in return. She'd told Anna-Grace only a fool would fall for Briley's charm, and apparently she was more foolish than she'd ever believed. Twice she'd let slip things she wished she hadn't, so now she stayed on her guard. He wouldn't trip her up again.

Today it would be easier to avoid his questions because she intended to spend the day with Anna-Grace. Of course, she'd still have to be on her guard, but at least she didn't suspect Anna-Grace of intentionally digging for information. And in all likelihood, Anna-Grace's focus would be on the house. The girls planned to go to the Meiers farm, take measurements of all the rooms, then drive to Wichita and shop for paint and wallpaper. Alexa found it somewhat amusing that Anna-Grace was nervous about making selections, but she didn't say so. No sense in hurting the girl's feelings. Besides, she enjoyed looking at paint and wallpaper samples. It should be a relaxing day. And after dealing with Nicole, whose moods changed faster than a chameleon racing through a flower garden, she'd earned it.

She waved good-bye to the Kirkleys, then hurried in to clean the kitchen so she and Anna-Grace could leave. Anna-Grace was already there, scraping and rinsing the dishes. She smiled when Alexa came in.

"Please don't chase me out. You're doing me a favor today, so I want to return it. Let me do the dishes."

"But —"

"Don't you need to go strip the beds and gather the towels?"

She should get the laundry started before they left. "Are you sure you don't mind?"

"I don't mind." Anna-Grace pointed imperiously toward the doorway and set her face in a mock scowl that perfectly mimicked Aunt Shelley. "Now *go.*"

Alexa dashed off. She pulled the rumpled

snarl of sheets from the bed in the room Nicole used and gathered a half-dozen towels from various places on the floor, including under the bed. She dumped the armload at the top of the stairs and then entered the 2 Corinthians 9:8 room. The bed was neatly made, and towels hung over the bars in the bathroom. If the towels hadn't been damp from recent use, she'd wonder if anyone had even stayed in the room. It looked vastly different from the hurricane Nicole left behind. As she began to strip the bed, she noticed an envelope marked *"For Alexa"* propped against one of the pillows.

Curious, she opened it and pulled out a folded sheet of the notepaper she'd placed on the dresser for guests' use. She unfolded the page and read:

Dear Alexa,
We're so grateful Mr. Plett brought us to your charming B and B. Although I'm sure it was a challenge having three people from such a different background staying under your roof, you were the perfect hostess and helped us feel very much at ease. Your grandmother told us we are some of your first guests, and we were so surprised. You have such a

natural hospitality, we assumed you'd been doing this for years. You truly have a sweet spirit, Alexa, and we wish you well in your future endeavors with the bed-and-breakfast and whatever else you choose to pursue. Please use the enclosed tip to do something special for yourself. I hope you will remember us fondly.

Sincerely, Kathy for all of the
Kirkleys —
Curtis, Kathy, and
Nicole (aka "Nicci K")

Warmed by the kind note, Alexa peeked into the envelope again. She gasped in surprise. A hundred dollar bill rested inside! She hadn't expected tips at all, and to receive such an extravagant one sent her pulse into a mad gallop. She forgot all about stripping the bed and raced for the stairs, leaping over the pile of laundry on the way.

She found her grandmother in her usual spot beside the front room window, embroidery hoop in hand. She waved the bill under her nose. "Look what the Kirkleys left for me. Can you believe it?"

Grandmother smiled. "Why, yes, I can believe it. The Lord knows you're concerned about finances, so He's showing you He's able to provide."

Alexa blinked back tears. "They left me a really nice note, too, thanking me for my hospitality." She sniffed and flattened the bill against her bodice. "Now I feel bad for thinking evil thoughts about the little would-be music star, Nicci K."

Grandmother laughed long and hard. "She was something, wasn't she? But she definitely has an amazing talent for one so young. I hope she'll use it wisely and not let it go to her head."

"Me, too."

Anna-Grace joined them. "The dishwasher is running, and I cleaned the table and countertops. Are you ready to go?"

Alexa shook her head. "I got sidetracked. Let me get a load of wash going, and —"

"Just go," Grandmother said. "The laundry can wait until you get back."

"Oh, Grandmother, I can't just leave the sheets and towels in a pile on the floor." Aunt Shelley would be mortified.

"Think about Anna-Grace." Grandmother looped her arm around the girl's waist and gave Alexa a puppy-dog look. "She's so eager to take you to the house, she's almost dancing in place. So go."

Alexa looked at Anna-Grace, who tipped her head and pleaded with her eyes. The two of them had begging down pat. She shook her head, grinning. "All right. I guess it won't hurt to wait a few hours to wash the sheets and towels. But if Aunt Shelley comes over, don't let her go upstairs."

Grandmother laughed.

Alexa turned to Anna-Grace. "Let's go."

Anna-Grace squealed. "Finally!" She grabbed both of their coats from the hooks and tossed Alexa's to her. "Good-bye, Aunt Abigail! We'll see you later."

"Enjoy your day, girls."

In the car Anna-Grace turned a beaming smile on Alexa. "This has been the longest week. I thought Thursday would never come. But Steven said the kitchen is done. Well, except for painting the walls. And the bedrooms are ready for paint, too. I can go over every day now and work, if I want to."

"I remember how much fun I had transforming the old summer kitchen into a little cottage." Alexa sighed. She missed living out there. "I know you'll enjoy seeing the changes in Steven's house, too." She turned into the lane leading to the farmhouse, and her heart leaped in her chest. She eased her car next to Paul Aldrich's truck and then left it idling, trying not to frown. "I thought you said the kitchen was done."

Anna-Grace's face pinched into a confused scowl. "I did."

"Then why is Mr. Aldrich still here?"

"Well, the bathroom isn't finished." The girl shuddered. "Steven's been using the *outhouse* all this time. Mr. Aldrich still has a lot of work to do in the bathroom."

Alexa's palms began to sweat. Could she be in the house with Anna-Grace's biological father and act naturally? Over her months in Arborville, she'd developed a comfortable friendship with the man and his son even though she still sometimes wished they were family. If she could handpick a father, she would choose someone like Paul Aldrich. But he wasn't her father. He belonged to Anna-Grace, too.

Anna-Grace touched Alexa's arm. "We won't be in the way if that's what has you worried. Steven said so. So let's go in, huh?"

Alexa shut off the engine. She drew a deep breath and sent up a silent prayer for God to guard her words and her expressions. Then she said, "Lead the way."

CHAPTER 31

Anna-Grace

The front door wasn't locked, so Anna-Grace stepped right on in with Alexa lagging at her heels. She'd expected more enthusiasm from her cousin. Obviously she had a knack for decorating, and she must enjoy it to have tackled enormous projects like Aunt Abigail's house and the summer kitchen. Maybe she just didn't like being with Anna-Grace. The last three nights of sharing a room hadn't brought them any closer together despite her best efforts. If they couldn't bond over choosing paint colors, something Aunt Abigail said Alexa loved to do, then it might be a lost cause. The thought made Anna-Grace sad.

But she pasted a smile on her face and drew Alexa to the center of the front room. "Steven! Alexa and I are here!"

He appeared at the head of the hallway. He moved directly to Anna-Grace and planted a kiss on her forehead. Then he turned to Alexa. "Did you bring your measuring tape?"

She patted her jacket pocket. "Got it." She looked around, shaking her head in wonder. "Wow. You've really been working hard. How many layers of wallpaper did you have to strip before you got to the plaster?"

Steven grimaced. "Depends on the room, but in here? Seven. Unbelievable." Scuffles and a *clink-clink* echoed from somewhere on the left. Steven looked in that direction. "We're putting up tile in the bathroom. I'd better get in there and help." He eased backward. "Do your measuring and be sure to let me know when you're done so I can tell you good-bye."

"We will." She blew Steven a kiss before he disappeared around the corner, then she took Alexa by the elbow. "Let's start in the kitchen. I want to see how it looks now that it's all finished."

They spent a few minutes *oohing* and *aahing* over the new cabinets, mossy-green tile backsplash, and the crisp gray-and-white squares on the floor. Anna-Grace couldn't resist opening and closing a few cupboards, envisioning the shelves filled with dishes and pots and home-canned goods. She aimed a smile at Alexa. "I think I can see myself cooking in here."

Alexa nodded. "It's a very nice kitchen. Will you want wallpaper or paint in here?"

Anna-Grace held out her hands in a gesture of helplessness. "I don't know. My mom's kitchen is painted, but the one at Aunt Abigail's has wallpaper. What do you think would be best?"

Alexa made a slow circle around the room. "Well, there isn't a lot of wall to cover. The doorways to the dining room and mudroom take away wall space left over by the cabinets. But there is the soffit above the cabinets . . . Maybe you could paint and put up a pretty wallpaper border along the ceiling that has the same colors as the wall paint and the tile." She peeked into the mudroom. "You could use the border in here, too, to dress it up a little bit, even if it is just an entry space." With a brisk pace she crossed to the doorway leading to the dining room. "If you choose a border that has matching wallpaper, then you could use the paper for the walls in the dining room and pull both spaces together."

Anna-Grace blew out a little breath. "I would never have thought of that, but I like the idea. I'm so glad you're here, Alexa."

A weak smile curved the girl's lips. She pulled out the tape measure and held it up.

"Let's get this done so we can go choose your colors, okay?"

Anna-Grace held the end of the tape while Alexa recorded the measurements. She took the task seriously, sucking in her lips and checking the numbers twice before writing them down. They measured every room in the house, starting with the mudroom and moving toward the bedrooms.

"We better get the hallway, too," Alexa said.

Anna-Grace pressed the end of the measuring tape to the corner next to the closed bathroom door. "And then the bathroom." She angled her head, listening to the soft scrape of tools and mutter of voices behind the door. She giggled and stage-whispered, "If they'll let us in there."

Alexa didn't laugh. She checked the tape and scratched some numbers onto the pad of paper. She put the pencil and paper in her pocket, but she didn't move toward the bathroom door.

Anna-Grace gave a little tug on the measuring tape. "Come on. One more to go."

Alexa stood her ground. "If they're putting up tile, we'll be in their way."

"But I have to know how much paint to buy." Anna-Grace turned the door handle and eased the door open a few inches.

417

"Steven? Can we measure the bathroom now?"

"Just a minute." A few more scuffling noises, these louder than before, and two soft *thuds* came from behind the door. Then Steven's face appeared in the gap. "How about you give me the tape, and Mr. Aldrich and I will measure for you? We're already tripping over each other with the boxes of tile and buckets of grout in the way."

Alexa scurried forward and thrust the measuring tape at Steven. "Just call out the numbers and I'll write them down."

"Perfect." The door closed. After a minute or two, Steven called, "Six feet, two inches wide. Eight feet, eight inches long. Six feet, ten inches from the top of the tile line to the ceiling."

Alexa repeated the measurements as she recorded them.

The door opened, and Anna-Grace couldn't resist sticking her head inside. Glossy squares of dove-gray tile marched along the bottom third of one wall, their sheeny, new appearance a stark contrast to the patched plaster surfaces. The carpenter stood halfway behind Steven. She held out her hand to him.

"Hello. I met you at Aunt Abigail's birthday party, but there were so many people there I don't know if you remember me. I'm Anna-Grace Braun."

The man moved toward her so slowly it appeared he was battling a strong wind. He extended his hand, then glanced at it as well as his splotchy clothes and grimaced. "I shouldn't touch anything. I'm pretty messy."

Anna-Grace linked her hands behind her back. "That's all right. I just wanted to thank you for the work you're doing on the house. Everything looks so nice."

"You're welcome. It's a . . . pleasure to work on the house where Steven and . . . and you will live." He gazed into her face with such intensity she felt he was measuring her, too.

She drew back slightly, unnerved. He hadn't behaved so strangely the first time they met. She would remember. "Well, now that we've got all our measurements, we can go paint shopping." She turned her attention to her beau, but she sensed that Mr. Aldrich's steady gaze remained pinned to her. "Steven, are you sure you trust me to make the selections?"

He stepped between her and the carpenter, and she nearly heaved a sigh of relief. "Get what you want. Except for pink. I'm not keen on pink."

Anna-Grace gestured to her dark-pink calico skirt hanging below the hem of her coat.

"Except on you," he corrected.

She laughed. "All right. No pink." She tipped her cheek for Steven's kiss. Then she started to leave. Mr. Aldrich pushed past Steven and reached toward her. He held a chipped gray tile. She looked at the tile and then at him in confusion. "What's that for?"

He bobbed the tile. "Take it with you. It will help you choose a color to coordinate with it." He seemed to watch her hand lift to take the tile from his grasp. Then he looked into her face again. Was there a shimmer of tears in his brown eyes? He blinked several times. "There are extra tiles from the kitchen backsplash in the mudroom. Please take one of those with you, too."

"A-All right." Anna-Grace backed away. "We'll do that. Thank you."

"You're welcome." His voice came out low, tight, emotional. "You're very welcome . . . Anna-Grace."

Every other man she'd met in Arborville had referred to her as Miss Braun. Paul Aldrich's use of her given name sent an uneasy prickle across her scalp. She turned toward Alexa, eager to retrieve the kitchen tile and leave, but the expression on her cousin's face — anger, resentment, maybe even a hint of worry — held her in place for several tense seconds. She flicked a glance over her shoulder to find Mr. Aldrich still looking at her even though Steven had returned to work.

Skewered between two confusing expressions, she wasn't sure what to do. But then Mr. Aldrich gave a little jolt, nodded once at her, and turned away. His response seemed to remove whatever odd emotion had come over Alexa, because her stiff shoulders wilted and she slipped the pad of paper and pencil into her pocket.

"Are you ready?" Alexa asked.

Anna-Grace darted forward. "Yes. Let's go."

Steven

Steven grabbed another mesh sheet of tiles and carried it to Mr. Aldrich. The carpenter crouched on his haunches, trowel held over the bucket of Spackle, but he didn't dip into the white paste. He seemed to stare at the blank space waiting the next arrangement of tiles. Steven looked at the wall, too. Had he set the last sheet crooked? Mr. Aldrich was a stickler for perfection. He carefully examined the placement of the sheets. He

421

couldn't see anything wrong.

Steven bent down on one knee next to the carpenter. "What's the matter with the tile?"

The man jolted as if he'd been shocked with a live wire. "What? Oh. Nothing. Nothing's the matter." He swiped his hand across his eyes.

Steven frowned. Had the man just wiped away tears? The idea left him uncomfortable. Maybe Mr. Aldrich needed a rest. "You want me to do the Spackle for a while?"

"No, I'll do it. We had a . . . a good routine going, and you're doing . . . doing . . ." He hung his head.

There was something wrong. Steven sat in silence, uncertain how to proceed. He'd never seen a grown man act so emotional.

Suddenly Mr. Aldrich angled his head and gave Steven a serious look. "Anna-Grace . . . you love her?" He nearly growled the question.

Even though he sometimes wondered if they were rushing into marriage, Steven knew how to answer. "Yes, I do. Very much."

For several seconds the carpenter glared into Steven's face, as if seeking hidden motives. Then he slumped forward, reminding Steven of a balloon losing its air. If he hadn't propped his elbow on his knee, he might have gone face first into the wall. "I'm glad. She . . . she's a beautiful girl. And I can tell she loves you." He bolted upright, his spine stiff and his expression stern. "You'll take good care of her?"

"Of course."

The intense expression cleared. He blinked several times, each blink seeming to ease a bit more tension. Then he nodded at the wall. "Well, let's get back to it, huh?" He spoke so normally, Steven might have thought he'd imagined the strange, edgy exchange of only moments ago. But he hadn't imagined it. Paul Aldrich had behaved like an overprotective —

Chills exploded across Steven's entire body. Was it possible Paul Aldrich was Anna-Grace's *father*? He pressed the sheet of tiles into the wet Spackle, his fingers trembling so badly the entire sheet went askew.

Mr. Aldrich chuckled. A guttural, unnatural chuckle that spoke volumes. "Here, now. No crooked tiles. Straighten that up."

Steven did so, grinding his teeth so fiercely together his jaw ached. Questions screamed for release. *Who is her mother? Why did you give her up? Do you want her to live in this town with you and your son?* But he kept his teeth clamped and held them inside. He couldn't let on he knew the truth. Not yet.

CHAPTER 32

Anna-Grace

Anna-Grace sat in silence for the first half of the drive to Wichita. She tried to recapture her former excitement, but the uncomfortable feelings raised by Paul Aldrich's strange behavior stole it away. Alexa was quiet, too. Had the man's actions left her on edge as well?

"How well do you know the carpenter?" Anna-Grace blasted the question.

Alexa visibly jumped, then took a firm grip on the steering wheel and sent a short look in Anna-Grace's direction. "How well? He spent a lot of time working at Grandmother's house, I've attended service with him every Sunday since I came to Arborville, and he's taken some meals with the family. So . . . pretty well, I guess." She scowled, her gaze on the road ahead. "Why?"

"The last time I met him, he wasn't so

weird." Anna-Grace shuddered and hugged herself. "The way he stared at me today . . . ugh. It was creepy."

"There's nothing *creepy* about Paul Aldrich."

Her tart response startled Anna-Grace and stirred defensiveness. "You don't think it's creepy when some man you hardly know looks at you so intensely you wonder if he can see your soul?"

Alexa huffed out a short laugh. "Don't be melodramatic."

"I'm not. You were there. You had to have seen how he . . ." She couldn't find words to describe the way he'd fixated on her face and didn't look away. Not even when his eyes began to water from staring so hard. "I've been stared at a lot. Anytime my family goes outside of Sommerfeld to the grocery store or discount store or mall, people stare. Because we look different to them. I've learned to ignore it. But I couldn't ignore Mr. Aldrich. I was half-scared he wanted to grab hold of me."

"He'd never do that."

"How do you know?"

"Because I know, okay? He's a gentle man. A kind and loving father."

"Then why'd he act like that? Like he was seeing a . . . a ghost or something?"

Alexa sent a quick sidelong look at Anna-Grace. Then she turned forward and set her lips in a firm line.

Anna-Grace turned her face to the passenger window and spoke to the passing landscape. "I didn't intend to make you angry, but I really don't know why my comments about Mr. Aldrich bother you so much."

Despite being given the opportunity to explain, Alexa didn't speak.

Anna-Grace chewed her lower lip, stared out the window, and sought a means of apologizing so she might be able to salvage the rest of the day. Before she could form a request for forgiveness, something Dad had said — just a few words in the midst of another conversation — raced from her memory and thumped her with understanding.

She jerked to face Alexa. "He's an old family friend, isn't he?"

After a moment's pause, Alexa gave a grim nod.

"I remember when Steven told my dad that Paul Aldrich had agreed to work on the house. Dad mentioned he'd once thought Mr. Aldrich might ask to marry your mother." She clapped her hand to her cheek. "Oh! Alexa, is Paul Aldrich your father?"

Alexa stared straight ahead and spoke through gritted teeth. "No."

"Oh." Anna-Grace frowned, confused. If Mr. Aldrich and Alexa had no relationship, why would she want to defend him? "Well, then —"

"Look, he isn't anything more than a friend." Alexa released a heavy sigh. "And I shouldn't have gotten upset with you." She whisked a contrite look at Anna-Grace. "Let's just forget it, okay?"

Although it wasn't exactly an apology, it was good enough. "Okay."

"And, Anna-Grace . . ."

"Yes?"

"If Mr. Aldrich looks at you strangely again, give him a little grace. He . . . he's lost a lot." Alexa glanced at Anna-Grace, and tears winked in her eyes. "He lost his wife when she died. Before that, he lost the girl he loved when my mom went away, and — Well, just a lot. So be nice, okay?"

Anna-Grace didn't plan to be unkind. She just wanted to keep her distance after the strange way he'd made her feel. But she nodded.

A home improvement store sat off the highway just ahead. Alexa slowed and made the turn into the parking lot. "And now let's have some fun choosing the right wall covering for every room in the house."

Anna-Grace wouldn't argue about setting aside the subject of the carpenter who'd once been sweet on Alexa's mother. She browsed the wallpaper bins first and chose rolls of sunflower border for the kitchen and mudroom, a coordinating plaid in pale yellows, greens, and cream for the dining room, and a muted gray-and-white-striped paper for the bathroom, even though it was among the patterns marked for bedrooms. "It looks more masculine than the wallpaper with seashells," she told Alexa, "and since the kitchen and dining room will be more feminine, I think the bathroom shouldn't be."

Alexa shrugged. "It's your decision. The gray and white will be a nice background for just about any color of towels. And you can mix it with a floral-print shower curtain for a touch of femininity if you want to."

She'd worry about shower curtains — and every other kind of curtain — another day. Steven probably wouldn't want to spend money on curtains if they decided to sell the place.

"What about the front room and bedrooms?" Alexa asked. "Paper or paint?"

Anna-Grace chewed her thumbnail. "What do you think I should do?"

Alexa folded her arms and crunched her forehead. "Honestly, I'd paint those rooms. Something light and neutral. They aren't terribly large, so a lighter color will make them feel bigger, and a neutral shade will blend well no matter what furniture you bring in."

"All right then. Neutral."

Alexa took control of the cart and pushed it toward the paint section. After perusing paint swatches and laying more than a dozen options across the bottom of the cart, Anna-Grace decided to go with various shades of taupe. Alexa suggested getting four or so little sample cans instead of buying gallons of paint.

"The light in a room can distort the color, so painting a few splotches on the wall will let you see whether you really like it or not."

Anna-Grace assumed Alexa knew what she was talking about, so she asked the person behind the counter to mix the samples for her. As the worker completed her request, she turned to Alexa. "This is a really good idea. Even though it means I have to come back another time for paint, Steven will be able to help choose, too. It is his house, after all."

A slow smile played on Alexa's mouth. "Well, it might be his house, but with all the couples I know, the wife does the decorating. So you'll probably end up doing most of the choosing."

Anna-Grace slumped against the edge of the counter. "Really? I don't think I'm up to that. Just this" — she waved her hand at the items in the cart — "taxed me to the limit of my abilities, and you were helping."

"You'll be fine." Alexa's gaze shifted to some unknown point beyond Anna-Grace, as if a secret thought had carried her away. "It's amazing what you can do when you really have to."

Although not even a smidgen of foreboding touched the other girl's tone, Anna-Grace still experienced a chill of apprehension. *When you really have to.* She didn't *have* to decorate the little house Steven had inherited. She didn't even *have* to live in it with him. But would she? That question remained unanswered.

Briley

When the old Buick Alexa drove pulled up the lane, Briley was waiting on the porch swing. Half-frozen from the wind — did it have to blow as hard as it did in Chicago? — and more than half-grumpy, but waiting anyway. Something she'd said yesterday led him to believe there was more to the story of her mother giving birth to an illegitimate child. Len had instructed him to uncover the full truth, and he had a plan. But he needed to talk to her alone, away from Mrs. Z's sharp-eyed gaze and any other listening ears.

She slid out of the car, extending both legs in a graceful sweep. She slammed the door, looped her purse strap over her shoulder, and moved nimbly over the steppingstones. Holding her jacket crisscrossed over her waist, she bounded up the steps and headed straight for the door. Briley cleared his throat. Loudly. And she came to a sudden stop and whirled in his direction, her brown eyes wide.

"Briley! You startled me." Her expression turned accusatory. "What are you doing out here?"

He gave the swing a gentle push. The chains creaked — a grating sound. He planted his feet against the porch boards. "Sitting." He glanced toward the empty car. "Where's Anna-Grace?"

"I left her at the house with Steven."

"Ah." Good. Complete privacy. He patted the seat. "Join me."

She didn't budge. "It's too cold to sit out

432

here in the wind. I bet it's at least ten degrees colder than it was this morning."

"It's not so bad." He tempered the lie with a smile. His leather coat protected his torso, but his legs were cold. "Come on. I have something important to tell you."

"You can't tell me inside?"

He rolled his eyes. "Do you always have to be so difficult? Don't make me print up another dozen of those pictures and post them in store windows in Arborville."

She set her lips in a scowl, but she scuffed across the porch and wriggled into the far corner of the swing. "All right. What?"

"I'll be leaving soon."

To his gratification her face fell. "Already? But you're on the schedule through the end of December."

"I know." Another blast of wind tossed her ponytail over her shoulder and a few strands caught in her lip gloss. She never wore lipstick — just something clear and shiny. She always looked so fresh — innocent and unspoiled. For a moment regret pricked. His article would expose her lack of innocence. But there was no turning back now. Len was counting on him. "I didn't expect to finish my research so quickly, but I think I've gathered enough information to write the article. My boss said to come on back to the office."

Her brow puckered. "Oh. Well . . ."

"Before I go, though, I'd like to take you to dinner."

Her mocha-colored eyes widened in obvious shock. "Dinner? Me?"

He feigned confusion and glanced around. "Is there anyone else here?" He grinned, shaking his head. "Yes, you." Laying his arm along the back of the swing, he leaned in. Just a bit. Not enough to send her running scared, just enough to capture her attention. "I know I'm not the easiest person in the world to get along with. Believe me, lots of people have made that clear. So before I go, I'd like to, you know, make amends. A nice dinner in Wichita, maybe even a show afterward if there's a movie you'd like to see. That is, if you're allowed to go to movies. What do you say?"

Apparently he'd rendered her speechless, because she sat for several seconds staring at him with her brow pinched in consternation. Her reaction brought his defenses up. He frowned. "I thought you'd enjoy a relaxing evening out. But if not —" *Easy, Forrester. Don't chase her off.* He pulled in a calming breath, the way Aunt Myrt had taught him. Forcing a teasing grin to his lips, he finished his sentence. "I totally understand. Give it some thought and let me know." He started to rise.

"When did you want to go?"

With a nonchalant shrug that was completely opposite of the exuberant leap of his pulse, he sank back onto the swing. "Tomorrow evening, if that fits your schedule."

"And . . ." She caught her ponytail with both hands and twisted it into a rope. "It's not a date — just a going-out-to-relax thing, right?"

His defenses wanted to rise again. Dating him would be such a horror? "That's right."

If she frowned any harder, she'd end up with her forehead as snarled as her hair. She released the ponytail, which flipped over her shoulder, and relaxed her face at the same time. "All right. I'll check with Grandmother just to make sure she doesn't mind, but . . . if she's okay with it, I'll go."

If any other girl had responded so noncommittally to his invitation to dinner, he would have snapped something like "Don't do me any favors" and stormed off. But he needed this girl. So he smiled. "Good. Tomorrow at six thirty. That way Mrs. Z won't be alone for long before the nurse arrives."

"Anna-Grace will be here."

She didn't look any happier about leaving

her grandmother with Anna-Grace than she had about going out with him. He might have to ask about that, too. "Ah yes, I forgot. Then we could go earlier if you want."

"I still need to fix supper for Grandmother, Anna-Grace, and Steven."

"So six thirty after all?"

She sighed. "Yes. That's fine."

He forced a cheery tone. "Great! Now you scoot inside. Your face is all pink — the cold air must be kissing you too hard."

The pink deepened to red. She jumped up and darted inside. He descended the steps in two wide strides and headed for the cottage with a bounce in his step. Success! If he turned on the Briley charm, proven time and again to coax what he wanted from someone of the female persuasion, he'd have the nitty-gritty for his article by tomorrow night. He envisioned Alexa's sweet face turned up to him, pink-cheeked and uncertain even while agreeing, and his steps slowed. Guilt tried to worm its way through him. What he planned to write would cause pain to the people of this small community.

Before he'd come to Arborville, he'd thought they were nothing more than a bunch of weird religious throwbacks to the 1800s. But now he knew them. He liked them. Some — like Alexa, and Steven, and Paul and Danny Aldrich, and maybe even Mrs. Z — had become friends. Could he expose them as no different than anyone else? *Should* he do it?

He jabbed his fist in the air and sent the unwelcome emotion spiraling away. He'd come to do a job. He owed Len — the man had given him his start. And how else would he finally see his name — the name of the punk kid everybody said was doomed to end up in juvenile hall — on a front page byline? He'd finish the article. These people didn't mean anything to him, after all. Saying it enough would eventually convince him it was true.

CHAPTER 33

Steven

Steven tried to focus on the blotches of paint Anna-Grace had carefully lined up on the wall in the front room. Instead of seeing shades of tan — she called them "taupe" — all he saw was Paul Aldrich's face when the man asked, *"You'll take good care of her?"*

Anna-Grace gave his elbow a little nudge. "Well, what do you think? Which do you like?"

He made himself concentrate on the blobs of tan, darker tan, lighter tan, and tannish-gray. In all honesty, they looked pretty much the same. He shrugged. "They're all . . . okay, I guess." He looked at her. "What do you like best?"

Instead of answering, she lifted his arm and fitted herself against his length. With her cheek pressed to his collarbone, she peered up at him and smiled. "I like you."

He should move her away. Having her so

near raised temptations a decent man shouldn't act on. The thought troubled him. He wouldn't have suspected Paul Aldrich of being anything but decent. If that man fell from grace, anybody could. Despite his inner worries Steven couldn't resist slipping his arm around her waist and smiling back at her.

"This is nice, isn't it? Just the two of us?" She flicked a glance left and right, then settled her cheek back in its spot. She looked so sweet with the white ribbons from her cap trailing past her jaw and her blue-eyed gaze aimed at him. She fit perfectly beneath his arm — as if they were two halves of one whole. She sighed softly. "I'm glad the carpenter left before Alexa and I returned."

"Why is that?"

"He makes me nervous. He's a very odd man."

Recalling the man's emotional reaction to spending a few minutes with the daughter he gave up for adoption nearly twenty years ago, Steven experienced a rush of sympathy. "Anna-Grace, that isn't very nice."

She stepped away from him and gave him a disgruntled look. "Are you going to get onto me about disliking Mr. Aldrich, too?"

"Who else got onto you?"

"Alexa." Anna-Grace folded her arms over her chest. "She called me melodramatic because I said I didn't like the way he ogled me."

Steven brushed his knuckles along her smooth cheek. "I don't think he meant to ogle you. I think he was just . . ." His hand froze beneath her chin.

She reached up and cupped his hand, pressing his palm firmly against her jaw. "He was just . . . what?"

What could he say? Anna-Grace hadn't wanted to read the letters from her birth parents, which meant she didn't want to know who they were. He wished he hadn't figured out Paul Aldrich's relationship to her. Sometimes ignorance really was bliss. He stroked the tender spot in front of her ear with his thumb. "Just trying to be friendly. I'm sure he didn't mean anything by it."

Hurt flickered in her eyes. "Why are you defending him? I understand why Alexa stood up for him — he's been friends with her family for a long time. But you —"

"He has?" Steven dropped his hand and moved a step back. "How long?"

She shrugged. "I don't know. I just remember my dad saying he'd once been sweet on my cousin Suzy, and when I asked

440

Alexa about it, she confirmed he and Suzy were good friends a long time ago."

Steven's mouth went dry. He forced a casual tone, his heart thudding. "Suzy is Alexa's mother, right?"

Anna-Grace nodded.

Bits of information began connecting in his mind like pieces of an algebraic equation. Paul Aldrich and Suzy Zimmerman had been sweet on each other. Could Alexa's mother be Anna-Grace's mother? If so, instead of cousins, the girls were sisters. Possibly even twins. But why had Suzy kept Alexa and given Anna-Grace up? Why didn't Mr. Aldrich openly claim Alexa? He obviously knew he'd fathered Anna-Grace, so didn't it stand to reason he'd know about Alexa, too? There were still too many unknown variables for the equation to take shape.

Her brows pinched together. "I thought it was kind of strange that Alexa was so supportive of the man who'd once spurned her mother. Or maybe her mother spurned him. I don't know. Either way, there had to have been some hurt feelings. But she still told me to be nice to him."

"That's always good advice."

"I'll be nice. But I also plan to keep my distance from him. Truthfully, Steven, he made my skin crawl."

Steven chose his words carefully. "If you intend to work over here, you won't be able to stay away from him. The house is pretty small, and he isn't going anywhere else until everything here is done." He remembered the man's request to bring his son along on Saturday. "When there's no school, he'll have his son, Danny, with him. It will probably bother the boy if he sees you being standoffish with his dad."

Anna-Grace tipped her head. Her eyes seemed to berate him. "You know I wouldn't be intentionally unkind. Especially not to a child. And I would appreciate it if you would support me and my feelings instead of sticking up for the carpenter who's working on your house."

He caught hold of her shoulders and drew her into his embrace. She didn't wrap her arms around him, but she allowed him to hold her close. He rested his chin against her temple. The mesh of her head covering felt abrasive against his flesh. "I didn't mean to make you think your feelings don't matter. Of course they do. But the carpenter has to be here every day until the work is done. If you'd rather not be around him, then you'll have to stay at your gra—" He bit the tip of his tongue to stop the word *grandmother* from escaping. ". . . great-aunt's house until his part of the renovation is finished."

She shifted slightly to look up at him. "But if I do that, it'll prolong doing the painting and wallpapering. I said I would help."

"It'll keep." Steven formed his next words carefully. "What about other people in town? You've been here almost a week now. Has anyone else made you feel uncomfortable?"

Her face formed a thoughtful pucker. "No. Not especially. A few have looked at me funny — questioningly, I guess. And sometimes I get the feeling Alexa doesn't really want me around. But no one else makes my skin crawl."

Steven couldn't decide if her answer made him happy or sad. He pulled her close again, his thoughts racing. Should he tell her why Paul Aldrich stared at her? It might ease her mind if she knew the reason he couldn't seem to take his eyes off of her. Better yet, it might send her running back to Sommerfeld, and he could follow. One thing he did know — if he told her now it would be more for himself than for her. As difficult as it was to keep the information a secret, he wouldn't tell her until he was sure it was something she wanted to know.

Once again he took her shoulders and set her aside. "I'm going to take you back to the B and B. It isn't wise for us to be here alone like this."

"We haven't done anything wrong."

In the fellowship's eyes being alone together was wrong because it could lead to sinful behavior. The fact that Anna-Grace now stood before him proved at least one Old Order Mennonite boy and girl had given in to temptation. Although he'd always surmised his fiancée had been born to an unwed mother, knowing her birth parents were Old Order — just like he and Anna-Grace were — increased his determination to remain above reproach.

He offered a gentle smile. "And I want to keep it that way. Come on. Let's go." He helped her into her coat, then escorted her to his pickup. He opened the door for her and took hold of her elbow to give her a little boost into the cab.

As she settled on the seat, she turned to him. A sad smile tipped up the corners of her lips. "I know how much this farmstead means to your family. I won't let my feelings about Mr. Aldrich keep me from being open-minded about living in Arborville. Don't worry."

He lifted her hand and kissed her fingertips. "I'm not worried." He closed the door, then blew out a breath. Not worried? A blatant lie. His biggest worry was he'd be stuck on this farm for the rest of his life, wishing his brother had stayed around to inherit this land instead. As he rounded the truck, his thoughts turned into a prayer.

Lord, forgive me for fibbing. And for withholding the truth about Paul Aldrich. Reveal it to Anna-Grace when the time is right. And, Lord? He paused with his hand on the driver's door handle and looked skyward. Not even a wisp of cloud hid him from his Father's view. *Let her decision about staying or not staying be the right one. For both of us.*

Briley

Friday morning Briley asked for a second helping of Alexa's special pumpkin pancakes. The first serving — three dessert plate–sized fluffy cakes with thin slivers of raw apple and chunky walnuts between the layers, smothered in warm, cinnamon-laced maple syrup, and served alongside sausage links — was enough to satisfy the heartiest appetite, but they tasted so good his mouth insisted on more. He'd just skip lunch later. Besides, he needed to get his fill of Alexa's good cooking before he returned to Chicago.

445

As he dug into the second stack of pancakes, Mrs. Zimmerman shot him a serious frown.

"Alexa tells me you're leaving us soon." She held her coffee cup beneath her chin but didn't take a sip. "Does that mean you've finished your article?"

Briley swallowed and swiped his mouth with his napkin. He noted both Steven and Anna-Grace paused in eating to turn attentive gazes on him. He answered cautiously. "Not quite. I still have one more loose thread to tie up." He shrugged. "Even so, I'll probably head out Monday morning."

"Well, I will tell you now, young man, I wasn't too sure about hosting you when you first showed up here." Mrs. Zimmerman spoke in her brisk, straightforward manner, but he detected a hint of apology in her expression. "If it hadn't been for Alexa needing the money your stay would bring in, I would have sent you right on down the road the first time you flirted with her." An impish twinkle brightened her faded blue eyes. "You are something of a scamp, Briley Forrester."

Her comment raised memories of Aunt Myrt. His lips twitched into a grin.

"I also worried your worldly wise ways might cause problems with some of our young people, but I've watched you with Alexa, with young Danny Aldrich, and now with Steven and Anna-Grace, and you know . . ." She lowered the coffee cup and pointed at him. "Instead of stirring discontent, I think you've made us examine our lifestyle and consider it through an outsider's eyes. You've given us a chance for self-examination. That's a good thing."

Alexa entered the room but remained near the doorway, seemingly unwilling to interrupt her grandmother.

"Of course, outsiders come to Arborville frequently to shop for handcrafted items or just to gawk at the Amish buggies, but none of them stay long enough to really understand how and why we live the way we do. Having you live among us gave us an opportunity to share every facet of our faith, and maybe let you discover we aren't so different from each other after all, hmm?"

Mrs. Z held her hand toward Alexa, and the young woman hurried across the floor to take it. She smiled up at her granddaughter for a moment before turning to Briley again. "As for me, you've let me see how Alexa's decision to turn my old farmhouse into a bed-and-breakfast inn is more than giving Arborville a hotel of sorts. It's a means of ministry. So thank you for staying here."

Briley stared at the wheelchair-bound woman. Oddly, a comment Paul Aldrich had made weeks ago tiptoed through the back of Briley's mind. Something about not being able to make the fish bite — you could only throw out the bait and wait. The cynical side of him tried to tell him she was toying with him. Misleading him. Even tricking him. But his deepest scrutiny uncovered not a shred of insincerity. Her honest admission impacted him deeply. Even so, he set his jaw to avoid clamping down on a dangling hook.

"Will you send us a copy of the article when it's printed?" The older woman raised one gray eyebrow. "We don't receive Chicago periodicals here in Arborville, you know."

Briley hoped they never saw the article. He needed a change of subjects, and he grasped the first question that entered his mind. "Why is this place called 'Grace Notes'?"

Mrs. Zimmerman and Alexa exchanged fond smiles. Still holding her grandmother's hand, Alexa answered. "First of all, God's grace is a precious gift. I think grace is the purest form of mercy, offered even when it's undeserved or rejected." She spoke with a seriousness that captured Briley's attention so thoroughly, he almost neglected to breathe. "We humans are so imperfect, and we mess up so many times —"

Mrs. Zimmerman released a throaty chuckle and nodded.

"But God continues to give us grace. So that's part of it. The other part comes from one of my favorite verses. Zephaniah 3:17 tells me the Lord takes delight in me, and that in His love He rejoices over me with singing." Tears winked in Alexa's dark eyes, turning the irises a deep chocolate brown. "I wanted the name of the inn to honor God for what He does and what He gives. Grace Notes just seemed to . . ." She shrugged, a trickle of soft laughter leaving her throat. "Fit."

The pancakes soured in his stomach. He pushed his plate aside. "Steven, are you ready to put me to work?"

Steven gave a jolt, as if he'd fallen asleep at the table. Red streaked his clean-shaven cheeks, and he jerkily pushed from his chair. "If you want to work today, I'm sure Mr. Aldrich and I will find something for you to do."

Briley headed around the table, eager to escape the strange pressure in his chest.

"Then let's go." Before he made it to the front door, Alexa's soft voice brought him to a stop. He turned to find her near, his lunch box in hand.

"You'll want this. Your last box lunch from Grace Notes."

Did she have any idea how much her statement bothered him? He took the lunch box and gripped the handle so tightly the fibers dug into his palm.

"And I asked Grandmother about going to Wichita with you this evening. She approved it, so I'll be ready at six thirty if you still want to go."

Briley closed his eyes for a moment. What was wrong with him? He needed the evening with Alexa. Without the nitty-gritty details of her illegitimacy, he couldn't finish the article. But he was sorely tempted to cancel. To forget the whole thing. Her simple statement — *"grace is the purest form of mercy, offered even when it's undeserved"* — taunted him. They'd been kind to him. Opened their lives to him. Trusted him. And he intended to repay them by exposing their imperfections.

"Briley?"

He opened his eyes.

Amusement showed in the quirk of her lips. "If you changed your mind, it won't hurt my feelings."

If he didn't change his mind, he'd definitely hurt her feelings. Hers, and Mrs. Z's, and every other person in this town who'd made him feel welcome. He shook his head. "I haven't changed my mind. I'll ring the front bell at six thirty, like a true gentleman would do." Even though he was no gentleman.

"All right." She backed slowly toward the dining room, her smile sweet. "Enjoy your day."

He headed onto the porch and turned his face toward the cool breeze washing from the north. He blew out a breath of aggravation. At himself. At her. At Len. At circumstances. He flicked a glance at the sky as he headed for his car. Would that grace Alexa talked about cover someone who deliberately hurt people who lived to serve God? Probably not. The realization made him sadder than he wanted to admit.

CHAPTER 34

Steven

Friday morning Steven drove Anna-Grace to the hardware store in town to buy wallpapering tools before going to the house. Paul Aldrich had offered the use of his tools, claiming Alexa had borrowed them when working in the B and B, but Anna-Grace declined the offer. She gave the excuse that if she broke something, she'd feel guilty, but he suspected she just didn't want to be beholden to the carpenter. He considered refusing to buy new. After all, she only intended to put up paper in the dining room and bathroom. They might never use those tools again. But twenty dollars was a small price to pay for her comfort.

As the cashier tallied up the purchases, the man said, "So you've got the walls all prepped for paper already, huh? I got a look at the place when we came out and repaired the barn. There was a lot of patching to do.

You must be working nonstop to have them patched and primed so soon."

Steven frowned. "Primed?"

He placed the trimmer and stiff brush inside the plastic water tray and slid it across the counter. "Well, sure. Wallpaper won't stick to unpainted plaster. And it sure won't stick wherever you've got Spackle. You have to prepare the walls with either paint or primer."

Steven grimaced and looked at Anna-Grace. "I wish Mr. Aldrich had said something about primer."

The cashier chuckled and scratched his chin. "He probably assumed you already knew. It's pretty common knowledge."

Gritting his teeth to hold back a growl, Steven cupped Anna-Grace's elbow and led her to the corner of the store where a freestanding metal shelf held gallons of ready-mixed paint. He picked up a can of flat white primer and read the label. "This says a gallon will cover two hundred square feet. Do you remember how big the dining room is?"

She nodded. "Fourteen feet long by eleven feet wide."

Steven tapped the can with one finger and muttered, "So twenty-eight and twenty-two equals fifty, times ten feet high comes out to five hundred square feet, which would mean two gallons plus two quarts of primer. But if we take away the door, the built-in cabinet, and window openings, two gallons should cover it all." He reached for a second gallon and then turned to find Anna-Grace staring at him, open mouthed. "What?"

She released a short huff of laughter. "You're so smart. I would never have figured that out in my head."

He snorted. "Smart, huh? I didn't even know we had to prime the walls first. 'Common knowledge,' the man said." The embarrassment still stung.

"Common knowledge for a carpenter. Not for a farmer."

Her words did little to comfort him. A teacher should know things that were considered common knowledge. "Let's get this paid for."

In the truck Anna-Grace reached across the console for his hand. He took it and she squeezed hard. "Thank you for buying everything. I know you think it was frivolous."

He thought it more foolish and prideful than frivolous, but he didn't say so.

"But it shouldn't be wasteful. After all, we might decide to paper the other rooms someday. Or if we end up living somewhere else, we'll have what we need to decorate those walls with paper if we want to. The tools will be used again someday, I'm sure."

Steven eased the truck off the highway onto the gravel road. "Will it be hard for you to think of living somewhere else after putting work into this house?"

She sat in thoughtful silence for a few seconds. "Maybe. I don't know. It was fun choosing the wallpaper and the paint colors, and the kitchen is so nice. I found myself imagining cooking in it. It felt . . . comfortable."

He wished he could feel comfortable. Mrs. Zimmerman had told Briley that his time in Arborville gave the Mennonites a chance for self-reflection. She was right. Meeting the reporter from Chicago had brought him face to face with the root of his dissatisfaction. People outside of Old Order communities could choose whatever career they wanted. They had *freedom* where he had none. Spending time with Briley had only served to magnify Steven's frustration.

He jammed on the brakes, nearly sending Anna-Grace into the windshield. He ignored her cry of surprise, slipped the gearshift into Park, and whirled on her. "I was thinking last night about the Zimmermans. They've rented my grandfather's farmland for more than twenty years. Now that I'm here, they have to find land somewhere else to plant crops. It's a hardship for them. I feel guilty taking the land away from them. Clete had already put in a winter wheat crop, and I've told him to plan to harvest it for himself. But if we aren't going to stay here — if I'm going to sell the house and the land — it would probably be good for them to know soon. Before they find some other land to rent. They should have first chance at my acreage since they've put so much work into it."

Anna-Grace gazed at him, her blue eyes wide. "Are you asking me to decide *now* whether or not I can live in Arborville?"

"I'm asking you to decide quickly. For the Zimmermans' sake." And for his sake, too.

She shook her head, the ribbons from her cap gently swaying beneath her chin. "I can't, Steven. I haven't even attended service with the local fellowship."

If he told her they were taking farmland away from her biological uncle, aunts, and grandmother, would she make up her mind more quickly? He was twenty-three — the age when English students graduated from college and began their adult vocations. The impatience to do, as Andrew Braun had phrased it, what he was meant to do nearly turned him inside out. *And if you'd just come right out and tell her you don't want to live here, you could end this frustration now.* His lips parted, the words ready to escape.

"I have to be sure, Steven, before I ask you to give up the land your parents gave you."

Her simple statement sent his desires scuttling into the shadows. How could he have forgotten his parents? He couldn't dishonor them by throwing their gift back in their faces.

She looked at him, confusion evident in the pinch of her brow. "I thought you were going to let me have time to decide. Do you really need to know right now?"

He hung his head. "No. Take the time you need. I'm sorry I pressured you."

She leaned across the console and placed a kiss on his jaw. "It's all right. I'm sorry things are so uncertain." She smiled, her expression hopeful. "But one thing I know for sure — I love you, and I want to be your wife. Wherever we decide to live, I know I'll be happy."

Steven nodded, put the truck in gear, and released the brake. Her final statement echoed in his mind. *"Wherever we decide to live, I know I'll be happy."* He wished he could make the same claim.

■ ■ ■ ■

Alexa

After serving supper to Grandmother, Steven, and Anna-Grace and receiving Anna-Grace's promise to clear the table and wash dishes, Alexa darted upstairs to change for her evening with Briley. She tossed her twill skirt and long-sleeved T-shirt in the dirty clothes basket, then stood in front of her closet, trying to decide what to wear. Even though this wasn't technically a date, she wanted to look nice. But not too nice. So she wouldn't make Briley think she thought it was a date. She laughed at herself. "Just pick something!"

She chose her ankle-length, straight, tan corduroy skirt and topped it with a sweater of deepest turquoise. The sweater's nubby texture and cowl neck provided a perfect setting for a multicolored gauzy scarf, which she looped around the cowl and left the ends dangling. Kind of like the ribbons from a Mennonite cap. Brown slouch boots completed her outfit.

In the bathroom she released her ponytail and brushed her hair until it snapped and glistened. For a moment she considered leaving it down, but the rubber band had left a crimp. So she touched up the ends with a curling iron and finger-combed it back into a tail. She gave her reflection a thorough examination and decided the loose curls made the hairstyle a little less stark. She'd do.

She glanced at the clock. Six twenty-two. Eight minutes to spare. She giggled. If she wore makeup like Nicole Kirkley, she'd need another thirty minutes to get ready. Sometimes it really was simpler to be Plain. She returned to her bedroom and slipped the strap from her hobo-style purse over her shoulder, then headed for the stairs. As her foot descended on the first tread, her cell phone rang out with Beethoven's "Für Elise" — Mom's ringtone. She stopped, fished out the phone, and pressed it to her ear.

"Hi, Mom!"

"Hi, honey. Are you busy?"

Alexa grimaced. "Actually, I'm getting ready to grab some dinner in Wichita with a friend. But I have a minute or two."

"I won't keep you long then. I just wanted to let you know I'll be in Arborville for Thanksgiving."

Alexa released a squeal. "I'm so glad!" Then she remembered why Mom had been uncertain about coming. "Did Bridget's daughter have her baby already? Is everyone all right?"

"Bridget's daughter hasn't had her baby yet, but —"

The doorbell rang. "Hold on a minute, Mom. Let me answer the door, and then you can finish your sentence." She bounded downstairs and swung the door open. Briley stepped over the threshold, bringing the spicy scent of aftershave with him, and her jaw dropped in shock. Unwittingly her gaze traveled from the toes of black leather cowboy-style boots up the length of creased black trousers, along the line of a boldly splashed yellow, turquoise, and fuchsia silk tie falling across the button placket of a sheeny steel-gray shirt, and finally to his freshly shaved, smiling face. His leather bomber jacket lay draped over his bent arm in readiness.

She gulped. A man didn't spruce up like that on a Friday night for anything except a date. A *real* date. Suddenly she felt very dowdy and way too young.

"Alexa?" Mom's voice came through the phone.

She held up her finger and mouthed to Briley, *One minute.* He nodded, and she rushed into the little enclosed landing at the base of the stairs. "I'm here." She tipped

460

sideways to peek at Briley, who'd moved to the window and seemed to be examining the shadowy side yard. Merciful heavens, no man had the right to look that good in a shirt and tie.

"Okay. I'll be in Arborville for Thanksgiving, and then I might be moving back there."

Alexa jolted upright. "What? Why?" Briley turned and sent a worried look in her direction. She angled herself toward the corner and lowered her voice to a whisper. "Why would you leave the hospital? You love that place!"

"It would take too long to explain right now, and you have someplace to be. But save a room for me, Miss Innkeeper." The forced joviality in Mom's tone stung Alexa's heart. "I'll call tomorrow and we can talk more then, okay?" She disconnected the call.

Alexa dropped the cell phone into her purse and moved slowly into the front room, her thoughts churning.

Briley flopped his jacket over the arm of Grandmother's chair and crossed the floor to meet her. "Is something wrong?"

"No. Yes." She laughed nervously. "I don't know."

He touched her arm, just a brush of his

fingertips against her sleeve. "Do you want to cancel? I'd say we could do this another time, but . . ." His lips curved into a half smile.

How could she refuse to go out with him when he'd fixed himself up like a *GQ* model? He'd even done something different with his hair — bringing a few strands of his bangs to the side so they formed an imperfect rooster tail that was somehow perfect in its rakish appearance. She shook her head, laughing softly to keep from crying. "No, we can go." She took a step back and gave him a deliberate, teasing head-to-toe look. "That is, if you don't mind being seen with me. I didn't realize this was going to be a dress-up event."

He grinned. "So, are you sayin' I look *good*?" He drew out the word and struck a pose.

She burst out laughing. Her worries over her mother's odd phone call shifted to the back of her mind for a few seconds. Instead of answering his facetious question, she moved to the coatrack and unhooked her unpretentious trench coat. Briley bustled over, plucked it from her hands, and then held it for her.

As she slipped her arms into the sleeves, he said, "You look very nice, Alexa — as pretty and fresh and unspoiled as always." Heat flooded her face, but she appreciated his gesture and the kind words delivered without so much as a hint of teasing. He'd promised to behave like a gentleman, and so far he'd hit the mark.

Remember, Alexa, this isn't a date!

She turned to thank him, but Grandmother rolled her chair into the front room, stopped next to Briley, and began an inquisition.

"So you're going to Wichita, hmm? What exactly are your plans for my granddaughter?"

Briley stood erect. "Dinner at an Italian restaurant."

"Is there drinking there?"

"Probably, but we won't be in the bar, and I won't order alcohol."

"Are you only going to dinner?"

"Possibly a movie afterward. It'll depend on how long it takes us to get served and what's playing."

Grandmother shook her finger. "Nothing R-rated, young man."

Briley saluted.

"You'll watch the speed in that sporty car of yours, and you'll make her wear her seat belt?"

"Of course I will."

"You'll wear yours, too?"

"Always do."

"And you'll treat her like the lady she is — no shenanigans?"

"Not one shenanigan. I promise."

Grandmother nodded. "All right then." She looked at Alexa and held open her arms. "Give me a hug."

Before Alexa could move, Briley bent over and embraced Grandmother. Alexa got a glimpse of Grandmother's stunned face over Briley's shoulder, her arms still widespread. The hug was short — perhaps two seconds — and he stepped aside.

Grandmother stared up at him, her jaw hanging slack. Then she snapped her mouth closed, fixed her face in a scowl, and pointed at Briley. "That, young man, classifies as a shenanigan." Then her lips formed a grin. "But I'll forgive you. Come here, Alexa."

Alexa leaned in for a hug. "We won't be late."

Grandmother patted Alexa's back. "Have fun."

Briley grabbed up his jacket and shrugged into it, the motion very masculine and self-assured. He touched his hand to Alexa's spine and turned her toward the door. "Here we go."

Alexa drew in a deep breath. *Here we go . . .*

CHAPTER 35

Briley

The entire ride to Wichita, Alexa sat with her hands linked tightly in her lap and her gaze aimed out the side window. Tension oozed from her stiff frame, and Briley developed a knot between his shoulder blades in response. Either she was really uncomfortable with him, or that phone call had rattled her good. He wished he knew which was the cause. He tried twice to get her to talk — loosen up a little bit — but his efforts failed.

In times past if a girl showed herself uncooperative, he just took her home and wrote her off. He considered taking Alexa home. But not out of anger or frustration. More out of sympathy. The unusual emotion surprised him. He deliberately tamped it down. He had a story to complete. This wasn't the time to get all sappy and soft. Even so, when they pulled into the restaurant's parking lot and he'd killed the engine, he rested his fingertips on her shoulder and said, very gently, "Hey."

She turned to face him, the silky ends of her ponytail drifting across his knuckles.

He smiled what he hoped would be interpreted as an encouraging, friendly smile. "If you're not up to an evening out, you can tell me. I won't hold it against you." But Len would hold it against Briley.

She sighed. "I'm sorry."

"Is it me?" He sniffed his armpit. "I showered and everything, but . . ."

His teasing did the trick. She laughed and lightly swatted his forearm. "It isn't you, goofy. It's my mom. That phone call."

"Ah." He formed a concerned grimace without effort. "Bad news?"

A frown pinched her brow. "I can't be sure. She said so little. But what she did say makes me wonder . . ."

"Wonder what?"

She shook her head. "It's silly to sit out here and talk. We came to eat, right? And I smell garlic bread. Can we go in?" Her lips formed a weak grin. She was trying to lose the doldrums.

He'd meet her halfway. "Absolutely." He hopped out and trotted around to the passenger side. He opened her door, giving a little bow as he did so, and she rewarded him with a more genuine smile. Clouds hid the stars from view, but round lamps mounted high on poles sent down as much light as an overhead sun. Their short, plump shadows accompanied them across the parking lot.

The foyer, lit by odd half-shell fixtures pointing toward the ceiling, seemed inadequate after walking under the spotlights outside, and Briley blinked a few times before he felt comfortable guiding her over the marble floor to the greeting counter. "Hi. Table for two."

"Name, please?" The greeter, a woman probably in her midtwenties, gave him a bold assessment.

Briley, embarrassed for Alexa, fidgeted beneath the girl's flirtatious grin. "Forrester."

She winked — winked! — before shifting her attention to the plastic board under her fingers. "It could be up to thirty minutes until we have a table ready for you." She locked gazes with Briley, not even glancing in Alexa's direction. The girl was cute — wavy blond hair pulled into a messy bun on top of her head with a few strands loose around her face and makeup artfully highlighting her big blue eyes and heart-shaped face. But the blatant way she ignored Alexa set Briley's teeth on edge. The girl fluttered her eyelashes. "You can wait at the bar if you like."

Briley shook his head, unnerved by the girl's attention but unsure why. What had happened to the Briley Forrester who knew how to take advantage of girls foolish enough to throw themselves at his feet? He put his hand on Alexa's back and aimed her for the foyer. "No, thanks. We'll wait out here."

He settled her on one of the pair of padded, armless settees inside the front door, then slid in beside her, keeping a good foot's distance between them. He frowned, recalling the way the greeter had eyeballed him and looked past Alexa. "I'm sorry that girl was so rude," he said without thinking.

"You don't need to apologize for her behavior. You didn't do anything wrong." Alexa held her hands outward in a gesture of acceptance. "You're a good-looking guy. Girls are bound to notice."

He considered thanking her for the compliment, but she'd spoken so matter-of-factly, he wasn't sure she meant to compliment him. He stretched his arm along the back of the settee and rested his ankle on his knee. "She had two customers standing in front of her. She should have acknowledged you, too."

Alexa just shrugged, apparently unconcerned. So he decided not to worry about it anymore. But he wouldn't give that girl the time of day, either. "While we're waiting, why don't you tell me about that phone call from your mom. It might help to get it off your chest."

She bit the corner of her lip. "I don't know . . ."

He gave her shoulder a light flick with his finger. "C'mon. Tell Big Brother Briley all about it. You'll feel better."

Her eyebrows rose, and a wry grin twitched on her lips. " 'Big Brother Briley'?"

He laughed, pleasant memories marching through his mind. "At my last foster home — I lived with a lady we all called Aunt Myrt — I was the oldest of all the kids. Kind of everybody's big brother. I liked it." With a jolt he realized he had liked it — liked the way the younger ones looked up to him, came to him with their problems, tried to emulate him. Not that he'd always set the best example. He pushed that remembrance aside. "Since I never had real brothers or sisters, Aunt Myrt's other foster kids became my family. But I haven't been able to play big brother to anybody since I moved out on my own." He flicked her again, twice, then poked her. "So c'mon, Alexa, let me relive those carefree days. Tell Big Brother Briley what's worrying you."

She drew in a breath, and her lips parted as if ready to speak. The doors opened, and two laughing couples spilled into the foyer, their arms wrapped around each other's waists. Alexa watched them pass, her lips clamped tight. He inwardly groaned. Why'd those people have to interrupt right then? They'd stolen the moment.

Then Alexa shifted to look at him and said, without any warning or preface, "I'm worried she's going to give up something else she loves."

Briley's reporter nose began to itch. Fiercely. He rubbed it with his finger. "What's that?"

"Her job."

He leaned in and lowered his voice. "What else has she given up?"

Twin tears winked in the corners of Alexa's dark eyes. "Her . . . her daughter."

The answer didn't make any sense. "What —"

"Forrester, party of two." The greeter's voice intruded. She sashayed so close her bare knee exposed by her short, tight, black pencil skirt brushed against Briley's shin.

She leaned in and whispered, "I bumped you up. Shh, don't tell." She touched her lips with her finger and winked again.

Briley cleared his throat and shifted his leg away from her. "That isn't necessary. We can wait."

The girl shrugged, the movement somehow provocative. "The booth is a smaller one, kind of a tight fit for four, so . . ."

Briley looked at Alexa. She made an it's-up-to-you face. It would be easier to talk within the private confines of a booth. He stood. "All right then."

Alexa rose, and Briley gestured her forward, putting her between him and the greeter. Apparently the pushy girl finally got the message, because she stuck her nose in the air and returned to her place behind the greeting table.

A slender young man carrying a pair of menus led them between tables to the back wall where an empty booth waited. Briley gestured Alexa to the first bench, and he slid onto the second. He couldn't wait to return to their conversation. It took great self-control to patiently allow the server to share the evening's special, which was portabella-stuffed tortellini, lightly coated with a rich asiago cheese, tomato, and basil

sauce and served with braised steak medal-
lions.

His description complete, he asked, "What
can I bring you to drink?"

"Water with lemon, please," Alexa said.

"The same," Briley said, even though he
preferred a soda.

"And would you care for an appetizer —
mozzarella sticks or fried mushrooms?"

Briley looked at Alexa. She shook her
head. He turned to the waiter. "No appetizer."

"All right. I'll be back in a few minutes to
take your order." The kid scurried off.

He'd never cared much for tortellini —
too doughy — but Briley decided to order
the special so he wouldn't have to waste
time looking at the menu. He set the plastic-
covered parchment aside, propped his
elbows on the table, and leaned toward the
fat jar flickering with an LED light in the
middle of the table. "Okay, you've got to
explain yourself. Your mom gave up her
daughter?" He raised one eyebrow and
forced a short chuckle. "Then what are you
— an imposter?"

In the muted light of the restaurant, Briley
watched Alexa's face turn pale and then
brighten with splashes of red. She aimed
her gaze at the menu and chewed the corner

of her bottom lip. His curiosity mounted even higher. He reached out to lower the top edge of the menu and capture her gaze.

"Alexa?"

Tears flooded her eyes. "That's exactly what I am. An imposter." A strangled sob broke from her throat. She slapped her hand over her mouth and fled the table.

"Alexa!" Briley charged after her, nearly plowing down the server who'd returned with two tall glasses of water. He ignored the kid's startled face and followed Alexa's escaping form, aware of the curious glances of other patrons observing their progress. He could imagine what they were thinking, and a wry thought formed in the back of his mind — *Sure am glad I'll never see these people again* — as he caught up to her and took hold of her elbow.

She wriggled. "Let me go, Briley, please?"

He held tight. "No." A good reporter wouldn't lose the chance to uncover the whole story. And a good big brother wouldn't let her run off upset and crying.

A middle-aged man in a three-piece suit bustled over to them. His nametag identified him as the manager. "Is there a problem here?" He dipped down slightly and peered into Alexa's face. "Is this man accosting you, miss?"

"No, he's my —" Alexa gulped. "I'm with him. I'm all right."

The man didn't look convinced, but he straightened and sent a glance across the restaurant. Briley glanced, too. A dozen faces peered back, some curious, others seemingly amused. The manager turned to the two of them. "I'd appreciate it if you'd take your scuffle elsewhere."

Briley wouldn't have used the word *scuffle* to describe their behavior, but he bit back an argument and simply nodded. The manager strode off, his shoulders square. With his departure the patrons apparently decided the show was over, because they returned to their quiet conversations, although a few continued to observe Briley and Alexa from the corners of their eyes.

Briley released Alexa's arm and leaned down. "Do you want to stay here and eat, or would you rather . . ."

She hugged herself. "Let's just go." Her eyes flew wide. "I left my coat and purse in the booth."

His jacket was there, too. He aimed her for the front doors. "I'll get our things. Meet me outside." Carrying a lady's coat and purse out of the restaurant couldn't embarrass him any worse than their theatrics already had. He kept his gaze averted as he

475

marched to the booth, dropped a couple of dollar bills on the table, and loaded his arms with their belongings. A few titters followed him as he exited, but he pretended he didn't hear.

Alexa waited right outside the doors, her shoulders hunched against the cold and tears trailing down her cheeks. She offered him a penitent look. "I'm so sorry, Briley."

She'd run away from him, made a spectacle of him in front of an entire restaurant full of strangers, and stolen the chance for him to enjoy a really good meal. But his heart turned over in compassion anyway. He draped her coat over her trembling frame, then chucked her under the chin. "Aw, it's okay, little sister." With his arm across her shoulders, he steered her toward his car. "Tell you what, we'll find a drive-through, order some greasy cheeseburgers and fries, and have a long talk in the car."

She looked up at him, her expression uncertain.

"You'll feel better after you've filled your stomach and spilled your worries." He opened the door for her and gestured for her to get in. "Trust me."

A wobbly smile curved her lips. "Okay, Briley."

She eased gracefully into the seat, and he

gave the door a slam. He trotted around to the driver's side, his heart thudding. Whatever she'd meant by her statement, his reporter instincts told him it was big. Really big. His instincts were never wrong. He could hardly wait to hear the story and then share it with Len.

He climbed behind the wheel and started the engine. He glanced over to teasingly remind her to buckle up, and his gaze met hers. All thoughts of teasing fled. Her face, still stained by tears, looked at him with complete trust. His stomach lurched. *Come into my parlor, said the spider to the fly . . .* The line from a children's poem rose from his memory, and he knew exactly which roles they each played. Could he really treat her so callously, spinning a web around her for his own selfish purposes?

Alexa pulled in a long breath and then let it out slowly. "Thank you for being understanding. And for being willing to listen to me."

He swallowed. "No problem."

"I think you're right. I think I will feel better after I've said it all out loud."

He should tell her to forget it. He should tell her the secret wouldn't be safe with him. He should — "Then let's get going so you can feel better as quickly as possible, huh?"

He put the car in gear and squealed out of the parking lot, determinedly keeping his gaze away from her sweetly trusting face.

The interior of his car would probably reek of grilled onions and grease for weeks, but it would be worth it. He'd pulled in to the first fast-food joint he encountered, afraid if he waited too long he'd talk himself out of prying information from Alexa.

With burgers, grease-splotched bags of french fries, and sodas balanced in their laps, they sat in the car at the back corner of the dark parking lot next to the trash bins. The dome light served as candle glow. Not exactly the evening he'd planned, but he wouldn't complain. He was still getting what he'd come for. Because Alexa hadn't stopped talking since he'd put the car in Park. His ever-present little voice recorder, hiding in the gap between his hip and the console, captured every word of her story about her mother giving up her real baby for adoption and then choosing to raise a baby girl abandoned by a stranger only hours after her birth.

"I didn't find out until this past summer that Mom isn't really my mom. But now that I know, I can't stop wondering who my real mother is. Where she is. Why she left me in that box behind the garage at the unwed mothers' home in Indiana."

The pain in Alexa's voice stabbed Briley. He understood abandonment. He'd never forgotten the day his mom had pulled up to the fire station, opened the door, and said, *"Get out, Briley. Go see the firemen."* And he'd never seen her again.

He had no desire to reconnect with the woman who'd left him, but clearly Alexa wanted to know the woman who'd given birth to her. "You know, you could probably find her. There are lots of private investigators who go snooping around, unraveling mysteries." Len had a half dozen on the payroll at the *Real Scoop.* "It might take some time, and probably cost you a pretty penny, but it could be done."

Alexa hung her head. "I can't."

Recalling her grandmother's comment about Alexa needing the money his stay would provide, he nodded. "Oh. Money woes, huh?" He wished he were independently wealthy. He'd buy an investigator for her.

"That, and . . ." She sent him a helpless look. "It would hurt my mom."

After listening to her tell about the upbringing she'd received, all the things her adoptive mother had done to provide for her without the support of a husband or other family, he really believed the woman would understand Alexa's desire to find her birth parents. "I think you're selling her short. She's been pretty unselfish up 'til now, hasn't she, always putting you first? Why would now be any different?" Alexa remained quiet, so he added, "Look, lots of adopted kids search for their real parents. Your mom's probably even considered the possibility that you'd want to look for them someday, and I bet if you told her, she'd —"

"I'm not adopted."

Briley drew back, surprised by the panic in her tone. "But you just said —"

"I said I was raised by my mom. She found me, and she raised me, but she never adopted me." The words poured out like a bucketful of water being emptied in one swoosh. "She even told the hospital that I was hers — hers by birth — and put her name on my birth certificate. But it was all a lie. She . . . she basically stole me. So I can't look for my real mother. Nobody can know I'm not really Suzanne Zimmerman's daughter. Mom could get in terrible trouble. Don't you see?"

He did see. His scalp sizzled with awareness. He'd thought the story would be revealing an illegitimate birth within a Plain community. But this was deeper. Bigger. Much more scandalous. An Old Order woman had not only given birth to an illegitimate child, she'd then taken someone else's child to raise as her own. He envisioned the headline: *A Lifetime of Lies — Kidnapping and Deceit in Mennonite Mecca.* He could imagine the buzz.

Alexa reached across the console and caught the sleeve of his jacket. Her fingers pinched down, the grip desperate. "And you can't tell anybody. I only told you because I was upset, and because I know you'll be leaving soon, and maybe even because you weren't raised by your parents, either, so you can kind of understand my feelings. But you have to keep this a secret, okay?"

He stared at her, a glib assurance hovering on his tongue but refusing to leave his lips.

She shook his sleeve. "Please, Briley. Please promise you won't tell anyone."

Chapter 36

Alexa

Briley offered to walk her from the barn to the front door, but Alexa shook her head. His gentlemanly treatment and big brother routine had already enticed her to say much more than she should have. She wouldn't give him a chance to weasel something else out of her.

She waved to Marjorie as she passed through the living room but didn't pause to chat. She wanted to close herself in her room and pretend she hadn't been stupid enough to tell Briley Forrester the truth of her parentage. Why hadn't she refused to leave the car until he gave his solemn vow to keep the information to himself? His throaty chuckle and glib response — *"Stop worrying, okay?"* — hadn't fooled her. Somehow her story would end up in his article, and she'd never be able to face her mom, her grandmother, or her uncle and aunts again. She'd just proven herself untrustworthy to the entire Zimmerman clan.

A band of light flooded the upstairs landing. Anna-Grace's door stood open, and the light meant she was awake. Alexa stifled a moan. Why couldn't the girl be asleep already? Alexa peeked around the corner. Anna-Grace sat propped against the headboard with a book in her lap. Hope flickered in Alexa's chest. If Anna-Grace was absorbed in the book, maybe she wouldn't notice Alexa sneaking past. She tiptoed onto the landing.

Anna-Grace glanced up. A smile broke over her face, and she set the book aside. "Hi! I've been watching for you." She patted the edge of the bed. "Come, sit, and tell me about your evening."

Alexa paused outside the door. She didn't want to hurt Anna-Grace's feelings, but how could she sit there and pretend all was well? She forced a laugh. "There's not much to tell, really. Just a drive to Wichita, dinner, and home again." Oh, such a blatant fib . . . Her conscience pricked.

"What did you eat? Something good?"

Anna-Grace's open expression and lighthearted questions deserved a kind response. Alexa sighed, defeated. She stepped into the room and fingered the brass finial on the footboard. "Actually we just had cheeseburgers and fries. Nothing special."

Anna-Grace burst out laughing. "He dressed up for cheeseburgers and fries? That's too funny!"

Alexa didn't find anything funny about it, but she made herself smile in reply. "Yeah, I guess so."

"So no movie?"

Alexa shook her head.

"Oh. Too bad. I —" Suddenly she frowned and leaned forward, peering into Alexa's face in concern. "Alexa, have you been crying?"

Alexa touched her face. Her cheeks were dry but felt stiff from the salty tears that had escaped earlier.

Anna-Grace bounced off the bed and came at her. "You have, haven't you? Why? What did he do? Did he —"

Alexa held up both hands to stop Anna-Grace's indignant flow of questions. "He didn't do anything." *Except listen to me.* "He was a perfect gentleman all evening." *And I trusted him way too much.* "Honest, he acted like a big brother." *A conniving big brother . . .*

Anna-Grace stared hard at her for several seconds. Her face finally relaxed. "All right.

But then why were you crying? Is it because . . ." She touched Alexa's hand, the
gesture laden with sympathy. "He's leaving
soon? Good-byes can be hard."

If he went back to Chicago and wrote
about Mom taking a baby who didn't belong
to her, she'd have to face some serious
good-byes. And they would be worse than
hard. They would be heartbreaking. Tears
threatened again. She sniffed. "You know
how girls get sometimes — emotional for
no good reason. I just had an emotional
night. That's all."

"Are you sure?"

"I'm sure." My, she had this lying thing
down pat. Guilt smacked hard, but she
didn't dare tell anyone else the truth. She
inched toward the doorway. "I'm going to
bed. I'll see you in the morning, okay?"

"All right. Good night, Alexa. Pleasant
dreams."

"Thanks. You, too." She hurried out as
fresh tears stung her sore eyes. After what
she'd done tonight, she deserved
nightmares.

In the middle of breakfast Saturday morning, Alexa's cell phone sang with Mom's
ringtone. *Saved by the bell* . . . Sitting at the
table and trying to act natural, as if she

485

hadn't been a blabby fool the night before, was torture. But she had to follow her usual routine. Grandmother's legs didn't work, but her mind was sharp — she'd wonder why Alexa hid in the kitchen. But now she had an excuse to escape.

She jumped up from the table and dashed out of the dining room. As she clattered up the stairs to her room, she answered. "Hello? Mom?"

"Good morning, sweetheart. I decided to call you before I went to sleep so you wouldn't have to wait until late afternoon to talk. I know I worried you yesterday."

Mom knew her so well. Alexa closed her bedroom door and sank onto the bed. "Yes, you did. I had a hard time sleeping last night, wondering why you'd give up your job and move to Arborville." She'd also worried about other things, but she couldn't bear to tell her mom how careless she'd been. Mom would be so disappointed in her.

"I'm sorry I ruined your sleep. And I don't want you to worry, okay? Often a closed door is God's way of moving us where He wants us to be, and I'm going to believe that's what is happening now."

The conversation was too cryptic for Alexa to follow. "What door is closing?"

"The doors to the hospital."

Alexa almost dropped the phone. "Your hospital? But why?"

"For the past several years they've had a hard time making ends meet. Even nonprofits have to meet certification requirements and purchase up-to-date equipment. It's a never-ending challenge." Mom spoke calmly, assuredly, her voice as soothing as a lullaby despite the difficult subject. "But with recent government changes and more stringent insurance rules, it's just become more than the church can handle. So they put the hospital up for sale. A corporation has already made an offer the church would be foolish to reject. We might close as early as the end of November. By the end of the year, for sure."

"Oh, Mom . . ." Alexa's chest ached. Mom had poured her heart into the patients at the small church-owned hospital. Leaving it would be like leaving a much-loved friend. She pressed her hand to her jumping stomach. "What about Linda? What will she do?" Mom had always called Linda the glue that held the entire hospital together. Linda would be rudderless without her job as administrator.

"She decided to take it as her time to retire. Tom retired last year already, and he's pestered her to do the same, but she didn't want to leave the place in a lurch." Mom's soft chuckle filtered through the phone. "She and Tom are already planning a lengthy road trip."

Alexa released a sigh. "At least she isn't in mourning."

"You know Linda — as usual when trials have come our way, she's encouraged me to see the silver lining instead of focusing on the dark cloud." Briefly silence fell, and then Mom spoke again, her voice hesitant. "She also suggested I look for a job near Arborville, where I can be closer to you and the rest of my family. What would you think of that?"

"I wouldn't complain if you were closer, and I'm sure Grandmother would be happy." After Briley printed the story, though, they might have to change their names and move to Canada. Or Siberia. She swallowed the unpleasant taste of fear and regret. "I wish you could bring Linda and Tom when you come at Thanksgiving. I'd love to see them."

"Oh, they'd love that, too. They miss their girl." A yawn met Alexa's ear. "Sweetheart, I'm bushed. We had three emergencies come in last night — not a minute to catch my breath between them. I need to get some rest. But please don't worry, all right? We have to trust that everything will work out in the end. Good-bye now. I love you."

"I love you, too, Mom." Alexa set the phone aside, then sat staring into nothing, various scenarios forming in her mind. If Briley divulged their secret, Mom might face criminal charges for baby-stealing. Kidnappers faced stiff penalties. She might even go to jail. If he didn't tell and Mom came here to stay, she'd be in the same town with Anna-Grace. Neither were pretty pictures.

A tap at the door pulled her from her reverie. "Who is it?"

"It's me — Anna-Grace. Aunt Abigail wanted me to see if you're okay."

"Come on in."

The door creaked open and Anna-Grace peeked in. "Are you all right?"

Alexa wearily pushed to her feet and crossed to the doorway. "As 'all right' as I can be, I suppose. My mom just told me the hospital where she's a nurse has to close. So she's losing her job."

Dismay widened Anna-Grace's eyes. "I'm so sorry. Does she know what she's going to do?"

"Not yet. She's coming to Arborville for Thanksgiving, and she's thinking about looking for a job around here."

"It would be so nice for you to have her here!"

Alexa wished she could catch Anna-Grace's enthusiasm. She moved toward the stairs, and Anna-Grace followed. Suddenly the other girl gasped. Alexa sent her a questioning look.

Anna-Grace said, "I don't suppose Cousin Suzy would want to be a teacher instead of a nurse."

Alexa stopped on the stairs and frowned. "A teacher?"

"Mm-hm. Clete came in while you were upstairs and told Aunt Abigail the teacher from Arborville received approval to be published to a man from Weaverly, and they want to marry at the end of February. Apparently he's a widower with two small children and doesn't want a long courtship. So Clete and some others are searching for a new teacher to finish the term."

"Mom has a nursing license, but she doesn't have a teaching certificate."

Anna-Grace shook her head. "She wouldn't need one for the church-run school. The rules are different. At least it would be a job right here in Arborville."

As much as Alexa enjoyed working at the grade-school cafeteria, Mom had never envied her position. "I don't think she'd be interested."

"Oh. Well." Anna-Grace shrugged, her smile intact. "I'm sure the right person will come along for the school." She squeezed Alexa's arm. "And I'll pray your mom finds a nursing position. Without a husband to provide for her, she must be worried about how she'll support herself."

Unexpectedly, defensiveness swelled. "Mom isn't a worrier. She *trusts.*"

Anna-Grace's smile turned tender. "You have a mother of strong faith. Like mine. My mom isn't a worrier, either, and she taught me to give my concerns to the Lord rather than fretting." Her fingers tightened once more on Alexa's arm and then slipped away. "We're lucky, aren't we?"

Lucky? Alexa was jolted as she processed the sweetly worded question. Before she could find an answer, Anna-Grace hurried down the stairs and around the corner. Alexa heard her call, "She's okay, Aunt Abigail. She's coming down."

Alexa stepped from the staircase to the living room and came nose to chest with Briley. She jerked backward so quickly she almost lost her footing. He reached for her, but she grabbed the piano and kept herself upright.

She glared at him. "You nearly knocked

491

me down."

"I'm sorry." The congenial big brother of last night had disappeared. In its place stood a storm cloud.

Alexa shivered. "Excuse me." She started to step around him, but he held out his hand. She froze in place.

"We need to talk." He kept his voice to a murmur, loud enough for only her ears.

She flicked a look toward the dining room, but Grandmother had her head turned away, conversing with Anna-Grace. She gave Briley a scowl. "I talked enough last night. I don't have anything else to say."

"Well, I do." His tone developed a bite. "When you've finished the breakfast cleanup, meet me in the barn. We can talk privately out there."

She didn't want to meet with him. But she would. Because somehow she had to convince him to keep her secret. Mom had already lost her beau, her daughter, and her job. She couldn't lose her freedom, too.

Briley

Briley paced back and forth across the hard-packed dirt floor, scuffing up bits of straw and coating the toes of his shoes with fine, powdery dust. After wrestling with himself all night, he knew what he wanted to say to

492

Alexa. He knew what he *had* to say. He also knew it would hurt her, make her angry, and ruin the friendship they'd formed. Her feelings shouldn't matter. He'd be back in Chicago soon, would never see her again, but it bothered him more than he cared to admit to leave on a sour note. Especially after her grandmother had given that flowery little speech about the "good" he'd done for the people in town.

He'd grown to admire Mrs. Z. She wasn't afraid to speak her mind, and she cared about her kids. She reminded him of Aunt Myrt. Without warning his former foster mother's voice crept from the recesses of his mind. *"Every man has two equal abilities, to build up or to tear down. The challenge lies in knowing which is the right choice."* As a teenager he'd rolled his eyes and inwardly called her old-fashioned. But now he understood the wisdom of her words. Telling the story Len expected would build himself up as a reporter, but it would tear down the integrity of the faith-based group of people he'd come to know and respect. Which was the better choice?

Another of Aunt Myrt's pieces of advice whispered to him. *"When you need answers, Briley Ray, there is One who knows all and who will never lead you astray. Talk to Him."*

Briley groaned and slapped his hand to the sturdy beam rising from the center of the barn floor. Aunt Myrt knew God well enough to talk to Him. So did the Mennonites in Arborville. But he didn't. He'd never taken the time to get to know God. Had never *wanted* to know Him. The title believers used for God — Father — had always tripped him up. His father, and the pseudofathers his mother had brought into their apartment, were never trustworthy or admirable or loving. So he'd pushed Aunt Myrt's Father aside, too. Why would God help him now? This decision was his and his alone.

CHAPTER 37

Steven

What a stupid decision he'd made, keeping secret his desire to be a teacher instead of a farmer. If he'd told someone — his parents, Anna-Grace, a friend — then one of them would point to Steven and tell Clete Zimmerman, "He'll do it." If others knew what he'd wanted since he was a young boy, they would all be happy for him, would say things like "God opened the door" or "This is the Father's will, for sure." But because he'd allowed his brother's derision and choice to abandon their home to keep him silent, he couldn't say anything now. They'd all be too shocked to consider it a real possibility.

He swallowed a groan. He'd thought his only chance to teach would be in a secular school, one that required its teachers to have a degree from a college. All of his thoughts had been to somehow get a degree. But the church-based school only needed a willing teacher. And he was willing. If they were willing to let a man teach their children.

Clete had left the dining room only a minute or two ago. Maybe Steven could catch up to him, find out how soon the fellowship wanted to put a teacher in place, find out whether they'd even consider a male teacher. Female teachers were common in the private, church-run schools, but most of them only taught for a short time and then chose marriage and a family over teaching other people's children. Maybe having a male teacher, one who would stick around, would appeal to the fellowship leaders in Arborville. He had to know.

He swiped his mouth with his napkin and leaped up. Anna-Grace gave him a curious look, and he paused long enough to assure her he'd be right back. Then he charged through the kitchen and out the back door, searching for Clete. He spotted the man at the far edge of the grassy yard climbing onto his tractor. He waved his hand over his head and yelled, "Clete! Clete, hold up!"

Clete, half on and half off of the old iron tractor, looked over his shoulder. As Steven ran across the yard toward him, he stepped back onto the ground and turned to face him. "Something wrong?"

"No, but I wondered . . ." A huge lump formed in Steven's throat, blocking his windpipe. He coughed into his hand, inwardly praying for courage. "You told your mom the church school will need a new teacher. Do you know when?"

"Well, by February for sure. Although Miss Reimer said she wouldn't mind going to Weaverly sooner, to get settled into the community before then."

"Would y-you" — *Don't stammer!* — "consider hiring a man to teach the school-children?"

A mild frown formed on Clete's face. "A man?" He shifted his ball cap on his head. "We've never had a man teacher, but I don't know that we would have anything against it. Do you know of a man who's interested in teaching?"

Steven's pulse doubled its pace. "I . . . I do."

"In some ways it might be a good thing to have a man in the schoolhouse. Someone stronger, who would keep the older boys in line a little better." Clete chuckled. "I know my kids behave better for me sometimes than they do for their mother — something about my deeper voice, probably." Then he gave a rueful scowl. "But the salary we can pay . . . We're a small fellowship. I doubt

497

we'd be able to offer enough for a man to take care of his family."

Ideas raced through Steven's mind, almost dizzying. He wouldn't need a big salary — not if he continued to receive rent for his farmland. And his house was paid for. He could afford to take a modest salary from the fellowship, thanks to the blessings he'd received from his parents.

Clete said, "There are a couple of younger ladies in town who aren't working right now and are the right age for teaching. The fellowship plans to ask them about filling in for Miss Reimer. Surely one of them will accept since it's only to finish out the year. Then we'll search harder for a new teacher to start next spring." He clapped Steven on the shoulder. "I'd better get to work now. The winter wheat won't plant itself, you know."

Steven backed up as Clete started the engine on the tractor. The rumble vibrated the ground and sent tremors up Steven's legs. He turned and walked slowly toward the house, replaying Clete's comments in his mind. *God, You know my desires. You always have. I didn't want to come to Arborville. I only came to honor my parents, but now Arborville needs a teacher. It all seems so perfect to me, but is it only my wishful thinking making it seem right?* He came to a stop beneath the clothesline and reached up to grip the thin wires, holding tight.

It's probably foolish of me to get my hopes up. I don't even know yet if Anna-Grace will want to stay here. All this time I've wanted her to choose no so I could sell the property and use the money for college. But now . . . He jerked his hand free of the line. The wire sent out a whine that slowly faded into silence. He lowered his head, uncertain what to say next. How he hated these jumbled thoughts and feelings. If only God would write the answer in the sky.

He sighed and ended his prayer the way his parents had taught, the way Jesus Himself had instructed His disciples. *Your will be done, my Father. Your will . . .*

Alexa

Even though she knew Briley was waiting, Alexa took her time cleaning up the breakfast mess. If only she could turn back the clock and redo her evening with Briley. If only he wasn't a reporter from Chicago who had the potential to expose Mom's wrongdoing. If only . . . She slapped the dishwasher's door closed and drooped over the countertop. If only she could truthfully call herself a Zimmerman — if not by blood, by legalities — so there wouldn't be a story to report.

She grabbed her sweater from a peg by the back door and headed for the barn. God didn't hold Mom's youthful indiscretions against her. Paul Aldrich and her family had forgiven her, too. They'd all offered grace, as had the Arborville fellowship, who included Alexa in their fold even though she wasn't a member of their church and of an illegitimate birth. But Briley wasn't family, and he wasn't part of the Mennonite fellowship. She was pretty sure he didn't possess a relationship with God at all. She wouldn't hope for grace from him.

The heavy barn door hung in the closed position. She pressed her palms to the edge and gave a mighty push. It resisted moving, the old rollers in the track rusty and stiff from age, but she put her full weight against the door and created a gap wide enough for her to step through. The outside air held a bite this morning, but the thick barn walls and insulating bales of hay made the barn's interior comfortable. It was quiet, too — a good place for a private conversation. If only the subject didn't promise to be so painful.

When she entered the barn, Briley rose from a short bench tucked in front of one of the stalls and moved toward her in his usual self-assured stride. If only he'd smile, tease, even wave a copy of that ridiculous photograph under her nose. But instead he approached with a solemn expression that sent chills from the base of her spine to the top of her head. She stopped short in the middle of the floor and allowed him to close the distance between them.

"I didn't think you were going to come." His words held a hint of criticism.

"I almost didn't. I really don't want to talk to you. I've already said too much." Far, far too much. The regret panged through her, and she folded her arms over her rib cage. "But I decided —"

He held up his hand. "Don't talk. I don't want you to talk. I want you to listen." He caught her elbow and led her to the bench. With a gentle push he settled her on it, then took a step away and faced her, his feet widespread and his arms crossed. His tall form created a formidable barrier between her and the door, and for a moment she questioned the wisdom of being out here alone with him. Uncle Clete was in the field, but the rumble of the tractor would keep him from hearing her yell if she needed him. Should she have insisted on meeting in the living room, where Grandmother was close by?

He began to speak, and his tone chased away her worry. He sounded more apologetic than antagonistic. "You knew all along I'm a reporter. You knew I came to Arborville so I could write an article about living the Plain lifestyle. So when you talked to me last night, you had to know that everything you said could be used in my article."

He'd told her not to talk, but she couldn't stay quiet. "But I didn't know! You called yourself 'Big Brother Briley,' and you told me I'd feel better if I talked about what was bothering me. You weren't being a reporter last night, you were being my friend. I . . . I *trusted* you."

He cringed, proving her protest hit its mark. But then he cleared the expression and pinned her with a stern look. "I'm sorry you feel that way, but what you have to accept is that we've only known each other for a few weeks. Sure, we've become friends. Sort of. But once I leave here, will our friendship continue? Doubtful. Chicago and Arborville are too far apart. Your lifestyle and mine are too far apart. So you can't expect me to throw away the best story of my career over a temporary, short-term relationship."

Alexa nodded wildly. "Yes, I can. Because your story will affect the most important, lifelong relationship I have!"

He let his head drop back and released a heavy breath. "Alexa . . ."

She jumped up and curled her hands over his muscular forearms. "Briley, please." She waited until he met her gaze. "You've been in Arborville for more than a month. You've gathered other information. Can't you write your article without including my mom or me?"

Anger flared in his dark eyes. He stepped free of her light grasp. "No, I can't. Because I didn't find anything else that proves what I set out to prove."

"And what is that?"

"That you people aren't perfect. That you're no different than anybody living in the cities. That you don't deserve the public's admiration and envy."

She gawked at him, too stunned to speak. He'd come hoping to find ways to denigrate the faith of the people living in Arborville? And she'd handed him a reason on a silver platter. *Lord, forgive me . . .* Tears flooded her eyes.

He released a low growl through his clenched teeth. He marched a few feet away and stood with his back to her. "I will not let you make me feel guilty about this. My boss sent me here to find dirt. I found it. I

503

did my *job.*" He spun to face her, his eyes flashing fire. "When I get back to Chicago and I write my story, my name will be on the front page for the first time. Front page, Alexa. Do you understand the significance of that?"

A snide laugh left his throat. "Of course you don't." His gaze narrowed and he jabbed his thumb against his chest. "But I do. Only the writers of merit get front-page coverage. It's a recognition I've wanted for . . . for years." His stiff frame wilted, and he shook his head, the fierce expression turning to one of longing. "You were raised by a woman who found you instead of birthed you, but I bet she encouraged you, didn't she? Told you how much she loved you, told you when you did well in school, praised you and made you feel important. Am I right?"

Mom's familiar endearment — *"You're my gift"* — rolled through her heart, followed by a wave of pleasant memories. Anna-Grace had been right. She was lucky to have such a wonderful mother. "Yes. Even though I didn't have a dad, Mom made sure she loved me enough for two parents. I never questioned that I was loved."

"Well, I can't say the same thing. I never felt loved. Never felt important or needed.

In fact, when I was a kid, they put me in special classes because it took me until I was nine years old before I learned to read. So I got called 'dummy' a lot." He grimaced, as if the voices from the past were tormenting him now. "Teachers, foster parents, social workers . . . they all said I'd never amount to anything. I was too wild, too lacking in intelligence and common sense, too uncaring. For a long time I acted out. I broke every rule my foster parents made. I refused to do my homework. I told everybody I didn't care what any of them thought. I figured, prove them right — why not? If I was unlovable, then it didn't matter that nobody loved me."

Even though his tone was brisk, businesslike, she sensed that the remembrances hurt. They hurt her, and they weren't her memories. "I'm sorry, Briley."

He huffed out a breath and waved his hand, dismissing her words. "It's over. Water under the bridge. And none of it really matters anymore. Except this." His face stony, he scuffed slowly toward her. "I made a promise to myself to prove them wrong. To show the teachers who thought I was stupid and the foster parents who thought I'd never amount to anything that I can be successful. I've been waiting for the chance to see my name under a front-page lead story, and now I have it. I can't give that up."

His hands descended on her shoulders, holding her in place. He lowered his voice to a raspy whisper. "I'll change the names. I'll do that much to protect you."

She released a sad laugh. "Changing the names won't protect me. Arborville is so small the people here will recognize my mom and me in a heartbeat. They live a simple lifestyle, but they aren't stupid, Briley." And eventually the authorities would figure it out, too, putting Mom at risk of prosecution.

His lips formed a grimace. He shook his head. "I'm sorry it'll be uncomfortable for you, but I'm telling the story. I've waited too long and worked too hard to just let it go."

She stood beneath the weight of his hands, beneath the weight of his painful past. She'd listened, as he'd asked her to do. Now she wanted the same courtesy from him.

CHAPTER 38

Briley

He braced himself for Alexa's protest. She would protest. Argue. Beg. Maybe even cry. He'd always hated seeing girls cry. Especially when he caused the tears. But he'd be strong. He would *not* give in.

She took hold of his wrists and lifted his hands from her shoulders. Then she moved behind him and gave him a little push. "Your turn."

He glanced at her over his shoulder with a raised brow. "For what?"

"To sit down and listen."

She pushed him again, the pressure insistent, and he huffed out a brief snort of laughter. He could listen. He owed her that much. Even though his eyes and nose itched from breathing in the musty scents of the old building, he moved to the bench, turned, and seated himself as if perching upon a throne. Palms on his thighs, he lifted his chin and gave her a haughty look. "Thouest may speak."

She frowned. "I'm not teasing, Briley."

So much for using levity to decrease his discomfort. "Sorry. Go ahead." He pointed at her, warning her with his scowl. "But keep in mind, Aunt Myrt said I'm as stubborn as a dozen mules, and she was right. You can't change my mind."

She stood for a moment, seeming to examine him, and he made it a point to gaze back without flinching, even though her somber perusal made him want to squirm. Finally she moved to the bench and sat on the end. Shifting sideways so she could face him, she linked her hands in her lap and fixed her gaze on his face.

"First of all, I'm sorry you never felt loved. I can't imagine anything worse. I didn't have a big family, and I was jealous of the kids who had a mom and a dad and brothers and sisters. I always wished I could be part of a family like that. Even so, I wouldn't have traded my mom for any other family in the world. I guess, even though it might sound a little weird, it was a good thing my birth mother threw me away, because the best mom I could hope for found me."

Briley gave a little start, a strange thought forming in the back of his mind. If his

508

mother hadn't booted him out, he'd have never met Aunt Myrt, the best person he'd known until coming to Arborville and meeting the Zimmermans. *Tear down or build up?* Alexa was talking, and he forced himself to listen.

"I knew how much Mom loved me, and I was fortunate to have other people in my life — people from church — who loved me, too. Most of all, my mom always told me how much God loves me."

Aunt Myrt had told him the same thing. Over and over and over . . .

"If I had grown up feeling like no one loved me, I'd probably be trying to find my self-worth and value in other things, like a job." She sucked in a sharp breath and looked away for a moment, as if something had poked her in the ribs. When she turned to him again, her cheeks wore a rosy glow. "I've kind of done that myself with the B and B . . . trying to make it a success so my aunt Shelley and uncle Clete would think more highly of me. They" — she blinked away tears — "didn't like me much when I first came to town." She touched his knee, just a brush of her fingers. "So I understand why the article is so important to you. I really do."

He didn't think his front-page article and

her cooking for guests carried the same importance, but arguing would only prolong their conversation. He clamped his teeth together and remained silent.

"But you're looking for recognition in the wrong place. The people who hurt you? They didn't care about you then, and they don't care about you now. Do you really think your estimation will go up in their eyes just because your name appears under an article on the front page of a newspaper?"

Defensiveness hit so hard he jolted. "Now, just a minute, I —"

"But let's say it does change their minds. Let's say they look at your name on that page and they realize they were wrong — that you aren't dumb or incompetent or worthless. Will that magically change you somehow?"

He tried to interrupt again, but she kept going, either unwilling or unable to stop her flow of words.

"Will that brief moment of reflection — of 'Hmm, so I was wrong' — by people who aren't even in your life anymore make any real difference? I don't think so. Because, Briley, *those people* don't define your worth."

The cocky teenager who'd resided under Aunt Myrt's roof roared from the past and aimed a sarcastic arrow at Alexa's heart. "Oh yeah? Says who?"

"Says God."

He bolted to his feet and moved to the opposite side of the bench, where he glowered at her. He wanted to roll his eyes. He wanted to bark out a derisive laugh. He wanted to storm out the door and not look back. But he couldn't. Some invisible, incomprehensible something — or was it Someone? — sealed him in place.

She rose and turned to face him, her movements so slow she seemed to be pushing through a wall of water. " 'For God so loved the world . . .' " Her voice was quiet, reedy. He had to strain to hear her quote a scripture he'd memorized to earn a candy bar from his Sunday school teacher when he was thirteen years old. He recited it in his mind along with her. " 'That he gave his only begotten Son, that whosoever believeth in him should not perish, but have everlasting life.' "

She reached across the little bench and touched his wrist. " 'Everlasting,' Briley. Did you hear that? What you're trying to do won't last forever. It will only give you momentary satisfaction — no longer than the amount of time it takes to read your name."

He ground his teeth together so tightly his jaw ached. He wished he could argue with her, but somehow the arrow he'd tried to fling had become a boomerang, spinning around and impaling him instead. The pain in his chest took all his focus. He couldn't form a coherent thought.

"I know you want to feel important. I know you want to feel loved." Tears rolled down Alexa's cheeks. Tears not for herself, but for *him.* "So listen to God's words. Believe them. He loved you enough to send His very own Son to take the penalty for your sins. If you accept His salvation, you'll have love — love that lasts through eternity. You'll be God's child, and there is no greater position than that."

Her fingers slipped around his wrist, a gentle tether pulling him toward the One Aunt Myrt had loved and served and tried so hard to make real to him. "God the Father wants to rejoice over you with singing, Briley. Will you let Him?"

Longing spiraled through his chest. *Will you let Him?* And then Len's warning about being taken in by a little Plain girl swooped into his memory. He was playing right into her hands. The longing unraveled. He yanked free of her grasp. "As I said, I'll use fictitious names, but the story's in. And that's final." He expected her expression to harden. For venomous words of protest to spew from her mouth. Maybe even for her to leap over the bench and pound her fists on him in rage. It wouldn't be the first time someone had physically attacked him in anger or frustration.

But she didn't.

Gazing up at him with tear-brightened eyes, she nodded. Then she sighed — an airy expulsion of breath that spoke of both resignation and acceptance. "All right. If you think that's the right thing to do, I won't argue with you. But, Briley?"

He stiffened his frame, steeling himself against a new feminine ploy.

"I'm going to pray for you. Not for you to change your mind about the article, but for you to change your mind about God. Because you need His love."

"You need His love, Briley Ray. It'll transform you if you'll only turn to Him." Aunt Myrt again, rising from the past. He'd had enough. Without a word, he spun on his heel and pounded for the barn door. He gave it a vicious two-handed thrust that sent it screeching along the iron rail. Chill air, heavy with the scent of fall, filled his lungs, and for one moment he savored the fresh essence — the smell of the plains. The smell

he now associated with the Plain.

Growling at himself under his breath, he aimed his feet for the cottage. He'd pack. Pay his bill. Throw in some extra to compensate for the income his early departure would take from Alexa and Mrs. Z. Then he'd hightail it back to Chicago and count down the minutes until his long-held dream became reality. He would see his name on a front-page byline. He would!

An unfamiliar car revved up the lane, stirring a cloud of dust. The car's horn blared out, an intrusion to the otherwise peaceful setting, and the passenger hung out the side window while waving both hands. Was someone in the middle of some kind of emergency? He moved backward to give the vehicle space to pull in, and he almost stepped on Alexa, who'd apparently trailed him out of the barn.

Before he could apologize to her, the passenger door flew open, and none other than Nicole Kirkley dashed directly at him, squealing at the top of her lungs. She leaped into his arms. "Briley, I won! I won!"

Anna-Grace

Anna-Grace might not like Paul Aldrich much, but it took less than an hour for her to fall in love with his son. Steven and the carpenter spent the morning putting the bathroom fixtures into place, and instead of helping his dad, Danny assigned himself as her assistant. With a seriousness that made her swallow giggles, he explained how to use half-inch-wide blue tape — painter's tape, he called it — to mask off the tops of the baseboards and along the window and door frames.

"You don't hafta put it along the ceiling this time since we're gonna paint the ceiling, too." Danny stood in the middle of the dining room with his hands on his hips and examined the newly Sheetrocked ceiling with a critical eye. "Dad had to take down the crown molding before he could fix the walls and ceiling, and that'll save us some time. But he kept it, and Mr. Braun wants to put it back up."

As he tucked the remaining tape in the pocket of his overalls, he said, "You ever painted a room before?"

She shook her head. "No. Never."

"Painting's not hard. Just takes planning, preparation, and patience." He aimed his businesslike gaze at Anna-Grace. "See, since the crown molding'll cover up the place where the walls meet the ceiling, it won't matter if the ceiling paint touches the wall. We just gotta make sure the wallpaper goes up almost to the ceiling line. Then the crown molding will hide the edge of the wallpaper and any little paint oopses."

What an adorable little man he was! Anna-Grace turned her back on him so he wouldn't see her smile. She pretended to press a short stretch of tape more snugly to the door casing and then, when she'd gotten her amusement under control, she faced him again. "You know a lot about fixing up houses. Are you going to be a carpenter when you grow up?"

Danny scratched his head. "I dunno. I like helping Dad. Mostly 'cause I just like being with him." The boy grinned sheepishly. "He's kind of my best friend even though he's my dad."

Anna-Grace's heart caught. The boy's sincerity tugged at her. Paul Aldrich must not be all bad if he possessed the admiration of this darling little boy.

Danny went on. "But Dad wants me to be what God wants me to be, and I'm not really sure what that is yet." Hunching his shoulders, he giggled. "But sometimes I hope God'll want me to be a baseball player. I like baseball a lot."

Anna-Grace didn't bother to hide her smile this time. "If you play ball as well as you prepare a room for paint, you'll be the best player ever."

Danny beamed at her. He swung his arms, brushing his blue-striped overall legs with his open palms. "So . . . ya ready to paint now? Dad's got extra rollers and paint trays in the truck. He said we should go ahead and use them, too, when I asked him for the painter's tape."

Anna-Grace cringed. "Can't we use brushes?" Steven had purchased brushes.

The boy made a face. "We could, but it sure goes slow. Rollers are better."

She hadn't wanted to use the carpenter's painter's tape, and she didn't want to borrow any of his equipment, but the boy seemed to know what he was doing. She sighed. "All right. I'll have Steven buy some to replace the ones we use today, as well as the tape. Okay?"

Danny offered a nonchalant shrug. "You'll hafta talk to Dad about it. He told me to make sure you got whatever you needed to get the job done."

The man was certainly considerate. Was he as generous with all the people who hired his help? Seeing him through Danny's eyes, she wished she could feel more comfortable around him.

Danny trotted out to the truck and carried back fuzzy rollers on bent handles which he attached to long poles. He made her shake the can of primer until she thought her arms would fall off, and then he poured paint into low metal trays with slanting bottoms. With great patience he explained how to dip the roller in the puddle of paint and glide it over the slope to remove the excess before applying the paint-drenched roller to the wall. "If we drip, we'll want to wipe it up real quick so it doesn't ruin your nice wood floors. Dad didn't have paint cloths in the truck." He frowned at her. "Will you be careful?"

She feigned great seriousness although laughter threatened. "I will. I promise."

"All right, then. Watch me for a minute, then you try."

She stood aside, linked her hands behind her back, and watched.

He held his tongue in the corner of his mouth, his brow puckering in concentration. With smooth, even sweeps he painted an up-and-down path on the wall. Then he looked at her and smiled. "See? It's not hard at all. Go ahead — you can do it."

Releasing a nervous giggle, she picked up the second pole and imitated his movements. When she managed to cover a small patch of wall with cream-colored primer without dripping on the floor or her clothes,

Danny let out a whoop.

"Woohoo, Anna-Grace! You're doin' great!"

His compliment warmed her to the center of her soul. She turned to give him a smile and caught a glimpse of the boy's father peeking around the corner at them. The expression on his face — a mix of deep pain and intense longing — melted her pleasure in one heartbeat. His gaze locked with hers. For long seconds they stared at each other while Danny whistled and went on painting, oblivious. Red mottled the man's cheeks, and he finally ducked out of sight.

A prickle of unease traveled across Anna-Grace's scalp. If every person in Arborville made her as comfortable as Danny did, she'd choose this town as her home without a moment's pause. But how could she stay in this town when Paul Aldrich lived here, too?

CHAPTER 39

Briley

By noon Briley had everything packed and stacked beside the door of the cottage for transport to his car. He checked his wallet to make sure his corporate credit card was in its slot, and then he headed across the yard to the back door. Clete's tractor — one that looked like it should have been retired twenty years ago — was parked under the elm tree at the edge of the stubbly field. Briley's steps slowed and then stopped.

Even though he'd walked this pathway countless times over the past weeks, the difference between Arborville and the city that had always been his home still startled him. He let his gaze drift over the dark, stubble-dotted soil stretching toward the horizon to the windbreak of scrubby trees in the north and finally settle on the tractor. Sunshine through empty tree limbs formed slashes of darkest russet across the implement's red-painted body. The scene before him seemed surreal, almost like a painting.

Although he'd been here long enough to know it was true, a disbelieving question still formed in his mind: *Do people really live like this?* He automatically reached for his camera to capture the image, but he'd already packed it. He allowed himself a few more minutes of absorption before forcing his feet to carry him to the house.

The porch door hinges squeaked, just like the one on the back door at Aunt Myrt's place. Had he ever remembered to oil them, the way she'd asked each time one of the kids slammed in or out? He didn't think so. Back then he hadn't cared much about pleasing anybody but himself. He gave a start. He hadn't changed much. Shaking his head to dispel the thought, he entered the kitchen.

Apparently Alexa had prepared a simple lunch today, because sandwich fixings — a few slices of bread wrapped in plastic, a package of slivered ham, and an open mayonnaise jar with a knife sticking out of it — and a rumpled potato chip bag were still sitting on the counter. A smile tickled his cheek as he remembered their teasing exchanges via his lunch box. He'd had fun. He'd miss it.

Voices carried from the dining room, and he remembered why he'd come in. *Pay your bill and move on, Forrester.* He headed through the little passageway, and as he entered the dining room, laughter erupted around the table. An unexpected wave of jealousy struck. He wanted to be part of their circle. But hadn't he made his choice? When he got back to Chicago, the other reporters would be jealous of him for landing such a controversial story. *Pay your bill and move on.*

"Hey." The laughter faded, and everyone turned to look at him. He aimed his attention at Alexa. "I need you to —"

"Briley, did you hear the news?" Mrs. Z flapped her hand toward Nicole, beaming as proudly as if her goose had just laid a golden egg. "Nicole won the contest in Missouri, and an agent wants to take her down!"

"Take me *on,* Mrs. Zimmerman," Nicole corrected, and the group gathered around the table laughed again. All except Alexa, who pinned Briley with a sad, disappointed expression.

He'd seen that same look on Aunt Myrt's face too many times. It pierced him as much now as it had back then. He shifted to clear her from his line of vision. "Yeah, I heard. She told me out in the yard." She'd almost squeezed his head off with her hug.

"But I didn't tell you everything." Nicole turned backward in the chair and cupped her fingers over the top. She peered at him with wide, sparkling eyes, resembling the cartoon drawing of Kilroy. "The agent who wants to sign me on? He lives in Nashville, and he works with some of the biggest recording studios in the business. He said he can get me on the radio and singing at rodeos and doing fund-raising concerts. He said he heard a rumor about a new talent-search program for television, kind of like *American Idol,* to discover the next big country-western star, and he said he'll put my name in for the first season." The girl bounced in the chair, her voice rising into a near squeal. "And if I win it or even make it to the finals, I could get a contract with a record company!"

"Wow." Briley injected as much enthusiasm as he could into his voice. "That would be something, wouldn't it?"

Nicole's father smiled at his daughter. "Kathy and I always thought Nicole had talent, but most parents think their kids are special. Even when they aren't. Hearing that agent go on and on about her natural ability and unique vocal tone, well . . ." The man gulped, his face staining with pink. "It

523

makes a father proud. Makes me want to break out in song."

Nicole giggled. "Please don't, Daddy. I didn't inherit my talent from you."

More laughter spilled, but Briley didn't join in. He found no humor in squelching the father's desire to sing for joy for his child. Alexa's teary statement about the Father God wanting to sing over him with rejoicing roared through his memory. A lump filled his throat. Without conscious thought he glanced in her direction and found her gazing at him. Something in her eyes — sadness, yes, but something more — held him captive. He finally recognized the emotion. Compassion.

She slowly stood, her gaze never wavering from his, and opened her mouth to speak. Instinctively he drew back, derisive voices from the past rising up in a chorus of criticism. "Briley, have you had lunch? I can make you a sandwich."

His chest tightened, his lungs refusing to draw air. How could she reach out to him in kindness when he'd openly stated his intention to broadcast her mother's sins? He knew why. She possessed a merciful heart. She offered mercy even though he didn't deserve so much as a shred of it.

He found his voice. "I'm not hungry. I

just came in to pay my bill. So I can check out."

"Check out? Today?" The dismay in Mrs. Z's face was a knife in his stomach. "But I thought you would go to service with us one more time before you left."

Mr. and Mrs. Kirkley pushed away from the table, and Mrs. Kirkley gestured for Nicole to rise, too. The woman flashed a smiled at Briley. "Alexa has work to do, so we'll get out of the way."

Mrs. Z rolled her chair toward the family. "You don't have to hurry off, either. Why don't all of you — Briley, you, too — stay the night and go to service with us in the morning."

Mrs. Kirkley shook her head. "Oh, we couldn't impose. Nicole just wanted to stop by on the way home and share her good news since you were all so kind to her when we were here before."

"Besides," Nicole added, "we hafta get back. The agent said he'd be calling to set up some gigs, and I need to clear my calendar."

"Mm-hm, your calendar." Mr. Kirkley hooked his elbow around Nicole's neck and tugged her close. "It's so cluttered, it will be a challenge to find an open day for performances."

The girl grinned sheepishly and shrugged out of her father's hold. Still smiling, the trio headed for the door. Mrs. Z accompanied them, but Alexa held back. She moved to the fold-down desk tucked in the corner of the room.

"It'll only take me a minute to total your bill. Do you want to pay it now, or do you want me to mail the newspaper an invoice?"

The civil, professional way she addressed him took him back to his first day, when she'd instructed him to call her Miss Zimmerman and calmly deflected his flirting. If he'd known then how he'd come to admire her, respect her, consider her a friend, he would have insisted on a different place to stay. But it was too late now. The damage was done.

He whipped out his wallet and slipped the credit card free. "Put it on here."

She grimaced. "I'm sorry. I don't have a credit card machine yet. I can only take cash or checks."

He didn't carry a checkbook — who did anymore? — but there was an ATM at the convenience store. He could draw cash off his card. He put it away. "All right. I'll get you cash. How much?"

She bent over the desk, wrote some figures on a small preprinted invoice, then tore it from the booklet and handed it to him.

He glanced at the amount. Something didn't look right. "Is this for a week or for my whole stay?"

"Your stay."

Briley shook his head in disgust. He'd paid more for a three-day weekend at a four-star hotel. "Are you sure that's enough?"

"It's what your boss and I settled on."

Len had obviously taken advantage of her youth and inexperience. He jammed the invoice in his pocket and silently vowed to double it. Maybe triple it. Len could afford it, and she deserved a decent payment for the story . . . and the grace she'd shown him. *And just how much is grace worth? The life of one Son.* Cringing against a stab of remorse, he turned toward the passageway. He'd get cash, pay her in full, then take himself back to Chicago, where he could write his story and then forget about the people he'd met in Arborville.

Steven

Steven pulled into the convenience store parking lot and parked alongside the brick building, next to a fire-engine-red sports car. He hopped out and glanced at the familiar vehicle as he strode up the sidewalk.

527

Briley must be picking up lunch, too. He'd laughingly confessed to developing a taste for the double-pepperoni pizza baked in the store's oven.

The smell of pizza and fried chicken wafting on the breeze enticed Steven to hurry his pace. He hoped there'd be a couple of whole pies ready to go so he wouldn't have to stand around and wait. He, Paul, Danny, and Anna-Grace were all hungry after their busy morning.

Inside, other customers crowded up to the pizza counter, and Steven stifled a groan. Obviously he'd be here for a while. He grabbed a Styrofoam cup and filled it with cola. He might as well sip while he waited his turn at the counter. As he secured a lid on the cup, Briley stepped up beside him.

"Steven, hi. I'm glad I ran into you."

He didn't sound glad, and he didn't look it, either. In fact, he seemed haggard. Steven frowned. "Are you okay?"

"What?" Briley's brows descended briefly, and then he laughed. One short blast of mirthless sound. "Sure. Sure, I'm fine. Just have a lot on my mind. But like I said, I'm glad I spotted you so I can tell you good-bye."

Other customers jostled him. Steven poked a straw into the center of the plastic lid and moved away from the soda machines. Briley followed him. They stopped in front of a rack of potato chips, and Steven propped his hand on top of the rack. "I thought you were going to stay through December."

Briley shrugged, gazing over Steven's shoulder as if lost in thought. "Yeah. Initially I figured I'd need to. But I've got my story — I know what I'm doing — so it's back to Chicago I go."

Steven wished he knew what he was going to do. Anna-Grace hadn't been too happy to stay at the house alone with Paul and Danny Aldrich, but she'd spattered primer on her skirt and resisted being seen in public even more than being left behind. Her reaction to the carpenter — to her *father* — bothered him. She was going to let one man keep her from settling in the town that could offer him a chance to do what he wanted to do. He swallowed a self-deprecating snort. Funny how that teaching position had changed things.

"Good for you." Steven clapped Briley on the shoulder, hoping his enthusiasm seemed genuine. "Glad you accomplished your goal. I bet you're happy."

"Yeah. Yeah, I am." But he frowned as he said it.

Steven sipped his cola, uncertain how to proceed. If Briley were a ten-year-old, he would know how to draw him out. He'd always had a way with kids. His mother laughingly called him a Pied Piper. But he wasn't sure what to do for Briley. He cleared his throat. "So . . . when are you leaving?"

"As soon as I get back to the B and B, I'm gonna pay my bill and then head out."

Steven raised his eyebrows in surprise. "Today? Now?"

Briley nodded.

"Why not stay one more night and go to service tomorrow so everyone can tell you good-bye?" At least four families had invited Briley over for meals, and the entire Zimmerman family had practically made him part of their clan. They'd all be disappointed if he took off without giving them a chance for a proper farewell.

Briley shook his head. "Nah. It's a long drive. I want to get started."

"Well, at least stop by my place and say good-bye to Paul and Danny Aldrich. They're working there today. Mr. Aldrich will want to thank you for the help, and Danny will be plenty upset if you just take off without letting him know. He really likes you."

Briley looked down, a sad smile curving

his lips. "I like him, too. He's a good kid." He lifted his head. "Okay. I'll swing by there before I leave."

"Good." Steven glanced over to the pizza counter and noticed it had cleared. He took a step in that direction. "I'm going to grab a couple of pizzas to take to the house. Have you had lunch?" He waited until Briley shook his head. "Plan to eat with us then. One last slice of Arborville pepperoni before you go home."

Briley pulled in a deep breath, closed his eyes for a moment, then released the breath and nodded.

Steven bustled over to the counter. "One full double pepperoni and one full cheese, please." He inwardly added, *And make it quick.* He needed to get back and play buffer between Anna-Grace and Mr. Aldrich before she made a rash decision that could cost him his dreams.

CHAPTER 40

Anna-Grace

The sound of an approaching vehicle brought an immediate rush of relief. Steven was back! Anna-Grace darted to the front window and looked out, but instead of Steven's pickup, Briley's sports car pulled up the lane. She sighed. She'd rather have Steven — she felt secure with Steven — but another person in the house to take Paul Aldrich's attention away from her would help. What was that man's problem? Arborville would not be big enough for the two of them if he didn't get his odd behavior under control.

She opened the door for Briley and gestured him in. "I didn't expect to see you today. Did you come to work?"

"Nope. To say good-bye."

A boy-sized squawk sounded from the dining room, followed by the patter of feet. Danny careened into the room and slid to a stop next to Briley. "Good-bye? Are you leaving?"

Briley clamped his large hand over Danny's head and tipped the boy's face upward. "You didn't think I'd stay in Arborville forever, did you?" He grinned, but Anna-Grace thought it seemed tense. "My job's done. Time to head on."

"But we're gonna fish at the pond tomorrow, and I wanted you to come." Disappointment colored the boy's tone and expression.

Briley dropped his hand and looked away from the boy. "I'm not much of a fisherman, kid."

Danny sagged forward. After his cheerful attitude all morning, his defeated appearance stung Anna-Grace. Just as she would have done to cheer Sunny, she slipped her arm around his shoulders and tugged him against her side for a brief hug.

Steven's truck pulled up, and at the same time Paul Aldrich entered the front room from the hallway. He and Briley greeted each other, and Anna-Grace took advantage of the distraction to run out to the truck and welcome Steven back. He opened the driver's door, and she stepped into the gap.

"Thank goodness you're back. Briley Forrester is in there, wanting to tell you good-bye."

Steven handed her a stack of two pizza boxes, then slid out, holding a fistful of paper napkins and a jug of fruit punch. "I know. I saw him at the store and invited him to eat with us. I can't believe he's leaving already."

Anna-Grace appreciated the warmth rising from the boxes. The outside air was cool, but more than that, she felt goosepimply from discomfort. "Instead of Briley, I wish Paul Aldrich would leave." She frowned at the house, envisioning the people inside. "How can such a nice little boy have such a weird father?"

"Anna-Grace, that man is not weird." Steven spoke so sharply, she jerked toward him in shock. He glared down at her. "Why are you so determined to dislike him?"

Chafed by his tone, she automatically defended herself. "I can't help it. He puts me on edge the way he watches me. It's been worse today. I've caught him spying on Danny and me, like he's afraid I'm going to do something or say something objectionable." She shivered. "I worried how people would treat me if they found out one of the fellowship members gave me up for adoption, and every time he looks at me I feel like he's thinking, *She's the one.* I hate it!"

Steven stared at her with his lips set in a grim line for several seconds. Then he dropped the items he was holding onto the driver's seat of the truck, yanked the pizzas from her, put them inside the cab, too, and took hold of her elbow. "C'mere."

He led her across the hard ground to the little toolshed between the house and barn. He guided her inside and then closed the door, sealing them in the dim, musty space. She shrank away from him, uncertain and more than a little nervous. "What are you doing?"

He set his feet wide and folded his arms over his chest. "I need to tell you something, and I didn't want anyone overhearing. We're safe in here."

She didn't feel safe. She pressed her back against the rough siding of the shed. "Tell me what?"

"You'll have to get used to be being around Paul Aldrich because Arborville is his home, and I intend to stay here, too."

"But I —"

"I know I said it was up to you, and I'm sorry if changing my mind feels high-handed. But there's a chance for me to do something — *be* something — that means a lot to me. I don't want to give it up."

He made no sense. And she didn't like the way he spoke to her, so gruff and forceful. What had happened to her sweet, gentle Steven? "W-what don't you want to give up?"

In the muted light filtering through cracks in the siding, she watched him close his eyes and crunch his lips together as if a secret pain seized him. After several tense seconds he spoke, still with his eyes shut tight. "Teaching."

Had she heard him correctly? "What?"

His eyes popped open. The blue pupils blazed with intensity. "Teaching, Anna-Grace. I want to be a teacher. Not a farmer, a teacher." He stepped forward and caught her upper arms. "When my folks gave me this land, all I wanted to do was sell it so I could take the money and use it to earn a teaching degree. But I knew if I told them so, they'd be hurt. Kevin already ran off to do whatever he wanted. How could I do the same thing?"

Anna-Grace stared at him, her mouth slightly open. He couldn't have surprised her more if he had picked up a stick and clonked her on the head. Her usually reticent beau continued, the words pouring out briskly and his chest heaving as if he were running a footrace.

"I hoped you'd decide you couldn't live here. If it was too hard for you, my folks would understand why I sold the land. But Arborville needs a teacher. They need a teacher *now*. And I want to take the job. I wouldn't even need a degree — not here. And even if it doesn't pay very well, it won't matter, because I can rent out the farmland and bring in money that way. So it makes sense to stay here, live in this house, and teach in the Arborville school."

Anna-Grace stood in silence, with the fibers of her dress catching on splinters in the rough boards behind her, and digested everything he'd said. They'd courted for over a year, she'd known him her entire life, and not once had he ever mentioned wanting to become a teacher. Only weeks ago he'd promised her wherever she wanted to live, he would go, too. And now everything had changed. She was published to this man, but with only a few sentences — more words than he'd ever strung together at one time before — he'd become a stranger.

His hands briefly tightened and then dropped from her arms. He stood straight and gave her a firm look. "You've got to get over your revulsion toward Paul Aldrich. As I said, Arborville is his home. It's going to be my home. And if we're going to be married, it will be your home, too."

Her heart ached. She loved him. But at that moment she didn't know him. She pulled in a ragged breath. "Then maybe we aren't going to be married."

Briley

Where was Steven and that pizza? Paul and Danny had gone into the dining room to peel the painter's tape from the woodwork, leaving Briley in the living room to wait alone. And he'd waited long enough. He'd said his good-byes. He should go pack his car and get on the road.

He stepped onto the porch, and Anna-Grace burst from a ramshackle building to the east of the house. Steven pounded behind her, calling her name, but she didn't pause. She ran straight to the house and looked up at Briley with tear-filled eyes.

"Are you going to Aunt Abigail's?"

He nodded.

"I'm going with you."

"Anna-Grace!" Steven reached for her, but she ducked away and darted for the front door.

"I just need my jacket. I'll meet you in your car."

Briley sent Steven a questioning look, but

the young man clamped his mouth closed and stomped toward his truck. He pulled out the pizzas and headed for the house, nearly colliding with Anna-Grace who scurried out with her head low. The two of them stopped, stared at each other for three seconds, then sidestepped away and went their separate directions.

Anna-Grace glanced at Briley. "Let's go."

In the car she hunched over her lap and cried. Briley considered asking if he could do anything for her, but fearful she might actually ask for his help, he decided it was better to stay quiet. He'd never been very good at handling weeping females.

When they reached the house, she straightened up and offered him a grateful look. "Thanks for bringing me back. S-Steven said you're l-l-leaving. I . . . I wish I could go, too."

And I wish I could stay. He gave a start. Where had that thought come from? He rubbed the underside of his nose with one finger and gathered his senses. "Did you two have a fight?"

She nodded. The ribbons of her cap were rumpled, strands of blond hair drooped along her cheeks, and tears formed twin tracks down her pale cheeks. She looked so forlorn, he couldn't resist offering a word of comfort.

"Lots of lovers have quarrels. You'll work it out."

She sniffled. "You think so?"

He popped open the console and dug out a crumpled but clean napkin. He pressed it into her hands. "Blow." She did. When she'd finished, he said, "Yes, I think so."

She released a long sigh. "I'm not so sure. Steven . . . Steven's changed."

He needed to load his car. He didn't have time to solve Anna-Grace and Steven's problems, nor did he want to. But she showed no signs of vacating his vehicle. So he sat and let her talk, even though he suspected she was talking to herself rather than to him.

"Everything is all upside down. I thought I was following what God wanted for me, but now I'm not sure. I'm in this town where I have family, but I don't know who they are. My mom and dad aren't my real mom and dad. Steven isn't the farmer I thought I was going to marry . . ." The tears started rolling again. She turned a look of misery on him. "I don't know what to do."

He didn't, either. Her comments didn't make much sense. But he offered what he hoped was a comforting smile. Her lips quirked into a sad smile in reply, and it struck him how much she resembled Mrs. Z's daughter Sandra. And Shelley. And — his pulse jumped as realization bloomed — probably the third Zimmerman daughter, too. The one who kept Alexa because she'd given her baby to a family member to raise.

He blurted, "It's you."

Her eyes — blue, like the other Zimmermans — flew wide. "W-what?"

He flopped limply against his seat and closed his eyes, pressing his memory. Anna-Grace had said she didn't know who her family members were, so she was unaware that the woman in the wheelchair was her grandmother. But did Mrs. Z know? She'd never said anything to indicate an awareness, but he'd watched the older woman gaze at Anna-Grace with affection — sometimes with a secretive smile on her face. She knew. And Alexa knew. Alexa had called herself an imposter and suffered the agony of not really being a Zimmerman while welcoming the real Zimmerman offspring into her home and —

"Mr. Forrester? What did you mean?" Anna-Grace's wavering voice derailed his thoughts.

He floundered for an answer. "It's you . . . Steven loves, so you two will be okay. Give it time."

She dabbed her nose with the napkin. "When are you leaving for Chicago?"

"As soon as I get loaded." His chest tightened. He wasn't ready to go. His story was finished, but there was something else he needed to do here.

"W-would you take me to the bus station in Wichita? I want to go back to Sommerfeld."

He started to agree, but then Aunt Myrt's advice came out of his mouth. "Are you sure you should? Running away from a problem never solved it." Wasn't that what he was doing — running back to Chicago to escape the odd yearnings that had nibbled at him from his first days in this town?

She chewed her lip, uncertainty marring her brow.

He smiled and lapsed into Big-Brother-Briley mode. "You know what? I think you need a night to sleep on it. Really decide if leaving is the best thing to do." He surprised himself by adding, "What would your father tell you?"

Shame crept across her features. She hung her head. "He'd tell me to pray about it."

The yearning returned, stronger than ever. He pushed it down. "Then maybe you should."

"I know I should." She aimed a sheepish

look at him. "My father isn't my birth father. I was adopted."

Briley held his breath. His recorder was in the console. Could he hit the Record button without disrupting the moment? She might give him something he could use. The lid was still up from when he pulled out the napkin. He reached in and snagged a packet of gum while unobtrusively punching the square button on the recorder with his knuckle. "Oh yeah?"

"Mm-hm. Somewhere out there I have another mom and dad, the ones who supposedly gave me life." Her gaze drifted out the window, as if the people would materialize from the scrub trees. "But honestly, the ones who really gave me life are Andrew and Olivia Braun. Because they're the ones who raised me and loved me and taught me and called me their child." She looked at Briley again. "They taught me, more than anything else, I am God's child. He has wonderful plans for me, because good fathers — and God is a very good Father — always want the best for their children."

Tears swam in her eyes, but they didn't spill. "I'm not sure what's going to happen with Steven and me. We have some big things to work out. But the God who gave me to Dad and Mom will give me a good future. And He'll do the same for Steven, because whether or not we become husband and wife, we'll always be God's children." She tipped her head. "Are *you* God's child, too, Mr. Forrester?"

Chapter 41

Briley

Briley stepped past his pile of belongings and sat in one of the vintage chairs. He laid the recorder on the table, lining it up with the checks on the little square of cloth, and hit the Play button. Then he listened. He listened to Alexa's voice. He listened to Anna-Grace's voice. He rewound it and listened again. But not to the words. To the emotions.

In both recordings when the girls spoke of God — the One they called Father — their voices changed. Even though both were distraught during the recordings, they calmed when they uttered God's name. A sense of peace, of serenity, of surety entered their tones. As he listened, his eyes slid closed, and a fleeting memory from a day he'd done his best to forget wiggled its way to the forefront of his thoughts.

He envisioned himself — tall even then

for his age but slight of build, in disheveled clothes a size too small, untied shoelaces dragging, and unwashed hair straggling over his dirty face. The remembrance carried him away, rolling like a movie screen behind his closed eyelids.

Mama reached across the seat, her elbow pressing into his stomach, and pushed the car door open. "Get out, Briley. Go see the firemen."

Briley looked through the wide opening into the fire station, at the shiny red trucks still wet from a fresh wash. He wanted to see those trucks up close. He clambered out of the car, then turned to Mama. "You comin'?"

She examined her fingernails, painted red and chipped on the edges. "No. Just go on."

Shyness clutched him. He reached for her. "You come, too."

She slapped his hand, fury pulsating from her. "Just go, Briley! Go!"

Her anger scared him. He started crying. "But, Mama . . ."

Mama growled and pushed him hard. His heels caught on the curb and he fell flat, scuffing the palms of his hands. He cradled them to his chest as Mama yanked the door closed and zoomed off.

Briley sat on the curb, staring after her, willing her to come back. But she didn't. So, scared and crying, he pushed himself to his feet and crept through the wide-open door, hunching his shoulders to make himself as small as possible.

An older guy with gray hair and the beginning of a potbelly spotted him and frowned. "What're you doing in here, kid?"

Briley peeked at the man through his thick, matted bangs. Would the fireman hit him? He rasped, his heart pounding, "M-my mama told me to come in here. An' then she drove away."

The man clomped toward him, and Briley let out a little squawk when the man scooped him up. He carried Briley to a chair, sat, and settled him on his lap. He held Briley — dirty, snot running down his lip, sour smelling from urine and sweat — close. So close Briley heard the man's heart beating in his ear. And the man whispered tenderly, "Now, don't you worry. Everything'll be all right. You just stick here with me, son, okay?"

Briley had huddled in the fireman's lap until a police officer and a lady he later learned was a social worker came along and took him. He hadn't wanted to leave the comfort of the man's lap. He'd never felt so secure.

The recorder reached the end, and Anna-Grace's voice echoed in the quiet room: *"Are you God's child, too, Mr. Forrester?"* Suddenly Briley was five years old again, wrapped in a pair of sturdy arms while a heart beat a comforting *thrum* in his ear. A voice whispered, *"You just stick here with me, son, okay?"* And Briley looked up and said, "Okay, Father."

Alexa

Alexa paused in rolling out crusts for tomorrow morning's quiche and looked out the window. The lights in the cottage still burned. She frowned and turned her attention back to the crust. When Anna-Grace came in almost three hours ago, she indicated Briley would be in soon to pay his bill. So why hadn't he come?

He was packed. She'd spotted his luggage in the cottage when she went out that morning to strip the bed and gather the dirty towels. He'd asked for his bill, and he had the notes for his story. *His story* . . . Worry stabbed, and she uttered another prayer to stave it off. Peace returned, and she added aloud, "Thank You, God."

She transferred the crust to a ceramic pie plate and crimped the edges of the soft dough, forming a rope pattern. She smiled as she pricked the bottom of the crust a few times with a fork, remembering Mom's relief when Alexa took over cooking duties.

"I can cook," Mom had said while pulling Alexa into a hug, *"but only because we have to eat to survive. For me, cooking is a chore."*

But for Alexa it was a joy. It always had been, from the time she received a toy Tasty Bake Oven for Christmas from Linda and Tom the year she turned six. She tucked the crust into the oven to brown and tipped her head, pondering which of her parents was the baker. Surely this interest in cooking was inherited because she hadn't learned it from Mom. She sank onto the stool next to the counter and rested her chin in her hand. The questions that had plagued her since the evening Mom divulged the truth of her parentage begged for answers. She hadn't pursued it because no one outside of Grandmother, Mom's siblings, and Paul knew the truth.

When Briley printed his story, the truth would extend beyond these walls to the entire community. Very soon her secret would no longer be a secret. Then would she be free to search for her parents? She couldn't honestly say she wanted to know them or claim them — she had Mom, and she didn't want a replacement — but she wanted to know where she came from. Her history. Mostly, she wanted to know why they hadn't kept her. Briley said there were people who would help. Should she ask for help?

Someone tapped on the back door and then cracked it open. Briley peeked in. He smiled — a heart-melting smile that made her forget for several seconds the torture he'd put her through with his decision to print Mom's wrongdoing. She stood quickly and waved him in.

He held up a stack of twenty-dollar bills. "I got cash from the ATM to pay you. Everything on the invoice and a little extra."

She took the bills, folded them in half without counting them, and slipped them into her apron pocket. Her stomach trembled, facing him after their disagreement. She wasn't sure how to act. She left her hand in her pocket around the wad of bills and fingered the crisp edges. "You didn't need to give me extra." Lifting one eyebrow, she managed to tease, "You didn't print them yourself, did you?"

He laughed, his white teeth flashing and a dimple briefly appearing in his whisker-dark cheek. "Ha! No. Not this time. You deserve the real deal. Because you, Miss Alexa Zimmerman, *are* the real deal." The humor faded, and he turned a serious look on her that sent her pulse scampering into double beats. "Alexa, there are three things I need to tell you. Well, the first thing is actually a question."

She gripped the bills and swallowed against her dry throat. "Okay. What?"

"First, is it all right if I stay one more night? Go to service with your family in the morning and maybe have lunch with all of you before I head out?"

Grandmother had already invited him, so she knew it would be all right. "Sure."

"Thanks."

He pulled in a breath, making the buttons on his shirt go taut across his chest. As usual, his recorder formed a bulge in his shirt pocket. She stared at the bulge while he talked.

"Second, you're not an imposter."

She whipped her attention from the recorder's bump to his fervent face.

"You are very much your mother's daughter. By your own admission, she loves you. She earned the title 'mother' by caring for you your entire life. Additionally, your grandmother loves you, your aunts and uncles and passel of little cousins love you. To them, you are *theirs*, and neither blood nor a legal document would make an ounce of difference."

His image wavered because tears clouded

her eyes. She choked out, "What's the third?"

He grinned and held up his finger. "I'm not finished with the second one yet. There's another part, and it's the most important part. Are you listening?"

She nodded.

"You're not an imposter because you are a member of God's family. He is your forever Father, and you are His child for eternity. Yes?"

For a moment she stared at him in open-mouthed amazement. He'd never spoken so easily of God before. Then the truth of his words washed her with a fresh rush of grace so sweet it became a lilting melody in her heart. God Himself must have given Briley that message for her. "Yes. Yes."

"Now the third . . ." He reached into his pocket and plucked out the recorder. He held it in his fist between them. "I told you I gave you a little extra in your payment, but there's another 'extra' I want you to have." He opened his fist and held the recorder flat in his palm. With his other hand he reached in and deliberately pushed the third button. The Delete button.

A *whirr* sounded, and Alexa gasped. She bounced her awed gaze from the recorder to Briley's face. "Did you . . ."

Slipping the recorder back into the pocket, he gave a slow nod. "It's gone. I also deleted the files from my computer. I decided I didn't need to tear you down in order to build myself up." A tender smile grew on his lips. Peace, joy, and contentment glowed in his dark eyes. "It's enough just to be the Father's child."

"Oh, Briley . . ." She clapped her hands to her cheeks and stared at him through a mist of happy tears. She would have stood there, silently celebrating forever, if he hadn't leaned sideways and aimed a grimace at something behind her.

"Um, Alexa? Whatever you put in the oven, I think it's burning."

She whirled around. A thin line of smoke snaked out from the oven door. "My quiche crust!" She yanked the door open and used her apron to pull out the pan holding a blackened facsimile of a pie crust. She dropped the pan on the counter, and chunks of charred pie crust bounced over the edge. She stomped her foot and turned to launch a complaint, but Briley's impish grin stilled her words.

He held his hands outward. "Hmm, can you say, 'well done'?"

She burst out laughing. She couldn't help herself. What did it matter that the crust was burned when she stood next to a new-born child of God? Chortling, she nodded and gave his arm a light whack. "Yes, Briley, I can say 'well done.' I would even say *very* well done."

Anna-Grace

Anna-Grace put down her pen and reached to rub the back of her neck. Knots of tension met her fingers, and she held her head low and kneaded for several minutes until the tightly bound muscles relaxed. When she lifted her head again, her gaze fell on the letters she'd spent the past hours hunched over the desk writing.

One for Mom and Dad, one for Steven.

Putting her thoughts down on paper had always helped her sort things through. She didn't know yet if she'd actually mail the letters. As Briley had advised, she intended to sleep on it. But she was sure by morning, after prayer and a night of rest, she'd know the right thing to do.

She picked up the letter for Steven, leaned back in the chair, and read what she'd penned.

Dear Steven,
I'm sorry for running out on you like I did today, but your sudden change in

plans pulled the rug out from under my feet, so to speak, and I needed to find a way to stand again. I suppose it shouldn't have been a complete surprise that you want to be a teacher. Now I can look back and see hints of it — the way you've always been good with younger children, your interest in math and history, even the way you sat down and started grading papers at my house that day as if it was the most natural thing in the world. I can see you being a good teacher, and if that's what you end up doing, I'm sure your students will be very lucky to have you.

But, Steven, I wonder why you never told me you wanted to teach. I understand you didn't want to hurt your parents, but really, would it have pained them as much as you think? Becoming a teacher isn't the same as what Kevin did, running off and never coming back again. They would have known where you were and what you were doing.

You claimed to love me, you asked me to share your life, but you didn't tell me what you wanted to do with your life. Instead, you tried to trick me into being the one to send you down a pathway other than farming. That hurts the most.

I keep thinking, shouldn't you trust the one who is going to be your wife? How can you really love me if you didn't trust me?

I love you. I've loved you for a long time, and I can't imagine my life without you. But right now I need some time to heal from this hurt. I need time to restore my trust in you. In us. I'm going back to Sommerfeld as soon as I can arrange travel. I will be praying for God to heal my heart and to restore our relationship if we're meant to be as one someday. I hope you will pray for the same thing.

Lovingly,
Anna-Grace

She set the letter aside and closed her eyes, trying to imagine Steven's response to it. She prayed he would take it well, would understand, and would want to work toward a reconciliation. But if he didn't, she would trust God had something else in store for her.

Her parents' letter was much shorter, essentially a request for them to bring her home at their earliest convenience. If she ended up mailing it, she would explain everything in person on the drive home.

She'd know by morning whether she would stay or go.

Guide my heart, God. Please guide my heart.

CHAPTER 42

Steven

Steven had always believed he would feel better once he let his secret out, but he didn't feel better. He wanted to be proud of himself for finally telling Anna-Grace the truth, but deep down he knew he'd gone about it all wrong. Her stunned look of betrayal played in his memory as he crossed the parking lot to the convenience store's pay phone and punched in his folks' phone number. He'd do better with his parents. But when his dad answered the telephone, and Steven blurted, "Dad, there's something I need you to know," then proceeded to share his long-held desire, Dad didn't say a word in response. Instead, Mom's voice came through the line, wary and worried.

"Son? Your dad just handed me the phone and went outside. What's going on?"

Steven leaned against the rough brick wall and told his mother the same thing he'd told Dad. "I should've said something before now, but I didn't want you to think I was like Kevin — selfish and disobedient."

Mom was silent for several seconds, and when she spoke, her words sounded tight. "Do you really think so little of us, Steven? God Himself put a call on your heart. You think we'd hold you back from following it?"

He hung his head. "I'm sorry, Mom."

"I'm sorry, too, that you didn't think you could trust us." A heavy sigh laden with regret carried through the line. "Son, I need to go talk to your father."

"He's probably really mad, huh?"

Mom released a short huff of humorless laughter. "No, if he was mad, he'd be spouting."

That was true. Dad was never short of words when he was angry. But when he was hurt? That's when he clammed up. Steven swallowed a knot of agony. "Please tell him I'm sorry I disappointed him. I'll call again tomorrow, okay?"

Back at the house he dressed for bed and flopped onto the mattress. All night he wrestled with God, alternately sleeping and praying. He awakened early Sunday and made use of his brand-new tub. But not even a steady flow of hot water over his aching muscles erased the heavy cloak of regret that had fallen over him when Anna-Grace drove off with Briley yesterday. He'd messed things up. He'd messed things up badly. But how to fix it?

He turned the squeaky spigots, dried off while steam formed a murky cloud around him, and then dressed for service even though the last thing he felt like doing was worshiping. But sometimes the thing a man least wanted to do was the best thing for him. So he plopped his hat over his freshly washed hair, climbed into his pickup, and made the drive to town.

Other vehicles, including Abigail Zimmerman's, were already in the lot. His chest pinched at the sight of the Zimmerman sedan. Had Anna-Grace come, or had she stayed out at the farm to hide? He hoped she'd come. Even if she was still angry, even if she turned up her nose and ignored him, he still wanted to see her.

I love her, God. He sent up the brief proclamation as he crossed the yard to the men's door. He knew God believed him. Now if he could only convince Anna-Grace he meant it.

He sat on the back bench next to Briley, who surprised him with his presence. He sang the hymns, recited the scriptures, knelt to pray, and sat attentively during the sermon, but afterward he couldn't recall what he'd sung, said, or heard. The entire time his thoughts were on Anna-Grace, who sat in the back with her great aunt. Would she speak to him when the service was over?

Afterward he waited in the yard close to the women's door for her. When she stepped out, her eyes met his — almost as if his gaze had lassoed her. And even though she hesitated for a moment, she walked toward him instead of away. She looked so sweet with her cap in place, her coat buttoned to the throat, and her hands locked behind her. Love swelled up, and he said the first thing that came to mind.

"I'm sorry."

A sad smile curved her lips. "Me, too."

Hope roared through him. Fellowship members milled on the lawn, close enough to overhear if they wanted to, but he had to ask. "Then you aren't mad at me anymore?"

A tiny sigh escaped her. "I'm not sure I was ever mad, Steven. I was hurt and confused." She squinted against a sunbeam that broke through the clouds. "I still am."

He ducked his head. "I understand. You have reason to be hurt and confused."

She reached into her pocket and pulled out a folded sheet of paper. "I wrote you a letter. Before I give it to you, I need to ask what you've decided to do. Are you going to teach at the school here?"

"I want to." The desire writhed within him. All night he'd begged God to drive the want from him if he wasn't meant to pursue it, but it was still there. "I don't know if they'll let me, but I'm going to talk to Clete about it again tomorrow. Tell him straight out that I want to teach."

She gazed into his face for several seconds, her expression unreadable. Then she gave a little nod and pushed the paper at him. "Read this when you get to your house. If you want to talk to me about it, I'm sure Aunt Abigail won't mind you coming to the house this evening."

He gripped the paper, curiosity burning.

She started to move away, and then she turned back with a winsome look on her heart-shaped face. "And, Steven? Whatever happens, even if it's hard, I believe it will be what's best. For both of us."

He watched her walk beneath the slanting rays of the sun to the Zimmerman's vehicle. She climbed in, turned her face to the glass, and she kept her sweet smile aimed at him until Alexa turned a corner that carried her from sight.

■ ■ ■ ■

Briley

When lunch, which took place at Clete and Tanya's, was over, Briley hugged Alexa, Anna-Grace, and Mrs. Z, shook hands with the men, and thanked Tanya, Sandra, and Shelley for their hospitality during his stay in Arborville. Then he folded himself behind the wheel of his sports car, gave a wave that was returned by more than a dozen enthusiastic hands, and took off up the road.

It was Sunday, but Len would be at his workplace. The man practically lived in his cubby at the *Real Scoop*'s suite of offices. Len really needed a life outside of the tabloid, and when Briley returned to Chicago he'd sit down and tell his boss how to find it. In the meantime he pulled out his cell phone and pushed the button for Len's number. Within seconds Len's gruff "hello" sounded in Briley's Bluetooth.

"Len, it's Briley. I'm on my way."

"Good! Good! I've saved half of the front page of next Saturday's edition for your story."

Briley sent up a silent prayer, double-fisted the steering wheel, and took the plunge. "About the story . . . I wanna kill it."

Len's guffaw blasted. "We must have a bad connection. I thought you said you wanted to kill the story."

"No, you heard me correctly."

"Whaddaya mean, you want to kill the story?" Right now Len was probably pulling out the few tufts of hair left on his head.

"Look, Len, I just think we need to . . ." Briley smiled. "Give 'em a little grace."

Several seconds of silence reigned, and then Len's fury exploded. "Have you completely lost your mind?"

Briley chuckled. "Yeah, I probably have." But he'd found his heart. And that was more important. "Listen, I've got another idea — something that could turn into a long-term serial and keep the readers coming back for more." And wouldn't Nicci K love having her journey to become the next country-western star chronicled? "But before I tell you about it, I have to do something. Go see someone. So I'm gonna use a couple of days of leave, okay?"

Len's disgusted snort carried clearly to Briley's ear. "Fine. Whatever. Go. But when you get back here, your idea better be good, because —" The signal faded, rescuing Briley from having to listen to the rest of his boss's wrath.

He unhooked his Bluetooth and tossed it onto the passenger seat, draped his wrist over the steering wheel, and settled in for the drive. It would be a long one, a long time coming, but he'd never anticipated a journey more than the one waiting for him now.

He ate meals from snack bars at convenience stores when he stopped to fill the tank with gas so he wouldn't waste time waiting for an order from a café, and he drove straight through the night. He reached the outskirts of Chicago as the sky bloomed as rosy as Alexa's cheeks when he teased her, and he smiled, envisioning the young woman who'd become his surrogate little sister. He drove through the early morning shadows, over streets where he used to skateboard, feelings of déjà vu making his flesh tingle.

Even though years had passed — a lifetime had passed — he found Covington Court as easily as if he'd visited it just yesterday. At the end of the cul-de-sac, the little ranch-style house that had provided his truest sense of home waited. The oak tree in the front yard still stood, taller than he remembered and spreading its empty branches wider, but the rope swing where he'd sent younger foster siblings soaring skyward was gone.

His heart lurched. Would she be gone, too? After all, she'd been old then — as old as Mrs. Z or maybe even older — and an entire decade had slipped by. *Let her be here.* The plea formed, a prayer really, and peace eased over him. If she wasn't here, he'd find her.

He pulled into the drive and shut off the engine. For a few minutes he sat and gazed at the dent in the white siding where he'd hit it with a baseball, the black shutters he'd given a fresh coat of paint the year before he aged out of the system, the wrought-iron porch posts and railings that had served as a makeshift jungle gym. Memories paraded through his mind so quickly that one barely had time to form before another replaced it.

Behind the picture window a movement caught his attention — the frothy curtain being lifted at the hem. A yellow-and-white whiskered face peered out. A grin grew on his cheeks without effort. She was still here. The cat proved it. She loved cats almost as much as she loved kids — especially stray ones.

Eagerness shot through him, and he smacked the car door open and strode up the cracked sidewalk, not even bothering to close the door behind him. He gave one leap onto the concrete porch, scaring the cat from its spot at the window. Pressing his finger to the doorbell, he sucked in a breath and held it.

Less than three seconds later the door opened, and there she stood in a stretchy purple pantsuit, older, more slope-shouldered, short gray curls forming little squiggles all over her head. Her gaze met his, and a smile of pure joy broke across her face.

"Briley Ray!" She threw her arms wide as the yellow-and-white cat shot out the door, between Briley's feet, and across the yard. "You've come home!"

His held breath whooshed out on a note of happy laughter. He scooped her off her feet and clung hard. "Yes, ma'am, I have. I've truly come Home."

ALEXA'S PEACH-PECAN PIE

Filling:
4 c. peaches, peeled and sliced
2/3 c. sugar
2 T. flour
1/2 t. lemon juice
1/4 t. cinnamon
1/4 c. butter, cut into small cubes
1 9″ unbaked deep-dish pie shell

Streusel:
1/2 c. brown sugar
1/2 t. cinnamon or apple pie spice
1/4 c. flour
3 T. cold butter
1/2 c. coarsely chopped pecans

Preheat oven to 425 degrees.

To make the streusel, mix the brown sugar, spice, and flour. Cut the butter into the mixture until it forms crumbles. Stir in the pecans. Sprinkle a third of the mixture into the bottom of the pie shell.

To make the filling, combine the peaches, sugar, flour, lemon juice, and cinnamon and pour into the pie shell over the streusel. Dot the peaches with the cubes of butter. Sprinkle the remaining streusel evenly over the peaches.

Bake for 45–50 minutes, until the syrupy topping boils in heavy bubbles that don't burst. Serve warm with or without fresh whipped cream or ice cream.

READERS GUIDE

1. Steven harbors a desire that began growing inside of him when he was still a child. His brother's discouraging words and the traditional roles of his faith community made him squelch the desire, which led to an underlying sense of dissatisfaction. How do we know when our desires are God-planted rather than self-chosen? How can we find the courage to follow God's will when those around us don't seem to understand or approve?

2. Alexa opened the B and B as a means of ministry, but at times she struggled with opening her doors to those who needed a place of refuge. Were her reasons for hesitation valid? How would you have advised Alexa?

3. Throughout the story Briley thinks of Aunt Myrt and reflects on different words of wisdom she imparted. Why did Aunt Myrt leave such an impression on Briley? Do you have an "Aunt Myrt" in your life who impacted you? How can you be "Aunt Myrt" to people in your life?

4. Anna-Grace goes to Arborville to "explore" whether or not she can be at ease in the town where her birth parents reside. Since she doesn't want to read the letters that would divulge their identities, is her plan wise or unwise? Why? If you were Anna-Grace's adoptive parents, how would you feel about her living so near her birth family? If you were Anna-Grace's birth parents, how would you feel being so near her and unable to claim her as yours?

5. Briley grew up feeling as if no one really cared about him, and it colored his opinion of himself. He developed a cocky veneer to hide his true feelings of insignificance and set a goal of becoming famous

within his vocation to prove himself worthy to those who had rejected him. Have you ever set out to prove someone wrong in their opinion of you? If you were successful, did it bring you satisfaction? Whose opinion is the best one to value — man's or God's? Why?

6. Unlike the other young people in the story who wanted to work at specific jobs, Anna-Grace wanted to be a wife and mother more than anything. She's caught up in her plans to marry Steven and build a family with him. Then when she discovers he wants something other than what she'd envisioned, her security crumbles. Were Anna-Grace's feelings of betrayal understandable, or should she have been more supportive? Has someone you trusted ever surprised you with an unexpected proclamation? How did you handle it?

7. Since Briley didn't have a father who was loving and involved in his life, he has difficulty believing God the Father could care about him.

Briley finds himself drawn to Paul Aldrich and Danny, and he watches the relationship between father and son. How does Paul, without being aware of it, model Father-God's attributes? What examples, besides Paul, did God place in Briley's pathway to help point him toward the care of a loving heavenly Father?

8. Alexa tells Briley that being "thrown away" was a good thing because she was found by a loving mother. Likewise, Briley reasoned he wouldn't have met Aunt Myrt if his mother hadn't abandoned him. Has God redeemed hurtful moments in your life and made them work for your good?

ACKNOWLEDGMENTS

I deeply appreciate the following . . .

Mom and Daddy, who modeled faith and led me toward a relationship with the Father.

Don, who handles the mundane so I can apply my fingers to the keyboard.

Kristian, Kaitlyn, and Kamryn, who humble me and challenge me and give me reasons to smile.

Judy Miller, who brainstormed with me and ignited my enthusiasm for this story.

The Posse, who consistently offer prayers, encouragement, or humor right when I need it.

The FSBC choir, who cheer me on when my spirit is lagging.

Shannon and the team at WaterBrook, who partner with me and make the stories shine.

My Father-God, who rejoices over me with singing and gives me grace beyond all deserving. May any praise or glory be reflected directly back to You.

ABOUT THE AUTHOR

Kim Vogel Sawyer is a best-selling, award-winning author highly acclaimed for her gentle stories of hope. More than one million copies of her books are currently in print. She lives in central Kansas where she and her retired military husband, Don, enjoy spoiling their ten granddarlings.

CPSIA information can be obtained
at www.ICGtesting.com
Printed in the USA
FFHW01n2022150918
48398262-52244FF